Also by Chris Dunn
in the *Contango* series

*Deadlines*

*Domus*

*Contango*

# TRICKS

## Chris Dunn

MINERVA PRESS

LONDON

MIAMI   RIO DE JANEIRO   SYDNEY

ISBN  0  75411  515  1




First Published 2001 by
MINERVA PRESS
315–317 Regent Street
London W1R 7YB




Printed in Great Britain for Minerva Press

# TRICKS

# ACKNOWLEDGEMENTS

Thanks are due to Penguin UK (London), Felicity Brown (Oxford) and Knopf US (New York) for kind permission to use the extract from *A History of Venice* by John Julius Norwich. Thanks are due to Blackwell Publishers Ltd (Oxford) for kind permission to use the extract from *Money and Empire* by Marcello de Cecco. Many thanks to Chris Moore and his team at Brompton Library, Kensington for their great and invaluable help on research. Likewise to the late and much-lamented Dr Richard Coghlan, formerly of the Bank of England, for his brilliant analysis of UK plc over twenty-five years of discussion.

PART ONE

# A COLD CONTRACT

# Chapter One

Joe played the nine of diamonds towards the ace in dummy and saw the heavy gold ring to his left tremble. I know that wobble, he thought. That's the housekeeping wobble. She's got it, but she'll hoard it. And he let the card run.

Elsewhere in the room, at the other three bridge tables of the Liz Playfair Bridge Academy, the women were intent as usual on their cards. A typical Wednesday evening gathering. They were crouched like cats over their hands. Nobody was watching for Joe's subterfuge, least of all Liz, patrolling the play from table to table in her awesome and statuesque six foot blonde majesty, eyes swivelling from hand to player's hand.

Outside, at the fashionable end of London's King's Road, down Lower Sloane Street, by the Duke of York barracks and a few doors away from the Sloane Club, it was night, a soft velvet blue of a night. An enticing night.

Joe was playing a treacherous game. The cards waved about somewhat to Joe's left and the two of diamonds floated on the table from Stella's hand. Stella failed to cover with the king – fatal error. After that it was all over. Duck and no dinner for Stella. Joe made his contract with overtricks to spare. For Joe's ploy to succeed it was vital that the king of diamonds lurked on his left and also that Stella ran away from the finesse. And run like crazy she duly did. So much for housekeeping. Evidently, even in Eden's flowery garden, the accounts had to be rendered.

Now the cards were heaped forlornly in the middle of the table, reds and blacks intermingled pell-mell. On either side of Joe and directly ahead, at the other tables, the play went on with semi-muted ferocity. Sacred time-out time for the high-heeled ladies of Chelsea and Knightsbridge. No time to lose before husbands returned from their counting houses in the City, in their customary state of fractious anxiety, or worse.

'You cheated me, Joe,' said Stella with her crooked bird-like smile and Levantine grace, reaching across to pat him a gentle rebuke on the arm. 'Joe, it was a swindle by you,' she added.

Joe shrugged and grinned back at Stella. 'Stella, I just wanted to introduce a spot of temptation. You know how it is.'

Lady Charley returned from the small kitchen behind the bridge room with the tea. An aureole of curls swayed about her cherubic face as she sashayed into the room. Gingerly she held three mugs of tea in one hand and a biscuit in the other. She munched at the biscuit in her light and airy way. She glanced round the room as if waiting for the band to strike up a polka. Deftly she distributed the mugs round the table, excluding Joe. Joe had not requested any tea.

'How did we get on?'

The question was posed more to the table as a whole than just to Joe, her partner. Lady Charley normally gave the impression that Joe was someone in the room who just happened to have fetched up at her table.

'You made it. Joe was very cunning. I was waiting for him to play a different diamond and I had my plan. But he played the nine! Can you imagine? I didn't know what on earth to do, and so of course I did nothing. That gave him the contract and it gives you the rubber too I think. Clever Joe.'

'Well done, Joe,' said Lady Charley, absently. She was dismissive of the tense play while she had been out of the room as so much ancient history. Joe should not have made his contract, not by a long chalk. It was a miracle of subterfuge the contract came home and a cause for some celebration that he had succeeded. But Lady Charley was oblivious to all that. After all, she had been making the tea in a noble act of self-sacrifice for the past five minutes. Now it was on with the motley, and time for something new.

'What did we make on the rubber?' Again a general question to the table at large.

'Plus five,' said Joe, glancing at the scorecard without scratching through the numbers.

'Are you sure? That doesn't sound very much at all to me.'

The two other women at the table confirmed Joe's guesstimate after much careful calculation.

'Well, that's far too little. That means we're only seven ahead now. Come along, Joe, we'll have to do better than that or the entire evening will be a washout. Heavens, is that the time? Come on girls, let's get a move on. We'll only have time for one more rubber, if my husband turns up on time. And I have a feeling that he's going to be punctual tonight. He's got a big client in tow and he said he'd be here on the dot of nine thirty. Middle East, you know.'

She stared at them meaningfully and the two women nodded in complicit understanding. Sir David, Lady Charley's husband, was a director of Global Aerospace, one of Britain's largest exporters. That meant long hours, snatched meals, broken timetables and good private schools; they knew all about it.

Lady Charley dealt the cards fast and skilfully and Joe watched them tumble to his right and his left. Lady Charley's long slightly bulbous fingers flew around and about, and her face, fringed by the curls, was rapt in concentration. Liz appeared at their side as Lady C dealt.

'How much did you go down by, Joe? One off, was it?'

'No, Joe made it, but it was my fault. He was just too subtle for me.'

Stella the penitent smiled at Liz, who gave Joe a proprietorial pat of congratulations on his shoulder. Lady C continued to deal the cards, but as she did so she glanced up at Liz with a hard expression on her face. No quarter to be glimpsed in those features. Lady C nodded her head in the direction of one of the other tables. Joe guessed what was coming. It had been coming for some time. Liz knew all about it too and most reluctantly would agree to go along with what Lady C requested and required. But she was not happy about the type of rough justice about to be meted out.

It was the old, old story. Joe had seen it more than just a few times at Liz Playfair's establishment – social customs versus bridge mores. Social customs won out every time. A ritual execution was being arranged.

Looking sweeter now, Lady C picked up her cards and arranged her hand into suits. The cream blouse was immaculate beneath the well-textured dark green cardigan. The rings on her finger flashed discreetly as she shuffled the cards around in her left hand. Joe picked up the heap of cards, barely looked at them, and put them back face down on the table. It was habitual with him. He knew what was in his hand. It took no more than a glance.

Years ago, before his fall from grace, when he played bridge in windy espionage lookout spots in cold war Berlin, that was what his mentor, the Fat Man, had taught him. 'Take the hand in immediately, and then watch the opposition – and that includes your partner. Bridge is like spying. Seize every tiny piece of information and build your picture. Watch the table. Pick up the cards as late as possible.'

Being a dutiful apprentice in those days, Joe had obeyed the Fat Man. Now, years later in this quiet but deadly Sloane Square haven, Joe realised just what a useless spy he must have been. Mannerisms like that are such a dead give-away, he thought to himself. Joe checked his cards again, this time in earnest, and the Fat Man faded from his mind with the usual touch of anguish. Joe had long since adjusted to the fact of the Fat Man's death, although the reality was a different matter.

Lady C started the bidding with confidence. She was smiling at her cards. Lady C and Joe reached three no trumps quite easily, without incident. A club was led and Joe's hand went down. It was a reasonable dummy. Lousy diamonds, some clubs, good hearts with luscious intermediates, and fair spades. Nothing to rave about, but again no complaints either.

Lady C started as usual with some gusto and then ran into problems. An excess of impetuosity was a fair description of her approach. Now she fingered her cards and stared unknowingly at the dummy. Joe knew that look. He had seen it many times before. It betokened blank incomprehension. Her mind was closing down. Lady C was floundering in the quicksand of her own making. After cashing her winners early, she was trapped in her own hand. She dared not play the diamond ace, and yet she had to make another spade trick in dummy. Archimedes himself would have had some problems unravelling the conundrum of Lady C's hand.

Arms folded, Joe looked across the table at Lady C

dispassionately as she chewed at her upper lip. In silence. 'Twas ever so. Any comment, however small, would provoke an outburst. Lady C stared at dummy some more and then solved her problem brilliantly. Holding her cards slightly away from her pert, well-cherished bosom, she called for help.

'Liz!' It was a voice that quavered on the edge of supplication while yet retaining in timbre just a slight necessary edge of authority. 'Liz, now what do you think I should do now?'

Liz was at her side. Clearly Liz and Lady C were together now on this one. A brief discussion, and Liz's blonde head bobbed up and down as it advised on strategy. Mumble, mumble, whisper, whisper. Much nodding of blonde hair intermingled with bobbling russet curls.

Satisfied, Lady C returned to the play. She did the only thing she could do to extricate herself from the mess. She led another spade.

Afterwards, as the cards were gathered in for another hand and the contract had been correctly made with nine tricks, Lady C explained it all brightly to the table. Truly, she had made her plan, but at that precise moment she needed confirmation from Liz that her plan had been correct. Which it had been, of course. Stella and the other woman at the table did not demur. They simply wrote down the score. In the ebb and flow of the game, everybody, including Joe on occasion, needed to consult Liz. Most of the time, nobody could make a contract without her counsel.

The buzzer sounded twice. That was Sir David's calling card. In two seconds he would be in the room, after bounding up the stairs two by two. Joe braced himself. The effort at self-control was considerable. Sir David was quite the most evil man Joe had ever encountered. Far worse than anything he had tangled with in his espionage days. Privately Joe called him the Black Pimpernel.

The door opened in a smooth rush and in came Sir David, all tanned sallow features, jet black hair swept back on the forehead, and a gracious, eager, even boyish smile of welcome. Good teeth and strong jaw. Beautiful shirt. Hearty, confident greeting, especially for Ursula, Lady C's friend from school, playing at the furthest table. A hug for Liz, and more smiles all round. Lots of smiles. The man had arrived. The women winced just a tiny fraction, as the male presence reappeared in reassertive mode.

Sir David glanced round the room like a conquistador and gathered up his wife who went to him willingly enough. Joe wondered where Lady C had parked her helicopter, the normal mode of transport to the academy, for the night. In the barracks, of course. Where else?

'Come along, darling, or we'll be late for our table. Good bridge, was it?'

'Marvellous. Stella played like a star.'

Sir David ignored Joe, the hired hand, and thanked the room quite gratuitously for having his wife. Covertly, Joe stole a glance at his eyes. Joe feasted on them every time he saw Sir David. They were hard and black like pebbles of dark midnight ice. The hardest, nastiest and most merciless eyes that Joe had ever seen. A killer's eyes, or worse, the eyes of someone who had always had – and enjoyed – precisely what he wanted. They were the eyes of a man beyond God. Joe hated Sir David, every well-bred, textured inch of him. He was certain too that the feeling was quite mutual.

Then they were gone, swooshing out from the room like royalty, but not before Lady C had given Joe her careful injunctive backward glance, unseen by Sir David. The glance was eloquent in its discretion. Don't forget to do what I asked you to do. It's important that you do this. I have trusted you, so please do it properly.

Few in the room would have noticed Lady C's look. It was for Joe alone. Always the same. Every week, quite casually, Lady C gave Joe an envelope to send the following day by recorded delivery from the local post office. The address was somewhere in South London. Lady C vouchsafed no further information about the envelope, nor did Joe make any further enquiries. It was a service that he performed for her. He did what she wanted. Every week he posted her letter for her. The envelope was addressed to a Madame le Pen. It was always the same. That was all Joe knew – or indeed cared. It was not a topic for discussion between them.

Now the bridge evening was breaking up. The women were rising from the tables, shaking themselves out of their rapt concentration, collecting their bags and packages, gossiping and moving with steady tread towards the door and familiar life and surroundings. Ursula, tall, queenly, capable and haughty, Lady C's special friend from school, was complaining, as usual, about her cards and her play and her partner as they all shuffled towards the exit, in high good humour. The evening had passed off with no outbursts of choler of any description. Nancy departed into the night still talking about her cookery book for charity.

Joe lingered, not because he relished the little social murder that was about to take place, but rather because he preferred to leave in the rear of the party. Fewer goodbyes to make that way in the street and thus fewer queries about the absolute destitution of his position. Joe took no winter break holidays in Verbier; nor did he spend his other evenings at Covent Garden. Joe was broke.

After the bridge was finished, the night yawned before him like an empty desert. Joe was more or less alone in that desert too. As things stood, Joe had more than just one foot in London's cardboard city. More like half his body. Life was very tough for him now that all his money and his career had vanished before his eyes.

Joe knew how Liz went about these things, but in the event Sybil did all the work for her. Sybil had been tricky from the start and was now impossible. She didn't fit in the bridge circle, even though she played the cards quite well. The wife of a Liverpool tycoon who had made his fortune manufacturing unmentionable things for women's bodies, Sybil was just too outspoken, just too enthusiastic and, in a word, just too loud for the diamond dames of Sloane Square. On one occasion she had turned up for the bridge session with an Instamatic, clicking away throughout the session in high good humour, and then handing the snaps round at the end. Jaws had dropped at the sheer scale of the impertinence. Finally, one of the women had called her brassy. That was the end for Sybil. The custom of the country prevailed over any subsidiary pre-eminence, especially in Sloane Square. Sybil had made the mistake of assuming that pots of money equated with easy access to social position. Now she was about to reap the reward of her bossiness.

Liz was seated at her table, collecting the fees for the evening in the room next door to the bridge tables, as the women eased their way out with many a cheery goodnight. Bookings were made for the following day, night or week as the cash was handed over.

Sybil bustled up to Liz, thrust a fifty-pound note at her and confirmed brightly that she planned to play at the same time the following week. Sybil waved her diary about under Liz's nose as she tried to make the booking, while bidding goodnight to all and sundry. Very much everybody's pal. Very much in control.

Looking at Sybil down her long nose, and very steadily indeed, as Joe noted, Liz refused to take the booking. Sybil failed to register the point at first and blustered like a bully.

'I said I'm free to play next week and I would like to play. So I plan to play. What's the matter with you, Liz?'

Still gazing at Sybil with slow and understated determination, Liz repeated what she had just said, namely that she had no gaps for the following week. She was full up. No room at the inn. Tough shit, but there it was. Or words to that effect.

Again, Sybil failed to register that she was being shown the door. But she was chippy by nature and she was bridling, nevertheless. The fifty-pound note lay disregarded on Liz's desk. I could do with that right now, thought Joe. That would fit snugly in my pocket.

Sybil powered ahead. 'Well, I'll play some other time. This is ridiculous. When do you have some vacancies?'

More notebook play, and Joe could see that Liz, for all her outward calm, was starting to lose control – and her temper. Her eyes were beginning to flash. Very gently, he intervened. Sybil turned on him with bewildered fury and yet some glimpse of camaraderie. Even she now could feel the ground starting to move beneath her feet. But Joe was, after all, a man. He could sort this silly woman out. It was time to bring in the heavy battalions. They never failed. Plainly Sybil just hadn't got the message at all.

'I think what Liz is trying to say, Sybil, is that Ursula and Lady Charley have pre-empted the entire situation by importing a whole host of their old school friends down to London to play bridge next week, so that Liz's booking system has gone haywire. It's been swamped, and poor old Liz here doesn't know whether she's coming or going.'

Pause, as the lie registered its impact on both women. Liz looked more relaxed all of a sudden. She nodded confirmation of the lie. These ritual executions were always messy. This sounded like a promising way out. Any port in a storm. The hair on Sybil's expensively coiffured head began to lie flat again. She started simmering down. Joe took her again, just as she was at her most vulnerable.

'Tell you what, Sybil, why don't you try that new bridge club in the Fulham Road, you know, Savage's. It's only just opened and it's said to be fantastic for its ambience. Try it once and report back. Or, if you like, I'll come along and play with you there.'

Sybil knew now that she was being dumped, but Joe's move had left her with no scope for manoeuvre. No way out for her. No spot on the bridge list for a start. And then she had always refused to play with Joe on the grounds that he intimidated her. What to do? Joe could see the thoughts coursing through her mind. Under pressure, she had become like an open book. Should she refuse his offer, she would be left with nothing. But how to rescue her wounded pride? Aye, that was the question.

She toyed briefly with the idea of falling on Liz's mercy and pleading for forgiveness, but then like any proud northerner she rejected a plea for clemency. Abruptly she reverted to type as the camouflage of social convention dropped away.

'I'll make up my own mind about that, Joe. I'll let you know. In the meantime, I'd like my change back, if you don't mind, Miss Playfair.'

The change from the fifty-pound note was counted out in silence, snatched from Liz's hand and then crammed into the proud but crestfallen Sybil's bag. Gucci, of course. Only the best. The door slammed behind her as she exited at top speed.

Joe looked at Liz, put his finger to his lips and motioned towards the door. Liz's eyes were shining with pure delight. The two of them waited about ten seconds, then Joe tiptoed to the door and opened it. Sybil was walking swiftly down the corridor but not so far away as she should have been. Ear to the door maybe? A little eavesdropping, perchance, just to poison the pill still more as she reported back to hubby that night on the dastardly behaviour of bridge circles in London?

Joe closed the door on Sybil in her rage and kissed Liz's hand. She said nothing. Her eyes spoke gratitude in volumes. Joe went into the night, but not before Liz had rebuked him for some of his more experimental bidding earlier in the session. Some things were just too important to pass without comment.

Joe left the bridge session wondering whether he had time to look again for Marcello that night. He decided that it was time for food.

## Chapter Two

High in a building on the other side of the Thames, not very far from Sloane Square, a man and a woman sat facing each other across a desk that stood perpendicular to the window and the river. They were talking together quietly at the same moment that Joe left Liz Playfair's, pondering Sybil and his quest for Marcello. It was just after nine thirty in the evening. The same velvet, plush night that had covered the sky over Sloane Square did likewise over their building. Both speakers were taut and alert, even though it was getting late.

'Always a tricky moment, the start of a mission, eh, Annie?'

'You can never tell what is going to happen. Missions are totally unpredictable. You know that. Braced for the worst, expecting the best, that's the most you can do. Sometimes it's just never enough.'

Annie spoke in short sentences, looking away from her companion and towards the dark river flowing steadily along some few feet away, outside the building. She was keyed up for the start. This was the moment they had all planned for during many months. The strategy was ambitious, imaginative and stood a fair chance of success. But there were gaps in it. Everybody acknowledged they were there. It was inevitable. Intelligence work and the tide of human affairs rarely coincided exactly. Those gaps could only be filled in by the human factor, that most mercurial of elements. She stared again at the river, thinking ahead, concentrating, trying to imagine the pitfalls to come.

Annie wanted a smooth start. No glitches at the off. If the mission could go wrong, it would go wrong from the start. She was concerned to prevent that. But her companion was inclined to chatter. She disliked and mistrusted such volubility. Intelligence work for Annie was not a cab ride but a journey right to the end of the road. The less said the better by the mission's handlers. That was her philosophy. She mistrusted the motivation of Bootface, her interlocutor, by more than just a tiny margin.

Bootface, as he was known up and down the building, had one of those squashed faces which descended, inevitably, to a proud and jutting jaw line. In the process the whole face took on the appearance of a cavalry boot – hence the nickname. Dead white in complexion, affable of manner and thoroughly experienced in this kind of work, Bootface seemed like a fine choice to make up the team. No obvious vices apart from a declared interest in horse-racing. But one of the girls had breathed a warning to Annie a week or so previously. Bootface, she had inferred, was not quite what he seemed. She thought he had some personal problem, like an expensive woman. She wasn't sure, but the warning had been clear.

'Face of a boot, but mind of a heel. Watch your step with him, Annie. He could turn quite nasty. I think he's out for what he can get.' And she had made a gesture that was quite unambiguous in its implications.

But, nevertheless, here they were together, Annie and Bootface, on this fine night, plotting the start of it all.

'You haven't told me the entire mission yet, have you, Annie?'

'I'm not certain I know it all myself. It will unfold by degrees, I think.'

That was a lie, the first of the mission. Annie did indeed know the whole mission. The lie did not augur well. But Annie was cautious. Bootface should not have asked the question. She felt obliged to be evasive. It was a very big mission indeed, the most important she had ever controlled. The sensitivity was such that no one could be trusted with the whole picture. Stuff Bootface, he could learn it as they went along. If he knew it all from the beginning, he would most likely panic, or do worse, so broad were the implications of the mission. So much hinged on Joe…

'You think Joe will be up to it? He's been around a fair enough time. You know what these agents are like. They get worn out; they just don't have the fizz for it any more.'

'He's the only one we've got and we're stuck with him. Nobody else can do it. Nobody else has the experience. All I'm worried about is his motivation. Will he feel like doing the job? That's the big question that I can't answer.'

Bootface laughed. 'Well, we've certainly put him through it.'

'He's tough. He can take it and still bounce back. He's done it before and he'll do it this time. That's what we're gambling on. The man is quality. But he may not play. After all, we're not exactly offering him the moon.'

Together Bootface and Annie had enforced the sale of Joe's villa in France because of alleged irregularities, blocked his bank accounts so that he had no way of getting at his considerable assets, and then blackguarded him in the City. That meant he could not find a job. Joe's passport had also been declared invalid through a neat deal struck with the Home Office.

Joe had been broken down stage by deliberate stage, all with the positive intent of putting him into a position where all he could do was the mission. No other options were available. To all intents and purposes, Joe was now a penniless prisoner, wandering forlornly without hopes in an open penal system that extended a mile square from Sloane Square. Busted down to his last pound and beyond. No way out without cash, or possessions, or a job, none of which he now had. Whether he liked it or not, Joe was part of the mission. Such were the rigours of modern espionage.

Joe still had bridge, thoughtfully provided for him by Annie and Bootface. But the bridge was part of the mission. It had been vital to effect an entry for Joe into the Liz Playfair establishment. That was where the key contacts for the mission would be made.

'I think it's the trapdoor for him, Annie. He stands no chance. He'll burn up. We need to position for that.'

'That's your view is it?'

Annie was thoughtful. She couldn't deny the justice of what Bootface had said. It was commonplace in the trade that there was always a final mission for a spy when the obligation of duality grew too oppressive and provoked mental breakdown. That was the risk. Or alternatively, when they could glimpse normality just across the creek, they ran for it, jettisoning the mission in the process. Such was the calculus built into spying. The more valuable and experienced a spy became, the more he wanted to enjoy the normality of his own life – and the more he had to be headed off from that option. But finally, and inevitably, a process of crystallisation took place. The spy went through the trapdoor. For him or her, it was over then. As for the mission... Wiser, for all concerned, to get that final mission well under way before the trapdoor loomed.

'Bootface, he's shown none of the signs. He seems healthy enough.'

'Appearances. You can't trust them.'

'Well, we'll see tonight, won't we?'

'Indeed we shall.'

'Appearances are all we have to go on. They're our only guide.'

Silence fell between them and Annie reflected that it was unlike a guy to become quite so combative and assertive so early on in a mission. Later on, certainly, when the mission looked to be succeeding, that was normally when the male assertion reared its head. But right at the start... It was odd. That whispered warning to her might well have been correct. Bootface certainly appeared to have an agenda more than slightly separate from the mission.

She would watch him all the time.

Joe caught the 22 bus which rattled down the King's Road. He recognised the conductor, who saluted him as he boarded the bus. Joe stuck out his tongue in response and climbed to the upper deck, reflecting that propinquity was the curse of poverty. You know everybody and you can't get away from them. Even the beggars... Figures stuck in a landscape. It's a solid old world down here below the salt, he cursed.

Leaving the bus, he climbed the stairs to his rickety flat situated close to the rough old game of the World's End housing estate. Across the street, in the small piazza, a couple of people had been murdered last week, quite casually, for the contents of their purse and wallet, most likely by crack fiends. But that night Joe was not deterred by fears of danger; he felt fleet and limber, almost invulnerable. High on survival hopes. He paused to stare at the crack in the wall beside his front door. The crack, a long scar running down the concrete, was a mental test for him, normally his first of the day. Sometimes the crack seemed longer, sometimes shorter, always depending on his mood. He could measure his paranoia about survival by the apparent length of the crack.

That night the bridge had been fun. He felt partly restored to himself, although the sight of Sybil's fifty-pound note floating idly on Liz's table still rankled with him. That fifty pounds equated to a couple of bills he had to pay very shortly for which he had no resources whatsoever. But no matter, God would provide. Or the stock market, or the cards. Or all three.

The crack had stayed where it was. No further subsidence; the building seemed intact. So far so good, Joe thought. Briefly reassured, he pushed into his flat. It was sparse, undecorated and only barely furnished. No place for smart parties. Apart from his gambling at cards and his trading on the Stock Exchange, Joe had no sources of income whatsoever. Home comforts came a long way down the list of spending priorities.

Joe wanted to check out a speech given that night at the Mansion House by the chancellor, Philip Snowden. Joe was running an open uncovered bear position on British Steel, which so far had grossed enough in profit to pay that month's mortgage instalment. He had sold four hundred thousand shares that day, shares which he did not own, in the expectation that they would fall in price over the next few days, on the back of Snowden's speech. Snowden, Joe reckoned, was both a fool and an obvious worthy fool. He had no conception of how markets worked. The speech, Joe had calculated, would be the usual dreary rehearsal of Labour's brilliant plans, and the pound would soar on the back of his words. The boys in the market could read Snowden easily enough – buffoon.

Joe flicked his TV to Ceefax, and read enough of the summary of Snowden's speech to convince him that the trade was correct. The pound had risen too, in New York, even before the chancellor had sat down. British Steel, as one of Britain's major exporters, would be clobbered by all this. Tomorrow the share price should get hammered.

Pleased, Joe thought about his dinner. Things were looking up and that crack outside should be shrinking now. A quick purchase of the British Steel shares around lunchtime tomorrow, a rapid closing out of his position, and some lovely cash would come tumbling his way. His abode would be safe for another month. It was perilous stuff, though. It would only take one wrong trade and Joe would be wiped out. Hurled forthwith into the gutters of London. Not so far to fall now.

Joe cleared such gloomy thoughts from his mind and prepared to sally out again. He was hungry and in a hurry; Zorba's souvlaki beckoned. He happened to glance at his phone, not expecting to find any messages. It was hard for anyone to call him now, even if they wanted to, since he had taken great pains to go to ground in maximum obscurity. His phone number was known to only about five people, he reckoned, and none of those, apart from his broker, would have called on an ordinary Wednesday evening.

The panel showed that he had received one message. The single digit winked at him accusingly. Joe took the message. It shocked him. The message was like a phantasm rising from the tomb to confront him over his rich and successful past. He had not expected the call.

'Joe, this is Emma here. You remember, Emma Bales. Yes, of course you do, you are as incapable of forgetting our little series of foot-tapping experiences as I am. Anyway, listen, Joe, I have had the greatest difficulty in tracking you down and you've been exceedingly naughty in not giving out your phone number to respectable people like me. What are you, some kind of spy or what? Anyway, now that I've run you to earth, I want to see you. No, not to make mad passionate love to you, that can come later. I want to see you about a quest I'm on…'

That makes two of us, babe, thought Joe wryly. Too few needles, so many haystacks. The voice from the past droned on. Such a mistake to revisit what's dead and done, thought Joe. This is going to cost me grief, of that I am certain.

The last time Joe had seen Emma Bales he'd been a force in the City, making one million pounds a year. Now he couldn't even pay his mortgage.

'…so will you please call me back on any of the following numbers. Be warned – I will pester you until you make contact. You are the only person I know who can help me over this. Please, Joe, my little runaway, don't be difficult over this. It's very important to me.'

Thereupon followed the usual galaxy of digits: mobile

number; a London number, which from the exchange configuration suggested that Emma lived quite close to Joe, somewhere in Kensington; and a final set of digits which Joe recognised as an exchange in Norfolk. But not the old number Joe had known just outside Norwich. She must have moved. Things had been happening to Emma Bales. In his high proud days of pomp, Joe and Emma had spent a blissful night together just outside Norwich. But that had been some years ago. How much now had changed.

Our Emma sounds as if she's done quite well for herself, thought Joe, reflecting that under no circumstances whatsoever would he ever return her call. The past is another country which I will not revisit. She can join the Fat Man, and other will-o'-the-wisps like Johnny and Spongo in my personal portfolio of ghosts. It always pays to leave the past alone. Only the future beckons, although what on earth that may bring, heaven only knows.

It was Joe's fixed intention to put enough money together from his gambling to sell up and leave. Australia, the United States, anywhere, just provided he could quit Britain. Nothing could be allowed to interfere with that plan. Britain had worked for him once; now it worked against him. He had chosen a route through and it had petered out. It was that simple. Time for fresh fields and pastures new.

Joe stood up, fumbling for his keys on the bed, and checked that everything was in place. His gaze travelled around the small flat. Slowly it stopped. It can't be true, he thought, I just don't believe this. No, no, no, not again. I just don't believe it. They must be kidding. Not now, not in the state I'm in. Go away, just go away and leave me alone.

He paused, then went outside the flat to stare at the crack. It did not appear to have moved. No comfort there. He stepped back into the flat and looked again. Rage and disappointment gripped him as he checked out what he had seen, realising only too clearly that his eyes had not deceived him. It was a signal. No doubt about that. It was certainly a signal. Not only that, but it was a signal that he alone knew, and only too well. The Fat Man had used it years ago in Berlin to warn him that something was afoot, something dangerous, something unexpected. It was far easier than a verbal warning. No need to talk at all.

The two clocks in Joe's bed-sitting room had been shifted from their spot beside the bed to a more prominent place on the mantelpiece. One had been put back exactly an hour and the second had been put forward by the same amount.

Still craving food, Joe walked forward and picked up the two clocks and stared at them. One read ten forty-five and the other eight forty-five. Impossible to be mistaken. Those clocks had been moved and reset deliberately.

By whom? Joe didn't care. When? At some point between mid-afternoon, when he had returned from his gambling with Joxer at the Jack of Hearts, and now. That was for sure. Those clocks always resided beside Joe's bed, one to wake up and one to get up. They were never moved. But the time was immaterial. The important point was that someone, or indeed perhaps some people, had entered the flat, with the purpose of giving him a warning signal. It was very discreetly done. It always was and it always would be. No point in checking for anything else in the flat that might have been moved, stolen, or broken. These boys were professionals. They would have left everything else as it was. They believed in an extreme economy of effects – just the signal and nothing else. No pantomime. No charades.

They weren't telling a story; they were making a point. Hello, Joe, they were saying, good to see you again. In good shape as always. Glad to see you're taking exercise. What nice weather we're having. Now about this mission... You're with us, of course, even though we've bust you down to your last pound and beyond. You have no problems about risking your neck, do you?

Deep in thought, Joe locked his flat behind him and wandered down the stairs out of the block and into the King's Road. The rate of exchange did not seem to be in his favour. But then, was it ever, dealing with the Gents?

Annie took the call.

'Yeah, he's left his flat and he's walking down the King's Road. Looks cool. Usual place I would think, yeah, Zorba's. That's where he normally goes on Wednesday evening. Any more you want?'

Annie let the watcher go. No point in tailing Joe now. He knew the game too well. He'd done enough tailing himself. Now it was important not to put any pressure on him. The algebra of espionage was grinding into position. Signals were all that were needed. But it was important that he went to Zorba's nevertheless. That too would constitute a signal – one of partial assent. Bootface and Annie waited high in their tower for fresh information, as the Thames ran fresh and quick at their feet.

They thought he would go to Zorba's. It would be more convenient. They had a surprise waiting for Joe at Zorba's.

Joe decided to go to Zorba's. Just by conforming to his usual routine he knew he was sending a signal back to the watchers. Yes, he had seen the clocks; yes, he was keen to play with them some more. That wasn't quite what he meant to indicate. But the alternative seemed too gross. Stay all night in the flat, like Achilles in his tent? No way. The swift leap onto a fast red and dinner in a strange new exotic restaurant? Hardly. He didn't have the cash for such an extravagant gesture. Besides, he might not enjoy his meal so much. Joe opted for a neutral position, determined to play along with events for the time being. That, at least, would cost him nothing.

The Fat Man rose from his tomb and gibbered a little at Joe in his imaginings as he thought again of the two clocks. Berlin came flooding back in a tide.

Joe walked on, a little more swiftly perhaps, as a basic sense of stimulus started to pulse within him. Skirting great-bellied Norman with his shaven bullet head, one of the most prominent and coarse-voiced beggars on the strip, and fortunately unseen by the tramp, Joe ambled into Zorba's and made for his usual table.

Nothing out of place so far as he could see. Darkness, bustle, sounds of hearty chomping. Faces smiling at the food and drink. Nothing to give the moment or the place a troubled sense of ambiguity, the hallmark of espionage. Nothing at all. Joe started to relax, his mind though still turning around the sight of the two clocks. After some swift injections of alcohol he would soon start seeing all that too in a different light. Returning briefly to the present, he realised that he still had Lady C's letter to post the following day. But Lady C seemed a cosmos away from Joe's sense of reality.

Pot-bellied Zorba waddled about as usual, poised to fetch him a glass of retsina; Charley was in the corner drooling over photos of his granddaughter in Sierra Leone; and the crack dealers were lurking at the far corner of the restaurant, white teeth glinting in the darkness, mobile phones waving about as they took eager calls from new clients in the area.

The crack dealers had moved in a few months previously and were finding rich pickings among the stockbrokers and merchant bankers on the strip. Joe wanted to be close to the dealers at moments like this. If he was going to disappear over the edge, as he had been frequently tempted to do during his stretch in the Sloane Square open prison, he wanted them to be there when he fell, to fill him so full of dope that it would take him out for ever. Just one fatal shudder of morale, he thought, followed by one massive fix. That's all it takes, and I'll be hooked, screaming for another shot like everyone else. Let the crack hit the brain in massive quantities.

His gaze travelled round the restaurant and took in a quiet studious-looking man in the far corner by the window, bent over some texts and fully absorbed in reading while he was eating. Then his eye stopped dead at the table in front of him. He hadn't noticed this at first. In fact he'd missed it completely.

A young man sat at the table with his head in his hands, weeping. Not loudly, not aggressively, but still sobbing. He was crying from the heart as only adults can do. Quite out of control. The man raised his unseeing eyes towards Joe, eyes that were red and blind with tears, and streams ran down his cheeks in furrows. Then down went his head again, and the body went up and down as the breathing grew staccato. In a very bad way indeed.

Charley held the menu up to Joe and said plaintively, 'He's been like that all evening. Just sitting there crying his eyes out. We've been walking on tiptoe. Nobody knows why he's crying but I think it's something to do with that book he's been reading. See, that one beside him on the table.'

A large book lay open and face down beside the man on the table. What Charley said was true. Just then the weeper gulped, took another look at the book, and this triggered a fresh source of whinging and weeping.

Charley continued remorselessly. 'Your usual, Joe?'

Joe nodded absently. The crack dealers stared at the weeping man with vacant looks of detached disdain. They were long inured to the spectacle of human tragedy. Indeed, it was an indispensable part of their world. Back to playing with the mobiles.

This is not a set-up, Joe thought. British intelligence does not revive long-lost agents by using men crying in public in Greek tavernas. That is something that is just not done. British intelligence is far too subtle for that. I'm safe here. I can enjoy some grub.

But as Joe ruminated, he reflected wryly that he was back in the spying game again, at least partially, whether or not he made a decision. The training and the exposure to risk were too profoundly embedded in him, the reflexes too heavily tuned in one specific direction. Already that sense of ambiguity was gripping him, that permanent impression that nothing was quite what it appeared to be. He was sliding back into that world where appearances were always deceptive. Where the garage forecourt attendant at the nearest petrol station might prove to be a key ally, indeed a god, in Joe's own little world. Joe was assenting to the signal involuntarily.

A couple of tough-looking young men wandered past the window outside, peered in, and then wandered off. The door of the restaurant opened again to admit a brisk, fresh alert young man aged perhaps twenty-five, who strode in followed by an equally smart and bright-looking young woman. They were charged with energy and grace. Out on the spree, bent on celebrating their considerable good fortune in being alive and together and beautiful.

At that moment the weeper looked up and his eyes met those of the newcomer through his tears. A sort of strangled 'Aaargh!' barked from his throat and the two held each other's gaze. They knew each other. Knew each other well.

'Pugh,' said the tall young man who had just entered. 'What are you doing here? And what on earth's the matter?'

'Oh Christ. Oh God!' was all the response he received. Then Pugh rose to his feet, eyes still dripping with tears, and pointing to the book beside him, half said, half croaked, 'Look. Named. Oh my God.'

Then Pugh hurried past the new entrants. He was soon out of the door. Joe looked out into the street from his table. He froze. He could see only too clearly what was about to happen.

Pugh, still waving his book, stood blindly on the pavement, as the traffic whipped past him. It stopped for a second and he tottered across the street, heading, in his shame, for one of the dark side roads off the strip. Silently the two toughs followed behind him. A mugging was about to take place. A commonplace event in the neighbourhood now that the drugs boys had moved in.

For reasons that had little to do with sense and everything to do with compassion, Joe found himself in the street. Slipping through the traffic, he followed the toughs. They had cornered Pugh by now; a knife had appeared.

Moving swiftly, Joe arrived behind the small knot of the trio. Without hesitation, he cracked the toughs' heads together hard. Then, bending down in a single movement, he brought the flat of his hand up in a scything arc that crashed into a groin. An awful scream from the victim, as Joe turned instantly to the other tough, knocking him straight against the wall before taking him with the left. Joe connected well as the fist swung from his pivoted hip with full weight behind the punch. It was all happening very fast, but also in slow motion. Joe's fist took the impact of the bone in the chin well, the knuckles riding the impact with a curve. His man sagged against the wall, then Joe swung round again very sharply, taking his first opponent on the bridge of his nose with the balled back of his hand.

Pugh gaped open-mouthed at the balletic cruelty of it all. He was quaking. Then Joe grabbed him and hustled him back across the street, then down another side street, moving at speed towards Battersea Bridge, obscurity and safety.

'Where is it that you want to go, Pugh? Best get out of here fast. They'll recover and come looking for you.'

'You know me too.'

'No way. I heard the name in the restaurant.'

'Yes, that was Archie. I was at school with him. A close rival. He will have enjoyed seeing me in tears.'

Always that sense of outraged *amour-propre* to the fore, thought Joe, as the two of them hurried through the dark streets. I've just saved this guy's wallet, if not his life, yet he's still brooding on ancient grudges. What a race of men we have here.

'Are we going the right way for you? I think maybe you should head for home.'

Now that the immediate danger of extinction was past, Pugh was recovering his assertiveness. Medium height, medium build, with gold pebble glasses and a boyish beguiling manner. Quite chunky in build but evidently no brawler. Joe recognised the type.

'Who are you?'

'My name's Joe. I'm a bridge player.'

'Just that? You play bridge and nothing else?'

'Just bridge.'

'How extraordinary. A friend of mine at school said he was going to do that, but he just wasn't good enough.'

Pugh paused and the tears started again. Joe could see the chain of thought. Friend at school, who failed, whereas Pugh had sailed on and on, until that day when… Joe guessed that the tears and the book were somehow connected to his career. Or absence of it now, by the look of things.

They moved quickly through the darkness and came to Battersea Bridge. It arched solidly across the Thames, with the river full and swirling beneath. To their left, the Albert Bridge gleamed like a pontoon to fairyland. Unreal. Joe prepared to say goodnight. He was thinking of the dinner at Zorba's which by now would have been returned to the kitchen. It was proving impossible that night to get even a morsel of food down his gullet. Time to hurry back. No thugs to be seen. All looked safe.

'I'll leave you, here, Pugh. Time for my dinner.'

'I can't thank you enough…'

'Not to worry. It was a pleasure. Well, almost a pleasure. Good to see the left is still working on cue. But best forget about all that now. Now you should hurry home and get to bed.'

Joe watched Pugh take the first few steps across the bridge and turned on his heel to return to Zorba's. He marched a few paces as quickly as possible, thinking about food. Then he heard a cry, panting, and more hurrying footsteps behind him. Gold-rimmed spectacles appeared at his elbow.

Pugh was humble, deflated and beseeching. He gripped Joe by the arm. 'Joe, I'm sorry, you have to help me. If you will, that is. I can't get over the bridge.'

Joe laughed. 'You put one foot after the other and you blow. It's easy.'

'Easy for you, but not for me. I'm afraid that if I get halfway across I'll throw myself into the river. I've had a terrible shock today. I just can't trust myself to get over that bridge alive.'

Pugh held up the dreaded book and looked wholly pathetic. He waved it at Joe as if in explanation. Joe could guess just how much the effort to call for help had cost him. He took pity on Pugh and shrugged.

'Come on, then, let's do it. Let's take whatever speed you like. There must be a gag in this somewhere about bridges and bridge, but I can't think of it.'

Together they trudged across the bridge, with Joe taking it slowly, measuring his pace to match Pugh's. Pugh trailed along, clutching his book and gazing with fascinated concentration at the waves beneath. Joe could gauge again just what was passing through his mind and offered silent sympathy. He had no desire for bonding with this haughty maimed individual, but nonetheless he felt obliged to offer some human succour. Suicide is about despair and despair is fatal to life, he thought. Must help a little.

They reached the middle of the bridge, and Pugh began to tremble. The urge to destroy himself was strong. Joe stood there beside him and waited against the wind and the tide as Pugh struggled with his conscience.

What on earth can there have been in that book for a man, and clearly quite a clever man poised for the best, to want to kill himself, Joe mused, struck at the same time that he too was virtually part of the same syndrome, courtesy of the two clocks earlier that evening. Death went dogging everywhere.

Pugh gazed down longingly at the waves.

'Don't do it; it's not worth it,' said Joe, trying to choose his moment.

Pugh nodded, and then shrugged, wondering clearly what Joe might do to prevent his leap from the bridge. He paused again. This was the critical moment.

'Pughs are never named. Our family is unseen,' he said very slowly.

Decisively but reluctantly, still moved by compassion, Joe very slowly took Pugh's hand in his and began to walk him firmly towards the Battersea side of the bridge. The hand did not dissent. With a sigh, Pugh suffered himself to be marched from the place of temptation. The clouds in the night sky blew about in random formations. The stuffing had gone out of Pugh. He complied with Joe's determination. He had chosen life, not the family heritage.

They reached the end of the bridge and Joe disengaged his hand. Pugh was silent for a second.

'I really wanted to do it, you know. I was going to jump, just when you took my hand. It was well timed of you.' The precision in Pugh's speech had not deserted him. It was like a part of his breeding.

Joe shrugged it off. 'I've seen that kind of thing before.'

'Oh, really.'

'Yes, the bridge world can get very intense.'

'I would never have thought it.' Pugh paused. 'Look, Joe, I think you may have saved my life twice over tonight. Can I take your phone number, at least? When I've recovered myself a little, I'll give you a call and tell you what it was all about. Will you let me do that? I owe you for all of this, not to mention our little matter back in the Fulham Road.'

Joe disclosed his telephone number with no manifest reluctance, thinking that his phone, after being dead for many, many months, was about to become red-hot.

'There's an answerphone on that too. You can always leave a message.'

'Yes, I suppose you'd need an answerphone, to pick up the bridge calls.'

Joe thought about Joxer Treadwell, his bridge gambling partner, he of the hyper-hypodermic. Well, not quite, sir, he thought; some arrangements have their own form of communication, irrespective of telephones.

Pugh shambled off and Joe watched him turn right at the pizza house some sixty yards away. Then it was back to Zorba's in three minutes flat, courtesy of a passing black cab.

'It should be quite a party by now. They should be chatting away quite merrily,' said Bootface confidently.

'Don't bank on it,' Annie growled in reply. She didn't mean to growl, but the blithe assumptions of Bootface that everything would automatically go smoothly were starting to grate. She felt like the Black Queen as she made her cautionary comments and she hated him for that as well. Playing Cassandra was not what she'd been brought up to expect.

'Simple enough situation, though,' replied Bootface. 'I can't see what can go wrong at this stage. Let's nip out and have a spot of dinner and a chat about something else apart from this blasted mission.'

Annie gaped at him. The idea of deserting her post in the middle of the fray would indeed never have occurred to her. 'Are you serious?'

'Perfectly. Tell you what then, if you want to play the Florrie Nightingale bit, you stay here and I'll go and feed. No sense in both of us wasting our time.' So saying, Bootface stood up, stretched elegantly and showily, and then wandered over to the door. 'See you in a few minutes then. God, will that Guinness taste good after all this hanging around.'

The door closed noisily behind him, leaving Annie in a state of considerable confusion. Truly this was going to be an awful mission, she thought to herself. He had no commitment whatsoever. She felt like a fool and an old maid saying this to herself, as if she'd turned into some crosspatch Mother Superior, but she had to face the truth of the situation. Bootface might just as well have been shopping at Marks for all the concern he felt about the outcome of Joe's mission. And Joe's mission was very, very dangerous. He had only to make one false move, and he would be dead in a flash. He was up against very ruthless guys indeed. No quarter even considered. Joe knew nothing about the mission because that was the easiest way of retaining his confidence. He needed to be eased into the whole thing slowly, with emphasis on the naturalness of it all. They were working with the grain of the situations as they arose. But it could all go very badly wrong. In a moment. So was there a jinx on this thing? She'd felt it sway a little from the word go. Everything which had happened subsequently confirmed her apprehensions. What disasters lay ahead, heaven alone knew. But Bootface was emphatically the wrong man for the assignment. No way either of changing him. She was stuck with him.

She was left alone in the vigil room with her thoughts, as the waves ran swiftly past.

'Where have you been?' asked Charley. 'We had to put your dinner back in the oven twice, and you've lost your table. You'll have to share with that man over there by the window, the one who's reading. We couldn't hold your table for ever. It's busy now. You can see that.'

Joe got the plaintive message and wandered across to the table by the window. The restaurant was full to bursting point now and the crack dealers had gone, he noticed. Off to ply their trade in the mansions of Redcliffe Square among the naive glitterati.

'Do you mind if I...?'

'Not at all. It'll be a pleasure. You can have all the table. I've finished eating. I'll clear a space away from my books. It'll be a pleasure to have some company.'

Joe noted a slight accent. German perhaps, or Austrian? The reference to company marked him out as almost certainly European, as did the careful way that he husbanded his books away, as if they were made of gold. And the English detested casual company. They would walk a million miles to avoid the rigours of a chat with a total stranger, something the Germans, in particular, relished.

'You disappeared very suddenly. What happened?'

Joe fell easily into conversation. 'I suddenly realised I had an urgent phone call to make. You can't telephone anyone from here. It's far too noisy. I had to go outside.'

'They were very worried about your absence. Charley – is it Charley? – kept taking your dinner away and then bringing it back. He was like a great hen. He should really just have sat upon it and kept it warm that way.' Again a slightly Germanic intonation.

They both laughed at the idea of Charley the hen. The stranger offered Joe a glass of retsina from his carafe.

Joe gave him a warning. 'Be careful. I can see you're not from these parts. This could be one of those nights. When Zorba's gets very full, the chef comes out for a breather, and tells jokes. In Anglo-Turkish. Bad jokes too. He can ruin a meal that he has just prepared with his jokes. Be warned.'

They clinked glasses, and the stranger introduced himself. 'Joachim. From Munich. I am here to complete my doctorate.'

'My name is Joe. I play bridge.'

'So Charley was telling me.'

Joe said nothing about his fluent German or his terrifying experiences in cold war Berlin. It made life easier for everyone.

'What is the doctorate about?'

'Twentieth-century British finance. Do you know anything about this?'

'Not a thing. Interesting stuff?'

For one moment Joe had overlooked his meteoric career in the City which had taken him right to the top of the merchant banking community. That was before his fall. Now he was just a bridge player. No more to be said. His one million pounds a year was just a distant memory, just as the Jews at Auschwitz, slaving in the mud, recalled their thriving businesses.

'It is proving to be somewhat tricky on occasion, Joe. Parts of it I just don't understand. British finance is a total mystery to me.'

'Not sure I can help you there. Not my subject,' Joe mumbled. His food had arrived. He was wolfing it down. Only now was he discovering just how hungry he was. He was happy enough with his role as dumb card player, now that he could get his gnashers around the lamb souvlaki.

'Do you mind if I talk?'

'Not at all, provided you don't mind my eating away at the same time.'

'Have some more wine.' Joachim poured out some more retsina, and began what was evidently a well-rehearsed piece of dialogue. 'Take Macmillan, for example. The means whereby he became prime minister are so odd. Really odd. I cannot write this, of course, in any thesis, but during the Suez crisis he behaved not as you might have expected. More like a spy.'

A huge bell clanged its chimes in Joe's head. He willed his face to remain still, his features to stay taut, his expression to remain unconcerned and his teeth to keep chewing. Spy, spy, why mention spy? His mind raced ahead. This was different. Two clocks. It was a pick-up. It had to be a pick-up. It could be nothing else. Two clocks... Give nothing away, he told himself. Just swallow. You're imagining things. Keep a straight face and then say ridiculous.

'Ridiculous.'

'I thought you'd say that.'

Two clocks, two clocks. So fast as well. He'd only received the signal about an hour previously. They must be in a hurry. A tearing hurry.

Joe drank down some more retsina and apologised for his concentration on the food.

'Just say all that to me again. So far as I can gather, Macmillan was one of our better prime ministers.'

Joachim smiled, a touch condescendingly. 'I know how proud you English are of your heritage, but the facts lead us to a far more ambivalent conclusion. Things are not what they appear to be.'

'They rarely are in this country.' I'll give him back some of his own currency, thought Joe. I'll assent to his thought process. That's highly invitational. Let's see how he copes with it.

Joachim coped very well. 'Yes, you're really getting the message. I'm very impressed. But let's look again, as I said, at the facts. Britain invades Suez, after Nasser seizes the Suez Canal. Anthony Eden, prime minister at the time and still fighting the wars against the dictators of 1938, is also critically ill; he has had a major operation, and the surgeon has sliced through his bile duct. He is in terrible pain. According to one view, he is at that moment clinically insane. Now what doesn't happen at this moment?'

Joe stared silently at Joachim, trying to look stupid, and feeling his way into this new situation. It was very high grade information that was passing across the table, though. He could feel that.

'Search me. I'm not a historian. You tell me.'

'The Americans do not intervene. Of course they don't. Britain and the US have run the world on a non-aggression basis since 1945. Just as the CIA overthrew Mossadeq in Persia in 1953, so too would the US refuse to intervene here. And my friend...'

Joachim paused dramatically, staring at Joe. Dumbly Joe gazed back while his mind raced ahead. This must be briefing, he told himself. But about what? My God, what on earth do they have in store for me?'

'Initially the Americans do not intervene. Why not? Because the work of recapturing the Canal is proceeding very well. The troops have landed, they are recapturing territory, and at a certain stage, the operation looks to be a certain success. As you might expect. That is not the situation as reported, nor indeed as perceived, but that is the truth of the matter.'

'What happened then?'

'The US changed its tune. Eisenhower, then US president, telephoned Eden. In the language of the camp, so I gather, he threatened to destroy the pound on the foreign exchanges if the UK did not pull out from the expedition.'

'And?'

'Of course, the UK was forced to comply with the US threats. Since 1945, it had been the junior partner in the US alliance. The expedition was a complete failure. It led directly to Eden's resignation, and the temporary collapse of the ruling Tory junta.'

'But where does Macmillan come into it?'

'I will tell you. You are not as dumb as you pretend to be, Joe. You catch on fast.'

Joe nodded at him. This was crazy, he thought, but it's proceeding at a very satisfactory clip. Say on, my sweet German brother, say on. This is fascinating.

'Macmillan had been the main force in the cabinet arguing in favour of armed intervention. Not only did he reverse his position on Suez almost overnight, just as Halifax did with Chamberlain over appeasement in 1938 and stabbing Chamberlain in the back in the process, but it is possible that Macmillan was also responsible for the switch in the American attitude. As the pressure began to build up on the pound, it is alleged that Macmillan telephoned the United States to enquire whether the administration would support a UK drawing from the IMF to support the pound. If that is true, then Macmillan himself was responsible for handing the US a weapon which, at the time of the crisis, it did not know it possessed.'

Joe stared at Joachim in silence, waiting for more. This was lamb souvlaki with a vengeance. Charley came bustling over to take away the plates and to show off photos of his granddaughter but Joe waved him away, still focusing on Joachim. Aggrieved, Charley slunk away.

'No one knows whether Macmillan made the call or not. Macmillan says he did, in his memoirs, but no other memoirs concur with that statement. It seems just too incredible for the British to take on board, that a chancellor should act like that to destroy his own prime minister. Both old Etonians, of course. Known each other from school. It's not as if they were strangers to each other. Mac did make notes and keep diaries on the Suez crisis but he destroyed everything early in 1957, after he had become prime minister. Now read this; it is an extract from the official history of the Bank of England for the period by John Fforde and is specifically about the mysterious telephone call. This is what I was reading over dinner. I still can't make sense of it, and nor, I suspect, could Fforde.'

Joachim continued to talk as Joe read over the page.

'He says something to the effect that there's an inherent implausibility in all of this. Would the chancellor have offered the Americans a card at this vital moment, a card which they themselves did not know they held in their hand? Well, of course, in Macmillan's case, nothing was inherently implausible. Again, would he have made the call when the exchange rate was not yet in crisis mode, without talking to colleagues, but when officials were advising against such an approach? Most certainly he would have done. During the war, according to one observer, he tore up a telegram from Churchill explicitly forbidding him to take part in – I think – the Italian campaign; drawled "You never saw that, did you?" threw the scraps in the fire, and went off on the campaign. Macmillan was a very lone operator. And he should have known what he himself actually did. So is Fforde right when he says it seems right to assume that no call was made on 6 November, although it remains a possibility that he might have done, pending the emergence of fresh evidence?'

'He doesn't know either,' said Joe handing the book back across the table. 'He does his best but he's fogged like the rest of us.'

'You can see why my thesis is so difficult. Nobody knows for certain what really took place. And the Suez crisis was one of the most important moments in the twentieth century for the UK, certainly in terms of its sheer power to change things. The Tory Party was split right down the middle and Eden, who'd been waiting for the job for twenty years, was thrown out overnight in favour of Macmillan, who in the 1930s had been viewed as certainly a socialist and perhaps even a communist.'

'A communist?'

'His trip to Moscow, wearing the famous white hat, was what made his early premiership. The Russians made him very welcome. Everybody saw that. But I digress. Nobody knows for sure what Macmillan was up to. But Macmillan the mad socialist of the thirties got the job as PM. The outsider burst through despite Suez and despite the travails of his marriage. His wife, as you know, had a thirty-year affair with Bob Boothby. "I am married to Harold but my heart is with Bob" is what she said, more or less. That kind of thing toughens a man up. It certainly put some steel into the foppish Macmillan, I can see that. But the key point is here. Without Suez, Macmillan would not have got the job. He took incredible risks to get that position and to manoeuvre Eden off the podium. For what? Would anyone have taken those risks just for himself alone? Was there some other interplay of factors taking place which we don't know about which would explain it all?'

Joachim paused. There was a lot to tell. Joe wondered just how much briefing he was going to get that night. But Joachim seemed genuinely puzzled.

'You see, I am beginning to think that the real significance of what Macmillan did over Suez lies elsewhere. We have perhaps to think on a broader scale and on a different time frame. We have to make a series of quite daring mental leaps. I will not tell you everything in my mind – and as you might have gathered, you are now getting some of the plums in my thesis – but let us agree on the simple proposition that by 1955 Britain was already a great power in decline. And living out the illusions that come with refusing to believe that decline is setting in. Shall we agree on that?'

'Agreed.' All this would sound much easier in German or even French, thought Joe, and it would also make better sense, but let it pass. Sufficient unto the moment...

'Now the most important thing about that year was the European conference at Messina, when by and large the problems of the European colonies, especially for the French, were sorted out in anticipation of the establishment of the Common Market a few years later. The British did not even send a junior civil servant. That was the level of British interest. Nil. Now around this time Macmillan takes this fantastic risk, this utterly fantastic risk, let us again assume, first by persuading his PM to lead the UK into the Suez expedition and then, by working the three card trick over the pound, becoming PM himself. An amazing business. But why?'

'You tell me, Joachim.'

Joe was careful not to sound too enthusiastic about the information drilling across the table to him, but he could feel great tracts of dead self beginning to awaken. A marsh in spring. It was like hearing the sound of distant trumpets.

'I have been doing some work on Britain's application to join the Common Market in the early sixties led by Ted Heath. Now we apparently negotiated in good faith, but the conclusion of some of the research papers I have read is unequivocal. Britain had no interest in joining and did its best to scupper the negotiations at every turn. It is all there in black and white. That is why, for example, Macmillan made his offer of US nuclear weapons to de Gaulle, on the eve of some crucial moment in the talks. Macmillan knew that the offer would so outrage de Gaulle that he would veto Britain's application. This is all very fuzzy. But at the end of the talks, when the veto had been announced, and de Gaulle saw Macmillan in for a private talk, the general was so moved by the state of anguish on Macmillan's face that he almost said *"Ne pleurez pas milord."* Do not weep, my lord.'

'Thank you,' said Joe. 'My French has never been that hot.'

'*"Ne pleurez pas, milord."* But was Macmillan really in such a state? All the research I have made about him suggests that he was a totally consummate stage actor, a man incapable of not playing to an audience. So if Macmillan was negotiating not to join the Common Market, it would have been natural to play the pathetic part that he did. That would have completed the picture. I think now – very, very tentatively, you understand – that Macmillan was bluffing the old general. He was putting on an act. He had been negotiating in very bad faith and he had succeeded. The general was not to know that at all. So the general was bluffed.'

'Why would Macmillan want to do that?'

Joachim played hard to get. 'You mustn't ask me that too quickly. My conclusions are fairly dynamic and I'm not at all certain that I can disclose them to you at this stage.'

'You could try.'

'No, I am too nervous about it all. I believe that I am on the brink of finding out something so shattering about Britain in the twentieth century, through its financial structures, that I want to be absolutely certain of my findings before I reveal them to anyone. It is a shocking conclusion that I am reaching.'

'Be brave. Try me. I'm very grown up about these things.'

'No, Joe, I daren't. But you have been a very good audience. I have enjoyed talking to you. We can meet again and discuss it a little further. I will dribble the truth out to you in stages. Or the truth as I see it, that is.' The way that Joachim rolled his r's suggested that he'd be paying a visit to a good dentist before long. The guttural sounds were quite nauseating.

'I'd like that,' Joe replied, wondering if, in his interest in Joachim's revelations, he'd been just a little too interested and a little too obviously more than just the no-braining bridge player he claimed to be. But so what?

Just as the two clocks had warned, contact had been made with something from the shadows in a way that betokened no questions. The whole thing had been very classy. It had been done in broad daylight, under the noses of Charley and Zorba, although Zorba's at close on midnight was not exactly the noonday sun. But the innocent happenstance way in which Joe and Joachim had met up together meant they could meet again quite naturally, without setting tongues wagging.

And there might be quite a few meetings to come. Lots of briefings. Joe found that already he was half assenting to the invitation winging its way from God knew where across the abyss of reality. He regretted the assent, but his soul had already betrayed him, thrilling at once to the thought of battle ahead.

Joachim then clinched it. He set up another meeting.

'Let me leave you my card, so that you can call me to fix another meeting. And let me leave you with a question. Who won the war? Now, Joe, you know the answer to that question, it is engraved on the hearts of every Englishman. Come on, who won the war?'

'We did, of course. But didn't we? Leastways, that's what I was taught at school, squire.'

'Wrong on both counts, Joe. There were two wars, and Britain lost them both. How about that?'

'Well, stripe me pink and colour me purple.'

'I'm sorry, what you pink?'

'Just an expression, Joachim. Well, you do know how to tell them, my son. I'll give you that. Now what were these wars?'

'Next time, Joe, next time. You will not be disappointed. And I, for my part, look forward to delivering another little lecture. The fruits of my research, so to speak, for a class of one.'

Joachim rose to go and Joe stumbled awkwardly to his feet as only the purblind English can when abroad. They shook hands. Then Joachim was off into the night, swinging his heavy briefcase as he walked briskly away. Joe watched him turn the corner and then found Charley at his elbow. He felt tired, it had been a long night. Charley was insistent about his photos, and Joe looked them over, cooing on cue.

A young wild-eyed woman, beautifully dressed but with haggard eyes and dishevelled hair, burst into the restaurant and looked around desperately. She wasn't after her man but her dope. It was tragic to observe. She was screaming for a fix. Her fingers twitched and played with her clothes. She was in a bad way.

'Oh,' she groaned, failing to spot the crack dealers, and then crashed out of the bar.

Joe left quietly a few minutes later. Truly, it had been a long night. Regretting the action already, he made certain that Joachim's card was safely stowed in his wallet. He knew he would make the call and he knew that he would turn up on time for any appointment they might make. Such was the carousel of espionage.

Annie was in better spirits as she turned the key to her front door. The first salvo of the mission had gone better than she could have hoped. Bootface had not absented himself for too long at the bar and didn't reek too strongly of booze on his return; he was functional. That was enough. He'd been back in time for the vital call. Perhaps she had been too harsh. Maybe he was one of those seat of the pants guys who just managed to get it right on the night, even if everything beforehand looked shambolic. Bootface had certainly been affable anyway, even going to the lengths of suggesting they dine together at some point in the future. That was polite of him, even though she had refused the invitation, as well she might.

And the call had been good. Ducks in a row. Joachim had made his contact with Joe. They had had a good meeting, and Annie approved of the Macmillan discussion. Not too fast an introduction to the world of total treachery; it would all come soon enough. Joachim had been impressed by Joe too, describing him as a total professional.

No trace of a German accent, in Joachim's telephone report to Annie. 'Never gave himself away once, not even by a flicker, did our Joe. We can do very good business together, I think.'

'And you, Joachim. No cockney rhyming slang?'

'No way. My German mother was dominant when I was talking to him. I was talking very good German English. Like that. But he's a cunning rascal, you know. At the end, he said "stripe me pink", and it was literally on the tip of my tongue to say something stupid like darn the rub-a-dub or some such crap. But I didn't. And there we are. We got the dialogue just about right, I think.'

He had signed off then. He had failed to mention Joe's

disappearance from Zorba's. A pity, really. Joe's encounter with Pugh was the single most life-threatening factor to the outcome of the whole mission. Nobody knew about it at control level. How could they? Pugh had chosen an out of the way pub, for him, so that he could do his weeping alone. It was pure bad luck that he had happened to run into Joe of all people that evening. An unfortunate combination of circumstances, as they would say, tight-lipped, in the spying game. These things just couldn't be helped.

But Annie had another more obvious, more immediate shock to cope with as she pushed through her front door. It was devastating. Right there on her mantelpiece, hitting the eye straight as she walked in, were two clocks, sited right next to each other. It was inexplicable. And through the half-light, Annie knew, without even looking, that one clock would be set an hour fast and the other an hour slow, just as Annie had set Joe's clocks that way during the afternoon as he played bridge with Lady C.

She stared at the clocks. It was impossible. It could not have happened in this way. She was not a subsidiary line in this structure, she was the final line. The line of support. No recourse beyond her. Beyond her lay chaos. That was the whole point about the intelligence game – behind it as a control structure there lay nothing. So things didn't happen to her, they happened further down the line. That was the reality of it all.

But here it was, an indisputable reality, two clocks set in their funny way. Someone had broken into her home and done to her exactly what she had done to Joe. The universe turned turtle for a few seconds.

She dropped her bag and picked them up, then turned them over. She was curious. No message, no, of course not. How foolish of her. The clocks themselves were... A simple deadly thought struck her, then went through her like a knife. It was so obvious.

She had warned Joe with the clocks. Now she too was being warned in her turn. It was so simple. Everything was clear now. It was going to be a very dangerous mission. Few if any of them would be alive at the end of it. It was as simple as that. She'd always thought the mission was more than tweaking the tiger's tail. And now she knew she was right. Death went dogging everywhere.

# Chapter Three

Joe woke up the following morning at around seven. His mind was crisp and clear. Sleep had washed away the effects of the alcohol. He lay in bed for a few moments, watching his breath condense in the cold morning air that gusted through his room and then slowly moved from the warmth beneath the duvet into the chill outside the bed. He had things to do. He had the mortgage to pay.

The markets opened in about an hour and a half. He would call Campbell his broker just before that moment, and tell him to sell the British Steel position. Take his profit, if there was one. How would the markets open? Joe was hoping for an initial mark down, which would squeeze the spreads and give him a good panic-driven price.

Forgetting about the big figure, if Joe saw 38p, and bought back at that price, then he would have paid the mortgage for next month. If he saw 37p, he could pay his gas bill and his council tax at the same time. He knew the numbers very precisely. And 40p? Bad, bad karma, 40p. Not a nice figure at all. No gains at all, so no mortgage payments could be made, and cardboard city was just a telephone call away. Perilous in the extreme.

Joe's bank had made its position very clear some months ago. It would repossess after just one missed payment. Just one. No further latitude was negotiable. *Lacrimae rerum*, dear boy, or words to that effect from the no-brainer of an account manager, who had requested the immediate return of Joe's chequebook. Credit, Joe? Credit, you fruit cake? You must be joking. Get out of my office.

So no credit. Money was a problem for Joe. That cooling of his bank's enthusiasm for the house of Joe was all of a part with the mysterious vendetta which had blighted his life so suddenly in the past few months. Everything had been soured as he had been swept from grace, power and affluence. But that was then. Joe was unrepentant. Today belonged to the fight back. Time to bob and weave.

He threw on a few clothes and wandered off down the street to the strip to buy his newspapers. Check the newspapers first, he thought, and that Snowden speech just to measure prospects. Then take in a little bit of instant, coarse meditation just to get the probabilities in line.

Treason was a matter of dates, and survival a question of morale; it went with the flow and against the odds. Early training in Berlin and other more mysterious points east meant Joe knew all about how to pump up morale just to meet the complex swirling requirements of the moment. His back was against the wall but he knew how to position against the bricks. So if he failed to sell at 38p? So that's tough, he thought. I'll have to think again. But something will happen, even if I screw up on the trade. In its odd way, life continued to throw up chances of survival. It was uncanny the way they arrived.

Eyes blinking with sleep, he stood in line in the newsagent's to buy his *Wall Street Journal* and his *Financial Chronicle*, willing himself not to make a sudden lunge for the information, forcing himself not to make foolish conjectures about events over the next hour, not to think at all, in fact, but to dissolve into the limitless possibilities of the present.

Anything could happen, he kept telling himself. Be prepared for that. Do not fail to reach out for the inexhaustible riches and vitality of the moment. Anything could happen.

Back once more in his flat, with the time ticking round to seven thirty, he made some tea and then very carefully opened the *Financial Chronicle*. Yup, there was the speech, second lead story on the front page. As usual the *Chron* reported it fairly straight without referring to any market reaction. This in a sense was good for Joe because it left the market to make up its own mind without obvious steer in the media from the authorities. But the gist of the report was pretty clear – more pie in the sky from the chancellor, which the traders would not like. The *Wall Street Journal* said pretty much the same thing. So far so good.

Joe drank his tea. Now for the karma. It was the only way. It stilled those terrible fears of imminent dissolution which came to haunt him at moments like these. Thoughts of what had happened the previous night and the beneficial implications of the contact were far from his mind. Anything could accrue from that, but this was here and now. He had to be ready for anything. He put the newspapers to one side, stretched out on his sofa, put the headphones on, and played Bach's Passacaglia in C minor, thirteen minutes of the purest architecture of sound it was possible to imagine, the music building inexorably from the first simple blocks of chord into a riot of baroque extravaganza, St Peter's Rome in the sky.

The organ thundered in his ears, and he drew quiet breath as Bach sketched out in solid lines the nave of his musical cathedral. With some mordant satisfaction, Joe thought of the event which would be revealed in a few minutes' time. Of the way that the future, with its hopes and aspirations, had been collapsed totally into the sempiternal present now that he was little more than a vagrant. Of how perhaps this was the apotheosis of his craft as lifetime spy and agent provocateur, because his poverty and absence of expectations enabled him to grapple even more strongly with the ambiguities of the fleeting moment. Given the moment, he could operate superbly, but given a longer perspective, he lacked any interest at all. Too much could happen in the meantime.

The clock crept round towards the time and Joe felt his mind grow tight and focused. Now for it, he thought; let's just find out how it plays. Gain or loss, who cares? The most important thing is to be there, up and running.

He thought of his stockbroker, Sid Campbell, he of the Scottish name and purest Jewish lineage, who in his kindness had rescued him from even greater penury some months ago. Out of the blue, just when Joe was about to go under for ever, Sid had telephoned him and in his crisp no-nonsense way had said, 'Joe, you were good to me when you were up there, so I'm going to repay a favour in a small way, now that you're down. You'll be back; everyone has their ups and downs. Don't worry too much about it. Failure is part of success. But in the meantime I'll let you do some account trading. If, as I think, you don't have a bank account now, you can use the trading account to make some money and you can draw on it for some cash. How about that?'

It had been a boon, like God reaching down to press a glass of clear water into the pilgrim's aching hands. No other word for it. Joe thought of the hordes of bewildered Jews fleeing the Nazis in terror across the North Sea from the shores of northern Europe, and landing at obscure towns in Scotland to be greeted by customs officers and mutual incomprehension. The customs officers solved the language problem by registering the refugees under their own names of MacDonald, and so on or, as in this case, Campbell. As Sid would say, 'I'm pure north London Scottish and proud of it.'

The Passacaglia drew to a quiet, mighty close, and Joe, his mind stilled of fears, began to make his call.

'Campbell. Can I help you?'

'Joe here. What are you calling them?'

Now for it. Now for the truth. A second of eternal tension. Campbell cleared his throat. The words came down the line and then the day broke into wreaths of smiles. 'So soon already to have such a good morning. What was all that trouble about?'

'Early mark down on Snowden's speech. I can get you 37½. That is if you're a buyer.'

'It's the Scot in you that makes you so cheeky, know that. If you can see 37½, I'm out.'

'Consider it done, Joe. I'll be back later in the morning to confirm the bargain. How does that leave you?'

'One mortgage payment better off and the gas bill to boot.'

'Good boy.'

'And the Pres…?'

Joe managed to get his question in at the last, with the trade looking so good. But Sid was a match for him in repartee.

'Hanging in and looking as good as you, Joe. River Plate here I come.'

'Rats, he's a broken man.'

'Not for a moment. Bye now. Don't let the bastards grind you down.'

Joe breathed more deeply now and lay back on his sofa, briefly shattered by the tension of the whole event. So close again. It had been very close this time. Joe had felt his dancing feet trail just very briefly over the edge of the cliff. For a few seconds he was actually foxtrotting in mid-air, defying gravity high above the waves. Not a pretty sight. But the exhaustion passed. Reality came rushing back. There were things to do. There was a day to plan, and perhaps more money to be made if he managed to meet up with Treadwell at the Jack of Hearts, he of the limitless aspirations, the very expensive girlfriend, and the twitching eyebrows as he went down a costly three in a cold three no trumps.

And then there was the President of the United States to think about for just a second, as one does…

Here the news was not so good for Joe. In a rash moment, he had bet Sid that Monica Lewinsky would sink Bill Clinton as allegations about the affair deepened. But Sid the older man, who had lived through Watergate and the Nixon years, was not convinced. History did not repeat itself, he argued. Joe had insisted and Sid had demurred. The upshot of all the wrangling had been a bet, notably that if Clinton was forced to resign over Lewinsky, then Sid, a Spurs fan, would take Joe to the football match of his choice. And vice versa. It was only after the terms of the bet had been struck that they both realised the shocking truth – it was open-ended. It could be any football game in the world. And naturally the longer Clinton resisted the allegations of impropriety, the more anxious Joe became. His finances simply would not run to a little jolly with Sid to Latin America. But there was always the chance that Sid might panic and close out this position, in which case Joe would settle for an Inter-Milan game, Clinton resignation or not.

Joe opened the newspapers. Now he could read them like a human being, rather than like some jackal skulking in the hedgerows. He turned to Tom Stone's column in the *Financial Chronicle*, pursing his lips almost immediately at an ill-phrased piece of market analysis.

Poor old Tom, he thought. He just doesn't know what he's on about in these markets. They're far too much for him nowadays. He's getting old. The US Treasuries market just doesn't work like that at all.

Markets renewed themselves with inexhaustible vitality, but not so the market practitioners, who little by little were pounded down by the thunderous power of the market's ebbs and flows, like rocks in the Atlantic tide. Tom had been on his market beat for a long time now and the strain of following the world's stock markets was beginning to show.

Joe felt younger by the minute as the impact of his successful trade started to filter through. He had a roof over his head for another month. Still in the warm. Just think about that. No cardboard city. A month is plenty enough. Anything can happen in a month, he reassured himself. I think I'm going to call Tom this morning and point out just what he might have said.

The thought pleased him and he went to make some toast as belated breakfast. His phone rang. Uncharacteristically, Joe took the call. It was Lady Charley.

'Oh, Joe, I'm sorry to call you at this ungodly hour, I suppose you're not even awake yet, but we're having a slight crisis over the bridge this morning. Sue can't make it because she's having a drama with her youngest and Trish is out of town so we're one short. We've tried Stella but she's up to her eyes in something so we wondered if you could fill in?'

From the depths to the heights, Joe thought as he assented to the invitation. One moment I'm hotfooting it into the gutters, the next I'm sitting at the bridge table of very nearly the noblest in the land. Truly never a dull moment.

'What time does it start?'

'We draw lots just before ten thirty, so if you could manage to be there at around twenty past, you can discuss your conventions with your partner.'

'I'll be there. I can make that time.'

'Thank you so much, Joe. You don't know how helpful this is. Oh, and I've been chatting to Liz this morning. She couldn't say so at the time, but she thanks you for being so helpful too over Sybil. Apparently you were quite diplomatic last night about the whole business. Surprisingly diplomatic, Joe.'

So far as Lady C was concerned, diplomacy, indeed, all the intellectual virtues known to man, reposed in the bosom of her set. Beyond that, nothing else existed, or if it did, that came as a complete surprise and shock to Lady C.

'A pleasure, Lady C. I gather Sybil won't be playing there this morning.'

Pause. Sharp intake of breath down the line, as Joe boobed by referring at all to the unfortunate Sybil. Lady C replied at her most injunctive. 'I gather Sybil has decided to play at this new club, Savage's. I, of course, won't be playing there, although some of the crowd have said they'll pop along to see what it's like.' Then Lady C moved without pause from the assertive to the suppliant and the mock submissive. 'Joe, you did remember to post that letter, didn't you? Or rather, since you wouldn't have had time last night, you won't forget this morning, will you? Just checking.'

A sudden pang on Joe's part as he thought for one ghastly second that he might have dropped the wretched thing during the scuffle last night. That would jar her Marie Antoinette bit a fair amount. But no, there it was, thank God, safe in his jacket inside pocket, albeit slightly tatty now.

'No fears, Lady C. I have it here.'

'Thank you, Joe, I hope we draw each other as partners this morning, but if we don't, then do have a good time. And thank you again for posting the letter.'

Was there just a hint of intimacy in the discussion? Joe decided there wasn't an inch of fraternity throughout the conversation. As for the letter, wild horses wouldn't drag the true reasons behind its existence out of Lady C. It was just a letter that had to be posted and Joe, as a convenient swain, had to do the posting so that life could go on at Lady C's hectic pace. Or something like that.

Joe thought about ringing Tom Stone at the *Financial Chronicle* and leaving an awkward message for him. Joe decided to risk it, to take an initiative that drew him briefly out of the routine plodding norm of his life, if only because it seemed to seal the signal triumph of the day so far. Mortgage paid for a month! Now that really was something.

His phone rang again but Joe declined to take the call. Better let the answerphone take the strain, he decided.

'This is a message for Joe from Rivers Pugh. I don't think you got my Christian name last night in the confusion, but that's what it is. I want to thank you for saving me last night and I also want to explain what it was all about. All the weeping and wailing, that sort of stuff. Perhaps you could call me on this number and we can fix up a meeting. Have a drink or something like that. I hope that I got your number down correctly last night and I hope to hear from you. I was hoping to catch you this morning; I didn't realise that bridge started so early in the day. I don't know whether you ever go out of town at all during your life as a bridge player, but if you ever do, I wonder if you'd care to come and spend a weekend with me at my home. It's not far to travel and I think you might enjoy Pugh Park. It's very easygoing. Very old too. Just my mother and sister to cope with. So do call and tell me what you'd like to do.'

Click. Joe was glad he hadn't taken that message in person. It was quite a pleasant message, but after his escape that morning from near oblivion, he had no desire to chat about the same thing with someone else close to the brink.

Which reminded him – there would be time today, despite the morning bridge, to do a little searching for Marcello. Did he owe it to Betty to continue his fruitless task? Hard to call; all he could say for certain was that once embarked on his quest he was still pretty determined to finish it. And that was that. He would call Betty later that day, after he had tramped a few more streets.

More bells. The phone rang again. More clicking, then a familiar voice this time, as Joe let the answerphone take the strain for a second time.

'Joe, this is Emma Bales again. Are you there? Joe, can you hear me? Oh bugger, why aren't you there. Don't you dare think you're going to escape me just by refusing to return my calls. I'm going to hound you until you respond. And if you're skulking there listening to all this, well, I think you're a louse for not inviting me to have breakfast with you.'

Click. This is a rather different Emma, thought Joe as he skulked nevertheless. She sounds rather more enfranchised. But he still refused to return her call. She is just not going to see me in this reduced poverty-stricken mode, he decided. She'll get bored eventually with trying to get in touch.

Eventually, as he was mulling over the bridge to come later that morning, Joe screwed up his courage and put a call through to Tom Stone's office. Too early, of course. There was no way that a journalist would surface before eleven at the earliest. But

Joe decided he had to do it, if only to retain some kind of contact with the life he had known and then lost so dramatically.

The switchboard put him through to Stone's extension where, in the absence of said Stone, he was invited to leave a message. Automatically he started to do so, got halfway through, realised with a start that he would be far away at the other end of the King's Road when Tom got the message and then left Liz Playfair's number as a contact. Tough if it interrupts the play, he thought, but then the play won't be much anyway. An interruption might be welcome. They play to affirm the status quo, not to explore change.

Finishing the call, he set off down the King's Road towards Sloane Square. It was just after nine thirty. The bus clattered round the World's End, and then swung over Beaufort Street. Joe was lost in thought as the bus jolted past Old Church Street.

He felt relieved at the British Steel profitable trade and it was fitting that he should spend the morning playing bridge with the dames. He looked forward to the fun. He'd been invited occasionally before, but as on this occasion only as a stopgap. Liz Playfair's Thursday morning duplicate was the social holy of holies in the area. Not everyone got to be invited. The dames were harried too, most of the time, but their Thursday bridge morning at Liz Playfair's was sacred. No husbands or children for that precious hour and a half, no dinners to arrange at very short notice, no egos to soothe or brows to sponge. It was approximately the only time in the week when they were guaranteed not to be on duty in one way or another. A number of the players had been at school together, and had grown together ever since across the great divide of husbands, families and the setbacks of life.

During this precious quality time the women regressed, not quite to pyjama parties in the dorm, but certainly to a more carefree state of play than they normally enjoyed. They romped just a little and there could be high jinks around the Playfair bridge tables, with Lady C leading the charge. Those were the times when Joe caught glimpses of a distant, drifting landscape of eternal dance, with Liz just outside the circle, beating a slow measure to the measured cadence of carefree dance steps.

Only about ten or twelve of them played together regularly,

although masses of well-heeled bridge players in Chelsea aspired to the honour of an invitation, or were even pushier than that in their attempts to get on the Playfair list, as the phrase went. What Joe had accepted so casually that morning was an invitation that other more socially aware players would have killed for. But that was his odd life now, Joe reflected, while the bus negotiated Sloane Square past Peter Jones and he jumped off at the corner of Upper Sloane Street and, after posting Lady C's precious letter, plodded over to Oriel for an early morning coffee – heights and depths and very sharp contrasts.

It was not true to say that all the social power of England reposed in that little group of women he was about to encounter in a few moments' time. That would be inaccurate. But equally there was very little that took place in the upper echelons of the country that was not known to them. Hatches, matches and dispatches; deaths and entrances; triumphs, disasters, peerages, bankruptcies or just small, rather dismal, unfulfilling lives after great early promise – all the news from the battle front flowed through those small elegant chambers of the Liz Playfair Bridge Academy. And mainly on a Thursday morning, when there was just a tiny bit more opportunity to chat and exchange information.

Liz Playfair's Thursday morning gathering was a social stock market. But, like all investors, the dames suffered from a fatal imbalance of their forces. They had long-range responsibilities but only short-range controls. Children and husbands would do as they were bidden when they were under the gaze of the memsahibs, but most frequently they were far, far away, either at work or at school, making their mischief. Out of sight, out of control was the maxim most frequently overheard at Liz Playfair's. So the women had to make shift accordingly and organise their skulduggery in a myriad of different ways, stabbing on the backstairs if need be.

No wonder they hung together as a group and were chary of outsiders. There was quite a fair amount of blood on those hands, all in that worthy cause of the hard business of society. In their own way, they led lives quite as hazardous as Joe's. Young men in whom a considerable investment has been made do not always make suitable matches and the same goes for the daughters.

Headstrong youth cannot be trusted to its own devices. Therefore unceasing vigilance was called for. That, together with long lines of communication, frequently renewed, was how the dames got round that imbalance in their forces.

They greeted him quietly as he eased into the academy, and offered him tea. It was a slow-moving vision of cardigans, blouses, jeans and hair not quite brushed the maximum number of times. In repose, the dames were practical, even rugged, in appearance and certainly not smart; that came later in the day.

Joe heard the end of a disparaging reference to the prime minister's wife, who had apparently not behaved well at the dinner table the previous evening, as he took the proffered draw ticket and found himself matched with Belinda, a woman with no cards judgement at all, although fully cognisant of all the arcane mysteries of British protocol. Belinda and Joe were drawn against Lady C and her great school friend Ursula.

Liz was seated between the two tables, invigilating. The hands were pre-dealt and selected from high-powered recent international bridge tournaments, where the greats of the bridge world competed. The cards sat in their little cases like so many depth charges.

Joe opened a no trump and heard two clubs from Ursula to his left, which showed hearts. Belinda fiddled around with her cards and Joe thought double sounded about right. Belinda was no poker player and her face spoke volumes; she had a good hand. Joe could feel Liz's eyes boring into Belinda's skull, willing her to make her bid correctly. Eventually the bid came out – four no trumps. Wrong bid by a mile.

Ah well, thought Joe, that's a safe seventeen hundred score drifting away from us, but too bad. They haven't been brought up to be quite so aggressive. Or not in that way. And they can't whistle through their teeth either.

Maximum for his opening, Joe bid six no trumps and down went dummy. High-bosomed Ursula, a woman who was never happy unless she bid at least four slams a session, correctly or otherwise, led the jack of clubs and Joe pondered his play. Eventually he went for a huge and beneficial split in the hearts. He played the queen against the ace on table, hoping to see the ten drop to his right. It all went according to plan. The queen was covered by Ursula's king, but the ten fell. Out of the corner of his eye, Joe spotted Lady C glaring at him as she gave up her singleton heart, but he persevered in his strategy. With just one loser in hearts, he had to get the clubs right, or play Lady C for the king of spades, taking a Chinese finesse in spades into his hand.

Impossible that she could have the king after Ursula's intervening bid, so Joe turned to the clubs. He paused. Defining moment coming up, he told himself. Only way to play it, he reckoned. It was a lot to hope for, but he was going for it. And so early in the morning and with such rapt concentration… Against king, queen and seven of clubs on table, he played his singleton club and finessed the seven – which held! It actually held! Totally and completely amazing. To Joe's great shock, he had made his slam. Impossible but true. Ursula had led from jack, ten, nine, eight of clubs. In sequence. He was flabbergasted. He stared in disbelief at the dummy as Lady C and Ursula bustled about with the cards.

'Next case, next case,' he could hear them burbling as he gawped at the cards. The thumping in his chest died to a steady pitter-patter and Belinda unbent sufficiently to give him a quick wan little smile of congratulation, like a beam of light shining behind a cloud.

Liz rose from her chair, and as she did so she winked at Joe. Now that was really something, Joe thought, a wink from Liz over his play. He must have done well! But he still felt weak.

Lady C and Ursula got to four spades in the next hand not without some bickering, glaring and snorting between them. They were playing a new convention like a new car, to be taken out for a spin and shown off, but as for what went on beneath the bonnet… Joe, with two small spades, led a spade and Lady C rebuked him for his unfriendly lead. Joe looked at the stiff diamond king in dummy and thought his spade lead represented an extremely hostile act indeed. Lady C huffed and puffed. Instead of covering Belinda's queen with her ace, she ducked it. Then Belinda's brow turned into a piece of corrugated iron as she frowned in concentration over the return.

Joe thought about the monkeys at their typewriters and *King*

*Lear* as Belinda fingered her cards. Anything could happen now and again so early in the morning. But miracle of miracles, Belinda found the correct return – the king of spades. That took some doing, since her husband kept her more or less in rags. But it took another spade off the table, killing the ruffs for Lady C.

The contract went one off. Catastrophe for Lady C and Ursula. Ursula wanted to rebuke Lady C, but since she was not quite clear in her own mind what had gone wrong she thought it wiser to keep a civil tongue in her head. She mumbled away to Joe's left. Belinda goggled at Joe, hoping for praise, fearing a tongue-lashing.

'If I were anywhere else, Belinda, I would leap across the table and give you a kiss for that king of spades return. It was brilliant.'

A rapid look of transcendental penitent gratitude spread across Belinda's face as she realised that someone was not angry with her that morning. She looked quite young again. Happy and aspirant, seeking approval. All to go for. Then the training kicked back in, as the experience of thirty years of marriage told heavily. She snapped back into mode. The smile died.

'Thank you, Joe. You are very kind.'

More hands, more play, more helter-skelter moves up and down the gamut of bridge bidding. Time marched on across the beautiful sunlit morning as the women played their bridge and Liz sat quietly in their midst, an imposing Sphinx. The square behind them and very nearly at their rear, basked in the slow awakening of the day. Peace, or a proxy for same, reigned in Chelsea and Belgravia.

It was getting close to the end of the session. Nearly time for the counting up, when one team or the other was pronounced winner; they played in groups of four. Although it all looked quite genteel, furious passions were kindled by these bridge sessions which only died after fulsome discussion over lunch. Faces could be very flushed. And before lunch there was Liz's summing-up of the hands and the play to endure as well, when the plaudits and the brickbats were ladled out, hand by hand, person by person. That was a chilling moment, even if heavily ritualised by custom. But the confessional moments were followed by conviviality in a local restaurant, always the same one, and that was something they all looked forward to as well by the end of the morning. It was a big treat for them all.

All, that is, except Joe. He was not invited. Lady C had put him straight on that one very early on. She knew the short sharp words of command English when she needed them.

'Girls only. Sorry, Joe. You're not invited. Such a shame but there you are. How else can we catch up on the gossip? We'd love you to come but you'd send out the wrong signal. Besides, you'd get in the way of the chat and you wouldn't understand any of it. Nobody you'd know. Anyway, you've seen far too much of us letting our hair down as it is. It wouldn't be fair if you came to lunch as well – you'd get too much of an advantage.'

That was the crisp way Lady C had made it clear to Joe that once the bridge was finished his role then was to walk out of the door very smartly and leave them all in peace. The chateau was shut. But Joe was content with this anyway. Lunch with the dames was truly impossible. And as they all played towards the end of that morning, his mind was straying forward to Marcello and his search for him that afternoon and then back again to the odd events of the previous evening. He drifted in space and time.

Contact again with the gents after so many months! Contact, yes, of course, it had to be contact. Nobody talked about Macmillan and spying in restaurants in Chelsea just like that. Come on, get real! But could it be real? And did it matter? He wasn't sure now, after the sufferings of the past few months. And Pugh! Who was he? Why had he been weeping in Zorba's? Did he connect in at all? On balance, Joe thought not. Pugh was just a random particle who happened to be there at that time when something else was happening. Joe could feel his spy's mind coming into play, working through the data, assessing the probabilities, weighing the evidence, gauging reality before reaching a conclusion. So much to take in, so much to be discarded. It was a long time since he had thought along these lines.

Ursula was playing the final board. She was in three spades and she was just about to go one off because of the appalling way she was playing the dummy, when the phone rang. Liz skipped lightly across the room into the adjoining kitchen to take the call.

'Yes, yes, of course, I'll get him. Yes, he's here. No, it's no trouble.' She called out to Joe. 'Joe, there's a Tom Stone on the phone for you.'

Ursula's cards shot from her hand and spread across the table and onto the floor. She stared at the dummy unknowing. She could have been anywhere, and she was certainly not playing bridge any more.

'What on earth's the matter with you, Ursula?' Lady C barked at her. 'There's something not quite right about you today. Pull yourself together.'

Ursula had gone quite white. Joe stood up, eased his way round the table apologetically and then vanished into the kitchen to take the call.

'Tom Stone?'

'Speaking. I got a message to call you.'

'Yes. I'm sorry, this is rather a bad moment actually. Thanks for calling. I wanted to check a detail with you about your column this morning, but we can talk again.'

'Sure.'

'Can I call you maybe this afternoon?'

Then the phone was wrenched from Joe's hand. It was Ursula standing right beside him. She spoke into the mouthpiece. Very confidently. A very different Ursula. She was on fire. Cheeks burning. Agog. The flames seemed to leap from her head.

'Tom, Tom, is that you? It's Ursula here. Yes, Ursula. You remember, don't you? Of course you do. It's been such a long time.'

A babble of high-pitched sound suggested that yes, indeed, Tom remembered. Joe glanced at Ursula before returning to his seat. Motherhood, all five times of it, had dropped from her like a shroud. Yet again she was a panting, ranting young woman, eager and anxious about her man, adrift on the high tide of London and on the loose. A slim young women could just be glimpsed through the necessary embonpoint conferred by so many years of testing, friction-full marriage.

Joe had unwittingly touched one of those key levers in some-one, the ones that remain motionless gathering dust for years, disregarded in the corner, until they are idly shifted from neutral to positive. By a chance remark or a casual meeting or a stray allusion. And then it's a firework display. All hell breaks loose... An alternative persona emerges, just as here a variant on the day-to-day queenly and responsible Ursula he knew so well was suddenly on display. A variable Ursula had been flushed out.

Even more surprising was Lady C's reaction when he returned to his seat. She seemed quite adjusted to the strange behaviour of Ursula. Hardly surprised at all. But cautious nevertheless.

'I always thought he'd turn up again, like the bad penny he is and always will be. God, how I hated Tom Stone when he was around. Such a sponger.'

So they did know each other, Joe thought stupidly, feeling like Inspector Clouseau. He made a sound of interrogation, but Lady C refused to be drawn further. The shutters were coming down already and the past was another country. Joe thought about the letter he had just posted and wondered if that too might have an explosive charge attached to it. But he dropped the idea. Perhaps a tad inappropriate. Lady C had fixed him with one of her angry eye-popping stares, which said: You'd better get on with the bridge if you know what's good for you. None of this malarkey concerns you, my boy.

Joe got on with the bridge. He picked up Ursula's cards very carefully, so that he couldn't spot the denominations, and replaced them on the table as Ursula returned. Her eyes were shining like stars but she was a miracle of self-control. She picked up her cards without a word and continued the play and indeed played so well that she almost made her contract.

What telephone call? Her face was a mask. Such powerful early training. That was the spirit, Joe reckoned, that made the empire what it had been. Fearful self-control!

No one else in the room had spoken. All had attended the interruption to Joe's phone call but none had commented. No one had whistled or shouted out something derogatory. This was not a gathering of the lower orders. The protocol was diamond hard. At the other table play had continued in seeming tranquillity. They might all have been back at school assembly with such innocent expressions. And Liz, who was of, but not in, this circle, but privy nonetheless to some of its deeper secrets, sat quizzically and sphinx-like at her spot between the two tables.

Then it was the end of the session. The laughter and conversation natural to the group erupted spontaneously as the tables broke up. Time in a few seconds for Liz's summing-up, accompanied by selected tongue-lashings, so Joe had first to scramble to another table and match up the scores with his team. He had little opportunity to question Ursula on her intervention in his telephone call. Not that he would have got very far. Ursula gazed straight ahead as Liz went through the cards and the play, clearly a world away from her exposition and oblivious to the present, her husband, his continuing financial difficulties and her five children, three of whom were still at boarding school. Her thoughts were far from the juggling act that constituted her life. She was thinking of what might have been, plainly with some affection as little smiles occasionally rippled across her lips. Nostalgia was a powerful, dangerous, tempting thing.

From time to time, Lady C glanced at Ursula with one of those looks which said: So it's happened then; what you've been hoping would come along for all this time has finally happened. Well, we'd better have a long talk about this before you go completely off the rails. This is your bosom buddy speaking now, so you'd better listen. We know each other. We've been around together, buddy babe. We have few secrets from each other. You don't get off so lightly as all that, you know.

Joe had seen this bullying look before in these women. And on occasion he had also encountered Ursula's expression as well – how what they had done in their past, frequently became turned into their futures in some odd transformation, as ever optimistic they endured the daily grind, living through – and via – something else.

But now this time it might all be somewhat stronger than that for Ursula. It could be quite catalytic. She had been rabid as she took the call from him. She had responded to something deeply primeval within her. Joe would wait upon events to find out how it all progressed. That was all he could do. He could hardly ring Tom Stone again after the interruption of Ursula and nobody at the Sloane Square end would tell him anything, of course. But he might pick up the odd hint as he went along. Ironically, for the time being, both he and Ursula might be rowing in the same boat as the two of them underwent rapid change. And who would have thought a simple phone call could have provoked all that?

No word of acknowledgement from Ursula as they closed for the morning. Joe hardly expected it. *Omertà* was in full sway. History was being rewritten. Joe had simply not received that telephone call – that was the long and short of it. Contact between Ursula and Tom Stone had been effected somehow via the medium of the Holy Spirit.

He did pick up a snippet as they all moved for the coats. He heard Ursula mutter to Lady C, 'Yes, I'm going to call him again after lunch. He's given me his direct line. We have such a lot to talk about. He sounds quite different now. You'd be amazed. Really. He's so polished, you just can't believe it's the same person. And he's been very successful. He's the top writer on the *Financial Chronicle*, so he tells me.'

Lady C emitted a sound which hesitated between outright disbelief and flat contempt for whatever reality Ursula cared to trump up involving Tom. Not many takers for Stone in that department, thought Joe. Poor guy. And he holds the City in his thrall every week. Her husband, the Black Pimpernel, probably reads him with complete devotion.

Then they all trooped off to lunch, a gay chuckling gaggle of women, handbags, mobile phones, sensible coats and gossip. One thing was certain – the discretion about Ursula's phone conversation which had been maintained during the bridge would not continue over lunch. There would be much riotous chat as Ursula was forced to disgorge all about Tom Stone, detail by detail. So much for the Liz Playfair bridge session that Thursday morning.

## Chapter Four

Joe was left with an empty afternoon after the entertainment of the morning with the dames. But he knew how to fill in his time and avoid the rough breakers of depression rolling home. He would go in search yet again of Marcello for a few hours. Then he would meet up with Treadwell at the Jack of Hearts for a spot of evil gambling. The force was with him that day. So nothing ventured, nothing gained.

Such were the shifts he been forced to contrive in the total absence of money, job and all the other trappings essential to life in London. But Joe was still at bottom optimistic. He hoped to depart the country to start again and he was confident that he would find a way out from the mess of his life. It was all just a matter of time and opportunity. He had to believe he could start a new life and he had to put all of this behind him. All that he was enduring now, he told himself, was a temporary period of living rough. And he, veteran of Soviet Berlin and countless espionage trips behind the Iron Curtain back in the bad old days of the cold war, could certainly cope with the odd tough year or two.

Just a matter of discipline and attitude, he told himself as he swung down the King's Road. And hadn't he done well that morning, taking his British Steel profit and securing the mortgage payment for another month? So smooth and cool that piece of profit-taking. Like velvet. This may be hand to mouth, Joe, my son, but it doesn't flag or pall for a second, he told himself again with great determination, realising that morale was now poised on a dangerous incline and ready to toboggan to the lower depths of despair unless he took his precautions. Thinking about the perils of his stock market operations of that morning did not constitute one of his precautions. Rather the opposite – it made his eyes widen in sudden fear at the risk he had taken. His precautions included clearing his head of the bridge and the dames by drinking a pint of Guinness at the Chelsea Potter, amongst people who had even more time to spare than he did, ahead of his meandering trip around London's seedier spots.

His search for Marcello had come about in a curious way. Some years previously, when Joe was in his pomp, he had thrown a party at his villa in France and found himself in deep conversation with someone he knew slightly, Betty, who just happened to have saved him from losing some two million pounds. It was a long story; it was the sort of kind gesture that people made in those days. But the upshot of his conversation was that Joe had promised Betty that he would seek and find her missing and errant son Marcello, the apple of his mother's eye, who had been driven from the Hertfordshire family home by a father seemingly possessed of a fury whenever he clapped eyes on the hapless boy.

Marcello lived somewhere in London. But how and whereabouts no one could fathom. What did he do? How did he survive? Again nobody knew. Marcello still rang his mother once a week on her mobile to confirm that he was still alive. Beyond that bland assertion of normality Betty knew nothing about her son. Nor did his sisters. And they grieved for him too. The entire mansion had been smitten with gloom by the overnight departure of Marcello.

So what should Betty do? Should she formalise the process of disappearance by posting him missing via the police and bring the whole machinery of bureaucracy grinding into action? Impossible. She couldn't do that, not in a million years. She was a rich women who lived in a mansion among fat acres of arable Hertfordshire. She couldn't bring in the snoopers of the state, asking their indelicate questions and submitting her family to the impersonal and judgmental gaze of outsiders. Impossible. It was not a feasible solution. Instead Betty had enlisted Joe's help, seeking and getting the support of someone who at the time had seemed rich, confident and independent. The rate of exchange was favourable; Betty had after all saved Joe some two million pounds.

Joe had assented to her request sitting on the pier, gazing like Caesar at his villa in the deep blue of a summer evening when the party was in full swing, as something he could accomplish in the plenitude of his power. Something of no great complexity and something which had to be done to repay his debt to Betty. His assent had been an expression of his magnificence.

Now, many months further on in his life and as yet no further advanced in the quest for Marcello, the search had taken on extra different dimensions. It was the link, the only link, which served to connect him to the old life which he had enjoyed. Everything had gone smash, apart from Joe's spirit. But Betty was unaware of this. When she spoke to him on the phone, she still assumed that she was talking to the old Joe, he of the careless rapture of fine gestures. And she was grateful for his time accordingly. She telephoned him frequently. Joe was gratified by that slight tiny balm of her deference and her attention. That alone could recall and validate the other time, the good time, when life was young and sweet and successful. It helped. Unknowingly, Betty was a boon. Joe was down otherwise, deep down in the gutter of life, struggling with all his energy in the kicking and gouging multitude, watching the crack in the wall beside his flat as a reality check on sanity and living on his gambling profits and the drawing facility he had with that oxymoron of his kind, a charitable and thoughtful stockbroker. Barely surviving on life in the raw.

So the search for Marcello went on. Joe had a number of photographs of Marcello which he showed around in pubs and clubs and wherever the young gathered in London. The photos revealed a tall, gentle young man, quite earnest but still athletic, smiling against sunny backgrounds, a happy and contented young man, in no sense out of the ordinary.

'Have you seen this young man? His name is Marcello,' Joe would ask as he passed among the groups of young people, sometimes affluent and confident, sometimes pinched and afraid, across the length and breadth of London. Always the same response: a long concerned scrutiny, especially by the girls, a short confabulation and then the sad, reluctant shake of the head. Smiles but apologies. 'Sorry, but we can't help.' Then Joe passed on. Very rarely was he questioned further about Marcello and this initially had surprised him. Gradually he came to realise that he was skirting the edges of a different tribe, the young, which had its own customs and lore, where uncertainty reigned. Where disappearance and failure were an everyday occurrence. Nobody wanted to know too much because of fear, fear that the contagion of oblivion might strike them as well. So no questions. Because no questions meant no voodoo, man, know what I mean?

Joe knew what that meant only too well. So he passed on. And on and on. And still Marcello remained elusive. Once Joe thought that he had found him, in a pub behind St Martin's Lane. He had offered the photos to the barman, who had immediately shouted out to the assembled young drinkers, 'Anyone here called Marcello?' A group in the far corner had disgorged its Marcello, a short, squat unsmiling Italian passing through London with his school group who was not enjoying the experience of being away from home one little bit. Not the real Marcello. Contact between Joe and the unwilling traveller had been brief and mutually upsetting. The false Marcello had wrongly assumed that his mother had come to fetch him home. He had not been pleased.

Joe had left the pub with more than just a tremor of uneasiness. It was a grim business. Marcello was lost and so too was Joe. But although Marcello might at some stage be found and reunited with his family, Joe thought he himself had become permanently dislocated. A spy could only function in ambiguity, among the cracks of life as it pounded away. If that life was taken away, the spy was faced with a hard choice, between living from moment to moment, with the future collapsed, embracing ambiguity wholeheartedly in the uncertainty of survival; or simply ceasing to exist, imploding somehow into the abyss of nothingness. Joe had chosen the former course, but it was hard for him to stick to the line of his commitment. Setbacks and circumstances and events and cataracts of depression buffeted him daily in their gusts.

Marcello in some respects had become the person that Joe had failed to become, years ago, after he had been sucked more and more into the treacherous world of espionage. In seeking Marcello, Joe was in fact looking for himself. Joe was aware of that. He realised there was a search for self, not exactly one of anguish but one more connected with an examination of possibilities and probabilities. Life might have gone this way but it in fact went the other way – that kind of thing. Joe could still just bring himself to be dispassionate about it all.

And he imagined constantly what kind of young man Marcello might turn out to be, fully aware at the same time that Marcello was doing exactly what Joe had done years ago, breaking away to make his own life. This was a small warning bell which couldn't be ignored. What Joe might find if he ever unearthed Marcello might turn out to be very different from the person whom Betty had earnestly and in good faith described to him as quiet, pleasant, agreeable and charming. Mothers, in Joe's experience, very rarely knew their own children. Or, to be more precise, they knew only that part of them which they chose to acknowledge as valid. So Joe could find a massive surprise or a terrible disappointment. He had no illusions on that score. In the meantime he continued the search. But the ending of that search could be profoundly upsetting.

'Yeah, Annie, I'm just about twenty yards behind him, but he won't pick me up. There are too many people between me and him now for that.'

'How's he walking?'

'Head up, not slouching. Seems fairly serene, I would say.'

'And heading for?'

'Sloane Square, I guess. He's off on one of those mooching trips of his, I guess. Showing the pics around, know what I mean?'

'Of course. Keep close. We're here all the time. Call us in half an hour, will you, anyway?'

'Will do. Out.'

The watcher clicked off. It was a smooth contact and Annie was pleased. These things all shaped a mission. Bootface prepared to speak. Annie could hear it coming. The body language did not augur well. His mind was not on the job. All morning he'd been shifting around like an animal with an itch, trying to get comfortable and failing. Now he was about to unburden himself. Annie dreaded the lapse in concentration.

'Why don't we hurry it all up, Annie? You know we don't have much time on this. Like show him he's being tailed. That would tell him something, wouldn't it?'

'Are you mad?'

'Not at all. But we don't have much time, as I said. He has to know that we're with him, that we want to bring him in.'

'Yes, but my dear Bootface, that all begs one vital question.'

'What's that, then?'

'We may be with him but he may not be with us.'

'Of course he's with us. He's part of the service, isn't he? That counts for everything. He's one of us.'

As Bootface flailed away, Annie saw those two clocks on her mantelpiece again, very clearly in her mind's eye, and realised that she would have to step very warily indeed with Bootface. There was something completely wrong here, something approaching a wilful failure to understand. A disregard for the mere humanity of the agent. That was new for her. His attitude was obscene. Agents were pure gold to be cherished and nurtured, because in the last analysis that was all they had by way of weaponry. They were the agents. But not to Bootface. To him they were expendable. Bootface just didn't class Joe as a human being at all. To him Joe was just an object. Something that came and went, something to be used. Or so she surmised, not as yet sure of her definition.

She took the high road of explanation, to be on the safe side. 'Because, my dear Bootface, we have smashed him into the ground, purely for our own purposes. We have taken everything we could from him and we have thrown him into the gutter.'

'Yes, yes, I know that. I'm not a complete fool, you know.'

'So we have to step warily. We have to encourage him to come to us. We are trying. But it all takes a long time. The psychology of the situation is crucial. You can't rush these things. We have to tempt him back into allegiance. We have to conjure allegiance because he is interested again in working for us. That makes sense, doesn't it?'

Bootface said nothing and merely nodded his head. But Annie saw a gleam of quiet triumph in his eye, as if he had forced an admission from her. So what did that mean? She was fogged. She had given him the bog standard line but that wasn't good enough for Bootface. This was unlike anything she had ever known on a mission. Bootface might have been working for Tesco or Boots for all his commitment to the mission, she thought.

The watcher buzzed through with more procedurals. Joe was boarding the tube; she would be close behind in the next carriage.

She would call again soon. She said Joe seemed fairly relaxed. Click and out.

Annie brooded on her little spat with Bootface. She felt nervous about it all. If someone had taken the trouble to warn her about something, using the clocks, then she'd better be careful about everything. Question all assumptions, including Bootface. This again was new for her. The point about the service was its sense of solidarity; they all worked together because they were the final line of defence to the country. If they started squabbling amongst themselves then that final line started to look very fractured indeed. But here it was before her eyes. Instead of sharing thoughts and ideas with Bootface she was going to have to withhold from him. So much was clear already. She felt chagrined by it all.

Joe stood at the entrance to the Jack of Hearts looking for Treadwell. It was four fifteen.

The trip in search of Marcello had not been a success. No sign of the boy for a start. Also he'd strayed into the wrong kind of pub, a gay pub, at least he thought it should be the wrong kind of pub for Marcello. Betty had never hinted that Marcello was gay. But then how would she know? Perhaps that was why Marcello had left home so suddenly, in which case they were all wasting their time grieving over him. For a young gay to leave home and get to London was like taking the first three steps to heaven.

The barman was very sympathetic. 'Yes, I know, dear, they come and they go. Like little fireflies, they are. You just can't hold them. I had a boyfriend like that once, not quite so good-looking, but very attractive. Very sexy. Beautiful tits, just beautiful. I just loved sucking his nipples. Very long they were. Of course, I was a lot younger then, not quite the bloated old tart I am now. Anyway, we had such a marvellous time together for about six months, such a good time, and then one day he just turned on me, called me all the names under the sun, including some new ones, said he'd found someone else and that was it. He was off. And off he went. Just like that. Phut!' And the barman clicked his fingers with a sad gesture of finality. 'How long were you with yours?'

Joe explained that he was looking for the boy on behalf of a friend, and the barman raised very slowly a highly quizzical eyebrow at Joe. It was a good lift of the eyebrow.

'Oh, it's like that, is it,' he said sceptically, moving away and further down the bar to wash an empty glass ostentatiously.

'Better try down the road then. I think the Fox and Faggot's straight, but then you never can tell these days, can you? Can you?' he said loudly and more theatrically to the whole bar.

A couple of muscular young men playing on the fruit machines turned round briefly.

'Can you fuck what, Norma, you old shagbag? You couldn't fuck your way out of a paper bag, you old queen,' said one of them offhandedly before turning back to the machine, running his hand with measured lust over his companion's bottom. The machine clunked and whirred as if in response.

Joe left the bar clutching the photos. London was becoming more and more like Berlin for him, a revisitation of his youth. For the scene to be complete all it needed now was for the Fat Man to rise out of the grating in the pavement and hover in front of him, like a piece of demented ectoplasm.

Yet again Joe saw the Fat Man lying dead in Fleet Street, with his gun sliding from his pocket to the road with a clunk and the bystanders gathering in a crowd. That was the Fat Man's final resting place and something like that would be his, unless his luck turned, thought Joe, abandoning the search for Marcello to seek out Joxer at the Jack of Hearts.

So it was on to stage two of the afternoon. Joe could feel the melancholy gathering like mist across a glen, but so far he had staved it off. And a little gambling might help morale along marvellously. No sense in feeling any guilt at all about the past. What was done was done. And the Fat Man, like Marley, was dead. Definitely dead.

So there he was standing in front of this seedy-looking gambling joint in west London. The Jack of Hearts was a hard gambling club with tough rules. Before it let the punters in, it wanted bank references, a deposit of two thousand pounds or upwards, depending on what the stakes at the table were, and a few more vital financial details, like credit card viability. The Jack of Hearts was less concerned about the bridge credentials. That was up to the punters. But payment was on the nail. Bridge was a cash business.

Joe could supply none of these details. He had no money, let alone a bank account. But Treadwell, or Joxer, as he was known at the tables, had money. Oodles of it, so far as Joe could gather. Joxer was a doctor, a junior consultant no less, who had taken his first sure steps on the ladder of medical success. He now had half a day's consulting in Harley Street. He was looking for two days there shortly, in the medical world's version of Arcadia. He was getting there. But the money came too slowly for Joxer. The girlfriend's red Porsche was always moving just a little too fast for him. And Joxer was no longer in quite the first flush of youth. Any window of opportunity which opened for him now might well provide the last glimmer of success he would ever see. So to keep up with the whole shebang – girlfriend, career and socialising – he needed to gamble. And he needed Joe. Joe was cool where he was too dashing. Together they formed a powerful partnership.

Needless to say, Joxer knew nothing of Joe's other life. To him Joe was just a gift from the gods, a bridge player available at almost any time during the afternoons, when he could slip away from his 'research' to the Jack of Hearts and try to make a few hundred. Colleagues said that Joxer had published too few papers. Joxer claimed to be working on his *magnum opus* that would astound them all, Hippocrates included.

He and Joe gambled hard together, splitting the winnings seventy–thirty, with Joxer taking the lion's share. They had been successful together. On a good day they would split a thousand pounds. And on a bad day? That was when Joxer disappeared back into the operating theatre to perform an urgent operation, post-haste, putting off his girlfriend for the evening en route.

Joe saw Joxer pacing up and down in the entrance hall. Joxer was tall and thin and looked manic. Eyes bulging behind the heavy frames. Black hair sprouting over the collar which was just a little too worn. Predestined to be choleric in later middle age. They made contact. Joxer rounded on Joe.

'Look, where have you been? We distinctly said four o'clock and now it's quarter past. We're losing time.'

'Relax. We've got all the time.'

'No we haven't. I've got to be back in the operating theatre at five fifteen. Something nasty. Anyway, come on, let's get going. Let's hope there aren't any Chinese around.'

Last week a couple of Chinese had taken the pair of them for a hiding, the first for many weeks. It had come as quite a shock. They had grown too complacent.

They fought their way through the smoke and the foursomes gathered somehow in inert silence round their tables and found a table up. They were playing at the twenty-five pounds a hundred tables. Quite small stakes. That was how they played, building up some scratch of winnings among the weaker players before moving on to the bigger fish. Sometimes it worked.

Joxer did the honours of the introduction. So did the opposition. Brief exchanges. The opposition had the pasty look of players who have been at the same table for about three weeks. But no body language at all. Quite silent. It could be tough opposition.

'Weak no trump. Twelve to fourteen points'

'Likewise.'

Joe dealt. He had a typical no trump hand: ace, king, small in spades, ace to two small in hearts, king, ten and six of diamonds, and four small clubs. Joe bid a no trump and Joxer raised to three no trumps. The king of hearts was led, and down went the dummy.

The smoke swirled around and Joxer sat there like the mask of Fu Manchu glittering in his intensity through the fog. He was perfectly still. No way he was going to jig up and down and disturb declarer. He was a good partner in that way. Joe studied the dummy full of suspicion, with that little fluttering sense of fear in his gut. Getting from his hand to dummy might be like advancing across no man's land in the Battle of the Somme. Very costly. It behoved him to take care. He looked some more, getting the feel of the hands.

Easy boy, easy, he was telling himself. This ought to make. But go carefully. Spades looked okay; clubs were just about tolerable; the play was really in the diamonds – ace, queen, nine, five, and four on the table. With five diamond tricks, the contract was home. But could he make five diamond tricks? He could if the jack of diamonds was on side and if the split could be handled.

And there was something else too about the hand which he couldn't quite discern.

Gently, he played a small heart and covered the king with his ace in hand. No sense in holding up – they'd see the club switch. Then Joe saw the booby traps in the hand; it came to him quite suddenly. He felt a lot happier. At least he could see the bomb now. First, the jack of diamonds had to be on his left, which was quite feasible since West had only shown a maximum of six points so far. Second, he had to make sure he wasn't blocked in his own hand in the event of a really crappy split, like four to one in the diamonds. Because he had to make five diamond tricks. No other way could he make it, with the clubs as they were, and the hearts.

Very carefully, like an animal putting forward a careful paw in the forest, Joe played the diamond ten – and it held. No pauses in the play from either of the opposition – these guys were really good. Next Joe played the king of diamonds and to his great relief East showed out.

Oh, frabjous day! Let the welkin ring, thought Joe, realising that he could claim. No sense in playing on. He had his nine tricks, including the spades, which he showed. Game and vulnerable. Joxer was expressionless and silent. But game up and vulnerable. Halfway to the rubber and some dosh.

The next hand was dealt through the smoke. The Armenian opposition, at least Joe thought they were Armenians, bid and made two spades, plus an overtrick. Then in the next hand Joxer opened one club, and after Joe's pass, bid two clubs. This looked awkward. Joxer was doubled for takeout, and East bid two spades. Joe at this point should have bid three clubs, but he held back for fear of getting doubled. Two spades was passed out – and made. Game all and both sides vulnerable. Joe's pass had been quite valuable. Three clubs would have gone two off, which doubled and vulnerable makes a very tidy figure above the line – for the opposition. That kind of woolly play sure cuts into the winnings, thought Joe, who at this stage was hoping for a repeat performance of the British Steel coup in the morning.

Some sundry play then followed with both sides hacking and scraping for an advantage. Both sides vulnerable, but neither side getting the cards quite right in order to make game and the rubber. Snow on the roof. No big fishes of hands coming up. Easier just to wait for the good cards to come round. But meanwhile time was marching on; Joe thought of Joxer's patient preparing himself mentally to be sliced open in about twenty minutes while the artist himself was slugging it out underground in a tough card school by way of focusing. Always go for the jugular, Joxer.

But Joe could hear it coming. The slam. Joxer was a man who liked to bid a slam when he was ahead. It meant he could wrap up the play faster than he'd anticipated. Joe could feel his slam bid in the wind, even though the cards might not be there to justify it. Just instinct perhaps. Or experience. Joxer was getting impatient. It was on its way, that was for sure, and then there it was. Joe bid a spade, Joxer replied two hearts and then there they were up in six hearts with not a flicker of interest from the opposition. They were both slumped in their chairs as if heavily winded by blows to the solar plexus. Or dead perhaps.

The jack of clubs was led, and Joxer screwed up his face. He had to play it carefully, because if the slam made then they could both quit with their winnings. Joxer could sidle into the operating theatre with a clear conscience and Joe could go home to sleep. But if the slam went down, then there would have to be more time spent at the table and that would cause complications. Joxer carried on staring at dummy and his hand, looming through the smoke. Joe liked the look of it. It meant he was taking it seriously. Joe had given him a fabulous dummy – fourteen points in all with a singleton club and ace, queen, jack of spades. Admittedly the hearts were a touch bedraggled. But Joxer must have five of the little buggers.

As if reaching a sudden and irrevocable decision, Joxer covered the jack of clubs with his queen and then played the queen of hearts towards Joe's king–jack in dummy. Oh shit, thought Joe, this is going off, I know this is going off, unless... unless... I've got it, I understand, but let's just see, shall we, let's just see. The queen of hearts glided on to the table, the three of hearts was played to Joxer's left and the other side showed out! Joxer had played for a four-nil break in the trump suit and the bugger had got it right. The slam made. Whoosh, whoosh, whoosh.

No story after that. Joxer's face briefly assumed human form and he allowed himself to smile. Until that moment he'd been somewhere in outer space. And a long way from the operating theatre; thinking about the Porsche, no doubt, his own this time.

Game set and match, or rather rubber. The Armenians paid up willingly enough and one of them said in halting but precise English, 'You know you two play very well. A little bit too well. But there is always another time. We shall meet again but next time at higher priced tables and then we—'

'Thrash you,' said Treadwell with a smile, flicking through the notes and easing them into his wallet. Joe could see a rather sumptuous dinner coming up that evening for Nicky with Joxer bragging heavily about his exploits in the operating theatre and the path to the golden mile in Harley Street.

They played a couple more rubbers for form's sake with the Armenians, but with no big swings against them they managed to hang on to the winnings, exiting at five o'clock in good order.

Outside the Jack of Hearts, Joxer pushed Joe's split of the winnings, a wad of purple notes, into his hand. Joe felt hungry already. That meant a good meal that night at Zorba's, for starters.

'Nice play, Joe,' Joxer said, marching down the street, looking more and more like a doctor with each step. The carriage of the head changed, with the personality. But so what? Joxer was an out and out *arriviste*. Anything went in the quest for position, having it all. So far as Joe knew, Nicky was unaware that her extravagant courtship was being financed by low gambling at the Jack of Hearts. And would she care if she knew? Fast rewinding to the events of the morning and a very different game of bridge, Joe rather thought she might. At some point, when the mansion in Hampshire had finally been paid for. Until then? For the time being Joe felt too exhausted to care. He sprang into a cab, planning to retire to bed for a few hours of sleep. British Steel was tough, but the Jack of Hearts had been nerve-racking. Had he got that diamond ten wrong, or had Joxer not played the queen of hearts – it just didn't bear further thinking about.

He ignored the crack in the wall as he passed into his flat. He knew it had not lengthened. Things were in their place. They look okay for the time being, he thought. I can take it for a few more hours. And the money will last until tomorrow. This lotus-eating life can just get too much for a man, he thought, his head crashing down on the pillow and his eyes closing immediately. But there again, it has its compensations, he mused, looking at the crisp bundle of notes under the lamp beside the bed.

Then he slept, sleeping that flat-out sleep of the totally exhausted. Later that night, he would be awake. But for the time being he preferred oblivion. If indeed he had any choice in the matter.

There was another call on his answerphone, another call from Pugh. This time more urgent and more injunctive. But Joe would find it in the morning. It would still be there.

# Chapter Five

It was Sunday and Joe was sitting on an early train heading south. He had received detailed instructions from his new friend, Rivers Pugh, regarding the exact train to take, what clothes to wear and how long he should expect to stay at Pugh Park. Not that he was likely to outstay his welcome. Rivers was revealing himself as a master of detailed planning. He wanted to get everything right and correct. Joe expected to be back in London by early evening.

Rivers had sounded much recovered on the phone when Joe finally, after much cogitating, opted to contact him. Voluble response and much explaining. Lots of self-justification. Joe had barely listened. He assented to all the instructions. It seemed easier. Friday had been a black day. The depression had come rolling in from the east, prostrating him in the process. He barely knew what day it had been, let alone where Pugh Park might be situated. It was easier to go with the flow. At some stage on Saturday the black clouds began to ease. Until then it had been hell. Even the Thames started to look attractive as a haven.

'Go to Waterloo, and catch the 11.05 train. They normally go from platform eight on a Sunday. Then wait at the station. I'll be there to pick you up.'

Joe arrived at Waterloo at eleven, more or less *compos mentis*, but with that jagged haphazard relationship with objects and phenomena which stems from extreme stress. Occasionally he banged into things as if his nerve ends had grown furry. Much seemed fuzzed. He stumbled about on the station concourse securing his ticket. He felt nervous and edgy too about the trip out of London. He had a poor expectation of it. It could prove fatal to morale if he happened to run into someone he had known from another life.

Imagine, he told himself, if someone breezes up to me and claps me on the back saying, 'Why, Joe, where have you been? Long time no see. And what about that bank of yours, you old devil, how is that shaping up? Still fighting it out with the Gilstons? They're an evil crowd, you know that?'

That would give him a jolt, he knew. All that City success had finished for Joe a long time ago. The Gilstons had taken their revenge on him, like many others, not only stabbing him in the back while he was out of the country but ensuring too that he never worked again in the City. Some form of blacklisting had taken place, a blacklisting that could never be pinned down. His name had never gone on a noticeboard, no one had ever publicly proclaimed his unsuitability. But a whisper here, a rumour there, a quiet shake of the head from that charming man in the corner of the Jamaica and there it was – he was out. Or rather, not so much out as not considered. He had become invisible so far as the City was concerned. It was as if he had never been. He had fallen from a great height and many had connived at the descent.

'What Joe, you, chief executive? I don't believe it. Surely not... And if you were what you claim to have been, how come you're applying for this terribly humble position as US equities analyst? A bit beneath you, I would have thought. You must have done something terribly wrong. Are you sure you're giving us the full story?' Meanwhile persons or people unknown had helped themselves to his fortune, so that here he was... Joe snapped to and focused on the present. Truly that way madness lay. He refused to think about it any more. The past was dead.

Joe had not rung Joachim, more or less because he had forgotten about him. Life ebbed and flowed around him but it had no hard sense of definition for him. Hard for him to make appointments, since he kept no diary. It was that kind of life he was leading. He would ring Joachim but not yet perhaps.

Thinking about how unfortunate it would be should he run into old City acquaintances, Joe opened the *Sunday Times* but he wearied of it quickly. He put it down on the seat beside him as the train rumbled into Woking and then, suddenly bored again, picked it up again to flick through the supplements. His eye was caught by a poem, which he started to read with no other interest than that it took his mind away from his own problems. It was called 'Jo bound' and it read as follows:

I knew a friend once who could write poetry.
It was brilliant stuff.
He showed me how to bend the words into a line of sense,
Curving reality through the verbs.
He wrote well, like Homer,
Scattering plump adjectives like a peasant sowing corn at autumn.
I need him now – urgently.
I've met someone with eyes like stars
And the smile of a hectic Trojan.
My icon, whom I in turn idolatrize.
But how to express, how to capture all of this?
How to get into words
Such grace, like a bird alighting on a slow flower,
Or the zest of such presence lighting up the room suddenly
On quick entry. Blown by the freshness of such a wind,
Wrapped in such sure embrace, I am bereft
Of tongue. And I am afraid
Of loss.
I need to borrow the words and talent
Of my friend, to work in a little
Careful, tactical plagiarism.
But he has departed,
Bound for Australia and a new life. Bizarre
Now to think of him mute and his words stowed away,
Chugging them both across silent seas,
Thinking of what is to come
While I court this star, new risen,
Warming the world with careless rays.
And I have no words. Only prayer of devotion.

Joe noted the name of the author, something Priest, before tossing the newspaper away on one of the other seats. He liked the poem and it moved him. Such a sophisticated work of composition to write such a simple poem he thought, and its tender feelings warmed him for a second. Priest and his girlfriend must be having a ball this morning, after rushing out at four in the morning to buy fifty copies, he thought. To amaze their friends. Who would be duly astonished – they'd always considered Priest to be such a good-for-nothing. Such magic *joie de vivre*... At this moment, the two of them will just be surfacing from beneath their bedclothes for a Sunday cup of coffee, all toasty warm, followed by a nice lingering grope, followed by... Joe's mind turned against the ensuing scene, blanking it out utterly. Well, his girlfriend will be pleased.

It was a long time since anyone had cleaved at all in any way like that to Joe. That kind of thing did not come cheap in London, if it came at all. So it didn't come to Joe these days. No wonder he'd noticed the name Priest. Joe lived like an ascetic.

The moment of ease fled and he was back in the old gut-gnawing sense of survival which rarely left him now. Always against the odds, he thought, that is the curse of it all. Rough work, this agent's game – *ne soyez pas de notre confrérie. Jamais, oh jamais*.

His train pulled in at the station. Mechanically he descended from the train and wandered along the platform; time to get on parade and receive the exaggerated attentions and gratitude of Rivers Pugh.

Bootface rang Annie at home as Joe's train pulled into the station. He'd been brooding. That was clear. He was alone in the office, keeping the Sunday vigil. He seemed agitated.

'So where is he then?' He spoke curtly.

Annie was fascinated by the assumption of guilt on her part; in some way, inferred but not stated, she had let the side down. Again. Again and again. Annie was not impressed. She was playing with her sister's new baby. It gurgled in delight at her as they all romped on the floor. Sunday morning's best time. Annie was not best pleased by the call.

'What do you mean, where is he? Heaven only knows – defecting probably.'

It was a bad joke. Bootface was not amused.

'Yes, but where is he? What's he doing? Haven't we got someone on him?'

'My dear Bootface, how many times do I have to tell you? Joe is a very grown-up operative. If he doesn't want to work for us again, then no power on earth that we possess will induce him to do that. He is not – I repeat, not – a baby.'

Her sister's new baby chose that moment to give out a deafening, truly ear-splitting, shriek of discontent.

'What on earth was that?' said Bootface.

'Wind,' said her sister. 'Turn him over.'

'Turn who over?' said Bootface, clearly alarmed.

'You'll find out. Speak to you on Monday. And for your information, I haven't a clue where he is,' said Annie, putting the phone down crisply.


Same Rivers Pugh, but no longer weeping this time. He seemed quite fresh-faced and young in the Sunday morning air. Same gold spectacles and air of fastidious concern. Same globular eyes. He can't be more than twenty-five, thought Joe. So young and so despairing. It was tragic.

He greeted Joe warmly. 'Oh, there you are, Joe. What a time I've had winkling you out of London. Do you play bridge all day and all night? You've been very hard to get hold of.'

His desire to see Joe and thank him formally was undiminished. But there was an extra timbre to what he said. He sounded plaintive and just a mite peeved at the amount of trouble he'd taken to run Joe to earth. Joe stored that tone of voice away. He had a sensitive ear and he knew well the terms of trade in this environment. Both shared equal time but though Joe's time was River's time, the same could not be said for Rivers. Joxer had the same failing. But it was early days to pass judgement.

'I'm sorry I haven't been around to take calls very much recently. The play goes on and on.'

'But do people play much bridge in London?'

They were driving now, down the winding country lanes flanked by green, but at some speed. Rivers drove with grace and dexterity. It was a fast car but he handled it well. To the manor born.

'In my neck of the woods they do nothing else. There are at least five or six bridge clubs within a mile of where I live.'

'My goodness, I'd never have guessed. It's like a warren. All of them carding away like rabbits. And where might that be, where you live?'

'World's End way.'

Joe was determined to play the bridge player role to the hilt, unless he found that circumstances, like running into one of the Gilstons, made that impossible. There was something about Rivers which encouraged duplicity, something about his angle of descent which contradicted the evident intelligence. He was just too eager to show off his superior brainpower. Sadly, he had not learned the dull virtue of concealment and it could prove fatal for him.

Joe could hear the old army phrase ring in his ears: bullshit baffles brains. And it had to be true in this case. For all his superlative intelligence, breeding and grooming, Rivers was a naïf. A Candide. An innocent abroad. And exactly how fatally naive Joe would no doubt garner a glimpse at some point during his visit.

What was it that Rivers had done to cause him to weep like that in public? Joe was willing to wait to find out. He felt old, cunning and wise in his company. Happy to let the young man frolic in the sunshine – and find the landmines of his own accord. So not especially friendly towards Rivers. Just too many unspoken assumptions for Joe's liking.

'We're getting quite close now.'

They turned in sharply at the gate, and sped up the drive of Pugh Park. Joe noticed trees, broad expanses and a small stream running through the drive. They sped over the bridge. The house was a solid but slightly understated Tudor pile, nestling shaded by trees, some one hundred and fifty yards up the drive. But then a surprise, which broke the line of nostalgic historicism. Running down the drive towards them, like a vision of sheer delight, came a young girl. Blouse and skirt ballooned around her in the breeze as she ran, almost on her points. Like travelling. Perhaps eighteen, or a young twenty. A fresh beautiful smile right across her face. Flowing blonde hair. She reminded Joe of one of those gloriously coloured hummingbirds in South America, landing with weightless ease on the flower's stamens. Balanced on her long slim legs and moving like the wind, she was a dryad girl from the woods. Close to Pan and his cronies. Joe felt better immediately.

Rivers stopped the car and the vision drew nearer. 'My sister, Perdita. She always comes to meet the car. She gets so excited by visitors. She just has to run down the drive to meet whoever comes in. My mother can't stop her, although she's tried. You'd think she was a maiden locked up in a chateau the way she rushes down the drive.'

Pause, as Perdita embraced her brother through the window. A big embrace, because she was also out of breath. She kissed him with great tenderness, her blonde hair falling across both their faces.

'I was afraid you were never coming back. Why were you away so long?'

'I wasn't away for long. Just about an hour. Anyway, this is Sunday. I told you I was going to pick Joe up at the station afterwards. My interview only lasted forty-five minutes. So I haven't been gone all that amount of time. But, Perdita, this is Joe. I told you about him. Joe saved my life.'

They shook hands across the steering wheel. She was briefly speechless at the very thought of it all. But not for long.

'Oh Joe,' she said, eyes popping like stars at him, 'I'm so grateful to you. Yes, just very, very grateful. I couldn't stand it if anything happened to him. We'd all die. Just pass away.'

'Just like that?'

'Bloody rude, I know. But it's true. Rivers is the man in our family. We couldn't have carried on living without him. It would have been impossible. We couldn't have coped. We missed him even this morning when he went off for his dreadful interview. At least I did. I think Mother was too busy in the veggie garden to miss anyone.'

She looked Joe straight in the eye as they shook hands and the sunlight fell across her face, moulding and blending the blue eyes and the pale lips and the broad forehead into some bucolic vision of the corn fields, reapers and the rolling acres. Ceres herself, perhaps? Unlikely, but a very beautiful girl nevertheless. A Guinevere still in love with her family and her home and the closed life of the domain.

Joe felt the loss of his fortune even more keenly. Such a pity about those lost millions. They would have come in useful this morning, he thought.

'Interview?'

'I'll tell you all about it. I was sacked last week. That's why I was so shocked. But it went well, I think, even though it was a bit of a come down. You know, having to sell yourself, that kind of thing. It's not really my cup of tea. At least, I don't know. I've never had to do it before, anyway.'

And Joe, who had been sacked, defenestrated, shown the door, shot at, beaten up, and generally abused throughout his working life, mumbled sympathy and support as they rode slowly up to the house, with Perdita perched, as seemed only natural, on the bonnet of the car, kicking her legs up. Rivers drove very carefully, steering with precision, so as not to crack or chip such a delicate piece of Dresden. Perdita turned back every so often to stare at them through the windscreen, laughing as she did so.

Joe realised as well that there had been steel fences ringing the estate as they drove in. That shocked him. There were no barriers here. The whole place was open to the sky and the road, merging in a quiet way into its surroundings.

Perdita sprang off the bonnet at the front door. 'Mother, they're here at last,' she cried out in the hallway.

'Coming!' echoed from the upstairs and a dignified figure descended the stairs in measured haste. She turned at the bottom of the stairs. Then Joe was face to face with Lady Pugh. She shook his hand warmly with unaffected directness. She made him feel welcome. He was across the threshold and into the warm. Joe started to feel at home, an unaccustomed sensation for one exposed to the cold for so long.

'Joe, it's you. I'm so pleased to see you. I'm so pleased you were able to come. We all owe you a debt of thanks. Do come in. You are very, very welcome.'

'Mother, Mother, come on, what do you think? You must tell.'

'Shut up, Perdita. He's only just arrived.'

Rivers spoke in that rough way that brothers adopt with their adored sisters. Lady Pugh had the unfeigned directness of the very aristocratic, more at home in the stables and the garden than in the drawing room. There were dark shadows under her eyes and she moved with a travelling grace. But without eschewing responsibility. And she had charm, that unlooked-for godlike ability to light up a room. It streamed from her, as it did from

Perdita.

Descended from badgers, I'll be bound, thought Joe unkindly and then repented of the thought as cheap and unworthy. Not for such an ambience, he told himself. He was enjoying the warm atmosphere. He resolved to avoid unnecessary displays of temperament.

'Give him a chance to take his coat off, I tell you.'

'No, no, Mother, come on do tell. He's just so fascinating. I can't keep my eyes off him. He looks so tough. Like a gangster. We thought you'd be a weed, even though you beat those two thugs up.'

Joe was taken aback for a second, but adjusted, realising that he was in the bosom of a family where things were said unscripted, where people spoke their minds, and where views were held in common. It was novel for him, he who was trained to keep his own counsel. But he joined in.

'Yes, do tell, Lady Pugh. Come on. First impressions are the ones that count.' Entering into the spirit of things, Joe posed alone and away from the group in the hall, head held high like a warrior. They all laughed. Lady Pugh stared at him for a few more seconds.

'Mother's psychic, you see. She has second sight. She's not often wrong, though she has been known to misunderstand it all. Come on Mother, what is it to be?'

Suddenly grave for a second, but with a reassuring smile, although it failed to reach the eyes, Lady Pugh passed monumental and accurate judgement. 'Joe, you are surrounded by death. Always. Even here in this house. Always death. He is your oldest friend. You don't love him, but he's always there. Yet you survive. You always do. And so do those who stay close to you. I don't understand it. There is death but no death. I've never seen this before, ever. And I am not afraid to welcome you into my house, even though I ought to show you the door.'

She held Joe's gaze again and there was no smile in the eyes. Just wary precaution. Joe shrugged and laughed, as did the other two at their mother.

Talk about having your cover blown, thought Joe. The Gents should have her on their books. There'd be no spy rings left by the time she'd sniffed them out. What did I say about badgers?

He grinned at Lady Pugh. Perdita, skipping about in the hall, hooted out again that her mother was the limit. 'I've never heard anything like it in my life. That's your best yet, Mother. It's all so obvious. Joe saved Rivers. That's what the death is all about. It's nothing more than that even though he looks so feral.'

'Feral?'

'Wild. It comes from the Latin *ferus*. Everyone knows that. But Joe, you're not a murderer, are you? You don't look like a murderer even though you do look tough. But you're more of a stage heavy. It's all for show, isn't it? They're not real muscles, are they?'

Still eyeing Lady Pugh, Joe posed away again flexing his muscles like a strongman and agreed with her daughter. In all their eyes he was still a bridge player, albeit a rather unusual one.

'Just a circus strongman. Total flab.'

'I thought so. I can detect these things.'

Then Lady Pugh invited him further into the house. 'Only then can I make a cup of tea for all you lot.'

'Even though you shouldn't banish me. Don't forget, death to be with.'

'And death to be without, too.'

'Touché.'

Meeting Lady Pugh was worse than falling in with the Stasi, Joe decided. He followed her into the kitchen, confident that the season of revelations was now past. Rivers and his sister lounged around the kitchen, making pretend gestures to help with the tea, but pretty soon they cleared off, leaving Joe alone with Lady Pugh. He passed things to her, fetching and carrying on request. She made the tea with slow deliberate grace. Her psychic powers had been laid to rest, that was clear. She was back in the real world again.

'Nobody in this household can make tea to save their lives. I'm the only one who knows how long it should be infused. It's what the French call tisonner.'

Joe shook his head. No French. He was a bridge player, apart from being the angel of death. No speaka da lingo...

'My children won't drink each other's tea, not even their own.

So I have to make it all the time. Their father was just the same.'

'Oh yes.'

'He's dead now, of course. And that's why it all came as such a shock to Rivers.'

'Forgive me, Lady Pugh, but I'm still a little bit foggy over all this. What exactly did Rivers do to get himself sacked?'

'He got himself named in a parliamentary report on the Foreign Office's conduct in one of the old colonies. The entire family went into mourning over it. We knew something like that was coming, because of the interviews with the Foreign Affairs Committee, but we had no idea the reprimand would be so severe. Rivers had to resign, of course. It's a terrible blot on the family.'

'I don't understand.'

'His father was a very senior figure in the Foreign Office. Very senior indeed. Beyond ambassador level. As indeed his father had been before him. The Pughs are a permanent presence at the FO. They've been mixed up with the FO almost since Walsingham's time. They practically own it. Indeed, if the family hadn't backed the wrong horse during the power struggle in Elizabeth's last years, the Pughs would have become a more powerful presence in the land than even the Cecils. The Cecils edged them out. So when a Pugh was criticised like this in a parliamentary report, Rivers had to resign. Had to. He had no choice.'

'I see. When you say Elizabeth, you mean, Elizabeth I?'

'Of course. You must forgive me. For a family like this – and I'm not a born Pugh, just co-opted by marriage, you understand – time is not measured in the conventional way. It has no breaks. It just stretches back as far as the eye can measure. Dynasties, alliances, land, ever onward and upward. So the family is still smarting over what happened in the late 1590s. It thinks it was outmanoeuvred. The 1590s was its big moment. It had just started to emerge as a force in the land after some pretty hair-raising times in the Middle Ages, backing both sides at once. And that's expensive. The Pughs think they might have done better when they tangled with the Cecils. But it's carried on going ever since, the feud, I mean. It is an intensely ambitious family, as you might have gathered.'

'Any good moments since the late 1590s?'

Lady Pugh laughed, and began the job of carrying in the tea. She whispered it to him with a smile, as she balanced the tea tray in front of the door. 'India. They did well in India. They got there before the Cecils through the East India Company. So India was a consolation for the Pughs.'

'Adequate compensation?'

'I think so. India's a big place. I believe they did well there. Hard not to, really. The odd jewel or two, you know, that kind of thing.'

She kicked the kitchen door open expertly and marched through carrying the tea tray high. Joe followed her, dangling some sundry mugs. It was that kind of household. You mucked in. He was much amused.

Rivers and Perdita were seated in a large room that opened out on to a lawn that ran down to a lake. She was stroking his hair for him and he was lying in a semi-supine posture in front of the huge windows. Animals seemed to wander back and forth at their ease across the sward. The Pughs seemed part of the animals and vice versa, like a *trompe l'oeil*. It was quite unbearably peaceful and reassuring. As Lady Pugh had said, the family had been there for centuries. It had merged with the territory.

Joe prepared to ask Rivers some questions. He wanted to learn more about the gaffe. It intrigued him. But Lady Pugh got there first. She opened her mouth to speak but Perdita interrupted her. 'Joe, you have to watch out for Mother. She likes to know about people, that is, what she hasn't already picked up on the psychic waves. She's going to ask you some questions.'

Lady Pugh was indignant. 'Perdita, I was not going to interrogate him. I was merely going to ask our visitor and saviour one or two questions about himself. People like to talk about themselves. It makes them feel at home. Sugar, Joe?'

'No, thank you. But I do take milk.'

'Help yourself. Now, Joe, have you always been a bridge player? What got you into it?'

Perdita rolled her eyes towards the skies at her mother's persistence and Joe reckoned it was all going to be terribly easy for him. They were just rolling around together. It was effortless. It was like being in a badger's cave, warm and friendly and a trifle musty. The weight of the centuries hung light over them all.

'Lady Pugh, it's so much better than working.'

'That's it, then. I'm going to be a bridge player too. You can start teaching me right away, Joe. I like the sound of it immediately.'

This from Perdita, who in truth it was hard to imagine toiling away in an office, even one in the King's Road, where opening the post took until lunchtime. Those long legs and slim thighs and shimmering energy were not made for drudgery and the measured day.

'But Joe, how do you get started at becoming a bridge player? I mean, what do you do for money, for instance. Are you sponsored?'

Joe felt that the whole Sunday was starting to come alive for him. Not that his guard was beginning to drop – that was impossible. The spy was too deep in him for that. But briefly he felt protected and cosseted and able to flower as something in alternative mode. And, as he kept telling himself, they didn't know who he was. He was new for them. He had possibilities. He could reinvent himself, just for a few moments, in fresh company.

He decided to tell them a story to explain what he did, just as he might have done in the old days at Martins Bank when he was rich and powerful.

'Imagine the Wild West, and think about a shanty town somewhere in the middle of nowhere.'

'This just too romantic for words. The Wild West, cor, how scrumptious. Joe, you're not drinking your tea. It'll get cold.'

'Perdita, stop interrupting him.'

'A stranger rides into town. He goes into the saloon and sits down at a table. They're playing poker and they cut him in on the deal. They've been there for days. No one has shaved. The personal odours are rank. Outerwear is far from casual and contains much ironmongery, which he eyes with some trepidation. He bets and bets. Sometimes he wins, and sometimes he loses. They all watch each other very cautiously. And outside as they play and as the day draws on, there is nothing but great acres of ground and the sky. Uninhabited. So he is alone with the cards and his luck and his money. Eventually he leaves the table. He has some winnings. He gets on his horse and leaves the town. Looking for another—'

'Change of clothes.'

They all laughed. Perdita had interrupted well.

'And that's how you get started playing bridge.'

Joe drank his tea. Then they all fell about with laughter again, tickled by Perdita's conceit. Lady Pugh looked pleased. Her family appeared to be delighted with the stranger.

'So you live by your wits, Joe, in a manner of speaking?'

'You could say that.' That statement was at least partly true, although it did contain resonances which Joe declined to amplify.

Rivers entered the conversation. 'It's a pity I hadn't met you before I got mixed up in all this wretched business. I could have used some of your nous, Joe. I wouldn't have been sucked in so deep.'

'Rivers, tell me about the interview this morning. How did it go? Are you going to get hired?'

'That's difficult after the pounding I took at the hands of the committee. There is a mark of Cain all right on me. They made sure of that. My man said he'd think about it. He's a connection from school. Somebody put me in touch with him. It may work out for me.'

Rivers paused. Plainly the idea that the automatic stepping stones to grace and light might somehow have been removed was novel for him. He failed more or less completely to connect with the reality that he had been branded. That he might conceivably fail. It was still just a concept for him. He had not been touched by it all profoundly. It had not changed him in outlook. The levers were still there, waiting to be pulled, as he thought.

'You know, the wonder of it all is that I didn't think I was doing anything wrong. I thought I was just doing my job. I was completely shocked when I was hauled up in front of the committee. And I'm still not certain that it all came out as it should have done.'

Little lights started to twinkle in Joe's head. He recognised this talk. It sounded like the old, old story. No matter how you sliced it in the UK, Joe reckoned, you always came back to perfidy. He knew immediately what Rivers was trying to say. But he refrained from indicating too much rapid familiarity with the situation.

'I don't understand. You must explain.'

Perdita again was quicker to the punch. 'What Rivers is trying to say in his unbearably pompous way is that he thinks he was fixed. Impossible to imagine it of such an organisation, and such a noble and well-established family, but certain things seemed to be going on, which he was too junior to understand.'

Joe could well imagine the FO fixing anything and anybody. He'd seen a fair amount of their handiwork in his time. Berlin had been a paradise for them.

Perdita continued. 'All of a rush, there were heaps of documents to look at, to sign, and to put before the minister, all in a tremendous hurry. Poor Rivers was overwhelmed. Some of it he did correctly, but some of it, inevitably, wasn't quite done to standard. But there was no time to check everything.'

'And that's where the trouble lay?'

Rivers came into the conversation. 'And it all led to this. Try looking at page twenty-seven. That's where the Pughs met their Crécy and their Waterloo.'

Rivers flung across to Joe a large blue-bound book which Joe took to be the book Rivers had been weeping over during their first meeting at Zorba's. The parliamentary report, dreaded by civil servants and ministers alike, if things were going wrong. Page twenty-seven was wrinkled and corrugated at the edges of the page and in large parts in the middle of the page, where the tears had cascaded on the paper and then dried.

It was easy to spot the passage Rivers wanted read. It had been highlighted in black bold by the committee itself in the middle of the page. It read:

We believe that the senior officials – Ms Blake and Mr Pugh – who received both the minutes of 22 February and the Project Monty document made serious errors of judgement and failed in their duty to Ministers by not acting promptly and decisively on the information they contained... We conclude that there was an appalling failure in the briefing of Ministers, which we recommend should not be repeated. It is on the basis of briefing that Ministers report to Parliament and, in the words of the

Resolution of the House, it is of paramount importance that Ministers give accurate and truthful information to Parliament.

Parliamentary committee reports didn't come stronger than that in Joe's experience.

'Golly, they really went for you, didn't they? The full monty all right with all barrels blazing. What on earth did you do to deserve all that shellacking?'

'Oh, there's more later on in the report; it gets worse if anything. But let's not dwell on that, shall we?' And Rivers held out his hand, requesting the return of the Pugh's history of shame.

'So what happened to Ms Blake?'

Silence in the room all round. The Pughs all looked at each other. It was the question that should not have been asked. The setting suddenly was less than bucolic.

Lady Pugh provided the information. 'She's been promoted.'

'What? Impossible.'

'Yes, she's moved up two grades in the FO. I'm in the street and she's higher up the ladder. What makes it all the more surprising is that it was her brother who gave me all the extra work to do. He made me take the extra responsibility. I had no choice. He was my boss. He just loaded the work on me. And all at the last minute, too.' It all came out in a rush.

'What could I do? I was at school with Jasper. So what could I do? Nothing, that's the answer. I had to do whatever he told me to do. I've known him since I was seven years old. He's always been a year ahead of me in everything. And now... I just can't believe that he could have dished me like that. I just can't believe it. But there it is. Something happened. His sister is on the way up and I'm out on the street. Finished at the FO. I still just can't believe it. There's been a Pugh there for four hundred years. And now we're the pariahs of the place. I doubt if they'd let me through the front door now, whereas before it was always young Rivers Pugh, the last and greatest of the Pughs, about to make his mark. Everyone said as such. I just can't stand it.'

Rivers looked at Joe in the same way as he must have looked at practically everybody in the past fortnight or so. The look said: Say it isn't so. Say that this is all a nasty dream and that I'm going to wake up safe and sound in a few minutes. It was a very sad look, one of infinite supplication. Rivers craved that reaffirmation of the status quo, the positive affirmation that nothing had really changed. And Joe could see by inspection that Rivers still thought that he would get reassurance from some quarter.

Lady Pugh bustled into the conversation and struck an upbeat note. It, presumably, was not the first time that the question of his fall and future had been debated at Pugh Park. 'But your meeting this morning went well, didn't it?'

'Oh, yes, he was fine. Sloane School looks after its own. No doubt about that. He was quite convinced that—'

Perdita interrupted her brother. The blonde hair frothed around. She was getting bored again. 'Do you think we ought to show Joe around. He hasn't come all this way on a Sunday just to hear the Pughs sobbing their little hearts out over some wretched stupid report from Parliament, has he? I'm sure he has better things to do with his time. Like do some gambling.' She rolled her eyes at Joe, who had the distinct impression that he was now a permanent fixture at Pugh Park – unnerving.

'I do love the thought of that gambling, Joe, I must say.'

'Quite right, Perdita. Joe, I'm sorry we were sidetracked.'

It was Joe's cue as well. He had had a simple idea. It related to the sward. Besides he too was getting a touch nervous by the discussion about failure. Rivers had clearly been fixed in some way by Master Blake, just as Joe had been fixed himself by powers and forces unknown. Any more of this and personal morale would start to suffer.

'Do either of you guys know how to play French cricket?'

They all shook their heads. 'Never heard of it.'

Lady Pugh looked approvingly at Joe. Fresh air – always a good solution to personal problems.

'I'll show you. Let's get out there and hack it. I just have to get into the fresh air for a few moments. I want to frolic on that grass in front of the lake. We'll need a bat or a tennis racket and a tennis ball. Got that kind of kit here?'

Perdita sprang out of the room in search of the equipment. Rivers looked once more wistfully at the report before following her.

So they played French cricket, the simple principle of which was that first, the batter's feet formed the stumps, defended by the bat; and second, once the batter had hit the ball, movement was permitted until the ball had been fielded. But the ball could be thrown at the feet from any angle by anyone. It was a boisterous game with lots of shouting. Perdita joined in the spirit of it with great gusto, flinging the ball like a cannonball at Rivers's feet. There was also the occasional lapse of aim, which drew great peals of laughter from everyone, as the ball fizzed into the trees and Perdita looked rueful.

And then, with just as much spirit, Rivers swatted the ball away into the long grass by the lake, scaring the birds into flight. He looked about twelve years old as he smacked the ball so hard away that he occasionally overbalanced. Joe played a foxy game when it fell to him to bat and they both found it hard to get him out. He kept shifting his position ever so subtly, which made the angle of attack difficult. Perdita used her bat like a frying pan. Her coordination was so poor that, by general agreement, she was given a few lets. Otherwise she would have been in tears because she was out so often. Even Lady Pugh, wearing her apron, joined in for a few minutes as the meat did its thing, cooking away in the Aga. She squealed as the ball tracked close to her and then flew over her head, as they all tried to outmanoeuvre her by attacking her feet from the rear. Her bat flailed about in the air, missing the ball completely. She was mortified.

'You're out, Mother,' they both cried out at the same time in jubilation and she handed over the bat reluctantly, complaining the while about the ruthless cruelty of her children. Silhouettes on the sward, dancing and cavorting through time…

The high jinks continued during the meal. Eating was boisterous. The odd bread roll was thrown in fun. It was a carefree moment, just four people seated amid history at a table, eating together in an amused way. Rivers started to perk up as the chat whirled around him. His shame began to evaporate. Joe did very little talking. Perdita caused most of the noise as she bullied her brother mercilessly. The omniscient Lady Pugh looked on in approval, bustling to and fro with the courses. She insisted on serving the entire meal herself. The wine was good Chardonnay and then better Amarone, served from the Pugh cellars. They went on, so Joe was told, for hundreds of feet below ground. 'Ever so ancient,' said Perdita. He took her word for it.

No more death at least, thought Joe as he munched his coleslaw. Wonder how she clocked me, though. She really must be psychic. And unbidden across the years, the image of the Fat Man rose again to confront him in his mind's eye. Not a good moment, his manifestation.

The leave-taking was joyful. Perdita scoffed at him as he went. The blonde cascade waved about her shoulders as she shrugged goodbye.

'I don't know why you're bothering to go at all. It's such a waste. We could carry on playing games down here. You're very welcome and yet you insist on going. I don't understand it and I feel quite put out about it. Yes, rejected, that's how I feel. Just think, Rivers, we're being traded in for a stupid game of bridge in London. How's that for a bargain? This Joe friend of yours must be insane, don't you think?' And Rivers was briefly all smiles, as Perdita strutted off down the station platform in something resembling high dudgeon.

Joe waved from the train as all three of them sat in a knot on the platform, waving back and escorting the train from the station by their well-wishing presence. Perdita hissed at him as they said goodbye that if he didn't return soon she would kill him. 'Truly, I mean it. I'll kill you,' she said, sounding horrible. And Joe believed her.

Afterwards, as the countryside ambled past and Joe sat in the train taking him back to London, he reflected on the possibilities of the encounter with Rivers and his family. He felt very exhilarated and yet cool about it all. The exhilaration faded swiftly as the stations flicked by and his soul returned to earth after a brief fling in the heavens. His training swung into play. Yes, there was no doubt that he had some sort of invitation to return to Pugh Park; and yes, it was equally clear that all three members of the family found him attractive each in their own different way.

He pictured Perdita and the thought of her crude banter and sharp wit wrenched at his heart. How he had loved her tyranny over Rivers! How he yearned for her scorn and contempt and disparaging shrugs of the shoulder! But he had no place for her. His priority was survival. Just that and no more. He very deliberately tore his mind away from her. She was just too exquisite for words. He wanted more, much more, of her and he acknowledged that. He glimpsed her again, rocking nonchalantly on the car bonnet as they drew near to the house, a study in casual blonde grace. It was all so very tempting. He could do with some tender loving care – he could use masses of TLC. And she wouldn't suffer by his presence, he knew that. So he should return there again and again? Should he? But did it mean anything? And would it last?

The train clattered over bridges en route for London. Joe sat in the empty carriage absorbed by his thoughts. He brooded on the resonances of the whole trip. He'd seen this before. There's such a thing as outstaying one's welcome, he warned himself. Yes, the Pughs were in some sort of trouble and yes, they had welcomed his presence as a kind of Figaro. But only for the time being. He was guessing now, but that was how he thought about it all. This was a show they had put on that morning and afternoon, just a one-off performance for their own benefit as much as his. They'd pull through. He was sure of that. That was what pedigree amounted to. It formed a network of support through which it was well nigh impossible in this country to slip and slither. Witness the Rivers interview that morning. What had he said again? 'Sloane School looks after its own.' That was it. And it was bound to be true. Sloane School, the most famous public school in the country, even better known than Eton, was bound to fly to Rivers's rescue. It sounded as if a helpful friend from Sloane School was standing by already, poised and probably even scripted to do some discreet, tactical propping.

But this was in the natural order of things. Rivers was the genuine article, and entitled to expect such help, whereas he, Joe, was no more than a piece of flotsam afloat on the great tide of English affairs. He had no claim on that delta of aid; he had to continue living by his wits. He mustn't forget that. He was an arriviste, a carpetbagger who had clambered up the winding backstairs of British life and who had now had his inevitable comeuppance. That was the truth of the matter. Well, more or less the truth.

So be it, he thought as the stations flickered, by one after the other. As for his fortune – well, it might come out of store one of these fine days and then he could go and bargain for Perdita's hand, all well and good. But until then he was jammed up and into the simple identity of a bridge player and there the matter ended.

The rate of exchange which caused his soul to fly up towards the stars after he met Perdita did not seem viable to him. As things stood, he didn't have enough to offer to justify the Pughs, still less Perdita, taking such an interest in him. He had helped out in a sticky moment and that had warranted an afternoon of great jollity in the countryside. But there it must end. No phone calls, no further communication, nothing.

His heart sank at the thought and he tasted the ashes of life in his mouth. More stations. But that was the sad obligatory reality of it all. Further intercourse wouldn't work, or at least it wouldn't work in the longer run, when Rivers was back on his feet and Joe was still thrashing about in the gutter. That was the time to think about, rather than the here and now. Joe might have been something big in the past, but he was very much something small now and that was how it looked set to remain.

And when Rivers was back and he was still down, that was when suddenly he would become a presence *chez* Pugh de trop by far. That was what he had to watch out for. He would have become dependent on their goodwill at just the moment when he had turned into someone whose calling card was distinctly tatty. Joe knew that he was a failure, a total write-off. That was indisputable. He knew also the appeal of Pugh Park and he knew too that he should resist it. So he ought not to be tempted by the embrace of the Pughs, however much he yearned to be taken to task at the dinner table by Perdita's sharp wit. He told himself he was a humble bridge player, and that's all he was, a trader trying to make his slams and his daily crust and that was how it ought to remain. Better to cut loose now than risk one of those ever so subtle rejections later on when he had become tiresome and predictable. Better to flee.

And yet... and yet... Was there no more to it than that? Joe knew there was and he knew that he would find his way into the centre of the argument by degrees. He hated the process of investigation but he felt little sharp thrills of excitement running through himself at the same time. His heart belied his head. This was living again, if only after a fashion.

*Perdita bene trovata*, he thought, if such a pun were possible.

A man climbed into the carriage at Woking and Joe eyed him stealthily from the other end of the carriage, attentive but unseeing. Then attention switched and he gazed at the sky. Joe thought about the two clocks and he thought about Joachim and the set-up dinner at Zorba's and he knew that there was more to it than he was granting the situation. He knew that he was lying like everyone else in this special part of the cosmos. But then there came a problem, one of logical fallacy. It took time to identify the problem which was real enough and he unravelled the bits and pieces meticulously. He was not afraid, just curious in a detached kind of way to see how he would react to the concept of an alternative reality stealing up alongside him.

He was surviving from day to day, largely because all his hopes and expectations had collapsed into the present. He had no hopes. He had nothing. All had been destroyed in his crash. To the extent that he could survive, indeed relish, the ambiguities of the passing moment, he could utilise all the ring craft he had learned in the espionage game. Spying equalled ambiguity equalled survival – that was the mantra. It had got him through so far; he could continue to survive. The mantra would not let him down. It was a passive state. He was like a log in the stream.

But Perdita represented expectations, big expectations. Movement and change. If he wanted to see her again, and he did, then he not only had to start building expectations into his life but he had to shift from the passive to the active. And that meant big alterations and big risk, because movement from his inert state was ultimately life-threatening. Joe did not exaggerate to himself. He knew by just how tenuous a thread his day-to-day existence hung. Sometimes even opening a door posed huge problems for him. Depression and despair stalked him at every moment. He knew that he could make a switch. That was the important point.

But it was dangerous. He knew that as well. To switch

emphasis and go for a state of activity, or something approaching the motors of normality, would pitch him into the abyss if it failed. He would have no defence against the deflation of his hopes if it all failed. But there was a way, which he knew very well, and of course, if he wanted to see Perdita again, he had to go down that route. Which he now thought, sitting alone on the train rattling back to London, that he would do, even if it meant taking a huge amount of risk on board. Therefore he had no choice... No choice at all... But even so he would be very, very careful. Even more careful than that, if possible. Being alone in the universe and then meeting a pretty girl and wanting to fall in love with her was no joke. Not humorous at all. He still didn't want to finish up floating down the Thames, dead from chagrin and despair. The desire to live was very strong in Joe.

Annie picked up the phone. It was early on Monday morning. Bootface was hovering around her, looking peaky. In fact, he looked ill. And he was angry. He had already made it clear that he had disapproved of Annie's reaction to his phone call on Sunday.

'Joachim here, Annie. I've had a call from Joe. He wants to meet for dinner. No urgency, but he is quite specific about making a date.'

'Wait one, Joachim.'

It was a simple enough message. But she was speechless. It was marvellous news – and right on cue. She hugged the phone to her and experienced the pure joy, in a flash, of an accurate prediction. She had read her man right. He was on line and in line. The scheme was working. Suddenly it all felt so good. Then she trusted herself to speak again.

'What are you going to give him?'

'I thought Callaghan, followed by some North Sea oil.'

'Callaghan, yes, but the North Sea is too quick and too up to date. You're rushing it. Macmillan is quite a hard pill to swallow. You need some more perspective. What else have you got?'

'Anglo-American loan? Yes, that would do, because I left him with some rhetorical questions at the end last time about the war. Yes, you're right. The North Sea strikes the wrong note.'

'Perfect. It sounds fine. And don't forget to work the Dexter

White angle in. That's absolutely crucial.'

'Will do, Annie. No probs. We'll meet around eight, when we do. Plenty of time for discussion.'

'Zorba's?'

'That's the place.'

'Good luck. That's very good news. We'll be in touch as soon as you call him to fix the date, yes?'

'Will do. Meanwhile, I'd better start boning up on the script. Bye for now.'

Annie turned to Bootface. She was smiling. She felt over the moon. It had all worked and the prodigal was back in the fold. Bingo!

'That was Joachim. He had a call from Joe. Joe wants to meet him. We're on our way, brother. Joe's back. And better still, he's come in of his own accord. Isn't that marvellous! He's not a pressed man. He's there of his own free will. He's on board again. It's worked, the softly softly approach. On this one at least the textbooks were right. Our man is in the frame.'

It was truly a sweet moment. But not for Bootface. Bootface just smiled his obligatory look of congratulations, but without any joy at all in his expression. Indeed Bootface seemed disappointed by the news. No, not disappointed, but lukewarm about it all. Half-hearted in his reactions. Tired about the whole thing...

Now what could the man be on about if this tremendous triumph for the mission meant nothing to him? Annie was baffled. Maybe there really was something tremendously wrong with his private life.

# Chapter Six

Joe made another call after he had spoken to Joachim. He returned Sybil's call on the answerphone and spoke to a quasi-hysterical woman for about twenty minutes. Sybil was in a state of considerable vexation and rage. She had taken her dismissal from the Liz Playfair Bridge Academy badly. In short, she was livid.

'What does it all mean, Joe? Why have I been shoved out? Do I smell? Is it something to do with that? What's wrong with me?'

'Sybil, I know nothing about the Liz Playfair set-up. I just go and play there. I'm the hired hand. So you can't ask me that, because I don't know the answer. And I certainly don't know the politics.'

'Yes, but you must have heard something?'

'I heard nothing. She may just have had no vacancies. It could be as simple as that.'

'I wasn't born yesterday, Joe. And you must know something. Why did you stay behind afterwards?'

'I was checking a hand with her that I misplayed.'

'Yes, but you're as thick as thieves with Liz and all that gang.'

'Don't believe in appearances, Sybil. We're not that close.' Best to temporise, thought Joe. Anyway, what he had said was partly true.

But Sybil was not shaken off so easily. 'It can't be that money is a problem. I have enough money to buy and sell that tinpot little shit-heap ten times over. Without thinking about it, or missing it for a moment, I can tell you. The money is always there. And who does Liz Playfair think she is, anyway. Little fucking tinpot goddess with her smart hairdos and her posh friends. I could tell you a few things about her, that I could. I've made some investigations about her. And I can tell you she's no more than a common trollop. Just a tart. At least that's what she was before she got married. She didn't have a bean and she was living down in Brixton of all places before she moved. And we all know what that means.'

Sybil had lately bought a very large house in SW3. Most people had heard about this event. The house-warming had been full of the most unlikely people, so Joe had heard. But it was a very large house nevertheless.

'And her marriage isn't what it's cracked up to be either. I've heard that too. They say her husband isn't at all happy with the way things are going. Not at all happy. But that's by the by. In the meantime I want to know why my money isn't good enough for that little poncy set of fucking bitches.'

Joe had often wondered how women discussed each other when far from the restraining influence of men. Now he knew. It was just as he had thought, only worse. Robust, and then some.

'Sybil, this is London. It's a funny place. It looks open on the surface but it isn't. It's full of snakes and whirlpools. Anyone can put their foot in anywhere and see it chewed off. It's full of traps for the unwary. You have to go carefully. You'll go to Liz Playfair's again, I'm certain of that. It's just a matter of waiting until there's a slot.'

'Fuck her slots. I wouldn't be seen dead in there again, not if you paid me. And fuck her. They can't play bridge anyway. They're all fools. I hate them.'

Brave words, Sybil, thought Joe, but complete lies. One telephone call to say there'd been a cancellation and you'd be dancing a tango across the desks, such is the power of social pull in London. Arrival – that's all that counts in this town, I'm sure of it.

'I'm going to screw that bitch if it's the last thing I do. I'll get even with her. And she'll regret the day she was born. I'm used to dealing with enemies.'

Sybil ranted on, this time employing the vocabulary of her husband. Some of the new words she was using seemed a touch unfamiliar. She couldn't quite spit them out with the easy venom she used for the more familiar, shorter words. She was reaching now into the love dictionary. It is curious, thought Joe, how frequently you get a fix on a relationship by casting the other partner out of mode and paying attention to the syntax. Just listening to Sybil curse and swear enabled him to gauge more or less exactly how Sybil's husband conducted his business affairs. Nastily, he guessed distractedly. His mind was elsewhere. He was thinking about Perdita and wondering where she was at that precise moment. Wearing clothes? Perish the thought. In the bath? Waking up? Drying her hair? His mind danced at the images. And was she thinking about him? He doubted it.

Sybil continued her abuse down the line. Joe interrupted her. 'Tell you what, Sybil, I've had an idea.'

She choked for a moment at his temerity. But Joe had to take his mind off Perdita. He'd go crazy thinking about her like this. The telephone was an instrument too full of temptation for him to resist. At that moment, he actually had it in his hand. He should have buried it deep in the dustbin or somewhere, well out of harm's way.

'That new bridge club, you know, Savage's, opened yesterday. Why don't we go and play there today? That could be fun. You never know, some of the Playfair crowd might be there and we could start easing you in that way.'

It was persiflage and Joe knew it. The idea of easing Sybil in anywhere was just too far-fetched for words. Sybil marched at the head of her troops. Diplomacy was something reserved for the infirm and the crippled. But she was too taken aback by Joe's idea to offer an alternative. She stuttered a bit and then accepted his offer.

The duplicate started at two in the afternoon. Joe knew about Tony Savage by repute. A brilliant young bridge player, Savage had stumbled across the bright idea of starting a fashionable bridge club in the Chelsea area, where the emphasis would be on ambience and atmosphere, and where players could enjoy their bridge. This was in contrast to the usual daggers drawn atmosphere which reigned in most bridge clubs, when civil war took place across the tables. It was a good moment to take Sybil. The club had barely started properly and she could get her foot in the door immediately and build up her own following, if that was how she wanted to develop her bridge in London. Joe had extended the invitation not wholly out of self-interest.

The two of them met outside the door to Savage's just before two. The new club was situated over a grocer's store in the

Fulham Road. Judging by the squads of women eagerly clambering up the stairs, the location was no deterrent. The club would be an instant hit. Savage had found a gap in the market. Within a month or so, Joe guessed the women would be leaving their shopping orders downstairs at the start of the bridge, to be collected on the way out.

Sybil was still heaving with rage. She stamped about on the pavement. Joe asked her what conventions she wanted to play.

'Anything you like. I play them all,' she snapped.

Looks like a weak no trump, Stayman, and an optional double over their threes, thought Joe. You can't get more basic than that. They ascended the stairs.

The room burst to his line of vision like a bomb. It was all a shock. There were women everywhere. Reds and greens and bronzes and lilacs; the room was a blaze of colour as well. It was like a scene from a Hollywood epic. And moving colour too. The women were restless; they were all over the place. They were impatient for the bridge to start. Not a man to be seen anywhere. There were women standing smoking, or just talking; some were arranging chairs, while others were chatting to their partners. A few already playing with the cards, seated at tables, while some were walking up and down the short stairs in the room or just staring out of the window. All the time they behaved with a studied disregard for anything like the male presence. It was a revelation for Joe. It was like a bathhouse, he thought, except that they were all fully clothed. No pandemonium, but complete order. Each in her own defined space, the women went about with detached but furious dedication, getting everything ready for the afternoon's duplicate. Joe had never seen so many women gathered together in a single room without men around. Their self-confidence was unmistakable. It was like another planet.

He felt just ever so slightly disarmed. Berlin had never been like this. And that had been bad. Sternly, he told himself to be a man and pull himself together. They could only eat him.

He found a table for Sybil who slammed her handbag down on the seat and glared at the opposition, two talkative American women who were worrying away about that night's dinner party. They answered her back brightly and then ignored her frown, as

Americans do when abroad. The play started.

Sybil was dreadful. It was the first time Joe had ever played with her as partner. He rapidly discovered that she had absorbed all the worst bridge habits going: she ticked her partner off for assumed mistakes; she questioned the opposition; she raised her eyebrows at the bidding; and then, in the middle of playing a hand, she pulled out a paper bag and started eating a cake. The Americans glanced at each other and then flicked an interrogative look at Joe. Joe ignored their gaze. He concentrated on the play.

Then of course it had to happen – Sybil revoked. All this at the first table. She revoked on the third board. The director was called. Sybil protested the ruling, the director grew testy, and Sybil was finally docked four tricks, still claiming that she was innocent and that she hadn't meant to play a diamond, instead of the obligatory spade. She huffed and she puffed and she perspired freely. It was gross to observe. Her face was like a puddle.

A poor start, Joe felt, and it could only get worse. It would be like competing in the Grand National on a horse without a saddle. He feared a very tough afternoon indeed.

Mercifully, the round came to an end. All the travellers had been marked up and the move was called. Like an expedition on the march Joe and Sybil moved to the next table. Clunk, clunk, ill-tempered clunk. Another shock, this time seismic.

'Well then, Joe, long time, no see. What a surprise. So why have you been hiding from me?'

Joe blinked. He had not been prepared for this. It was always traumatic to come upon someone unexpectedly whom you hadn't seen for some years; worse, to meet them in tricky surroundings, when you had been refusing to acknowledge their telephone calls; and truly the veritable pits to meet said person in the company of a social barbarian like Sybil. Hardly staking out the high ground in the discussion.

Emma Bales smiled sweetly at Joe as Sybil shot a look of thunderous rage at the interloper. 'Who is this women?' she queried, as if Emma had just returned from transportation.

Joe grinned at Emma. It was good to see her again. 'Oh, a very old friend. Nothing more or less. I've been avoiding her. But I can't think why. Emma, you look marvellous. Why haven't you been in touch with me all these months? You're a disgrace.'

A snort from Sybil and an injunction to play some bridge. But a radiant smile from Emma in recognition of Joe's astuteness. They picked up the cards.

'You've lost none of your quick wit, have you, Joe? How long is it now?'

'Would you mind not talking to my partner. I'm trying to concentrate on my cards, if you don't mind.'

Joe ignored her. 'It's a fair cop, Emma. I'll give you that at least.'

Sybil's eyeballs began to bulge as Joe added another very cheeky comment. 'Our co-op divvy number was 12,792. I thought I'd just mention that. I know you wanted to know.'

Joe made the comment as he sorted his cards, as if in response to a long-posed question from Emma. But it had been directed at Sybil. It scored a bullseye. At the reference to divvy numbers, she started like a guilty thing, glared again at Joe and went back to try to evaluate her hand. Early training will out, thought Joe as they began to play. Her life began on one side of the grocery counter or the other. And with malice aforethought.

It was not the same Emma Bales. That was evident from the first glance. The merriment was still there and the eyes still sparkled. Three years of absence had not impaired the intelligence. But her face was rounder and her appearance had changed. Emma in the past, in her legal days, had been trim but unkempt beneath. There was always a rowdy schoolgirl trying to wrestle her way out from underneath the chaste lawyer's outfits. Her clothes had been simultaneously a size too large and a size too small. She competed with her clothes as she did with the briefs. And the hair had been a study in disorder. Everything had been put together in a hurry.

But not now. There was something svelte and chic and well cared for about her appearance, something almost pampered. The expensive materials clung lovingly to her body, folding themselves obediently around her curves; the hair was simply cut, and lay in full-shaped contours on her head, a feat which no coiffeur would have attempted below one hundred and fifty pounds a session; and the rings on her finger were such as to induce any number of housekeeping wobbles. Such affluence breathes its own message. Emma had made it.

Joe felt ill for a second. When they had first met, Joe had been making around one million pounds a year and Emma had been struggling to buy her house in the off-fashionable part of Chelsea. No more. Now Emma looked as if she could afford the whole of Belgravia for starters. While he, Joe, was struggling to pay his mortgage, month by month. Again Joe felt the disgrace of his position and his poverty. It didn't matter what the reason might be for his lack of resources. That was immaterial. He was nearly penniless; she was clearly very rich now. The progress of their fortunes had been radically different. It galled him. Yet again, he thought, the Gents have a great deal to answer for over this.

She played the cards passably well too. Her bidding was well up to standard. True, she failed to spot a diamond switch, which would have given her a top on the traveller, but she sailed along quite well with the table. She knew the bids backwards, that was clear. Sybil, of course, was looking for slams in the sky, all part of her grand scheme, mentioned in confidence over the phone, to get on the Riviera bridge circuit soonest.

But the slams at Savage's were tough. It was a tough obstacle course. Sybil tried for a slam, got the club break wrong, and went one off. So a bottom for Joe and Sybil. The table, led by Emma who had spotted her madness early, murmured, 'Hard luck. Oh, bad luck!' which in truth showed reasonable sympathy, since she had made a brave bid.

Sybil huffed and puffed as the slam went down, and her eyeballs stood out on stalks. That was when the sawdust, Joe swore later, began to dribble slowly from her left ear. But she was too mortified to interfere any more in the enchanting dialogue which Joe saw opening up between himself and Emma – Orpheus and Eurydice, Part II.

'Joe, we'll talk later. At the end of the play today. And don't you dare try doing a runner on me. I will give you such a hard time if you try and give me the slip. But before you go and the move is called, did you see this? I have to ask you. You're the only connection I have left with him. Isn't it good news?'

She fished in her bag and drew out a slip of newspaper which

Joe eventually recognised as *The Sunday Times*. She smoothed out the page and pointed to the final columns.

'You see, he's made it.'

'What do you mean? Who's made it?'

'Look at the poem, you dunderhead, and look at who it's by. God, Joe, you're so slow these days. You'd think you lived in Norfolk.'

Joe looked. He recognised that poem. He'd been quite impressed by it at the time. He'd read it on the train down to Pugh Park. Now he started reading it again across the bridge table, none the wiser. Then the penny dropped. It was a slow penny at first, but then it fell faster and faster.

He saw what he was meant to see. He recalled a brave man, taken unawares by time and circumstances and a malign influence, walking slowly and sadly away from Emma and Joe some years ago, out of the kitchen and into the cold of the streets. He had departed alone. Gregory, of course. Not Greg Priest, whoever he might be, the author of the poem, but Gregory, Emma's Gregory, that Gregory, who had also, in a fresh reality, written the poem.

Recognition dawned. It was that Gregory, of course, the one who was thin, pedagogical and resolute in his own way. It was Gregory, the Greek teacher by day and the poet by night, the man who had shared Emma's life for many years before his disastrous encounter with Emma's brother, who had bought Emma's first house with her. That was the man who had written the poem.

Joe nodded at Emma. 'Yes, I see.'

Emma was full of impatience. 'Yes, but you don't see half as much as I do. The fact that he's been published in *The Sunday Times* means that he's made it. He's got where he wanted to be.'

'I think you're right.'

'Not only that. I want to know who he's dedicated the poem to. If it's another women – and it must be – then I want to know more about it.'

A mistake, this chasing after the past, thought Joe. It will end in tears. Of that, I'm certain. He changed the subject. 'And you, Emma? Not quite the original Emma, I think.'

She glanced at the rings and the bracelets. 'Oh, those. Huh!'

Joe saw that the old demons were starting to drive her as

before. She and Gregory had been lovers for years until Emma had attained some degree of success. That among other things had contributed to the break-up, which had been tragic. Was reconciliation in the air? Perhaps. Emma was clearly hinting that some sense of discontinuity existed in her life, some unfinished business. Another search might definitely be in the offing. He for Marcello and she for Gregory. And what larks!

The move was called and Joe and Sybil stood up to shift to the next table.

'I'll see you at the end, Joe. Don't you dare try and escape me. I warn you.'

'I wouldn't dare, Emma. You're far too awesome now for me even to think about it.'

'Who on earth was that extraordinarily overdressed women?' asked Sybil, who normally wore enough clothes for a trip to the Arctic.

'Just someone I used to know a long time ago. I thought she was full of embonpoint, rather than overdressed, if you see what I mean.'

'Don't you start talking Latin to me.'

'I'm sorry, Sybil. It just slipped out.'

'That kind of thing offends people and upsets them. Anyway, who is she?'

'Just an old friend, as I told you.'

'I can see that. Well, I hope she doesn't want to play bridge with you as well.'

That was Joe's first introduction to the unlikely passions which smouldered among the bridge-playing crowd of Chelsea. It wouldn't be his last exposure to it.

He and Sybil limped round the rest of the tables in some disarray. By the close, Sybil was not returning her partner's suit and she was ruffing Joe's winners; Riviera bridge seemed quite a bit further off. But not to Sybil. At the close, she rebuked Joe for his poor play and promised to give him some tips when they next managed to play again together. Joe hoped she'd give him the tips in Latin – but he said that to himself.

They waited for the results, and Joe could see Emma standing some way off. She was within contactable distance, which pleased

Joe. He wanted to hear the whole story. Her presence reassured him. He was not looking forward to his cold solo supper that evening. None of the Playfair crowd had been there that afternoon, which made him feel quite isolated.

Out came the results. They stood in groups and clapped the winners dutifully. It had been a disaster for Joe and Sybil. They were placed nowhere. She was angry. Without a word of thanks, she turned on her heel and departed, a snarl on her lips. And in soft bosoms dwell such mighty rages, thought Joe, lifting from Alexander Pope. Emma bore down on him.

'Retired, Joe? Is that what brings you here?' She came straight to the point.

'Not quite, Emma. Forcibly put out to grass is a better way of expressing it.'

Her face fell. 'Not quite the success I had envisaged for you.'

'There was a modification to the pro forma progression, I have to admit.'

'I did wonder what had happened to you. That was a marvellous night we spent together. But you never wrote, you know, or called. You just disappeared and left me to my fate in Norwich. Dear old Norwich. I was very disappointed. And now I find you have regressed.'

'Regressed badly. That's the problem with least squares analysis.'

'Poor you. You do look a bit haggard, I must say. So you're badly broke now, but still as witty as ever?'

'Pretty much broke, I guess, and the jokes are wearing thin.' Joe was careful not to be too specific.

'Whatever happened to all that money you were making? Unimaginable to lose all that. And you being so smart. Extraordinary. Well, I won't labour the point. It must be very painful for you even to have to think about it, especially if you're playing with partners like that dreadful woman today. And I suppose that's why you refused to return my phone calls?'

'Quite so. The shame of it, my dear, is just too, too blush-making. Really embarrassing. But Emma, shall we talk? You must have quite a story to tell.'

'That's a good idea. Why don't we pop across the road and

have a drink. I've got an hour to spare until my next appointment. It would be a pleasure. Since you're so broke, the Milky Bars are on me, so don't even think about putting hand to pocket. I know about these things. I've been poor myself. It's ghastly. Life is just so drab.'

They settled down together in Disraeli's in front of a bottle of red that normally Joe couldn't afford. The good wine, fat and full-bodied, sloshed down his throat, hit the brain and he felt better. Things were looking up for Joe if only for an hour. They talked together with quiet confident intimacy, as if the gap in their relationship had been three minutes, not three years.

'And the Reform Club? Are you still a member there?'

'Just about, although I never dare go there. Too risky for morale. I can't afford the drinks, let alone the contact with the members.'

'Yes, I can see how that could be. And we had such a good time together there. While I was in Norfolk I thought about it quite a lot. It was almost the high point of my life in London. And now, well, let's not talk about it, Joe. Poverty is just too awful to discuss. Nothing ever happens when you're poor, or, if it does, it's usually catastrophic.'

They clinked glasses in a sign of friendship restored. Joe asked her about Norfolk. She laughed the full throaty laugh of a women in full possession of her independence.

'The inevitable happened. I started practising in Norfolk if you remember, well set up on the proceeds of the house which you very neatly sold for me. You do remember that, don't you, Joe? Spongo, yes.'

Joe nodded. She continued.

'I was involved in lots of litigation. I started to meet the local gentry and, before I knew it, I was married to a nice large man with a red face, who brought with him another mother, who then died, and a very large farm. So a big change in lifestyle for our Emma.'

'And?' Joe liked the sound of the assets. Wealth like that always cheers.

'Bliss for two years, up until three months ago. I was enjoying a very pleasant life indeed. I wasn't called upon to do a great deal either, apart from opening fêtes. Geoffrey was a pillar of the community, almost a nave all on his own. And then one day, Geoffrey, who was a very stubborn determined man, went into his garden, his enormous garden, and fell out with one of the inhabitants of the soil, one of the tiniest and most insignificant members. A root. He wanted to pull it out and the root refused to be pulled. He started wrestling with it as I left to see a neighbour and I'm afraid the root won. Geoffrey collapsed with a cardiac arrest and died on the spot, or rather in the hall, where I found him twenty minutes later. It all happened in a flash. So, no Geoffrey... And no marriage, and really no farm.'

'No farm?' Joe was alarmed at the thought of the assets disappearing.

'I've more or less sold the farm. It's on the market, and I've got a buyer. As soon as the sale goes through, I will leave Norfolk and take my ill-gotten gains with me. It's a beautiful county and I was very keen on Geoffrey. Now that he's gone, I don't want to stay in the county. I thought I'd be there for ever. Now I find it's not to be. So I'm departing. I'm returning to London, not in quite the same way that I left it, but I'm back and once again Emma Bales will joust with the capital. Not quite the same tournament, though. As you might gather from my appearance, Geoff didn't exactly leave me penniless. Quite the opposite. I won't discuss the precise settlement with you, Joe, but it did run into a considerable number of noughts. So here I am.'

'Emma redux?'

'And occasionally the bountiful if you play your cards right. I think I must owe you something for that house sale you rail-roaded through. It was so slick. Assume that the odd cheque in need can fly your way, Joe. It will be a pleasure. No need to ask – it'll be there.'

'But where does Gregory fit into all this?'

Joe scored a hit. All the carefully constructed fiction of Emma the bold and brave disintegrated as soon as Joe mentioned his name. But Emma was courageous. 'I miss him,' she said simply.

'You were together a long time.'

As they spoke, Joe was thinking. He was full of thoughts. Poverty had sharpened his wits to a degree that affluence might have dulled Emma's. He was alert to the off chance. He was picking things up about Emma from the conversation that were surprising. She was just a shade different, just a fraction slower and more vulnerable than she had been before. Or perhaps Joe had speeded up. He had formed no hard and fast view. He continued to listen. He soothed her by his attention. But the chat did not have that challenging edge to it of before. It dwelt too much on the past. Joe stared at her very hard to conceal his wandering attention. He could guess what was coming. Back to Gregory...

'Yes, a very long time. We fought our way up from poverty together. And all the time that I was married to Geoffrey, I found myself thinking about Gregory. I still feel pledged to him, even though it all finished a long time ago. You know how it is in these long-term relationships. You grow together even when you're most apart.'

Joe could guess now why the offer of the money had been made so speedily. It was really money she was offering to Gregory, but through a proxy. She obviously felt as guilty as hell after throwing him out in a rage as she had done. And so the whirligig of time brings in its revenges... This was not good. Joe thought the whole conversation indicated a capacity for disaster that chilled him. Don't go backwards Emma, he found himself thinking as she ploughed on through the muddied fields of her reflections, throwing off in a cloud of fine chat the heavy thoughts of Norfolk years.

'And the poem?'

'Oh, you liked it? I did too. I'm so pleased. Seeing that poem was the clincher. I just have to see him now. I have no choice. When I read it, I was sitting in my garden, enjoying a cup of tea, and I noticed the poem and started reading it, thinking, as one does, I wonder if I recognise this... The page was folded across, so that I didn't see the name at the bottom. As I read it, though, I thought I recognise this tone, I know this sound, because Gregory always had a very distinct timbre to his style and to me it was unmistakable. So I took a peek at the author and there his name was. I was overjoyed for him.'

This was all like the enthusiasm of the Emma he had known in the past but it was still subtly different. Joe thought the money had changed her but in a most unobtrusive way. She had not adjusted to the change in status which money conferred. She liked the money – that was obvious. But she was too active and too eager to get things done. She was making a mistake about her money. In the US money was a dynamic thing which created freedom, but in the UK it was the opposite. In the UK it was a static factor, generating not freedom but obligation, and in exchange for that constraint it created patronage. So Emma wanted to go charging about, looking for Gregory instead of allowing him to come softly on bended knee into her presence. Along with another crowd of hangers-on.

Joe filed all these thoughts away for future use. He liked Emma very much but he suspected that prolonged exposure to Norfolk life and ways might have turned her into a fool, at least so far as London was concerned. He couldn't be sure but he suspected that he was right. He wouldn't bet on her timing in London or her chances of success.

She continued to talk about Gregory, as indeed she had every right to do. She had made some enquiries of the newspaper which had advised her to write to Gregory, care of the paper, but she had no wish to do that. She wanted to come across him unawares, and take him by surprise. It was clear that she was afraid that Gregory would turn tail and flee at the sight of her. She was afraid that he would reject her. And she wouldn't blame him if he did.

Remorse was working away there inside her and all the dollars in the world couldn't put that one right. It was she after all who had put him on the street. And it wasn't a very great sin that he had committed. You can't just buy peace of mind, reflected Joe as he realised how completely he had forgotten Pascal, his ex-girlfriend, over the years. No, he wouldn't be going in search of her. Even an open prison, such as he now experienced, changed a man.

Emma was also smitten by jealousy. She was quite explicit about this after the third glass. It all came spilling out. She was finding she had lots to say to Joe now that she had decided to unbosom herself. Joe listened patiently, fearing the worst. His thoughts grew blacker as she spoke. Joe reflected from the vantage point of his despair, a handy spot in such moments for clairvoyance.

'If I found that he really was shacked up with someone else, I don't think I could stand it.'

'But Emma, it's been a few years since you saw him. People change out of all recognition in that time in London. This sounds like madness. You may be fooling yourself. You may be terribly disappointed. You could get badly hurt. Be careful. This is good advice I'm giving you. Are you sure it's such a good idea to revisit the past in this way? You've got the dollars now. You can do anything you want. Just leave well alone. Let the past bury itself.'

'Unfinished business, Joe. Don't interfere.'

That's all she would say. Joe could see that her mind was resolved. Far be it for him to interfere. He had lived among these women for too long now to believe that a mere male could hope to change their minds once the fundamental – and wrong – decision had been taken.

'Fine, I'll say no more. So how are you going to find him?'

'Joe, I rather hoped... Well, the thought did occur to me as we were playing bridge. You don't seem to have too much on your plate at this moment in time. We could possibly search together. It would be fun. And I'd pay your expenses, of course.'

She hadn't needed to say that at the end. It smacked too much of Sybil and her vile concupiscence. But Joe forgave her. After a few drinks she was a sad sight. She was miserable and she was lonely and she seemed ever so slightly to be coming apart at the seams. The clothes were riding up and the hair was coming adrift. Collapse, in a flash, of morale. Joe knew the symptoms.

Yes, he would help her to find Gregory; they were both going the same way anyway. If she felt inclined in the meantime to cough up some spondulicks in the process, well, that would be a boon. But it wasn't essential. Joe was so absolutely poor now that the odd pound here or there meant nothing to him. It could hardly raise him from the depths.

He began to tell her about Marcello, to show that to some extent they had problems in common which they might share. She was amused by the story about the gay pub. She seemed relieved that she had found somebody with whom she could share something. She began to resurface. Her eyes grew merrier. The clothes sat easier on her.

'So you're in this little game as well? We could set up an academy for missing persons. But no luck so far?'

'Not so far, but it's a funny thing, Emma, this searching for someone. There are days when I think he's just around the corner and then others when he's clearly far, far away. I know it in my bones. You get a feel for these things. It's a primitive thing. I can almost scent him sometimes even though I've never met him. And recently I've had a feeling that I'm getting closer. I'm moving in on him. I'll find him. So we can find Gregory too.'

'What will you do when you find Marcello?'

'Go missing myself in a way that no one could ever find me. I know how it's done. I'm beginning to think it's about time I faded away.'

'I'm sure you do. You have that look to you. But you shouldn't, you know, not when we've found each other again.' Emma was clearly very, very disoriented.

Joe remembered what he had wanted to ask her. 'Your mother? What happened to her?'

Emma was offhand, but it cost her considerably to appear so blithe. 'Oh, she met someone at the same time that I met Geoffrey. So she got married as well. But the difference between us is that she died, while her husband lived. So how's that for coincidence.'

'I'm so sorry. Please forgive the question.'

'Nonsense, you had to ask. We have fallen out of communication. You have to catch up with things. There is a backlog. You have to know. It would have cropped up.'

Emma had cared deeply for her mother, putting her welfare to a large extent above her own when Emma had been poor. Now that she was rich her mother was dead. So to what end had she tended her mother, now that she found herself, to all practical effect, alone in the world? A very good question. Emma shook her head at the implicit note of interrogation. She was still very tough-minded about all that, Joe concluded.

'So when shall we start looking for Gregory, Joe?'

'Shortly. But in the mornings.'

'Why the mornings?'

'I gamble in the afternoons. Sometimes I play social bridge in the mornings, but not very often.'

'Where?'

'At Liz Playfair's. I mean, I play at Liz Playfair's but only as a hired hand and I gamble at the Jack of Hearts. It's a vile den.'

'Joe, you mean you have wheedled your way into Liz Playfair's establishment? You may be broke, but you're very select. It's the most exclusive bridge club in the area. Everyone I know wants to play there. She only takes the people she likes, I gather.'

'Really, I'd never have guessed.'

'Anyway, enough of that. What about Gregory? Tomorrow? Shall we meet tomorrow? We might as well make a start.'

'Not tomorrow. Too soon. But let's do it soon. It sounds like fun. I'll ring you.'

'I've heard that before. The last time you said that I didn't hear from you for three years. So when will you ring?'

They squabbled away together contentedly. She knew for certain that Joe would ring. He knew that once brought to the block, as he had been, that he would behave as he should. So he knew he would ring too. They chatted about how well Emma had learned to play bridge. She asked Joe where he had learned bridge.

'In prison.'

It was only partially untrue. Emma knew nothing about his alternative existence, the Fat Man or his early life as a spy with the Fat Man in Berlin. Not ever for consumption that particular box of tricks, Joe reasoned.

A shadow fell across them. It was Sybil. Not so much a chastened Sybil as a more thoughtful Liverpudlian. She twisted her face into a smile. It did not come easily to her.

'Joe, I wanted to thank you for playing today with me. I'm sorry I lost my temper. I shouldn't have done. Can we play again?'

'Of course, Sybil. Give me a call and we'll fix a date.'

'Thank you. I appreciate that. And Emma, it was Emma, wasn't it? Perhaps we could play together as well.'

Emma, surprised but willing, assented. Telephone numbers were exchanged. Covenants of friendship were pledged. Even kisses, on Sybil's departure.

Sybil turned away. Joe would have been impressed by her show of friendship had it not been for the sly look of malice in her eye. She's acting out of calculation, Joe thought, and I'm sure of that. There's not an ounce of goodness in the woman. She only says thank you if she wants something. Something very badly. Something so badly that she's prepared to kiss and make up with Emma – amazing. It must be a very bad thing that she wants. And he stored that thought too in his mind.

Then he bade Emma a swift goodnight, after she insisted on paying the bill. They arranged to meet at a day of Joe's specification at ten in the morning in the coffee shop at Peter Jones, to concert tactics. All very civilised.

## Chapter Seven

Thursday morning. Joe sat in his flat at the wrong end of the King's Road wondering, among other things, how he was going to make enough money out of the markets to pay his bills that month. He knew his finances down to the last farthing. Which was just about where they were. But no time for jokes. Time was marching on. He needed to trade. He had to find a good idea in the markets and make some money before the end of the month.

The phone rang.

'Joe?'

'*Oui, c'est moi à l'appareil.*'

'Joe, it's Liz, if it is Joe that's spouting all that rubbish. Can I call you back in five minutes? I have a drama. Hold yourself ready, young man.'

'What a thing to say to a young man. Sure you can call back. I'll be here.'

It was a bright sunny day. Some clouds in a blue, windy sky. A day for optimism. He felt good about things. He felt clear-sighted about the markets. Not lucky, but balanced and cool. Not that hot-headed feel which just obliged you to buy big when the animal spirits were in full rampage.

He scanned the newspapers, thinking about Thailand and wondering if it was time to go back in. He liked the way the forwards were closing in on the spot rate and he liked the way that the Bank of Thailand kept making such good news comments about the banking system. Pretty soon they'd be telling the world how all those bad loans had just floated away. Time to buy, time to buy?

But would his canny Jewish Scottish broker allow him to trade stock so far away? Hard to say; it would take some selling. Thailand was a good idea so far, at least on paper. It could be highly profitable. He could but try his man. Meanwhile he had to transform the glimmerings of an idea into a solid investment proposition. Joe was nothing if not sceptical about his flights of fancy. And methodical. Time for some scribbling.

He reached for a pencil and paper and started working out some figures. He was fiddling with the exchange rates, projecting a spot rate forward in time a few months and then linking it in with a possible move in the stock market via the assumed rate differentials. Taxing work. Joe reckoned the arbs were moving back in on Thailand and he knew those hungry boys – he'd been one himself once. Even now they'd be working out their carry costs. Doing the same sums that he was. Feeling greedy. Licking their chops. Wolf pack time. Hunting time.

His cup of tea cooled at his side, ignored. He scribbled on. The numbers looked okay. He started feeling optimistic. He decided to make a call to his broker. He reached out but his phone rang again before he picked it up. It was Liz.

'Joe, we've had a drama, and Lisa's stranded somewhere outside Windsor. So she can't make it. Or at least she can't make it until about eleven fifteen, if she makes it at all. I wonder, could you possibly…?'

'Liz, I'd be delighted. What time does it start again?'

'You know very well. Ten thirty, as I've told you on many an occasion.'

'Of course. I'll be there.'

'Joe, you're a star. You may have to be booted out midway through, if her ladyship does manage to make it. Does that bother you?'

'Not the slightest bit. I have things on my mind anyway. And I can take a hint.'

'Oh, Joe, you know we think the world of you…'

'You are too gross in your flattery, you bridge player, you.'

'Not necessarily. But, Joe, while you're on the phone, I wanted to ask you, how was Savage's?'

The local bridge world was a small but intense one. News had travelled swiftly from the Fulham Road to Sloane Square, at the speed of native bearer, that another cavern of afternoon delights was available.

'Well, I played with Sybil the—'

'Savage?'

'Nice one, Liz. Well said. Sybil the sadist more likely. Not a happy lady and not a happy afternoon. But apart from that, it was great fun. Lots of very very nice people and good bridge. Some of the hands were fiendish. He must have a really good bridge computer program.'

'So I've heard. Savage used to work in Knightsbridge for a time, you know that.'

'Such a small world. Did he really?'

'Indeed he did. But enough of that. I will talk to you some more later. None of my crowd there, I suppose.'

'Not one, Liz. But they will be, they will be. It's tailor-made for them. Lots of people for them to get their teeth into.'

'Until ten thirty then, Joe. And Joe, you were much missed yesterday. Lady Charley in particular was deeply miffed that you didn't turn up. Expect some black looks from that quarter.'

Joe went back to his calculations. Lady C could wait. Then he wearied of them. Thailand didn't quite seem to fly as yet. He needed to do more work. Maybe he should look at India instead. He picked up the *Financial Chronicle*. Time to read Tom Stone to see if he, the journalist, had any ideas.

He opened the paper with the habit of years, looking for Tom's column, ready for the fix. His attention was briefly elsewhere. At the back of Joe's mind there lurked, unbidden and uncontrolled, just like the hungry arbs out there prowling around in the stock markets of the world, the thought that later on that day, at seven thirty in the evening to be precise, he had a date with something approaching the important and the perilous. Called Joachim.

Just a simple name, a simple sound. But it resonated in his head. Not like a bell, more like the rattle of machine-gun fire. It wouldn't even be Joachim's own name. Just a *nom de guerre*. But the string of vocables sufficed to awaken all the fear and excitement of spying. Back in the groove. Trained to function split-wise. Heading back towards it.

Joachim and Joe were scheduled to dine together. At Zorba's as before. Surrounded by the crack dealers, the flotsam and jetsam of London society, and assorted drunks, pimps and tarts. What better setting for a spot of hot briefing?

It was their first meeting after Joe's recantation, the word he used to describe what he had done. He was recanting, like Cranmer and all the other martyrs burned at the stake. Returning to the Gents after they'd busted him. He thought he was a fool. He shouldn't go back in. But again, as he saw it, he had no choice. He knew what he was doing. He'd thought about it, no question. He was going back into the espionage game. Ready to be flayed, he was going back into that slow remorseless chess play of fear and terror, wits pitted against the unknown, the vicious and the terrifying in every dark corner of the room. He was going back into the snake pit. That was certain. For one reason, he reckoned, although he acknowledged he might be fooling himself here. It was because of Perdita. No other reason. He wanted to do something which would make him feel closer to her, more worthy of her than just being this spineless, flaccid old fool sitting around bemoaning his fate. Too old and too stupid maybe but perhaps worth the gambit. She had put an incalculable amount of zing into him, even though he refused even to consider telephoning Pugh Park in order to make some conversation. That was just too stupid a move for him to consider. She was far more of an idealised creature, someone he might have met in another life, that kind of tasteful thing.

So he was picking up the gauntlet which had been left so carefully in his path, just beneath his stride. With all the right kit to justify his move. He told himself he was under no illusions. He had been in – and out – of the espionage game a lot during his career. They were using him as they had used him all along. But he had no choice. He was not a pressed man; he was a desperate man. Anything was better than this lingering atrophy. He had to go back in.

And there was another reason which he dared not mention, not even to himself. That would come later, during the reconciliation of the accounts. He knew the books and he knew they didn't square as they stood. There had to be reconciliation. Of that he had no doubt. It was the ultimate equivalent of debriefing. A line had to be drawn under one account in particular. Balance sheets had to balance. And that was why he was meeting Joachim.

Two clocks had done it, followed by Joachim, followed, he assumed, by briefing. That was how it had been done. What kind of briefing there might be, he refused even to contemplate. He would learn soon enough. There would be a mission, one that was possibly life threatening and certainly dangerous. Once more the vision struck him of the bullets tearing into his quivering flesh. Briefly he felt old and tired. But then the resilience of the day recaptured him and he revived. Only one mission to go – now there was a thought. Nobody got used beyond this point. It was just impossible. So just one mission to go. This would be the last mission.

He turned the pages again in search of Tom Stone's piece. He found it and read it. He was shocked. He read it again. He was even more shocked. It was rubbish. Pure drivel from beginning to end. He felt cheated.

Not a single reference to the markets, no hints about likely moves in the Latin American markets, no clever allusions to the mind, or otherwise, of the Fed. None of the stuff at all from Tom's usual beat. Instead, the column was stuffed full of reminiscences of life years ago, when he'd been a young journalist on the way up. How times had changed and how everyone grew older – that kind of thing. Pure tripe. No hard-nosed crap about the markets at all. Some of the phrases Tom used seemed quite questionable, stuck in more for effect's sake than to enhance the thrust of the idea. Things like 'Every wrinkle tells a story' and 'He should be stuffed'. What on earth was that rubbish doing there?

Joe threw the newspaper across the room and then struck by a thought stood up and walked over to retrieve it. In mid-stride he laughed with delight and kicked the paper full with his foot. Of course, he knew what was going on, perhaps one of only three on the planet who did! How foolish he'd been, and there again how touching of Tom to have done it! Such a clever idea, seen in that light.

It was a love letter, written to none other than dear Ursula, against whom he was due to play bridge in just a few minutes' time! Ursula the babbler of last week, she of the ultra-cool disposition who had snatched the phone from his hand and jabbered at Tom. Now they had met, Tom and Ursula, of course they'd met, and they'd enjoyed the reunion. It had been great fun for both of them. Talking about what they'd done together so many years before. And now Tom, across the years and the space of London, was sending a little billet-doux to his ex-beloved in the shape of his column. Telling her that some things had changed, like his face and his hair and his girth, but that other things, like his affections, remained exactly as they had been. Hoping for forgiveness on account of his age. And why had they split up in the first place. And hoping that all his regular readers, like Joe, would overlook this one lapse. As indeed all, bar one, would refuse to do. And that one knew too much... Joe squinted again at the column looking for more clues.

Yes, yes, it had to be. Some of the other phrases were unmistakable. Tom and Ursula were planning to elope together. That was why he'd taken such risks with the column. He was planning to end it all for himself in Fleet Street and move in with Ursula and start a new life together with her.

Wrong, wrong, wrong thought Joe. There are no new lives. Only infinite repetition. Don't do it, Tom. You're feeding an illusion. Tom had only seen one side of Ursula, perhaps, the new Ursula who had evolved over the past twenty years of child-rearing, but he, Joe, had seen more or less all the sides of Ursula the prismatic. The snobbery, the uncontrolled loss of temper when the cards went wrong; the lament about her poor stupid partners... Tom was nurturing an illusion. He wouldn't enjoy the reality when he came hard up against it. Still less the visceral hatred of the jilted husband, to whom Ursula was far more than just a wife, even though she ranked a mere number six in the pecking order, a long way after the car and the mother. Ursula was a possession. Mr Ursula wouldn't let his drudge go without a struggle. A very bitter struggle. Poor Tom with his hopeless optimism about the future would not be able to take that point on board, Joe estimated.

Thirty minutes later, as Joe passed through the fair portals of the Liz Playfair Bridge Academy, he received additional proof of his surmises. Excitement was in the air. It was an Ursula transformed. There had been a visit to the coiffeur, and Joe had to admit that the visit had been a success; the hair had been trimmed back from its usual snakes and ladders game to a very fair approximation of a well-cut lawn. There was a new outfit, and there was a copy of the *Financial Chronicle* under her arm. She too had heard the message. She trilled good morning, while Lady C scowled her greeting at him. Liz had been right. He was deep in Lady C's bad books. Something to do with non-appearance and possession as well?

No, on the face of it, it was simpler than that. Lady C handed him a letter and asked him gruffly whether he wouldn't mind posting it for her. She had to rush off to lunch with her husband immediately after the bridge and she wouldn't have the time. All of this more or less unseen by anyone else in the room, where the ladies milled about like ponies in a paddock, pacing about in stately measure, drinking tea and gossiping about their families before taking their places for the bridge. No doubt about it, Joe fulfilled some weird and unknown function in Lady C's life. But a necessary function.

'Of course I'll post it. And I'm sorry that I wasn't around yesterday to take it for you.'

Lady C handed over the letter with its usual address with obvious relief. Then her mind cleared of that tedious little chore, she launched into an harangue of her good friend Lisa's bidding techniques, the said Lisa being in no position to defend herself since she was stuck somewhere on the Hammersmith Flyover by that stage.

The play began. Lady C was in fine form and the first on the attack, criticising Joe for his way of floating the cards down onto the table instead of placing them squarely on the green baize.

'I hate it when you play the cards like that, it's just so rude, Joe,' she said unequivocally.

She's really got it in for somebody, thought Joe, and I think I know who it is. I'm just the proxy for all of this. It's really Tom Stone she's got her knife into, that ghost from her past. Tom is disturbing the natural symmetry of life within the compound where we all laugh and play like primal fauns of the forest. He represents choices. No wonder she hates him. He's a disruptive influence from the outside world, a wicked Pied Piper.

And all the while Ursula sat there next to Tom, partnering

Lady C and playing her bridge as if in a dream. She too quite clearly had to rush off after the bridge, but for an encounter that would have far different vibes to the one that Lady C was planning to attend. An afternoon encounter with her beau.

Just then the phone rang. Liz went to take the call. But Ursula beat her to the punch. She was across the room and chattering into the receiver before anyone could say six no trumps. She flew like a bird, the creak and rustle of the new outfit accompanying her in flight.

No prizes for guessing who the mystery caller was, thought Joe. That must be our old friend Tom Stone making his confirmatory call of the lunch to the bridge room, rather than to the family home where hubby might just conceivably have taken a day off from the rigours of a struggling City stockbroking partnership and have intercepted the call from the errant swain. Lots of explanations to be called for from Ursula in that case. Far easier to use the Playfair facilities as a risk-free intermediary. Joe had a sudden vision of just how much trouble and disruption this headstrong fling of Ursula's might cause, when the vision faded. It was suddenly time to go.

The door opened and in strolled Lisa fresh from the fight with London traffic. She'd made it sooner than she'd expected. Lady C leaped to her feet and embraced Lisa fulsomely as if years had passed since they met. In fact they'd played bridge together the previous evening. But Lady C had to make some sort of gesture to compensate for the attention that Ursula was generating with her clandestine phone call. And Ursula, it had to be said, was pushing it just ever so slightly. Liz would not tolerate indefinitely her place being used as an assignation postbox. Not everybody there wanted to be a blind accessory after the fact of Ursula's infidelity. On the wind from the street outside came the silent susurration: Think of the children and the husband and the in-laws and the house and the holidays and the sheer fag of running the chateau and all the disruption and all the explanations if you do your flit. Lady C's rapturous welcome to Lisa contained more than a hint of rebuke to Ursula. No man was worth all that chaos, she was proclaiming to an Ursula still talking on the phone with an urgent, stupid smile painted right across her face. Society was rocking just ever so slightly and that tilt had to be removed. Only even keels could anchor here.

It was time for Joe to depart. The table was full now. He stood up gracefully and Lisa, after thanking him sweetly for standing in for her, sat down in his spot. A full house. He pushed his way through the baggage surrounding the table and headed towards the door. A kiss blown to Liz and a look exchanged with Lady C and he was close to the door. Ursula, returning to her spot, barely acknowledged his departure. Her eyes sparkled with excitement. The lunch was on! The trip to the coiffeur that morning had been worth it! She took her place at the table and turned to Lady C.

Once again reality twinkled. Joe in a snap out-take from the humdrum of day-to-day perceptions conceived the three women in a flash as seated together in a separate vision, like an engraving in stone on the exterior of a medieval cathedral. Ursula was bent over Lady C's bowed neck like an avenging angel poised to strike a killing blow of execution which would decapitate Lady C in an orgy of fury. She seemed possessed. Lady C was bent half forward in submission. And Lisa was kneeling beneath them both, as in some Old Testament fable, poised and ready to catch the tumbling head in a basket. And Lady C was ready for the blow so that justice was both done and seen to be done! She knew she had done evil! Joe had half glimpsed that frieze effect before but never so clearly and so wantonly as on the day of the Tom Stone luncheon telephone call. Clearly those women had got up to some very special kind of nasty business in their younger days. But then Joe was out of the door and into the street. It was no business of his to investigate their monkey tricks of a heady youth. He had other concerns on his mind.

Shades of grey night fell on his soul as he contemplated yet again the spectre of the meeting that evening. He took it in stages. He posted Lady C's letter and made his way back to the flat. Far easier to contemplate an infinity of wrong moves from the safety of familiar surroundings. Far, far easier...

But two shocks awaited him as he pushed through the door, only one of which might have been anticipated. The clocks were back in their threatening spot over the mantelpiece, wrongly set as before. So familiar and so predictable. The Gents' calling card, courtesy of the Fat Man, briefly risen from his tomb again to say hi. Good morning, Joe, and here is your phased introduction to the killing fields. You knew we'd come to call and so here we are, now that you've renewed your Faustian pact with us. Good to see you again, really good to see you. You knew, didn't you, that we wouldn't fail with the calling card?

Joe ignored the clocks. But on the answerphone, another shock. There was a message from Tom Stone! Joe knew only too well what that meant. It was a very serious mission indeed. Very, very dangerous. He went out for a long walk to rest his head and his nerves before the dinner, feeling just for a few moments fraught and isolated and nervous. The wonder of the call was clear because Joe had not left his own phone number for Tom to call but Liz Playfair's. So somebody had given somebody something to play with... And who would have thought it of Tom? And Tom wouldn't be pleased either, just when he'd found his long-lost girlfriend and the human condition was easing up a fraction for him. Now would he?

## Chapter Eight

Joe got to Zorba's at around seven twenty-five. He was a touch early. That looked good to the watchers. They would report him as being keen to keep his appointments punctually. No sense in doing anything else, but it went down well on the timesheet.

Nothing had changed at Zorba's. Same darkness, same smell of food wafting down from the kitchen in the heights above, same Zorba waddling about and same Charley waving the photos. Same crack dealers glinting in the darkness at the back of the restaurant, waiting for the anguished calls about supply. The earlier the better, so far as they were concerned.

Nothing had changed but then everything had changed. Only time would tell by how much. But all was different now. A tiny twitch on the thread and the whole pattern had changed.

Joe looked round for the mad-eyed blonde. No sign of her as yet. But she'd be there soon enough. And for her too it was only a matter of time. Gradually but with increasing speed the drugs would take her down. Another two months perhaps and she'd be screaming for her fix. That would be the crucial time for her. Both the money and the job would be on the rocks. There was a choice of routes then. Either her parents reclaimed her at that point and stuck her in The Priory down the road to dry out: that was the support route. Or, to finance and feed her habit, she went on the streets for the dealers and changed from a human being into a lump of meat. As simple and as straightforward as that. That was the normal outcome. That was what dope did. It gave you the illusion of freedom but in reality it imposed the harshest of choices. And there was no getting away from those choices either. It wasn't a game at all then.

Not yet there for me, thought Joe, but it's always just round the corner. Reassuring to think that the dope is always just so close. Right now it's about six feet away. You can't get closer than that.

Joe grabbed the corner table next to the window and waited for Joachim. He ordered some wine. Zorba waddled over. He told him a young man had been looking for him earlier in the evening and that he would either call back later on or leave a message for him at his flat. Drats, thought Joe facetiously. It had to be Pugh. Joe cursed him and his perseverance. He had refused to make any calls to Pugh Park and the memory of Perdita was slowly easing in his mind from total pain to just slow ache. He had hoped his silence would subtly convey its own diplomatic message. But plainly not so.

'He seemed very excited. He said he had things to tell you. It was the same young man who was weeping in here. But he was different tonight. More alive. No tears. More like a human being. He wanted to get hold of you and he was very insistent that I gave you that message. How have you bewitched him, Joe, eh? What is the secret of your charm?'

'Two hundred units of alcohol per week, Zorba. Without fail. Now fetch me that wine, pronto.'

Then Joachim was at the table, apologising for being late. Same stooped and scholarly look. Full briefcase that was emptied on the table. They changed places so that Joe could give him pole position by the window. That again looked better. Joe was being a very good boy indeed over all this.

Joachim went through the motions of smoothing out his papers and preparing to make his dissertation. Joe drank his wine and waited. The briefing would be subtle and well prepared. The obvious points would be hidden away in asides. He concentrated on looking attentive. Then Joachim started, part Germanic accent well to the fore.

'When I left you last time, I asked you who won the war in a rather jokey way. Now I want to come back to that in a second, but in the meantime I want to concentrate on someone you know pretty well. I want to talk about Callaghan who was prime minister in the late seventies, before Margaret Thatcher. Now how do you perceive Callaghan?'

'Bluff old guy, fatally attractive to other elder statesmen, clever in a way that I could never quite fathom.'

'Quite so, that is the answer I was hoping you would make.

Now let's look at his career in a different way. Callaghan is always the man on the way up right from the word. He is a deeply ambitious man. So much is clear from all the Crossman Diaries, which I am now reading. And his early background is terrifying. His father dies leaving the family in difficult circumstances, so that the young Callaghan more or less has to beg for his food on the quayside. So much is clear from his autobiography. And what happens to this young man?'

'You tell me, Joachim.'

'He comes up through the Labour movement, or more accurately through the trade union movement. But he is also deeply involved almost from the beginning with financiers. You would not guess this from his autobiography. But Callaghan finishes up as a rich man. He farms acres. Not everybody who got to be prime minister achieved that as well. He does well out of the system. He is rewarded. You're with me so far?'

'Perfectly.' Joe thought the Germanic accent had slipped a fraction.

'Now let's be more specific. During the sixties, when Callaghan is chancellor, he makes a terrible hash of the sterling crisis. A total mess. He is quivering under the shock of it all. As indeed is Wilson, the prime minister, and of course Cromer, governor of the Bank of England. Cromer, if some reports are to be believed, actively conspires to destabilise the pound when Wilson is prime minister. Dropping those damaging hints about the parity, that sort of thing. And of course at the death, when the pound is finally devalued, the Bank of England manages to lose the country an enormous chunk of the country's reserves by its unbelievable stupidity in the foreign exchange market.

'But back to Wilson and Cromer. The two of them just did not get on and Wilson was hated, almost throughout the City, because of his reformist desires and his critical attitude struck when he was president of the Board of Trade in the late forties. But Callaghan was different. The City liked him. He went along with the City. They saw him either as one of them, or just as a greedy socialist and capable of being manipulated. You begin to see what I'm driving at?'

'Not quite Joachim, but keep going. It makes for a marvellous tale.'

Joe saw very well what the thrust of Joachim's tale might be. But he preferred to take his time and fine-tune his judgement as the speech went along. He was still thinking about the call from Tom Stone which he had not yet returned. He would do that after his meeting with Joachim. But everything that Joachim had said so far conformed to pattern. It was marvellous to see the pattern unfold in this way.

'Loosely speaking, and this is painting with a broad brush, Callaghan outmanoeuvres his principal rivals for the leadership when Wilson goes, rivals like Barbara Castle and Roy Jenkins, and this mainly by opposing Wilson's move to introduce trade union legislation which will tie the brothers into a more legalistic framework. Callaghan at a crucial point plays the union card. It is a winning card. He splits the Labour movement by forcing the Fabian middle-class element to confront the trade union wing and thus emerges as the only viable candidate. So he becomes prime minister. Now before we fast-forward to 1979 and the events of that peculiar year, what was it that Callaghan did as prime minister that was utterly characteristic, for which in all probability he had been placed in the job?'

'Signed the IMF loan agreement?'

'No, that's what everyone thinks. That's the obvious thing. No, it was far more devious, but also essential in terms of continuity, so much so that it was never presented to cabinet, I gather, and it is the one thing that Healey bitterly regrets about his period as chancellor. So what was it?'

'Search me.'

'Sanctioning Chevaline. He approved Chevaline.'

'Chevaline?'

'An incremental programme regarding Britain's nuclear capacity.'

'I'm baffled.'

'You won't be. I refer you to Healey's autobiography, page thirty, for chapter and verse. According to Healey it was the worst thing he did as chancellor. Now let's continue. On to 1979, or rather 1978. We can come back to Chevaline. And we will. Chevaline is crucial. But ever onward just for the time being. In

1979, the election was held in the spring and Labour were routed by the radical Tories led by Mrs Thatcher. An entirely new era began. But let's take a step back to the autumn of 1978, at which point it was assumed that Callaghan would go to the country. Labour and the Tories were neck and neck in the opinion polls and the country felt quite good about Labour. It was recovering fast from the debacle of the IMF loans and the economic data was getting better and better. Labour stood a very good chance of winning the election. So what did Callaghan do? He told the Labour Conference that autumn that he wasn't going to the country immediately in what must have been a complete about-turn, taken by him personally, I guess, that took everyone by surprise. His move stunned the whole country. It was quite unexpected. Everything had been arranged for an autumn election. All the numbers that were published in late September and October were brilliant, so the whole affair had been programmed for months. Callaghan ran away from the election and what happened?'

'Winter of discontent?'

'Spot on, Joe. The dead weren't buried, the cancer patients weren't tended and the rubbish was piled high in the streets. The trade union movement, that movement which had carried Callaghan to power in the first place, experienced a moment of collective madness, either because of the presence of government agents provocateurs or natural spontaneous lunacy. But whatever it was, this proved Callaghan's ultimate and total undoing. The country turned against Labour and voted in Mrs Thatcher. So the key question is—'

'Did PC Jim throw the election?'

'We can't tell, Joe. He might have done, he might not have done. Apart from the pleasing symmetry of it all, from playing the trade union card to get the job of PM, which is then the crucial factor behind his downfall, I'm less concerned by that point. No, I'm more fascinated by the importance of Callaghan as an element of continuity. Wilson represented change, as did Jenkins, and both of these men were clever, formidable statesmen. So they could have achieved change. But not Callaghan. He was a polished performer but no radical. No, certainly not. He went to bed early as PM and only read the briefs that he wanted to. And he was a bully. But he got the top job. In some odd way the machinery of permanent government appears to have eliminated the movers and shakers in favour of the status quo element. Wilson, a truly brilliant man, really wanted to do things, but he was very quickly muzzled, partly it must be said because of the quixotic elements in his own temperament. But the odds were against him from the start as soon as Cromer started dropping hints in the City about the pound.'

'And Jenkins?'

'Now that was a different story entirely. Jenkins was a reformer: witness his performance as home secretary and witness his formation of a new party at the start of the eighties. Jenkins, of course, failed in his endeavours with the Gang of Four. It was too late by then and in any case the whole endeavour was undermined by the saturnine and over-promoted Dr Owen. So Jenkins was marginalised too. Chancellor of Oxford is no substitute for being PM. His whole career threw a kind of S-bend at the end of the sixties and the 1970 election, which Wilson managed, we think, to lose. But at the end of the day, and this must be the irony of the whole business, Callaghan, the pure product of the Labour movement which made him, every tiny particle of him, managed to destroy the whole socialist edifice so painfully constructed for one hundred years or longer. In the process, he eliminated that one element in the British political spectrum that acted and functioned for change.'

'Just amplify that, will you for me?'

'Very simply. The UK at the end of the twentieth century is almost the only country in the world, apart from the US, which is recognisably the same as it was at the start. Still runs a monarchy, still has the same vast differences between rich and poor, still functions in terms of massive inequality of opportunity and still slides down the world league. The UK formula doesn't really work except for a few. That's a strong statement but verifiable by the data. Don't forget that at the start of the century it was still the richest and most powerful country in the world by far. Far more so than the US. But no more. Yet the incredible thing is that the UK still makes the same mistakes at home and abroad. It hasn't learned a thing from its terrifying experiences in the twentieth century.'

'And so...'

'Most of my recent work has focused on just how that may have come about. In other words, whatever the tendency to change coming in from elsewhere or driving up from the grass roots of the country itself, these movements have all been systematically trampled on or asphyxiated, so that in the end there is no change. Well, that's not quite true, there has been change, but probably for the worse. But it's true enough for our purposes. Britain is a study throughout the century in inertia and incompetence. It tries to change but when it does it is always for the worse. Unlike Germany, France, Italy, or almost any country you care to mention, which tries and which sometimes gets it right, sometimes wrong. But with the UK it's different; it never works here. There's no getting away from it.'

'Indonesia? There's a country that hasn't changed.'

'Joe, you're being silly now. You know perfectly correctly what has happened in Indonesia, you of all people.'

'I jest. Yes, I do know about Indonesia. All right then West Hartlepool, how about that?'

Joe lightened the atmosphere just fractionally with his gag. He wanted a slight pause and it worked. Joachim dived into his wine and drank half a glass down at one gulp. It had been a long speech. Some silence reigned between them. At their back the restaurant bustled to and fro. People came and went in busy hungry throngs. But Joachim was a professional. He didn't pause for long. The Gents had sent the very best of them all to give him this briefing. This happened very rarely, that they disgorged their top men like this. It was like the Fat Man all over again, although Joe had some problems with that idea.

More wine, more quaffing, more sparkle in the restaurant. Joachim stared at the ceiling, waiting to begin again. Joe was beginning to see what this briefing session was about. Ever so discreetly, it was a consciousness raising exercise. He was getting a fresh outlook. He was being taught a new approach. He was being shown how to look at the UK from a different angle. That was why they had sent the top man. What Joachim was telling him, via various metaphors like Callaghan and Wilson, was that things were never quite what they appeared to be in the UK. Joe was deeply aware of that. The UK was a sphinx, a riddle, an enigma. It contradicted itself at every turn and it strained loyalties to breaking point and beyond. That at least had been Joe's experience. But he had never had his suppositions confirmed on such a grand panoramic scale before.

But there was something else as well. That was the hint behind Joachim's comments, it had to be. Behind the waterfall, where the spray dripped and flashed, there lay a secret path of understanding and survival. That was the key element in Joachim's speech. That was the nub of it all. What Joe was about to get was the secret – and true – history of the UK. No frills and no prejudice, just the plain unvarnished truth. That would be what Joachim recounted, in a very roundabout fashion, after he'd finished slurping his wine. But it would be rambling, Joe guessed, at least at first.

'And the continuity, Joachim? How do you start analysing that?'

Joe was right. Joachim temporised. He gave a great speech instead of the facts. 'Joe, that is my great discovery. I stand back, I clear my mind of all the extraneous day-to-day historical detail and I say to myself, What is actually going on? What is the pattern? I tell you the exercise bears fruit. Quite remarkable fruit, yes, indeed.'

'So, say on. I am quite fascinated by your x-ray capacity.'

'Right, Joe,' said Joachim, clearing his throat, 'let's flick to the end of the war. World War II, that is. Now what was the state of the UK?'

'Jubilant, I guess.'

'Yes, but from a statistical point of view?'

This was better. More facts. Joe liked a fix of data. But he played safe. 'Still jubilant?'

'Yes, of course, but also something else. You don't know? I'll tell you. The country was more or less bankrupt. It had fought the war on borrowed money from the colonies, creating what came to be known in time as the sterling balances, and using Lend-Lease from the United States. Many of its overseas assets had been sold to pay for the war. At the end of the war, the cupboard was bare.

The cupboard wouldn't have been quite so bare if Churchill hadn't prolonged the war quite unnecessarily some two years, because of his fear that the men wouldn't fight, but that's another story. So the UK went into the war as a great power and emerged with enormous debts – nothing more and nothing less. The war, of course, was a total failure. It should never have been fought. Britain achieved nothing, beyond selling the empire at knock-down prices. It was a quite unnecessary war. Britain went to war to defend Poland and ended up giving it away to Russia. Not a lot to show for six years' fighting, eh? And Britain was broke. The US had even confiscated its gold. Roosevelt sent a destroyer to pick the gold up from South Africa as collateral for Lend-Lease. Can you imagine the humiliation?

'Anyway, come the end of the war, and the scrapping overnight of Lend-Lease by Truman, the UK decided that it must have a loan from the United States. Now, it is by no means certain that the UK actually needed this loan and there were voices in the Treasury which argued against it; the accounts would have tolerated instead a devaluation of the pound to boost the export drive. But at this stage in the war, Maynard Keynes was the intellectual supremo of the Treasury and he decided, using a set of assumptions that were, incidentally, quite inaccurate, that he could raise money in the United States. Quite, quite wrong. The US saw the UK correctly as a client and profligate state, after its experience of the UK's borrowing programme in World War I. But the UK did not see things in quite the same way. So the UK pressed for a loan. And Keynes headed the negotiations, which went badly. The initial terms of the loan, which were very generous, were turned down by the British delegation, quite huffily. Then finally after many, many months of wrangling, fresh terms were agreed that were sharply worse than the original conditions. At this point, therefore, we are examining another concept which underlies the UK approach in the post-war period – the initial rejection of reality.'

'What happened to the loan?'

'A good question. And a tragic reply. It was squandered, largely because of the infighting in government between the Treasury and the Bank of England. That, plus problems of administration.

The Bank of England was running at the same time something called the sterling area which related to the empire and where all dollar earnings and holdings were pooled in London. But capital was free to move around in the sterling area, which it did. But there were leakages and frauds which could not be policed. The whole world was hungry for dollars because there was a shortage of greenbacks, not a surplus as Keynes had predicted. But London had dollars. Essentially, London stood guarantor via the US loan for the colonies' heavy post-war consumption and supplied liquidity to them in the shape of dollars, as they consumed. It has to do this because, bottom line, the UK was being blackmailed by the colonies. All those pounds created during the war to pay for Indian or South African guns and bullets, et cetera, were just sitting there waiting to be unloaded on the markets. So the UK was caught between a rock and a hard place. It was running a very loose system of controls and it lacked both the imagination and the talent to police its worldwide system. So the dollars kept flowing out. Here, look at this.'

Joachim handed across a document to Joe, marked TOP SECRET. It detailed the destiny of the US loan. It all appeared to have gone out through South Africa and India. Joachim nodded.

'Such a waste, eh? And all in vain. Two years after the huge run on the pound in 1947, sterling was devalued, some say, in the teeth of Bank of England opposition. But exports started to recover very sharply. Meanwhile the British people were suffering unimaginable austerities but that again is another story. The key point here is that the permanent government of the UK was not exactly incompetent and not exactly fraudulent, but it was divided. And as such it malfunctioned – as it always does. It would be harsh to say that it divided along class lines, but it is more or less true. But that in turn is of less importance than the fact that key parts of the executive were divided and some of them lived in cloud cuckoo land. All this at a time when the country had been stripped of its assets and had to compete on the one hand with a new world power like the United States and on the other with a hostile and very astute Soviet Union, equally determined to secure world domination. No contest. Basically despite all its efforts and all its deep pool of talent, the UK is not up to the job. Perhaps that is too harsh. Yes, let us just say that the UK cannot deliver in this new post-war environment. Its problems rush upon it from every corner. The equation of politico-economic success just does not factor for the British. So we reach another powerful and profound point. For all its vaunted longevity and tradition, the British system just doesn't work. Or doesn't work without endeavour correctly applied, which it never is. The UK doesn't deliver the goods. I mean, it doesn't work in the modern world. We have to take that as given so far as my system is concerned. It functioned perhaps quite well in a bygone age, like the age of Pitt, but in the harsh search for competitive advantage of the second half of the twentieth century, it is an also-ran. But what do you expect of a country that has a complete medieval monarchy in full working order?'

'Nice point, Joachim.'

'So what do we have so far? Well, let us summarise. We have a reluctance to face reality which we can analyse in some depth. First, the a priori assumptions. So for the American loan we can substitute the Suez fiasco, or the refusal to enter the Common Market in the mid-fifties, or the Wilson refusal to devalue, or the various attempts to hold the pound at overvalued and unsustainable levels. This is axiomatic. The UK will always position on the wrong side of the street. Next, the painful collision with external reality. So for the realisation that Johnny Foreigner is knocking off your dollar loan in great chunks, in the forties, substitute the horrified realisation that the US will not support the UK in its mad venture over Suez; or in the seventies, the dawning of the appreciation that the cost of belonging to the EEC is unacceptably high. Next comes the attempt to row back from this exposed position which always costs. Always costs enormously. Finally, when failure stares the country and the enterprise in the face, the search for a scapegoat, the change of personnel and the dash into new escapades to divert attention from the previous mess. That is the pattern which emerges. It is always very expensive. Next, we have a divided permanent government. And then, finally wonder of wonders, we have continuity. Nothing seems to change. The secretary of the man who runs the country still reads the *Daily Mail*, and the *Sun* is still read by someone who doesn't care who runs the country provided she's got big tits. You know it all as well as I do. There'll always be an England, white cliffs of Dover, the whole fakeness, if you want, of the thing.'

Joachim paused for breath and Charley brought the food and set it down in front of them both. The food, masses of it, looked good. The retsina sparkled against the light from the street. The table was inviting and Joe was hungry. He was enjoying the ambience and the briefing, in particular the sensation of tiptoeing around something quite bizarre and impenetrable, something vast and huge, but which nevertheless had secret entrances, passages and causeways. It was intriguing. To the initiated, the shape changed internally. It was not how it appeared from the outside. There were surprises. Joe could feel a desire growing upon him to learn that hidden shape in much the same way that he had learned from the Fat Man during his early days in espionage. But this was different. He and the Fat Man had dined together like this frequently in Berlin, after some routine work of espionage, like surveillance, and it had been exciting then. They had shared the thrill of it. But like everything it had developed its own sense of routine, even within the danger. And it had been physical. Or so at least it seemed with the hindsight of memory. Not so now. There was something here to grasp in the recesses of the mind, like a piece of algebra, something almost tangible but at the same time deeply elusive and changing in its shape, which required patient analysis and quiet understanding. It was a new idea with huge potential.

Joe had taken on some pretty nasty people in the past, but never an entire country before. It felt almost as daunting as playing bridge with the women at Savage's. But it was challenging. The effort to grasp the picture of the whole brought forth a response from him. He felt himself starting to rise to the occasion. His previous fears about survival started, inch by inch, to diminish, if only for a few moments.

'Tell me some more about Keynes and the loan.'

'You ask good questions, Joe. I was just about to come back to that. It's an important example of our double take on the UK, the "now you see it, now you don't" aspect that I mentioned. But just one moment.' Joachim fought with a piece of lamb briefly, swallowed some more retsina and began the briefing again.

'Back to the loan, as you say. Now much of my background to this is drawn from Sayers' great work, *Financial Policy 1939–1945*. It is a magnificent piece of writing and it is fair to say that the presiding genius throughout the book is of course Keynes himself. I mention this because it is important. Keynes is everywhere during the war. He is tireless; it is his war. But something seems to desert Keynes when he embarks on the negotiations with the Americans and it shows through, I fancy, in Sayers' prose. For once Sayers is not quite sure what he is describing because the genius Keynes during the war is not the numbskull in Washington at the end of it. I fancy… it is just my idea, you understand… it is certainly not conclusive. But let us look at some more background.

'Now Keynes was an odd fish. Life-long member of the Bloomsbury Group and intellectual maverick certainly, but also very very promiscuous. A homosexual, who was frequently in love with young men and who kept a diary detailing his sexual encounters; and these were very considerable at a time when homosexuality in England was a criminal offence. So he was used to living beyond the law as well as beyond the known intellectual limits. But he was also married to a Russian ballerina, with whom I think he did not enjoy conventional sex, although they were devoted to each other, and he was also an Apostle, that is to say he belonged to the Cambridge secret society which gave the world the Cambridge spy ring, including Burgess and Maclean, Stalin's super spies.

'Now none of this amounts to a row of beans until we build into the equation Keynes' opposite number in the US loan negotiations, Harry Dexter White. Harry Dexter White was Truman's right-hand man, who also just happened to be Stalin's man in the White House, it is thought. I stress, it is thought. But think about it, if you can, assuming it to be true. And don't forget it was Maclean who leaked the nuclear secrets to the Russians in Washington in the early fifties. So now a different scenario begins to emerge. The Russians knew about the atomic bomb. They were terrified of it. They knew that the US had a winning weapons' lead in the cold war which might or might not break out after 1945. They had to get their hands on the data. Otherwise Stalin was far too exposed by his thrust through Central Europe. But what to do? Well, one obvious way was to try and tie the UK as closely as possible to America by forcing it to borrow money from the Americans. Drag the negotiations out as long as possible, so that the juxtaposition of Britain to America became an established fact, and so that the British presence in Washington and New York would grow and look quite natural. That certainly happened too.'

'How solid is this idea that Keynes worked for Stalin?'

'Impossible to ascribe any total certainty to it. We do know that at one stage in the negotiations Keynes and Dexter White took a walk in the woods together with no one around at all from either side to check on what they said to each other. Chilling isn't it? They might well have been comparing their briefing notes from the Kremlin. But Keynes was untouchable by that stage. He was far too far up the tree ever to be exposed to anything like a positive vetting. So we can't tell whether Keynes worked for the Russians or not, although circumstantially it looks about as certain as can be. No, that's not quite the basic idea I'm trying to get across. It's more the thought that at a crucial moment in the UK's experience, when all the flags were flying, bands playing and everybody was standing to attention, the reality was very different, and very much more grim. The country was broke beyond repair. And more to the point, other people knew this. More than just the odd disinterested bystander was around to take advantage. Men like Stalin knew; they must have known.

'So Stalin at this particular juncture could take control of a country's destiny, even one with the heritage and tradition of the UK and change that destiny. He could push the UK into the lap of the Americans to serve his own purposes, using the great men of England to achieve that aim. That was a big shift on the world's geopolitical map, equivalent in its way to the Norman Conquest of England, which of course transformed the entire political map of Western Europe at the time. For what it is worth, and I am quite aware that you can go mad working out these intelligence theses, I incline to the truth of the theory, if only because of its simplicity. And its efficacy. It's all a question of the angle of approach. From the UK's angle it is clearly impossible that Keynes might have been a Russian spy. But from the Russian angle it is clearly highly probable that he was. Certainly a target. Gay, polymath, iconoclast, Russian wife, Apostle, and an advocate of greater state involvement and state control via higher government expenditure and borrowing, approaches that look incredibly ham-fisted and suspect in this more sceptical age. It all looks fishy to me. But just think of how the whole thing paid off for Stalin. By the early fifties, after Maclean, the Russians had the bomb. They could relax. Back on level terms again. That must have been a relief in the Kremlin. And Keynes may have helped them get there even though we just don't know for certain.'

Joachim paused and Joe took in the implications of what he had just heard. Simple, direct and breathtaking. His country, for which he had risked his life on more than just one occasion, was a patsy. No more, no less. Just a patsy. And, more galling, Joachim's words were so hard to gainsay. All the facts so far fitted, and there would be other facts, realms of them, all angled to back up the central thesis. Whether the briefing was true was quite another matter. The thrust of the briefing would not change, Joe could see that. These were the terms on which he was to trade during the mission. It was a hard pill to swallow – the UK, with all its pomp and pageantry and power and arrogance, was just a pawn in the game, just a small stupid thing to be pushed around from one square to another on the world's chessboard at the behest of other more powerful and invisible forces. Forces that were very smart. Forces that had worked out correctly where all the break points lay in the UK so that these weaknesses could be used as strengths to buttress the alternative usage of the UK. Forces that didn't miss.

Joe saw parts of it all very quickly. Like the UK's obsession with secrecy and cover-ups and failure to allocate responsibility. Should a hostile power ever get behind that wall, well then, it could use that obsession for its own purposes and bear down on any investigators to protect itself...

Joachim continued quite softly, now that he saw that he had Joe's imagination in thrall. 'There are twists and turns to all this which I will try to identify for you. But it is not easy. Language is hard to use here in order to convey the subtlety of the analysis. Where the emphasis falls is important, in order to grasp motivation which in turn is never wholly straightforward. Truly we are dealing with shadow land. Creatures that flit from shade to shade in the twilight. So let me use an analogy. Let us take a famous family in the land – no, not the Cecils, we will come back to them – let us take the Cairncross family. Very highly regarded indeed within the British Establishment. Sir Alec Cairncross was economic adviser to the government, afterwards head of the government's economic service and then later he became master of St Peter's College, Oxford. He was a very charming man and he went through the card – civil servant, don, administrator, author, a true member of the great and good. His daughter, Frances Cairncross, is a very senior journalist on the *The Economist* and her husband, Hamish McRae, is also a very senior journalist on the *Independent*. So the family as a whole is solidly entrenched within the nexus of relationships that we call the Establishment. As indeed was Keynes, with whom incidentally Alec Cairncross was associated in the thirties.

'Now, Joe, granted the thrust of our discussion this evening, it will not come to you as any surprise to find out that there is an alternative side to the Cairncrosses, notably Sir Alec's brother, John, who is normally reckoned to have been the most successful spy for the old Soviet Union of all time. The details of John Cairncross's spying activities need not concern us, suffice it to say that he was trusted at the most senior level of the British executive and that means he had access to pretty well everything that was classified. He took the classified stuff out in barrow loads, including the Bletchley Park decrypts to give to the Russians. There can't have been much the Russians didn't know about the UK after John Cairncross had finished giving them the goods. So there you have it – an astonishing contrast. At one level a brilliant academic and civil servant is twinned with a traitor. Both functioning simultaneously. The family table talk must have been hilarious.

'But there is another level to all this, which will intrigue you. Sir Alec wrote a very powerful book, called *Years of Recovery* dealing with Britain's economy from 1945 to the early fifties. By itself, the book is very strong meat. He follows the numbers through very rigorously and so far as I can gather he is the only historian of the period to do so. It is a unique piece of analysis. But it does not stand alone. I only discovered recently that *Years of Recovery* needs to be read in conjunction with another book that Cairncross edited, namely the memoirs of Sir Richard Clarke, the only man in the Treasury at the time to stand up to Keynes and the man who proposed another course of action to the one that Keynes pursued at the end of the war. So far as I can gather, the two books fuse and form a secret text which acts as a guide to what really happened to Britain in those crucial post-war years. It is dynamite. The numbers contained in one book and the commentary on them in the other is quite, quite unprecedented. Almost a justification by one Cairncross for the treacherous activities of the other? Extraordinary. And this is real life. The books are readily available. Now, for example...'

Joe and Joachim became aware of another presence at the table – Rivers Pugh. A transformed Pugh, whose eyes glinted and sparkled behind the gold-rimmed spectacles. A Pugh exuberant. Pugh looked pleased to see Joe again, but also exasperated because tracking Joe down had caused him so much trouble. Pugh was bursting with news to pass on to his new-found bridge-playing friend, but equally he was displeased to find that Joe was deep in conversation with a stranger. That was very clear from his expression. He didn't want Joe to stray too far from his aegis. In other words, Joe was out of his control. Pugh blinked his concern but finally the effort of containment was too much for him. The words burst out from him.

'Joe, where have you been? And why have you fallen out of communication with us? My mother is really very saddened by it all. She doesn't know what she's done to upset you and nor does Perdita. She is really very upset too. They both want to talk to you, but you don't return any of our calls. And we're all very distressed after we had such a good time with you when you came down to see us. We all want to play French cricket again but we're not very sure of the rules. So we can't play. And we don't know why. And we don't know why you are ignoring us? Why are you?'

He sounded like a boy of twelve. For a twelve-year-old it was a tremendous outburst.

Behind him, Joe could hear Joachim starting to put his books and papers away. The briefing was drawing to a close. There would be others though. So much was clear. But Joachim was bustling. He didn't want to be mixed up in any of this. Like Rivers, he didn't want to talk to outsiders. But he would be taking in all this byplay, for passing on later to his bosses. Joe knew that very well. It was part of the system. Nothing personal but the Gents liked to know everything about their precious agents when they entrusted them with a mission. Just in case. Just in case…

Joe motioned Joachim to Rivers. 'Friend of mine. A historian. We were talking about the First World War. He's got some interesting theories.'

Rivers was even more indignant. 'That's another reason why you should call my mother. She's fascinated by the war. She's compiling an anthology of the family's letters which she plans to publish. You must talk to her about it. She'd be delighted. I didn't know you were interested in the First World War. The family had four brothers and cousins at the front and they were all killed in action. The Pugh family was nearly wiped out. But they wrote home all the time. There are heaps of letters which my mother came across quite unexpectedly in the attic. She says they're extraordinary. Some of them have even got blood on them, imagine it, blood from the battlefield and the trenches. My mother even found that one of the letters was timed at ten thirty in the morning, just about an hour before one of my uncles was killed. She can't get over it. She keeps reading and rereading the letter, even though we tell her to stop it.' Pugh paused and then said emphatically, 'I hate that whole business.'

Then he fell silent. He felt he was talking too much about his family in front of strangers. It was time to pull down the portcullis. But it hardly mattered. Joachim was on his feet now and, bags packed, was moving swiftly. Normal life was climbing back in through the door, and through the window and down the chimney. The atmosphere had been broken. Joachim handed some pages to Joe as he manoeuvred round the table with his briefcase.

'Joe, I'll call you, or you call me, and we'll make another date. Meanwhile, I've prepared some photostats for you of all that statistical data.'

Then Joachim was gone, sliding through the door at high speed, after waving to Rivers and leaving his contribution to the meal on the table in an untidy heap of piled-up banknotes.

'Who was that? Friend of yours?' Rivers spoke more assertively now that the two of them were together. Joe nodded and Charley came over to take any orders that might be offered.

'You're looking better tonight than you did last time,' he said to Rivers in his barking kind of way.

Rivers blushed slightly and looked uncomfortable. 'I'd received a shock,' he said a touch inadequately. He didn't want to be reminded of his lapses. He wanted only to talk about his successes that evening.

'Leave him alone, Charley, and get him a drink. You'd think it was unheard of for people to burst into tears in this establishment.'

Charley sniffed and returned to the bar to bring some more retsina as Pugh exploded with delight. 'Guess what, Joe, I've got a new job.'

'Congratulations. What does it pay? That's the important thing.'

'Oh, only quite well to start with, but there are lots of opportunities to make extra by commission.'

'What are you doing?'

'I'm not quite certain, but it's very similar to what I was doing at the Foreign Office, you know, liaison with foreign countries, that sort of thing. But it's more on the commercial side, rather than the diplomatic bit. So it won't be exactly like the FO. Also it's a bit junior compared to what I was doing, but I'm told that as I learn more about the whole set-up, as time goes on, then I get more responsibility. Isn't that exciting? I'm off the streets and I'm back on the payroll. So no more weeping in public. Of that you can be assured. Rivers Pugh is a reformed character. Henceforth…'

Pugh seized his glass and held it high, looking slight but powerful, and then he and Joe stood up to clink together, ignored by the crack dealers who were jabbering into their mobiles.

'Here's to Pugh power.'

'To Pugh power then. May the force of Pugh be with you.'

They both drank down their retsina with gusto. Then Rivers, before Joe had time to question him further about the job, crashed the glass down on the table and said to him aggressively, 'Now come on, Joe, you are going to call my mother aren't you? She really wants to hear from you. She wants to tell you her favourite Macmillan story. She's told everyone else so there's no reason why you should escape. It's quite a good story, too. He was staying at the embassy, when she was there in Washington. And Perdita wants to bully you. She said so herself at the breakfast table this morning. She said you looked like the kind of person who would respond well to a good tongue-lashing. She said she couldn't wait to start. She bet you had some good lines of repartee stored up in that mug of yours. Those were her exact words. Imagine, my sister talking like that. I was shocked. That's your influence already.'

'I'll bet. She must be psychic, your sister, just like her mother. She's got me in one. I've travelled the world and the seven seas looking for a good tongue-lasher. "Seek and ye shall find," as the Good Lord said, and JC would have known, after casting out the money changers. But tell me, Pugh, how did you get the job? It fell out of the sky, or what?'

Pugh looked shifty for a second. Apprehension twisted his features into something quite unpleasantly powerful and demanding as an expression. Someone who was used to getting his own way, willy-nilly. He looked dark and froward. Then the look passed. He was young and sunny again.

'You remember when you came down to see us? Well, you remember that I told you I'd just been to see someone from Sloane School about a job?'

Joe admitted, falsely, that he had forgotten. Rivers looked relieved to find himself dealing with someone who could only recall card sequences. More frankly, he then told Joe very quickly that he'd been put in touch with someone else from Sloane School almost immediately, an interview had been arranged and the meeting had gone very smoothly, and he was due to start work the following week, since he was available on the spot. Oddly, despite his evident excitement, Pugh stressed the low salary, the setback to his ambitions at the FO, and some of the other drawbacks to the job. Joe put it all down to shame, for the time being.

'I don't want to say any more at this stage because it may all not work out, so forgive me if I'm a tiny bit evasive on some of the finer points. I'm being like that with everyone, even my old school friends, so it's not just you, Joe. The job, I'm told, may take me out of the UK for a while. Initially I'm told there's quite a lot of travelling, but that's no bad thing since I think I ought to lie low and let the report blow over. Out of sight out of mind, that sort of thing. Let the noble house of Pugh slumber for a while in people's minds. That's why I was so keen to make contact with you again. I'm leaving for the continent quite shortly, and I'm going to be away for some time. You could look after my mother and Perdita while I'm away, at least that's if you want to. You may have other ideas, and you may not want to, but I have to tell you you've made quite a hit with my family. Think about it, Joe. If you get bored with your bridge you can nip down to Pugh Park as I do and be waited upon hand and foot. Not such a poor prospect, eh? And Perdita wants to learn bridge, how about that?'

He looked at Joe, suggesting that anyone who turned down an offer like that would have to be mad. But Joe was mad. He wanted to complete his mission and then leave town and he didn't want anything to stand in the way of that plan. He had resolved not to be lured into the Pugh bosom. He avoided a direct reply. He particularly did not want to teach bridge to Perdita.

'When did you say they were coming up to town?'

'That's just the thing, Joe. They're coming up in two days time. So we could all meet for lunch and have a good chat and my mother can tell you—'

'Her favourite Macmillan story?'

'Oh, more than that. She'll tell you the Macmillan joke in the first five minutes. No, better. She's found some letters from French soldiers at the front and she's planning to translate them into English and add them to the collection. Make a contrast, you understand. She says they're quite superb. A pity you don't speak

French; you could help her with the translation.'

And Joe, whose French was fluent, like his German, could feel languages shrinking in his brain to the size of a pea as Rivers made his rapid, false assumptions. This agent does not speak French, Joe told himself. No French, he told himself again, just no French. I am a brainless provincial English idiot. I do not know what *va te faire enculer à sec* means – and I never have done. Nor *ceux qui sont pas jouasses je vais leur claquer le baigneur*. Still less have I ever read François Villon, no, not a single line, ever. Ever, ever, ever.

Rivers was starting to irritate Joe with his effortless optimism. Joe had started thinking about Thailand again and whether it would make a trade to pay for that month's mortgage. Rivers chattered on, confident that he had secured the vital bridgehead towards making contact with Joe. The wine flowed freely. He made merry and insisted on paying for the drinks. Joe did not put up too great a resistance.

Out of the corner of his eye Joe glimpsed the sad, mad, formerly haughty blonde make her dreary, uncertain and confused way into the restaurant and then drag her steps in the direction of the dealers. Who were, of course, waiting for her. Not at all surprised either. She still had some money with which to pay them, but not a great deal. She was beginning to look tatty at the edges, Joe thought, and the eyes were becoming more glazed and more fixed. She kept running her hand restlessly through her hair as though she had some small bug hidden among the tresses. Won't be long now, he thought, as Rivers chatted on about his sister.

Joachim reported back to Annie. Bootface had left the room a few moments previously and she was pleased by his departure. She felt in greater control when he was absent. Everything went more smoothly, especially the dialogue with the agents and watchers outside the listening post.

'Joachim, thanks for calling. How did it go?'

'Good, very good. I gave him World War II stuff as we agreed, and I started him off on the Cairncross story. He's a smart lad, Joe. He didn't say more than a few words. He just sat there and drank it all in. I left him some of the Cairncross writings so that he can start reading it. He'll read it too. He liked the sound of those big numbers, I could tell.'

'How long did it last? What kind of atmosphere was there?'

'The atmosphere was good. Very relaxed. And he was there early. I was impressed by that. It was a pity that I had to leave when I did.'

'What do you mean?'

Suddenly the air was turning icy for Annie. She tried to keep the anxiety out of her voice, but to no avail. Joachim caught the panic.

'Don't worry, Annie. One of his pals turned up at the table and rather commandeered the situation. So I cleared off.'

'Very wise. What time would that have been?'

With great care Annie tried to frame her next question nonchalantly. It was hard to do. She didn't want to disturb Joachim so that he inevitably would start framing his replies differently. But she could feel deep apprehension beating away in her mind. Intelligence work involved hunches. Sixth senses. Intuition. Something like that. Flashes of perception. But Annie had more than a hunch. She felt a deep tremor of unease at the thought that Joe had odd friends who turned up unexpectedly in search of him. He wasn't supposed to have any friends by now. He was supposed to be alone. And what friends he still possessed, she knew all about. That was the deal. He had been closely monitored. Care was beating now at the windows. She needed reassurance. Joachim said that he had left Zorba's at around ten thirty.

'And the friend? Any thoughts?'

'Young chap. Very excited. Full of himself. He'd just landed a new job and naturally he was grateful to Joe because of what happened last week. So he wanted to thank him for saving him.'

Care had become a bird of prey beating at the windowpanes.

'What happened last week? What's this business of saving him? You never mentioned that in your report.' Annie was very precise about these things.

'Didn't I tell you? I thought I did.'

'You didn't.'

'I'm sorry. The young man was in Zorba's, weeping over

something, a report I think, and then he left and was lucky not to get himself beaten up by some thugs. Joe intervened. He was out of the restaurant for about half an hour and then he returned alone, so I assume that he'd seen him home.'

'Name of the young man? Did you manage to catch that?'

Bootface came back into the room looking supremely bored. Annie was not on the speakerphone. She nodded her head noncommittally.

'Name of Pugh, at least I think that's what he was called. Yes, I'm certain of it. It was Pugh. He talked about his four uncles getting killed in the First World War. Yes, it was Pugh.'

'Sure of that.'

'Yes, I'm sure. It's Pugh.'

'Thanks, Joachim. And well done.'

Bootface made to take the extension but Annie motioned him away. Bootface frowned. Annie concluded the discussion with Joachim and clicked out. Bootface looked angry and excluded. But Annie disregarded him. She didn't want Bootface hearing about Pugh. It would create just too much hassle. Bootface would not grasp the importance of checking every available fact about the reality out there. He would carp at the suggestion. But for Annie, Joachim's unexpected revelation about what sounded like Joe's fisticuffs was pure gold. It enlightened everything with a future glow. Bootface was not meticulous about detail whereas Annie was fanatical about the reconstruction of what was really going on out there, far from the gazebo. On this occasion she preferred to do her own fieldwork. If nothing substantial materialised, she could not be accused of being alarmist or womanly or anything else derogatory that Bootface cared to invent and throw at her. And if something did turn up, well, then she had some extra edge over Bootface, when push came to shove. Wouldn't that be nice!

'Joachim was pleased with the way it all went. He got the stuff across to Joe and Joe took it all in quite easily according to Joachim. Joachim said that Joe was very receptive...'

Annie continued to talk, knowing that Bootface had already switched off. Bootface was the original top-down intelligence operative. He was devoured by concept, a dangerously simple approach, in Annie's opinion. It disregarded – consistently – the human factor. Annie was far more painstaking. Only time would tell who was right.

Joe left the restaurant with Rivers. Rivers was drunk and happy and paid far too much of the bill. Joe let him get on with it. He was too thoughtful to interfere. The night was dark but warm. Not hostile or threatening. Or not yet anyway. Joe had forgotten about the blonde who had left the restaurant long since, clutching her foil. He had things on his mind.

Rivers wanted to skip about on the pavement in joy at being retrieved and wanted while Joe was more concerned to lock the bits and pieces of his own personal jigsaw into place. Suddenly his world had become more crowded. And more urgent. And perilous. He had Tom Stone to contact; there was Emma to accommodate; he had some briefing to absorb about a strange country he had once heard tell of, namely the UK, situated somewhere in the North Sea; and there was a mission out there too, which was pulling him in very fast, almost as fast as the Pugh family was trying to rope him in. A dangerous mission, as well. Joe had no illusions on that score. He could feel his skin crawling at the fear to come as it used to flinch in the old days, in Berlin. And wasn't it about time he tried to make some more money from the markets, not to mention the little matter of finding Marcello? He inhabited a busy old world all of a sudden.

Rivers capered about on the pavement in his carefree exuberance. He began to irritate Joe, not least because he had interrupted the tête-à-tête with Joachim. Joe wanted to learn more about the strange vision which Joachim had conjured up for him. Rivers had interrupted all that with his plea for attention.

Very carefully, Joe arranged to cross the road where Stormin' Norman, the huge and ferocious tramp with a dirty shaven bullet head like the top of a post, was still seated on the pavement despite the late hour, begging furiously and abusively. Norman was in the unreconstructed section of beggary. He greeted Joe with cordiality. 'Hello, you fat cunt. So where's that money you promised me?'

Rivers stepped back and aside instinctively. Norman noted the fear. He was on him in a flash. 'Who's your boyfriend then? I didn't think you were like that, Joe, but then you never can tell, can you? 'Ere, pretty boy, come 'ere and I'll give you a good belting as well as a blow job, you little fairy. What you need is a good thrashing, you know that. Yes, you do, you'd love it, wouldn't you, you fucking pansy? Where d'you find him, Joe, down what little lavatory, eh, eh?'

Norman scowled at Rivers as he abused him. The correct course of response was for Rivers to give as good as he got and really lay into Stormin'. But he couldn't do it. Rivers looked sick. He was silent.

Joe wished Norman a pleasant evening in the language of the street. 'Look, Norman, you piece of shit, don't you fucking dare talk to anyone I'm with like that, or I'll kick your sodding goolies so hard they'll come out of your ears. So watch it!'

Norman laughed his hollow booming Newgate laugh at the repartee and breathed out in a great wheeze of contempt, a detestable look of loathing spreading across his countenance at the idea of taking a whip to Rivers.

''Ere, look, come here, fairy, I want to tell you something.' The gross Norman leaned forward invitingly. His great belly wobbled like a waterbed round his waist as he leaned forward.

'Don't go near him, Rivers; he'll grab your ankle.'

Rivers kept his distance. He looked as if he'd seen a troll. He was white with rage. Stormin' laughed again and made to undo his flies and flash his prick at Rivers but then he wearied of the game. He buttoned up his flies.

''Ere, Joe, tell you what, guess what I just seen. And guess what I just got. Eh? Go on, guess.'

'I don't know and I don't care, you great piece of shit. Fuck right off and die.'

'No seriously, look what I got.'

Norman held up a ten-pound note. He leered again at the two of them from his seat on the pavement.

'I got it from a woman. She went by just a minute ago. And I'll tell you why. See, I love big dominant women, right. You know, really huge women who shout and swear at you. I love it. Angry women. Can't get enough of them. It makes me feel so ohhhhh! Know what I mean? Anyway, I go to those orgies when I can

156

afford it, you know with spikes and knives and all that kind of gear, and I have just a great time. The women go crazy all night. Anyway, like I was saying, this woman went past just now and I recognised her. She was at one of those orgies. I think it was in Shepherd's Bush but I can't be quite sure. I still recognised her. Who she was with tonight looked ever so respectable, and he certainly doesn't know about what she gets up to when he's not around, I can tell you. What she was doing to the man she was with I couldn't even start to tell you. Not nice though for him. She gave me such a look as she went past with her head up there in the air. But she sees me and she knows it's me and she suddenly comes back in a great hurry and thrusts this note into my hand and then rushes off again in a terrible hurry. Not a word to me, though. She's bought my silence. Hah, hah, hah.'

Norman gave another spine-chilling rendition of the Newgate laugh and Joe started to giggle at the idea of Stormin' capering round in his mask and tutu.

'Maybe she gave you the money because she was grateful for what you did to her, Stormin'.'

Stormin' grew vexed at Joe's laughter and made another attempt to grab his ankles. Joe kicked his hand hard and caught it on the volley.

Norman snarled at him. 'So come on, you fat cunt, give me some money.'

'What'll you settle for? Fifty pence?'

'More, you bastard, more, I've got to get home tonight. Make it a pound and I'll give you a copy of the *Big Issue*. Go on, give me a pound.'

'Done. Here's a pound, but only provided you don't give me a copy of the *Big Issue*.'

'We're not all rich like you, Joe.'

'That's because you don't have my brains, you twat. Here, take your pound.'

Joe reached into his pocket and pulled out three pound coins, and rolled them across the pavement just beyond Norman's reach. The tramp scrabbled nimbly on the ground as they rolled by and grabbed them. He rammed them fast into his pocket.

'And I'll never call you a fat cunt again, Joe. And I won't call you a fairy no more either, you little fairy.'

Joe laughed again, aimed another kick at Norman and then passed back across the street, followed by a wondering Rivers.

'Why did you give him any money? I never give them anything at all. They're just lazy. They shouldn't be encouraged. You shouldn't help them like that.'

Sober by now, Rivers disapproved of Joe's generosity but Joe just shrugged, wondering if he'd gone too far in allowing Rivers to pay so much of the bill. Joe was about ten pounds ahead, in terms of what he should have paid, so indirectly and net-net it was Rivers who had paid the tramp. Joe did not point this quiet piece of irony out to Rivers. Instead he wandered down with him to Battersea Bridge gradually disentangling himself from Pugh but not before promising to call Lady Pugh at some early point in the next few days. Rivers was too insistent for Joe to demur. Distrustful of his own reactions in the direction of one Perdita Pugh, Joe promised that he would make the call. So Rivers succeeded in pinning him down at last. But Joe thought he'd had the last laugh because Rivers had been truly shocked and appalled by his brief encounter with Norman, wholly engineered in turn by Joe.

## Chapter Nine

Joe had two phone calls to make the next morning and then immediately afterwards he had a date to keep with Emma at Peter Jones. Up on the top floor of Peter Jones in the coffee room, where the ladies gossiped about their families, perched high above Sloane Square.

Emma and Joe were going in search of Gregory. It would be quite a busy morning. Almost the life of a very rich man in its spartan simplicity, he told himself, except for the fact that he had no money at all. Just a detail, Joe; the money's on hold, he told himself firmly as he debated which call to make first. Like death, the money will come. Eventually, he hoped. That was his mantra. He sang it to himself most days. He was not superstitious in the slightest bit. He didn't really care which call he did make first but he wanted to ease his way into the morning. He was taking precautions. A setback, a harsh atmosphere or a cross word of exasperation, and the ambience would be destroyed. He would start the day ruffled. And that would hit morale. He had to tread warily, because morale was a flighty bird.

Mindful of the crack, he made his decision carefully. He called his broker. Get some market feel, he thought, before I wander through the looking glass into the alternative world I know and love so much. He planned to call the Pughs a good deal later in the day.

He dialled his number. He connected.

'Campbell.'

'Joe here. Good morning.'

'I was wondering what had happened to you. How are you?'

'Very fit, Sid, very fit indeed.'

'Still above the arches, are we?'

'Treading water, Sid. The arches look lovely from this distance. I could eat them. Mind you, the president is even closer to the water than I am now.'

Joe heard an intake of breath by Sid. Get the frighteners on him quick, he thought.

'Sid, it stands to reason. No way can he wiggle out of this one. There's the dress; there's Starr; there's all this testimony. It's getting closer all the time. He'll step down before he's impeached. I know it.'

More heavy breathing by Sid.

'Look Sid, I'll make it easy for you. Close out your position and I'll settle for a trip to see Inter-Milan. Now you can't get fairer than that, can you?'

Pause from Sid, an awkward pause, followed by a long, slow and deeply felt sigh down the line. The Clinton situation was testing Sid's mettle sorely. But he wouldn't budge.

'No, Joe, I'm not trading this one. I'm hanging in there.'

Damn, thought Joe.

'Don't say you weren't offered an out on this... But meanwhile I have an idea.'

'When was the day when you didn't have an idea, Joe? That's why we get on so well together. You pitch and I catch. Come on, sell it to me, baby.'

'How does the account look, Sid? Tell me that first.'

'How much do you need?'

'The usual for the usual payments. I'm not going in big on this one. Not to start with anyway.'

'Wait one.'

Joe heard Sid click on his screen and pull up his account details. Joe knew the numbers as well as Sid. He was playing for time, trying to get the feel of the market through Sid's tone of voice. It might help him a little.

'Joe, when you say the usual, you mean your mortgage and the council tax and all that sort of thing, right?'

'Right.'

'You've got about five thousand over and above that. How does that square with your numbers?'

'Sounds about right.'

Joe used to keep about two million on special deposit or parked in the market. He was a far cry from that kind of money now.

'Okay, Sid, send Visa a cheque for the usual.'

Without a bank account, Joe had to work all his payments through a credit card. Complicated and expensive but so far it had worked.

'Will do, Joe. Now, what's the big idea?'

'I was thinking of buying Thailand.' Joe heard a sharp intake of breath at the mention of Thailand, whose near bankruptcy had rocked all markets nearly to destruction about six months ago. Sid was not a risk-taker in that league. 'Fortunately I thought better of it.'

A relieved exhalation of breath. Sid felt better now. He liked to follow Joe into a situation and that was one of the reasons why he had been so generous in extending the line of credit to one of the City's ex-movers and shakers. Sid knew Joe had an eye for a market situation and so far Sid had been right – Joe had made money for him by his stock-picking. So Sid in turn was popular with the clients. Because they had made money out of Sid's recommendations, that is, Joe's ideas. They all followed him into the situations that he picked out. And so the great investment world went round.

But Thailand? Oh, no, Joe, anything but Thailand… That was Sid's reaction. He had a wife and kids and a business to tend. Not Thailand.

Joe hit him squarely on the volley. 'I thought I'd go for South Korea instead. Only kidding about Thailand. There's a currency play, because the won is starting to recover against the dollar, profits are beginning to come through for the chaebols, as the trade account recovers, and I just like the look of that particular emerging market. Could be a good trade, Sid. I'm poised to buy. It's an in and outer, I'll tell you. I'm not there for long. But the emergings look hot. The Americans are pushing like crazy to get the Asian credit rating back in line, because their own current account looks so bad, so it's time…'

'All right, all right, I'll go along with you, Joe.' Sid sounded resigned. Joe could be very persuasive. 'I am not happy with any of this but the boy must have his head. So South Korea it is. But you have to tell me some more about how you're going to buy into the country. Have you got a vehicle?'

'Just the one but you'll like it. It'll kill you. It came to me in a dream last night.'

'That's more than what came to me last night.'

'Sid, your one and only Big Bang was ten years ago. Since then, nothing. Anyway, listen to me. About a year ago, I don't know if you remember, there was a real fuckwit of a guy who set up an investment trust based exclusively on Asian discounts, name of Praliffer. You remember Guy Praliffer?'

'Used to be a flash git broker in the old days, is that the one? Wasn't he with Panmure's?'

'Exactly. The man himself. Except that he wasn't with Panmure's. Try Brasenose.'

'Joe, such an eye for detail you have. But Praliffer, we haven't heard too much about him recently, come to think of it.'

'I'm not surprised, Sid. He very nearly went under last year. He got the Asian debt thing completely wrong and went into it loaded with Korean stock up to the eyeballs.'

'So. That means he's the wrong way all the way up.'

'Yes, but Sid, I happen to know, because I read the newspapers every day, that Praliffer is planning to merge all his Asian trusts with Marshall Morgan, whose funds are completely liquid. So Praliffer can average immediately and watch the market chase itself all the way up. It's a small deal but very highly geared. Even the discount looks good. It's about twenty-six per cent, so really bomberooboo territory. We can't go wrong.'

Sid was impressed. He whistled. 'Joe, where did you find this out? It's a beauty. I've heard "Can't go wrong" before, but I have to admit that this does sound good.'

'It was in the weekend *Chron*. I nearly missed it myself and even when I did see it, it didn't register immediately. Then it all clicked together. Round about four in the morning, but it still clicked.'

'As they do, just when she turns over again and says—'

'Give us another one, just like the other one.'

'Joe, I'm surprised at you. You know all the words as well. And here's me thinking you were such a well-brought-up boy. What's the name of the Praliffer fund?'

'Chaebol Trust, would you believe? So imaginative, isn't it?

The last price I saw was around 120p, so why don't we say ten thousand at 122p. Or thereabouts. That shouldn't hit the account too badly.'

'No, you've got a safety margin. I'll grant you that. Want to hang on while I check the price?'

'Go right ahead.'

Joe waited while Sid went and checked prices with his dealer. A good conversation. It all augured well. Sid sounded happy enough. But he was coming up to Becher's Brook very shortly and he didn't relish it one little bit; he had to make his little phone call to Tom Stone. That could be very tricky indeed because of the implications. He felt just a little bit like a rat in a trap. Trading stock was easy by comparison. Far easier.

Sid came bustling back to the phone. 'Joe, I'm sorry, but it looks as if someone else has had your idea as well. They're 132p choice.'

'Okay, that's fine, just buy me fifteen thousand at that price.'

Sid was on his guard. 'I thought we said ten thousand.'

'This is a fast-moving situation, Sid. I'm not going to hang around. I want stock and I want it now. You know how it is. I'll have fifteen thousand now and I'm out at 160p or thereabouts, if they look as if they're going to get there, that is.'

Sid was sufficiently impressed by Joe's idea and the ongoing speed of the market's reaction to Chaebol Trust that he meekly took the order, much to Joe's surprise but also to his considerable relief. He didn't want to miss the offer. He also wanted to get on with talking to Tom Stone.

'I'll do what I can, Joe. Can't do better than that.'

'Good on you, Sid. Call me back with the prices.'

They were parting on reasonably good terms. Down went the phone, and Joe returned to his dismal little flat just off the King's Road with the crack in the wall outside. But Joe ignored the dusty walls. He was back in the market and he felt better for that. A bit of trade and a bit of fear and a bit of excitement – that knocked the cobwebs of doubt away with one blow.

He sat by the phone. Now for Monsieur Stone and a different kind of girl entirely. He paused a few minutes before he made the call. It was back in the dark labyrinth again. He gathered himself.

This was real, or at least real enough to die through. More times of uncertainty and lack of trust. Groping on tiptoe and in silence through the dark rooms, one after the other, and all identical to each other, except that one room contained a killer. That was how it was usually. No reason this time why it should be any different. Joe had been here before, many times.

He composed himself and then fully cognisant of his actions, and the setting thereto, he dialled Tom Stone's number.

'*Chron*, Stone.'

'Tom Stone, it's Joe here. You left a message for me to call you last night. I'm afraid I got back too late to return your call.'

'And of course I'm returning your previous call. Joe, I never quite got to the bottom of your call. There was a slight disturbance at your end.'

That was nicely put, thought Joe as the image of a suddenly rejuvenated Ursula grabbing the phone from him flashed through his mind. I'm going to be as easy as possible with him over this double-talk of a conversation. Make it simple for him.

'Yes, there was something in your column that I couldn't quite grasp, but it doesn't matter now. It was something about the US bond market, but no matter.'

He must play to me now, thought Joe, if he's anything of a professional at this. And if he's not a professional, then I'm really and truly in deep shit all of a sudden. This is no place for an amateur. Have they sent me a professional or not? Have they?

'Yes, these ideas come and go, don't they? One minute they're very hot and then almost at once they're as cold as ice. I imagine you're an investor, are you?'

'Something like that. But a reader as well.'

This sounds good, thought Joe. It's worth being a bit glib. He's very polished. He's doing it well. No questions about background, nothing about Ursula, just an easy acceptance of the existence of the relationship. Very promising. No wonder we get journalists.

'Got any thoughts at all on the market now, Joe? I'm always looking around for something to write about in the column.'

This sounds great. Completely fabulous. Your time is too absorbed now with a certain somebody, thought Joe, for you to bother with doing any work. So you're going to play me as a feed.

Excellent. Acting on instruction? Or not? Who cares; it sounds good. That's all that matters. Well, let me try this on you. The first cut is always the cheapest, so they say, and they should know.

'Tom, I'm doing some trading in the Asian emergings. I won't be too stock-specific because that would compromise you, although Chaebol Trust does look a honey of a stock.' Joe spoke easily and with assurance as he slid the puff for his investment into the discussion. 'Enough of that, though. On a macro level the region may be on the turn. The US is pushing like crazy to restore the credit ratings of these countries and in the process reduce the risk aversion levels of the average fund manager. I think the US is succeeding here, so I see spreads against US Treasuries coming in very sharply. It'll be done through the bonds, of course. It looks very obvious to me. I think the spreads are about one thousand basis points at the moment and I guess they'll narrow maybe to six hundred bepees. That makes for a strong local stock market rally in anyone's money. I've bought a little bit of stock just to get my feet wet. I'm happy to hold...'

'Of course.'

'So there's no question of a quick in and out.'

Like I'm a holder for a week, thought Joe. An eternity or something similar. But what a beautiful scam, if you buy the idea and then run it in the column.

'I'll certainly look into it. It might make an idea for the column.'

Joe felt a massive sense of relief overhaul him like a warm wave. Wow. Just wow, wow, wow! Think of the money, he thought. Think of the profit. If you had the backing of the Stone weekly column, think how much easier it might be for you to stay afloat. He could puff your ideas as and when, up they would go in the market and out you would come... With a nice fat profit. Maybe this is what the Gents had in mind when they set up the connection. Oh, precious Gents, swine of my life...

'Let's be in touch, Joe. The more I think about the Asians, the more I like it. I'll do some work on it. There could be some mileage in this. For the column, you understand. Let's stay in touch. You've got my number and I've got yours, so we can communicate.'

'We could always meet for lunch.'

'Not just yet, I think. I'm terribly booked up for the next month or so. Not a single space in my diary. But we can certainly speak over the phone.'

It was the right answer. Joe felt even better. Quite giddy almost, all of a sudden. Had Tom accepted Joe's artfully posed invitation, that would have been sudden death for the whole idea of a go-between in the mission. Tom would have revealed himself to be an idiot. Quite unsuitable for the mission. There could be no meeting ever between them. Their contact was strictly impersonal. Anything more intimate was too dangerous. Emotions got involved. They might like each other, which would be fatal. Or loathe each other, which would be marginally better, but only just.

For the mission to succeed and for the communication line to get off the ground, it was absolutely and completely axiomatic that they should both remain invisible to each other. Just voices down a line attached to a tube. Nothing more. Those were the rules and that was how it was played. Always. Without exception. And Tom Stone had played absolutely right down the line, Joe thought. Bully for him.

They exchanged a few more pleasantries, and then Tom hung up. Joe paced about in his flat, feeling pensive. He liked the idea of the contact with Tom Stone and he liked the idea of making some money out of it, but he could not conceal from himself, now that the discussion was over, that it left him feeling thoughtful. Deep in puzzled reflection. Very poised, indeed almost balletic on his toes, such was his sense of alertness. It was perilous. No question. He had to be right about this one, and right on the ball, on top of it all the time. Snipers. Berlin. Empty squares. Death on parade. It was all one to him.

His phone rang again. It was Sid.

'Good and bad news, I'm afraid, Joe. We bought your stock for you and we paid 135p a share. The market was tight but we got the order in. But as soon as we'd done the bargain, someone came along and dumped a whole load of stock on the market, so Chaebol Trust is back down now to 128p in the middle and heading south.'

'Fuck it, Sid, I want some more.'

'What? You're averaging already. I don't like the sound of that. You normally throw an enormous wobbly if the price starts moving against you, right at the start. What's got into you?'

Sid did not know that Joe might just be in a position to ramp the price via the good offices of Tom Stone and his column. Sid could be very prim on occasion. And he was behind the times this bright and sunny morning. That was for sure.

'Look, fuck you, Sid and just—' Joe heard the brakes screech in his mind. No time to get smart with Sid. This was not cool. Haul back and then more so again. He couldn't afford to upset Sid. Without Sid, he had no money at all. He had to resist the onrush of power, the massive thump-thump of which had returned instantly, just because he'd made contact with a stupid hack. Who very likely would do him no end of harm. Joe closed down his mind. He backed off.

'Forgive me, Sid. I'm having trouble with transitive verbs this morning. When I said "Fuck you", what I really meant to say was, "How wise you are to query the buying order of your impetuous and loutish client." A mere slip of the tongue. Verbally, I was maladroit. Consider it forgotten.'

Sid laughed and sounded mollified, more than just a fraction. Joe heard him gurgle into the phone. Sid was Jewish as well as being a tough broker. He could recognise a spot of tactical grovelling. Chutzpah in spades to him. Also Sid liked the rough and tumble with clients. It made him feel more alive, always provided the clients came up with good market ideas after giving him verbal. That made it worthwhile.

'Well, Joe, do you want the extra stock or not?'

'Maybe not, Sid. The urge to trade has left me. I am detached now. Tell you what, if they get back to 120p, I'll have some more, say another five thousand. But not before that price.'

'For one moment, Joe, I thought you were human when you started slagging me off. But I should have known better from the ice cube.'

'I was starved on a hillside as a child, Sid. Iron rations and no mother's milk. No cradle tit. That's what does it. It gives you a basic lack of humanity.'

'Enough of your foul-tongued rubbish. I have business to transact. Good luck with the trade, Joe.'

'Thanks, Sid. We'll see. Tell me, Sid, what's my stop-loss position on Chaebol?'

'For you, Joe, around 110p.'

'You'll call me before you cut the position? Promise me. It feels good to me. You can't see these things. You're too close. And you're just a broker.'

'Pshaw!' or its north London Scottish equivalent came floating down the line as Sid rang off. Joe could see Sid almost instantly picking up the phone to another client.

'Oh, good morning, Lady Jolligobarmy, and isn't it a wonderful morning? Yes, of course, but I wonder if you're interested in a little situation I've been watching for some time and which is now maturing. It's called Chaebol Trust. Yes, you know it? Fascinating, isn't it. Such a shrewd operator old Praliffer. Well, I've got a little line of stock to place – yes, about fifteen thousand – and I can let you have them at 130p, if you're interested. The discount is very attractive... You'll take five thousand? Splendid. I know you won't be disappointed. No, the emergings are coming back into their own very forcefully all of a sudden. Thank you Lady Jolligobarmy.'

Joe paced about, envying Sid his quiet life of churning stock, and wondering about Tom Stone. Not as an individual but as a piece of the action. Tom Stone was suddenly very important to Joe, Ursula or otherwise.

In certain circumstances, British intelligence would send in a two-man team, one as a front man, the other as the discreet back-up. That meant there were four possible permutations available at any given moment: change the front man and keep the back-up; do the opposite; change both of them; or keep them both in place, depending on the maturity of the mission. The mission could go ahead quite gaily as all these options were being explored, almost as an independent concept. But for really big missions, two men were too cumbersome and too easily detected. More flexible was the system of sending in one man but with dual back-up, one to receive and one to transmit. That way the secrecy was optimal. Neither of the two back-ups would be aware of the other; neither had any more than limited knowledge of the whole operation. Only control had that luxury. And the flow of information was circular. All very neat and tidy.

So in this case the structure was obvious. Joachim would receive Joe's messages and Tom would transmit instructions, as and when required. This would be done very rarely since the progress of the mission would be murky and hard to define. No point in giving instructions if they might turn out to be false. But Joe's contact with Tom could be pretty continuous, because they had a common interest in the markets. And likewise with Joachim. This had taken a lot of patient work and planning, so much was obvious.

And to what end? The Gents wouldn't go to that kind of trouble just for the theoretical pleasures of the exercise. There had to be real danger attached to what he was supposed to be doing for this little cat's cradle to be set up. And ditto the rationale behind his incarceration in his Sloane Square open prison, one of the best and most beautiful nicks in town. Yes, real danger, with real bullets and real deaths and tragedies. And when would the shooting start? And would he survive? And would he ever see his money and his possessions and normality ever again?

Joe suppressed these thoughts focusing on anything that came to mind in order to drive the sick sense of time utterly wasted and trashed right out from his mind. He knew full well at that moment, in a blinding flash of clarity, that only the Gents could have busted him down to this point. Only the Gents had the power to place his assets under lock and key. Only the Gents could have brought him with such accuracy to this precise point in space and time. Because he had a job to do for them. And what job? Oh, to get himself half killed most likely, if not wholly wasted. A child could have answered that question. And would Joe play ball? Joe knew without blinking that he would play along. He had no choice. That was the beauty of the whole procedure. He had only one way to go in order to survive. Only one way out from the nick, otherwise he was stuck in poverty playing bridge with the dames for the rest of his life. He had to play the game. Also there was no sense in grieving over any of that. What was done was done. He had only one direction in which to walk in order to exit from his prison – even if there were shooters aimed at him along the route. Such a cool little fate the Gents had cooked up for him. So sweet and elegant...

Joe slammed the door of his flat behind him, gazed for a second at the crack in the wall, found that it had remained unchanged from where it had been during the night, concluded that he was still sane, albeit perhaps partially, and hastened down the King's Road to meet Emma Bales, bent on a quite different mission.

At least he was back in the market and trading stock. That was something. He wondered what those Chaebol shares were selling at right now as he jumped onto a bus heading fast for Sloane Square. He was out at 160p, that was for sure. The bus crashed the lights very brutally at the junction of the King's Road and Beaufort Street, jerking Joe's mind on to a different track. He mused with some irony on the possibility that Tom Stone's little romance with Ursula might have to take second place in the column to other more pressing requirements.

Joe hoped fervently to be invited to another Thursday morning bridge session. Would Ursula be clutching the *Financial Chronicle* on this occasion, he wondered, if the billets-doux of Stone weren't going to be there? Pray God one of the dames found herself marooned on the hard shoulder of the M4, just by Junction 12. He wanted to see Ursula's long face. Or joyous face – Stone might not run his idea at all. Stone had a lot of scope on this one. Joe might be totally mistaken about the whole thing. Only time would tell.

Meanwhile he had a small surprise for young Emma Bales. Best to let the conversation flow before he made his small gesture. Joe had done some homework on the likely whereabouts of the missing Gregory. He might only be a phone call away. But he wasn't going to tell that to Emma straight away. Joe knew about finding missing people by now; it should be a long process.

The bus crashed along the King's Road narrowly missing four or five pedestrians taking the morning air as they wandered across sundry zebra crossings. Much gesticulation in both directions from driver and SW3 denizens. Much mutual loathing.

They arrived all of a heap at Sloane Square and the bus

smashed to a halt. After narrowly escaping head-butting an octogenarian nun as the brakes went on, Joe wandered into Peter Jones. It had the dark cool feel of a cathedral in the early morning as shoppers sauntered among the departments, touching a fabric here, feeling a length of curtain material there, amid a myriad of quizzical appraisals. Joe was familiar with the Peter Jones ambience. He had been dragged the length and breadth of the store by Liz Playfair's bridge dames, while discussing some foul bridge convention, as they hunted down a birthday present for a god-daughter who had just had some very bad news over her A levels and desperately needed cheering up. 'Yes, I'll take that now. Here's my card. Yes, I would like it wrapped. Yes, I'll wait. Now, Joe, the principal of Stayman is what? I just don't seem to be able to grasp it. Do explain again. If I open a weak no trump, what happens then?'

Joe stood in the lift hemmed in by three pushchairs and babies, mothers standing resolutely behind each chair like dog handlers. No sound in the lift as all eyes focused on the guide to the floors above the doors. Lift doors slamming shut, then opening, then slamming. Joe reached the top floor alone. He wandered past the carpets, spread out in their enticing dark respectability and went into the coffee room. No sign of Emma Bales.

Joe joined the queue and bought two coffees, one for himself and one for Emma. It saved time, although by now she was only five minutes late. If she didn't want the coffee, it could always be changed. Joe found a spot over by the window overlooking the leafy spread of Sloane Square. Bright sunlight streamed through the leaves below in the square. Children played solemnly on the café floor watched with great vigilance by their mothers for any indications of excess exuberance. The odd passing Peter Jones domestic added a friendly hand to the children at play and was watched in turn with stiffening alarm by the mothers. The great English country house charivari, which can take root anywhere that people know each other or have mutual connections, was in full swing and the atmosphere was well strung with carefully modulated performances, even at that early hour.

Joe watched a trim but bulky figure swing through the entrance with heart-skipping vim and recognised Emma in her jeans and T-shirt, wholly unrepentant for her unpunctuality, looking like a cross between a rich woman and a student.

'I think it's the bag that does it, Emma.'

'Sorry I'm late, Joe. What d'you mean, the bag? Oh, you are such a thoughtful angel for getting the coffee in. What do I owe you?'

'The Exchequer will run to coffees this morning, ma'am.'

'I can't get over you being so poor, Joe. It's really upset me, you don't know how much. I thought about you all last night, and I was worried. But what do you mean, the bag does it?' She stirred the cream into her coffee. No sugar.

'Most of the women in this neighbourhood, even if they wear jeans, make sure that you know that they're still worth fifty million bucks. The jeans always look expensive, just so that you don't make a mistake and think they're part of the hoi polloi. But you wear jeans as if you grew up in them, No give-away. None elsewhere either, apart from the bag.'

Emma looked at her bag, and shrugged at the showcase aspect of it all.

'The bag is by Deliss. In case you ever need one, Joe, they're in St Alban's Grove, W8. But you missed the shoes. From the same stable.' She looked down at her shoes which were cut, as Joe now noticed, to match the bag in colour and styling. 'I have fat feet, you see, Joe, which need careful attention from cobblers. Which they didn't get in the past. But which they do now. The bonus from my wealth. My feet no longer hurt, thanks to them. Bliss from Deliss. The bag is extra. So there, clever clogs.'

She put her tongue out at Joe, fished in the bag and brought out a packet of Silk Cut, a lighter and a mobile phone.

'You talk rot, Joe. I look just like everyone else in my jeans. D'you mind if I smoke?'

'You never used to smoke.'

'There's a lot of things I never used to do, which I do now. When will men get used to the idea that women... I'm sorry, Joe, forgive me. I mustn't jump on my hobby horse and I must stop using that line. It's ridiculous. It worked in Norwich society but it sounds silly here. No, as you were saying, smoking; let's get back to that. I started in Norfolk because all the girls smoked and I felt a fool sitting around waving my hands and looking virtuous, so I joined the gang. I don't really like smoking to be honest, but I find that it does soothe my nerves. And they need soothing this morning. That's why I'm late.'

'Because you've been smoking.'

'No, you ninny, because—' Emma's phone rang. She picked it up.

'Emma Winterthorn.'

Joe's eyes widened. No, of course not, she wasn't Emma Bales any longer. She'd changed her name. That was what happened to women when they married. He remembered now. And a lot of other things changed too. As Emma had just told him.

Emma sounded in full control. 'No, I quite understand, Mrs Poole, I quite understand, and believe me, if I'd been in Arabella's position, I think I'd have done the same... Yes, of course, but Mrs Poole, it's only a dress after all. No, it'll come out in the cleaning, I'm sure of it... Well, I'd be delighted to. That's very kind... Right now? I'm sorry, let me rummage. One second, I'm going to put the phone down on the table. No, I'm having a coffee with a girlfriend in Peter Jones, I'm not at home, but my diary ought to be here somewhere.'

Emma put the phone down on the table, placed her finger to her lips and stared at Joe, nodding towards the mobile phone, then disgorged the contents of her bag onto the table. A red diary duly appeared. Contents of bag were shovelled back into bag, which sagged on the table with the grace that only the softest leather allowed. Dialogue resumed on the mobile. The two telephonic correspondents hunted for a date of mutual convenience, found one and agreed the time with much cooing. Emma closed the conversation on a pleasant note, smiling goodbye into the phone, and snapped the mobile shut. She turned the phone off and put it back in her bag.

'No more calls. The answerphone can take the strain.' She looked at Joe meaningfully and put her tongue out at him again. 'Thank you for being my girlfriend for a few seconds. A more unlikely one I can't imagine, but there you are. My cover would have been well and truly blown if she'd known I was with a bloke. It just wouldn't have paid.'

Then she smiled at him again and drank some more coffee. She looked as if she'd been quelling a native uprising. Emma was always resolutely and triumphantly Emma. Joe decided she knew nothing about cover. For her it was just a phrase. No spook about her.

'I'm in the most awful trouble here in London, you know,' she announced noncommittally.

'Do tell. Impossible for you to go wrong, I'd say.'

'You're not going to believe it, but I'll tell you anyway. Or shall I tell you on the way. No, we've got some time, haven't we? We'll have to go in about five minutes, I have a tight itinerary today. I have to do lunch with my mother-in-law, or should say, my mother-in-law that was. She's coming down from Norwich to keep tabs on me and check out how I'm spending Geoffrey's money. But let me start the painful saga of Mrs Poole. We were at the opera last night—'

'Who's we?'

'Teddy and I.'

'Teddy?'

'One of my suitors. Or should I say one of *the* suitors. Homer was not wrong, you know. Take a rich widow, and you have to find about two hundred extra suitors to add on and make up the supporting cast. They just swarm around me. And I don't believe I'm any exception.'

'How did you find Teddy?'

'Not through my beautician, that's for sure. No, I was introduced to him after a bridge soirée somewhere in Knightsbridge. Anyway, Teddy, like every other male in the area with good pedigree and no brains, takes a fancy to me and gets involved in the most elaborate chat-up procedure you have ever in your life experienced. Driven on, no doubt, by his fearsome mother. Finally, after he's gone forty-eight times round the mulberry bush, he invites me to go to the opera with him. No...' Emma held up a hand. Joe had his question ready. Emma forestalled him.

'I will not tell you the name of the opera because it was a private production held in the grounds of Lord So-and-So's manor out in the countryside. Berkshire. Beautiful setting. Good sunset as well. We girls get around, you know. Anyway, you can picture the scene. More like something out of *Hello!* than anything in real life. A lot of bowing and even more scraping. But suffice it to say that as soon as we arrive, Teddy's ex-girlfriend, or so he assured me, suddenly materialises from somewhere out of the bushes. Swooping décolletage, eyes like a tigress, in a rage. Snarls at him, snarls at me and then disappears. We take a deep breath, we indulge in some light petting and some measured explanation, and we settle down to a fraught time in a stunning setting. The opera starts, and by the interval the audience is pretty high on Donizetti – tough love and then some, you've been there yourself, I'm sure.

'So, drinks on the sward, the usual thing, hiss of high heel sinking into the turf. Merry clink of glasses and high pitched laughter. Then the ex reappears with an expression of manic hysteria and hurls a glass of wine at Teddy. It misses, of course, and goes all over me. She throws a fit, and lies on the ground screeching and Teddy, poor dear, is helpless with indecision. The women take over, and roll her about and start swabbing me down. She's carted off, God knows where. I watch the rest of the opera with a carpet wrapped round me, and Teddy looks about thirteen years old. Talk about master of the universe.'

'You know how to string a sentence together, don't you, Emma?'

'I didn't fight my way through the London legal jungle for fifteen years without learning the odd quirky phrase you know, Joe. Something stuck as I swung from brief to brief through the forest.'

'So who was that on the phone?'

'That was Mrs Poole, the mother of the ex, who is doing the social necessary and inviting me out for a heart to heart. She is going to give me the full unexpurgated truth about her wretched daughter and the wretched Teddy, even though she assures me it all finished, oh yonks ago, as she just said to me now on the phone, quite unconvincingly and lying through her teeth. The truth is—'

'That you're a misfit in this town. No way a Miss Fit.'

'Joe, you're a genius. You've got it in one. Come on, we'd better go if we're going to find Gregory.'

'Before lunch.'

Emma laughed. 'As if... But let me tell you, as we go, about my misfitting and your Miss Fit. God, how I love puns. That's one of the best I've heard recently. But it's tragic what I'm experiencing in London. You'd never have expected it.'

She stubbed out the cigarette which, Joe noted, she had smoked right down to the butt. But her skin didn't have that dried-up look of the heavy smoker so she was most likely just jangled. Emma hauled her belongings together and they walked together out of the coffee room. They waited for the lift in front of the subfusc of the carpets. Emma picked up her theme. 'You see, nobody apart from you and a few old friends knows that I used to be Emma Bales, upwardly socially mobile daughter of a failed master engineer and tanks inventor. You know, a blood-hound on the case and very tough on the whole legal bit. Christ, I was a junior partner for God's sake. But that's all gone. I'm introduced as Mrs Emma Winterthorn, from Norwich, and recently bereaved. All those legal qualifications that I swotted and sweated blood to get have been airbrushed out of the frame. They just don't exist any longer. You wouldn't believe that anyone could change their identity so completely in such a narrow area of space.'

Joe politely and silently agreed to differ with her on that point. But he did not interrupt her.

'So I'm thought of as a jolly provincial airhead who needs helping. Mrs Moneybags Winterthorn. And by God do those suitors know how to help. They're asphyxiating. And so good mannered I could scream. They hem you in so much you can scarcely breathe. Attention here, phone call there – nothing is too much trouble until, that is, you sign on the dotted line and the assets are jointly held. Then the control freak will step out from behind the screen. I can see it all coming. It all has the air of something ghastly and inevitable. I wouldn't mind so much if it wasn't considered so much the done thing. Do you understand what I mean?'

'Not quite Emma. Explain.'

'This is why I want to find Gregory. Otherwise I'm just supposed to keel over and marry the most eligible man who presents himself, irrespective of any intrinsic qualities. It's almost an arrangement, like a Hindu wedding. Because I have the money, I'm supposed to do the decent thing. Haven't you found that, Joe? From your angle, I mean. You still look pretty eligible.'

Joe thought about the careful way that he had been steered away from the social sweetmeats and agreed with her. 'Well, yes, in an inverted kind of way. Because I'm so broke…'

'It's strictly tradesman's entrance. I understand. Incidentally, your bridge was much commented on at Savage's, you know, Joe. You should go there more often. There's many a lass there with an eye that would roll for you.'

'And me without two farthings.'

'You must tell me more about that. Maybe I can help, I don't know. I feel very strongly about your poverty, Joe.'

They were on the pavement outside Peter Jones now, trying to hail a cab. They waited about fifteen seconds, no more, before one obligingly stopped. 'Where to, ma'am?' said the cab driver cheerfully.

In Fulham, it might have been a different story, thought Joe as they clambered in. But he was enjoying the outing with Emma, not least because there was no spook in her whatsoever. That was crystal clear – no spook. She spoke her mind too readily. Her reactions were as pure as they were outspoken. Joe had had his fill of spooks for the time being.

'Earl's Court, Hogarth Road,' said Emma and then lolled back in her seat as the cab swung round the back of Peter Jones.

'I thought we'd start from his haunts such as I knew them. This may be wrong and dear old Gregory may have changed completely, but he loved Earl's Court and that's where we used to drink in the old days, before I bought the house in Chelsea. So there's just a chance he may have returned there. It's worth a try anyway. I just have to find out some news about him before I make my big decision.'

'You were saying, Emma, about the English male.'

They were heading up past South Kensington tube station now, and turning into the Old Brompton Road.

'Was I? Oh yes, the attentions… Ugh, they make you sick. Cigarette lighters at the ready, twenty-four hours of the day. And there's always some damn mother hovering and crooning away in the background taking up the slack. No sooner have you seen Teddy off for the afternoon, than you'll have mother of Teddy on the phone, asking you how everything is and whether you can cope and "It must be difficult for you being so alone and I hope Teddy isn't being a bore. Do pop in for a coffee if you're feeling low, darling." It makes me want to scream. Your reactions have been programmed according to some template that just doesn't fit. I am a young – well, youngish, let's not fool ourselves – capable and professional women who may have landed on her feet through an accident of fate, not an hysterical wallflower straight out of the nineteenth century. Just because they're helpless and hopeless and can't do a hand's turn doesn't mean the whole world is like that.'

Emma stopped talking and stared out of the cab window. She started talking again but more musingly. 'We lived everywhere, you know, Gregory and me. We never had any money at all but we had lots of fun together. Bread and scrape and laughs. It was very tough at times; you must know those moments when you're down to the bare boards of everything and you just have each other. But bliss in retrospect and certainly marvellous compared to all this messing about.' She smiled ruefully. 'Poor Teddy. He must be getting hell from all sides this morning. There'll be fourteen messages from him on the answerphone already, I bet.'

More pause as the cab turned right off the Old Brompton Road. Then she resumed her comments about Gregory. 'We lived in north London, in a flat in Highgate underneath some terrifying cartoonist with his boyfriend; and then in east London, when I had the bright idea of buying a cheap house. Well, that didn't work out, but I had some very interesting times. Got to know some real villains in east London, Joe. Sawn-off shotgun stuff, blood on the floor, all the business, know what I mean, John. The nick was a second home for most of them. I did lots of legal business for them in the end. All straight and above board as well. They were always very straight with me, even old Clem, and I don't think he had ever been straight with anyone in his life. "Makes a change for me," he said, "acting like a gentleman," as he produced some amazing documentation that looked as if it had been through a shredder backwards. "Makes me want to send my son to Sloane School and give him an education, it does, dealing with you, Miss Bales." And as he said that, I knew that he had a gun in his jacket pocket. I could see it bulging out of his top pocket. I never told you the story about the furniture, did I?'

'I don't think you did, Emma.'

'I'll tell you as we go on the search. It'll liven things up. And here we are…'

They had reached Hogarth Road. They clambered out. Emma paid the fare.

'Number 67. Here we are. I remember it well. Just look at how dingy it is. It hasn't changed a bit. That's where he lived once, after being dumped on the pavement one night, and it's from here that we'll start our search, I think. Now the pub that he used to drink in at first was the one immediately behind us…'

She wheeled round and headed off down the street. Joe kept pace.

'What's this huge decision you plan to make, Emma?'

She was walking quite swiftly but not so fast as to be out of breath. 'To stay or to go. Either I marry someone in the UK, which is what I'm expected to do, or I chuck it all in and go travelling for a year or so. Go on a cruise and sort myself out. Sit in the sun in the West Indies. Do what all the other rich old biddies do and fill in time in the most agreeable way possible and eventually become as selfish as they are, poor lambs.'

Joe said nothing. He bided his time. He could see possibilities in all this. Not immediately. But he could glimpse a certain dynamic from Emma contributing in the future, in ways that he failed as yet to specify. She was so decisive and upfront that she just had to be of some use to him in his alternative role. That was axiomatic. Characters like Emma were rare and needed to be utilised correctly and speedily. The spy in him saw Emma's potential as a tethered target, in very much the same way that Joe would spot and mark dead ground automatically. But Joe said nothing about any of this to Emma, who continued to stride along.

She pushed into the pub ahead of him, and then paused. In fact, she stopped dead. Joe noted her reactions. They didn't surprise him. Half of her was rich woman, expecting the whole world to drop dead in appreciation at her feet, just because she was there. But half of her was still the tough lawyer on the way up, whose calling card was by no means acceptable. The tough lawyer still expected to work the room, the rich woman the room to work for her. So she stopped dead, paralysed by uncertainty.

The pub, which was very quiet and empty and still, despite the sunshine streaming through the windows, managed to ignore Emma's dramatic entry. Joe eased past her and went up to the bar. An old, fat and greasy Irishman with knowing eyes stared at him from behind the bar as he approached. A thin, dead roll-up balanced itself unsteadily on his lower lip. Not yet chucking-out time my friend, but you'll be among the first to go, his expression betokened. He was not friendly. But then this was Earl's Court. It was cautious about strangers; they brought trouble as often as not.

'I wonder if you could help us,' Joe began.

No reply from the Irishman. His expression did not change. He could spot a deadbeat.

Emma bustled up behind Joe. She had recovered her poise. 'Did you explain to him, Joe?'

'I was just starting on the saga.'

'Wait. Let me show him the photographs. We're looking for this man. Have you seen him?'

Emma opened her bag and pulled out a wad of pictures which she spread out across the bar. Gregory, Gregory, Gregory – about forty thousand Gregories in all. Joe recognised him from afar across time, the lean face, the slim frame, the tight eyes, the careful disposition within the photo frame. Scholar, poet, traveller, and perhaps even athlete – he had the figure for it. But Gregory inhabited the frames with circumspection; he was withdrawn from the beholder, even though it was Emma, his lover, who had taken the photos. There was something inner and covert about his expressions, Joe decided, although his impressions were fleeting. He was watching the barman who had leaned forward to study the portfolio spread out all down the bar.

The pictures depicted Gregory in almost every conceivable pose and location. They were a thesaurus of a love that used to be. Impossible not to remember him, once seen. Joe contrasted

Emma's approach with his own pathetic efforts towards finding Marcello. Joe had just two or three grubby and slightly soiled photos of Marcello which he showed around fairly furtively. Maybe he had adopted the wrong approach. Maybe the block-buster approach was the one that counted. Emma was going to find Gregory – so much was clear.

'Fine-looking man,' said the barman. 'I'd remember him if I'd seen him. 'Ere, Terry, come down here.' He shouted up the stairs. Clatter of boots on the stairs. Terry, wholly dishevelled, material-ised through the door like a sprite.

'You ever seen this man, Terry, drinking in here or around the area?'

More scrutiny from Terry who looked at the photos willingly enough. He raised his gaze towards Emma, standing at the bar alert in her well-made shoes but nevertheless anxious and hoping for good news.

'I don't want to disappoint you, lady, but I can't say that I do recognise him. But I can't positively say that I haven't seen him either. I think I may have seen him, although it may have been a long time ago. I just can't place him, even though he does ring a little bell for me.'

Emma looked wonderfully grateful and poised to speak but then the senior barman intervened. 'That's enough, Terry, and thank you. Now go back upstairs, will you.'

Terry scuttled out.

'Now, will you be wanting anything more, madam and sir? No? Well, I'll wish you a good morning, if you'll excuse me.'

Emma scooped up the photos with a huge show of reluctance and the barman went down the other end of the bar to serve a customer. Then they were out on the street again. Perhaps Joe's approach was the better one. More discreet.

'What was all that about?' Emma was baffled.

Joe was quick to interpret. 'Maybe he thought we were informers. I don't know. There must be lots of people passing through here and, by the same token, lots of people in hot pursuit. It's a shifting population. Nobody wants to get drawn into something that they can't control. Silence is best. You did well getting him to talk at all. He didn't look the type.'

Emma was silent. Then she said hopefully, 'But Terry did say that he might have seen him. He sort of recognised him, didn't he? That must be a good sign, don't you think, Joe?'

She needed some encouragement. She looked very down. Quite deflated. Joe put his arm round her briefly and hugged her. She clung to him gratefully.

'Emma, it was a good start. Believe me, I know about these things. He thought he recognised him; that's the best you'll get at this stage. Best not to dwell over much on the detail. Let's find another pub.'

Encouraged by Joe's comments, she started walking again. 'Yes, we have lots of pubs to try. This ought to be fun. Let's go into another boozer.'

They wandered off together down the street, with Emma trying to remember the next pub the two of them, Gregory and Emma, used to go to in the dead and glorious past during the course of their evening's drinking.

'I think it would have been—'

'What did you drink in those days, Emma?'

'Oh, Guinness, of course. For strength. I never really wanted to be slim. I just wanted to get on. Gregory was always the slim one. It didn't matter how much he drank, he never seemed to put on any weight, although he went haywire beyond a certain point in his consumption. But he was a permanent beanpole. We could never understand it.'

They went from pub to pub in Earl's Court. At first with elation but then with growing disenchantment. Always the same reaction; it became predictable. Photos spread out on the bar, intense interest, always the half recognition and then the clamming up. Gregory started turning into a Pimpernel for them, always just out of the frame and just out of focus, an elusive wraith of a man. Eventually Emma decided they ought to call a halt.

'It's getting late, Joe. I'm not meeting Ma Winterthorn until two thirty, but it'll take me an age to get over to Liverpool Street, even by tube. I'll have to change first as well. I can't meet Ma Winterthorn looking like this. She'd be very disapproving and I don't want to fall out with her just yet. She still has a lingering suspicion that I put arsenic in Geoffrey's morning brew. Let's have a coffee and call it a day, for today at least. It's fun, but it's hard.'

'Tell you what, Emma, let me take you to the Troubadour. It's a coffee house very close to here, and we can take a break there. It's an arty place too, and it has all sorts of people dropping in from time to time so it's possible someone there might just have seen Gregory. People actually read books in there, so you can't rule it out. And if we do find him in there, such an appropriate title of a place to run him to earth.'

Emma squeezed his hand. 'Joe, you're being a real pal over this. It's much appreciated. I couldn't do this on my own. You know that, don't you? Emma the capable would have to admit defeat on this one, without you. Thank you very much. But how far is the Troubadour from the tube?'

'Very close if you go in by the back entrance.'

'You know all the dodges, don't you, Joe! I've never met anyone who knew his way around London quite so well.'

'Even the blind consult me. But only at night. Come on, in we go.'

He pushed on the heavy door of the Troubadour and they entered its strange enigmatic atmosphere, with a thousand violins and lutes hanging from the ceiling. People were scattered here and there in relaxed mode, reading or simply staring into space. Emma was enchanted. She forbade any more of the quest.

'This place is too nice. Stuff Gregory for the time being. I just want to have a coffee. We can start here the next time. In the meantime, I want to rest my feet.'

'I thought Deliss…'

'Think how they'd be without Deliss. Joe, please, a cappuccino. My fat little feet ache to buggery.'

Joe ordered the coffees. He returned to find Emma staring at him fixedly.

'Joe, you're very good company. I've enjoyed this morning very much. I know it must be a bore for you traipsing round Earl's Court with this daffy bird, but I've got a lot out of it. Thank you very much.'

Joe could hear interrogation in the wind. He positioned

himself appropriately. Sure enough, the questioning started with the first sip of her cappuccino. Emma was seated with her back to the wall. She looked relaxed. Her feet wiggled free in trotter ecstasy.

'Joe, tell me, how is it that you've fallen on such hard times? You don't seem to have changed all that much from the time you were riding high. You're not exactly a mental paraplegic. So what went wrong?'

Joe gave her a little boy grin. It was crafted to mislead. 'I think these things happen. My face fitted once and then it didn't fit. So I was turfed out. And once you're turfed out, there is a long way to fall. The descent is very steep, especially since the UK is so unforgiving.' Joe was thinking spook. His mind was only half on what he was saying.

'Yes, but this doesn't add up. One minute you're the boss of whatever it was called, making over one million a year, and the next you're practically walking the streets. There must be a half-way house somewhere along the road here.'

Yes, thought Joe, and it's called British intelligence. But don't let that bother you.

'You may be right in general, but not in my case,' said Joe soothingly. He didn't want the conversation to get too close to basic causality.

'But how do you live, Joe, apart from gambling at bridge, which presumably you do on a huge scale?'

'I trade the stock market.' Joe realised that a whole two hours had gone by without him wondering where the price of Chaebol Trust was lurking. He must have been having fun. But where was the price now? His negligence was criminal. Little flutters of panic grabbed him in the pit of his stomach. What were the shares doing?

A smile lit up Emma's face. 'Of course, Joe. How stupid of me. Now I see it. You're a speculator. And I can also see how I can help you.'

Joe raised an eyebrow. This sounded awful to him. He didn't want helping. He just wanted to be free.

'Geoffrey's estate has just coughed up another million, and I'm a bit loath to keep putting it all with Brasenose. They're good, but they're not that good. Far too cautious. Why don't I put some of it with you to manage? I could pay you some commission and that might help.'

Joe waved his hands in negation. It was time to change the subject. He didn't want to manage anybody's money, thank you very much. He wanted to get his hands on his own loot. It was nothing more than that, just something personal and imperative.

'Emma, thank you very much for the suggestion. I'll think it over. There might be administrative problems here. But I'll certainly think about it.'

Emma looked helpless and puzzled. Didn't the man want to be helped? Was he just a teeny bit touched?

'Emma, I had a thought about Gregory.'

'You don't think I should be looking for him at all, do you?'

'I think it's very dangerous. You may get badly hurt. There's a risk to it all. The past is the past, and you can't revisit it. You just cannot go back. You have to look to the future. That is our curse, if you like. But perhaps you're afraid of the future because of the decisions and the commitment you will have to make and so you're retreating into the past. You're looking for Gregory because you can't face Teddy. Teddy and his mother, I should say. That may be an oversimplification but it's possibly right. So that's why I'm just a touch sceptical about looking after your money. It means revisiting the City with all its pomp and circumstance and I don't want anything of that. They kicked me out and I don't want to go back in. I've finished with it. I just want to get on my feet and then get out. Leave the country, flee and start a new life.'

Joe noted a responsive gleam come into Emma's eye and realised that he was pushing a perilous line of argument. Money and travel and adventure were in the air. He regretted his digression. He had been too explicit.

'So you may be chasing a dream and on the other hand you may not. Only time will tell. But in the meantime, I thought of a risk-free way for you to track Gregory down and to keep your options open, if you like.'

'All right, Mr Cool Cat, what is this Teflon-coated wheeze? I have very specific reasons for wanting to catch up with Gregory, but we'll let them pass for the time being. So what's the big idea?'

'You were alerted to him by his poem in *The Sunday Times*, right?'

'Right.'

'I thought that if we approached the Confederation of Authors – he's bound to be registered with them, because he's such a meticulous kind of guy, at least that's what you always said – if we approach the Confederation, we can suggest that we want to commission a poem from him on the strength of his piece in *The Sunday Times*. We, or rather you, offer quite good money for the poem, so they know that it's serious. They scramble. Poets are poor. This is important for one of their members. They get in touch with him, and I leave my number as a contact, so they come back to you via me. No connection with you at all. That way we find out a lot about him, including some personal details like his phone number and perhaps even his address, and that gives us some leeway to stake him out, without you being totally committed to the Gregory concept.'

Without a word, Emma stood up and in her bare feet waded around the table and kissed Joe full on the lips, cupping her hands round his chin the better to hold him as she did so. It was a very big kiss and it came from the heart.

'I thought you were charming, Joe, when we first met; I thought you were even more charming when we had that dinner at the Reform Club; and as for our night of passion in Norwich… You keep growing on me every time we meet. And every time we're talking about the wretched Gregory. It's the same old damn situation, isn't it? Our big kiss outside the Reform Club when we spent all night talking about him – and then he goes and lets us down. Then there was that chaste night we spent together in your flat in Notting Hill Gate, remember? And you always dance just that little fraction out of reach. Like a will-o'-the-wisp. Always back into the shadows for you. But what can I say, Joe? That is such a smart suggestion. You hit the spot every time. You are just so damned clever. That is such a good idea. I congratulate you.'

She was leaning over and across him as she spoke. Her bosom lay massively on Joe's cheek. It felt comfortable. More than maternal. Friendly even, within its supporting cups. But Joe thought of freedom and rejected the ideas that flamed immediately through his mind. All that, sadly, was over for him. He wanted to depart.

As Emma clambered back to her seat opposite Joe, she was obliged to negotiate a passage between the tables as Joe shifted position to let her through. His line of vision altered as he looked up. He froze. It was incredible. Journey's end, babe.

There on the wall, not two or three feet away, pinned to the noticeboard and unmistakable in its simplicity, hung Gregory's *Sunday Times* poem. Not only was it there for all with eyes to see, it was also signed. Joe could see the signature and a message at the bottom of the sheet.

Emma hadn't seen it. And Joe wasn't telling. Some instinct drove him to silence. He pouted at her as she sat down. 'Thank you, Emma. That was very nice.'

'You deserved it,' she replied, oblivious to the fact that the solution to at least one of her problems hung exposed for all the world to see just six inches from her left ear lobe.

And still Joe wasn't telling. He was not certain why he wasn't telling but he wasn't. He was keeping schtum. As schtum as schtum could be. Still smiling at him, Emma asked him where the Confederation of Authors might be located.

Conscious that Gregory might walk into the Troubadour at any second, and conscious of his imminent presence all around, and also feeling alive at all the possibilities which that suggested, Joe kept his voice very noncommittal, although his mind was racing. 'About five minutes' walk away. They're in the Old Brompton Road.'

'Joe, you're a miracle worker. So…'

'I can ring them and then call you and tell you how I got on. Then, if necessary, we can visit the premises. Nothing in writing, I guess. I think we'll just wave cheques at them.'

Emma rose to her feet again. She looked pleased and rejuvenated by it all. 'Joe, I really must be going. I'm going to have to dash. Maybe I'll take a cab.'

'Where do you have to get to in order to change?'

'You mean where do I live?'

'Something like that.'

'Pelham Crescent, where else? What, did you think I'd be

slumming it in Sumner Place? Purrlease... But I warn you, if you're thinking of moving into the Crescent, the neighbours can be noisy. Even frisky from time to time. And you, Joe. Where is your abode? Or are you going to be as evasive over that as you are over everything else?'

"Fraid so, Emma. Discretion is the better part of—'

'Bullshit, Joe, and you know it.' She was not yet resigned to the idea of going to meet her mother-in-law. She was keener to trade insults with Joe.

It would be Pelham Crescent, wouldn't it, thought Joe ruefully, recalling the crack in his wall now and his villa in the South of France, now sold at fire sale prices. Role reversal had its limitations. Pelham Crescent was perhaps the most sought-after address in the whole of Chelsea, which said a lot in itself. Emma was not just well off, she was very, very rich indeed.

'Joe, that money I talked to you about...'

'Yes, Emma?'

'If you don't want to manage it for me, you could just tell me what you're trading and we can split the profits, if there are any.'

She was indefatigable. Joe gave in. 'Okay, Emma, you win.'

He eased her through the door of the Troubadour and into the street, still wondering why he hadn't revealed the presence of the poem on the wall. Basic training, or just plain savvy caution? He couldn't fathom it at all. But he knew that he wasn't going to breath a word about it to Emma, not at least for the time being. Dead ground, but this time hanging on the wall.

'Emma, I'll tell you what I'm in. I bought them this morning. Quite a big position. Chaebol Trust. A good story, but a bit spivvy.'

'Oh good, that's just the thing to shake Brasenose up. Let's ramp it to the skies. I'll buy some on the way to the station. Consider it done, Joe. Goodbye. We'll talk this evening. And don't you dare do your disappearing act on me this time. I won't stand for it. What did you call them?'

Another cab pulled up. Emma clambered in. She leaned out of the window. 'What were they called again? Chaebol Trust? Good, I'm going to have some fun with Brasenose over this. Approximate price?'

'I paid over the odds this morning at about 130p.'

'We'll soon see about that.'

And the cab sped off, with Emma busy already making her call to Brasenose on the mobile. One little broker at least that afternoon was going to find himself with a tough order.

The same afternoon, Annie had made it clear to Bootface that she was not to be disturbed. She needed an hour left alone in the office so that she could reach a final judgement on the data she had gathered on Joe and his involvement with Rivers Pugh. Data which Bootface knew nothing about but whose existence he sensed.

Bootface would not be denied. He was like a small child. Impossible to fob him off. He continued to bustle in and out of the office, asking her time and again whether she had finished. Was she available for consultation yet? And if not, why not? That was his little joke, which he repeated about five times in the course of the afternoon. Annie was steadily losing her temper with him. Sooner or later there would be an explosion. She knew that and so, obscurely, did he. They were both waiting for the bust-up. Fatal for any espionage mission.

Bootface knew full well that Annie had extra information that she was refusing to share with him. That was why she wanted to be alone. And he resented the fact that she wouldn't trust him with her extra information. So he made trouble quite persistently and deliberately. A fine example of an intelligence officer going off his head. Finally she shooed him out and locked the door. She needed time to think, unimpeded by his presence.

The news was very bad. Rivers was about the one person in the capital with whom Joe should not be in any relationship whatsoever. The relationship was not life-threatening – yet. But as it matured and as the mission surged forward, it could all too easily get to be like that. An extra variable of risk had been added to the equation. Joe only had to make one false move, just one clumsy statement, and they would kill him. Just one sentence indicating that he was very much more than just a dumb bridge player – that was all it would take.

All too clearly Annie could see the shooter coming out behind

Joe's head, could see the trigger being pulled, could see his brains splattering across the opposite wall. These things happened. End of mission, end of Joe, perhaps even the end of lots of other things too. A lot, an enormous amount, was riding on this mission. And there was no way round the fact that Joe's encounter had taken place. He had met Rivers by an unlucky quirk of fate. That had happened; that was fact. No sense in trying to unscramble that by assumption. It was all very fraught. Unnecessary too, but that was what happened in missions. The trivial got in the way of the crucial and fouled it up. It was something to do with that thing called daily life. Weaving the thread of espionage into the pattern of daily life was always a very tricky business. Well-nigh impossible most of the time. This mission was no exception.

Rivers was moving in entirely the wrong company. He had fallen from grace and he had not redeemed himself by his choice of new job. Or rather his induction into his new job, because that was what it really amounted to. He was working with very dangerous people indeed, people who would not hesitate to kill – or rather, have people killed. And no wonder they killed easily; they had a lot to lose. They themselves were too powerful to have anything to do with something so mundane as the taking of life. They left that to the numerous hit men and assassins on the books. So as Rivers was sucked in more deeply, he seemed certain to confide in Joe and hence involve him by association. Joe was bound to start coming into contact with Rivers's associates and…

That would be when the damage would be done. It could happen in a flash. Joe had been a prominent man in the City and it had taken a lot of camouflaging to hide him away among the dames at Liz Playfair's. That alone had taken enormous patience and perseverance. Almost as much planning as mulcting him of his wealth. But it had worked. Joe had passed unrecognised for many months. The cover had been brilliant and totally effective. Now just when he was starting to get close to the action, or, more specifically, closer to Lady C, who was dangerous enough in her own right, the whole mission had lurched a foot or so in the wrong direction. These people, these new associates of Rivers's, they were City people too. Joe could quite easily be recognised by one of his erstwhile associates from his City days, and that would be it. In a flash. It would take just one glance of recognition and then they really would fry him. Of course they'd fry him. He'd have to account for the fact that he never admitted to Rivers what his other life had been. Which he couldn't do. So they'd all smell a rat. So would anybody. Even the man in the street would question why a big shot financier was trying to pass himself off as an ignorant bum of a bridge player. Especially a big shot financier who had come from nothing and shot to the top with no background at all in the English sense of the word. As for these hoodlums, they wouldn't think twice... Yes, they'd fry him.

As for the girl, Perdita, Annie knew enough about her feelings towards Joe from the wire taps to start shuddering with fear and apprehension. It was bad enough having him mixed up with Rivers, but Perdita... She was the one who could really sink him. Just one false word from Joe to Perdita, just one piece of injudicious pillow talk, and he was a dead man. Annie would bet a million dollars on that one. Such was the hazard in the operation.

She decided that at this stage there was nothing to be done. She had to trust to luck. That was all she had riding for her. They were barely close to the inner core of the mission – the suborning of Lady C – and Annie was in no position to start issuing instructions to Joe. Not after what she had done to him and his wealth. It was too soon. He was still too wild over what had happened to him. He had to come to her, under the stress of circumstance, and ask for guidance. That was how the relationship must develop henceforth. That was what the textbooks prescribed and they were normally correct. Until that happened she was powerless, unless something quite terrifying started to happen, in which case... But she must not intervene at this stage. That was quite clear.

Suddenly Annie thought about the two clocks on her own mantelpiece and realised that not only was Joe out on his own in this mission, but so too was she. This was no ordinary situation; the ambiguities were all around. She was not above the battle, directing the chariots, not this time.

She realised that Bootface had been banging on the door for quite a while and she paced across to let him in. She was still full of thoughts. He barged in with some asperity.

'So what's the big idea? Why did you lock me out?'

He was not a happy intelligence operative. Annie paid him little heed. She was still turning the whole question of the probabilities over in her mind, and what might be the optimal course of action. His presence did not wholly register. She mumbled a reply at him. This enraged Bootface still more.

'I want to get to the bottom of all this.'

'All of what?'

'All this secrecy. You're concealing things from me, Annie, things that you've found out, and haven't discussed with me. I'm not fully briefed at all times. How can I do the job without a proper briefing?'

'Don't be so pompous, Bootface, I'm not concealing anything from you. It's just that these missions are not linear. They have their little quantum moments and I'm just afraid that we're running up against one of them right now. And the reason I'm vague is that I really don't know what to do. Does that make sense? No point in discussing it with you until I've worked it all out in my own mind. Otherwise I might be wasting your time.'

Barely placated, Bootface paused. Then a look of extraordinary cunning came into his eyes. For a moment, he looked truly crazy. He seemed to turn inwards on himself quite physically.

'I've found out something too. Something that I've been turning over in my mind. So if you tell me your thoughts, I'll tell you mine.'

Annie stared at him speechless. It was all getting completely out of hand. And this was a mission, for God's sake, not a Turkish bazaar.

Bootface spoke some more. 'It's about Joe...'

'We know everything about Joe. What is there that's new that you've found out?'

Bootface seized his advantage. 'Tell you what, since you're so interested, why don't we have a drink and talk about it. Yes?'

Annie nodded, dumbfounded.

'Say next Thursday for our drink?'

'Why the delay?'

'I have to do some more checking. But Thursday will do. Until then, you can hold the fort can't you?'

'What do you mean?'

'I'll be back Thursday. Until then, just say that I'm sick, will you? You can do that. Especially as I count for nothing in this mission. And especially since you don't want anyone to know that you locked the door on a fellow officer working on the same mission, do you?'

'All right, Bootface, have it your own way. We'll meet on Thursday. But this had better be good.'

Again the look of amazing craftiness on Bootface's features. His whole face seemed to crinkle up into a grimace. 'You won't be disappointed. I can assure you of that. Joe's my boy, that's for sure.'

And then he was gone, out of the door, leaving Annie alone with her thoughts, her fears and the waves, running in their silent compulsive rhythms outside in the Thames, through space, through time. She stared at the river unseeingly. Inertia was not enough, she decided. She had to take some action. It was time she thought some more about Bootface, and got that little variable into the frame as well. Bootface was very dangerous. He was about to break the mission up from the inside just as surely as Joe could torpedo it from the outside. It was like watching a pack of wild dogs pursue a quarry, except that she had an uncomfortable suspicion that she was about to become the fugitive.

Those two clocks on her mantelpiece told her everything, in a sense, that she wanted to know. She was in danger as well. Joe could go down now quite easily; Bootface was going mad – or worse; and something strange and unknown was lying in wait for her. Her closed world of intelligence, where ploy and counter-ploy took place in a series of set and almost predefined gambits, was being broken wide open. This was very new. But it looked true.

She didn't feel afraid at all. But she felt vigilant. All these factors needed to be taken into account. She felt quiet and poised on the edge of the unknown. But she acknowledged too, as far as she dared, that the mission was internal to her as well as to Joe. She was just as involved as he was. And that never ever happened. No, it was no longer true that she was above the battle. Far from it. She was down in the arena with everyone else now, kicking and gouging. Those were her perceptions and her hunches and it was on the basis of these that she was preparing a new game plan. But also she reminded herself, there had to be someone out there looking after her. That was what the two clocks told her. She had to gamble on that factor as well. It could not be overlooked, not after Bootface's extraordinary behaviour.

What was it the gladiators said before they did battle? *Morituri te salutamus.* We who are about to die salute you. And in her ivory tower, as she now saw it, she had always admired that use of the future participle. Things were a lot more imminent than that right now.

Eventually, after a long inner tussle with himself, Joe rang Lady Pugh. He received a rapturous reception. No hint of criticism about the time it had taken him to come back to them after his visit to Pugh Park. Just a sort of quiet contentment coming down the line to Joe that he had decided to stay in touch with the family.

'And how are you, Joe? We've missed talking to you. How is the bridge?'

'I'm playing well at the moment Lady Pugh, so it's not too painful. Quite profitable, in fact.'

This was true. He had had a session at the Jack of Hearts with Joxer which had netted him some three hundred pounds. The two of them had departed in high delight. It had been fairly obvious that they would win some money that afternoon. Joxer had quite unnerved the opposition by rolling up his sleeve in mid-session and requesting permission to inject himself – there and then at the table.

'It's only sucrose, nothing but sugar concentrate. I'm very tired. You won't believe it, Joe, but there was a fight in the operating theatre between the anaesthetist and the registrar,' Joxer had informed him and the opposition who, to tell the truth, had been shaken quite out of their stride by Joxer's antics.

'Blood on the walls, would you believe. The patient woke up in the middle of the operation. Not enough oxygen. She had to fend for herself.'

The spectacle of the hypodermic driving into his arm as Joxer grimaced had been too much for them. One of the players had turned quite white at the sight of the blood. Their play had collapsed. Three hundred pounds of hot little smackers had cascaded into Joe's equally hot little hand.

But he rather gilded the lily over the bridge play with Lady Pugh. No mention of hypodermics – not good for ladies of a certain age and of a delicate disposition to hear such talk. Lady Pugh had talked rather ineffectively for a minute or so, plainly unsure how to drive the conversation forward. Then the phone was snatched from her hand and a familiar, much missed and already much cherished voice came on the line.

'Joe, I am really very pissed off with you indeed. Where have you been, you toad? You come down here, entertain us marvellously in all sorts of ways and then just disappear back into your rabbit hole in London without so much as a word. Bridge, my foot. You've been hiding from us. Well, it just won't do. It's not good enough. I demand more. More jokes and more French cricket. How about that? Where is it to be, our next meeting?'

Joe could hear a rather bleating 'Perdita, Perdita' of rebuke in the background, but he didn't care. He was very happy again to talk to the Boadicea of Pugh Park.

'To listen to you, anyone would think that you led a completely monastic existence. There is an outside world, you know, and you get to it by foot, bus or motor car. All you have to do is travel.'

'Yes, but without our Joe, there's no point, is there? What's the point in going out if you yourself are not going to be there? Yes, you, Joe, nobody else, just you. You're the one who makes up the game and plays on the pipes and that's why we like you so much.'

He had obviously been much discussed by Lady Pugh and Perdita and approved. He had secured entry deep into the bosom of the family without any of the normal vetting procedures being applied. He was of the Pughs now. They would not let him go without a struggle.

'Okay, then, Perdita, it's a fair cop. When are we going to have lunch in London? I'll treat you – and your mother too if she wants to come.'

'Oh, Mother comes too, she most certainly does. We hunt together. Don't we, Momma dearest…'

Joe heard a large, slightly ill-aimed kiss landing with a smack on someone's cheek. Perdita returned to the phone. 'She wants to talk to you some more about death. You speak French don't you?'

Carried away by the pleasure of the discussion with Perdita, Joe was on the point of revealing his fluency. He wanted so much to excel in her eyes and it was something which she expected from him. That was obvious. But he stopped. Training counted. The cold hand of reason descended on his heart.

'It's negligible,' he said, lowering his voice a fraction. 'I'm so ashamed of my French, it's so useless. Never got further than *amo, amas*. I can bid in French at bridge, but that's about as far as it goes.' It cost him an enormous effort to denigrate himself in her eyes.

'Well, a fat lot of good that is, I'll be bound. I expected better, but that's just too bad. You can't do everything. Mother wants to talk to you about these letters she's been translating from France. All about the French soldiers at the front. She wants you to read her translation. I can't think of anything more ghoulish myself, but then it does take all sorts. Her translations, I warn you, are a bit hit or miss. That's why she—'

Lady Pugh came back on the line. 'You know, Joe, one of these days I think I'm going to have to discipline my daughter, she gets so uppity.'

'Yes, I think you should give her a good thrashing. With the stable whip, Lady Pugh. That's what she needs. A firm hand. You should show her who's boss, Lady Pugh.'

'Perdita, Joe thinks I ought to give you a good thrashing and show you who's boss. Perdita…'

There was a sound in the background. A rather porcine sound.

'Did you hear that, Joe? I am really quite shocked. What an extraordinary sound for a young girl to make. Perdita, Perdita, come here. No, she won't come, Joe. She's left the room in a hurry. And I'm not surprised she's departed after that exhibition of poor taste. I'm not even certain I know which… Anyway, to business. I know you must be busy. Some lunch in London, Joe? We'd be delighted. That would be a real treat for us both. You tell us where to be and what time and we'll be there.'

They agreed a date and a time and Joe promised to call back with a suggestion for the venue. He rang off in high good humour. Apart from Rivers Pugh, about whom he felt most ambivalent, almost hostile, the rest of the family filled him with delight. He looked forward immensely now to the next meeting with Perdita. He was pleased to be such a hit with the Pughs. It was all most gratifying. Talking to Perdita was like sparring with a docker – *mano a mano* with no holds barred. He warmed to the whole experience. He felt cherished.

He put the phone down and it rang again immediately. It was Emma.

'Joe, thanks for a wonderful morning. I truly enjoyed it immensely. I got to meet Ma Winterthorn on time and that all went off rather smoothly and I also got to buy your Chaebol Trust and that wasn't too bad either. What did you pay for yours again?'

'About 132p each, I think.'

'Well, then, my dear Joe, I have good news for you. I had to pay 135p for mine. And they were still going up at the close of business. I've just had my little man from Brasenose on the phone, telling me what a strange purchase it was for me to make but that it didn't seem to have done me any harm. He thinks they'll trade above 140p next week. Isn't that grand?'

'It certainly makes me feel richer, Emma.'

'A pleasure, Joe. And the Confederation of Authors? When are you going to phone?'

'Shortly. I'll do it over the next few days. I have to think about these things before I actually get round to doing them. I have to prepare myself. You'll hear from me by the end of next week at the latest.'

'As long as that, Joe? I'm impatient to hear some news. Why can't you do it sooner?'

'I may be playing bridge.'

'Of course, how foolish of me. I almost forgot. With your smart friends at Liz Playfair's. I know – forgive me for making the enquiry. Everything stops for that, doesn't it.'

Confronted by a totally unexpected flash of temperament, Joe was taken aback. Something in the lower depths of Emma's character had suddenly heaved to the surface.

'Well, not entirely, Emma. It's just that Liz…'

Emma recollected herself. Her outburst had evaporated. 'I'm

sorry, Joe. Forgive me. That was unfair. I think the excitement must be getting to me. Goodnight and thanks again. We'll track that Gregory to his lair, don't you worry. And wasn't it fun, that Troubadour place of yours. We'll start from there next time. What do you think?'

'Indubitably, Emma. And my love to Teddy.'

'Actually, it's not Teddy this evening. It's Alex. Don't tell a soul but he thinks he's on a winner. You know better, though, don't you?'

'He'll be going home empty-handed?'

'He'll have to enjoy the dinner because that's as far as he gets.'

'You're very cold about all of this, Emma.'

'Don't forget I'm an old married woman now, having fun playing the field, not the helpless waif you knew in the old days. Anyway, I'm off soon from this country, remember.'

'Helpless, Emma?'

'Goodnight, Joe. You know what I mean.'

'Goodnight, Zuleika Winterthorn.' And Joe put the phone down quickly before Emma could get the last word.

# Chapter Ten

Early Thursday morning. Another Thursday morning in the continuing sequence and not long after the last Thursday morning. Ursula called Joe early, around nine o'clock. She sounded pent-up, excited but confused. Sounds of boisterous children revving up for the day could be heard in the background. Mentally she might have been half out of the nest, but physically she was well ensconced – and under pressure.

'Joe, it's Ursula. Could you help me? I have a small problem.'

'Ursula, I'd be delighted to help you if I can. What can be the matter?'

Joe was lying when he acted the ignoramus. He was too quick for her. He'd been up with the lark and he was fully briefed. He knew full well what her problem was. He knew about the Latin tag. What a silly cow she is, he thought.

Joe had bought his *Chron* early and Tom Stone's article was there for all to see. Oh frabjous day, thought Joe after seeing the piece. Lots about Asia... He had also acquired, by accident, a random copy of the *Daily Mail* which featured on the front page a handsome photo of Sir David and his charming wife, Lady Charley, emerging from a Chelsea restaurant late the previous night. Sir David was in line for some troubleshooting job in the new Labour government. Lady Charley looked suitably radiant. But that hardly concerned Joe. Tom had done him proud. A long exposition of the attractions of the Asian markets culminated in a series of share recommendations which just happened to squeeze in, almost as an afterthought, a reference to Chaebol Trust.

Puff, puff for Monsieur Praliffer. *Mais oui, mais oui!* But puff, puff for Joe as well. That was far more important. This feels like a spot of profit on the way, thought Joe, who immediately started to calculate just how much he would make if the shares hit 160p and he sold out. More than enough to pay the mortgage for a month, that was for sure. Time to talk to Sid... Or maybe let Sid come to him?

Tom had also been faithful in the column to Ursula, his long lost love. The swain had been active. Hence the Latin. He had not devoted the column to a series of mawkish personal reminiscences, perhaps on the pressing advice of his editor. Instead he had included, nicely in context but with a stunning double entendre for those who had eyes to see, a Latin quotation, obviously intended as his touching and personal message to Ursula, his newly rediscovered beloved.

It was a line from a famous Horace ode and in the *Chron* it read: *Qui nunc te fruitur credulus auream*. And Ursula was now phoning for help with the translation.

'Have you got a pencil and paper handy, Joe?' she asked, as children's voices boomed fractiously in the background. 'You know Latin, don't you? Of course you do. Well, you should do. You're a man after all. Now what does this mean?'

And she read the Latin line out to him over the phone without acknowledging that it came from the *Chron*, which was foolish in itself. Did nobody read newspapers in her world? But there was worse to come. Tom in his eagerness to impress, had actually misquoted the line so that the final word was *auream* not *aurea*. As the line stood in the *Chron*, it was nonsense. *Fruitur* should take the ablative, as Joe well recalled.

Typical of these two middle-aged star-crossed lovers, thought Joe as he huffed to Ursula in simulated effort at writing the line down. In fact, he did nothing, but stared at the *Chron*, giggling to himself as Ursula dictated the incorrect phrases to him meticulously, as if to a child.

'Have you got that now, Joe?' she asked sharply. Then her voice moved up an octave. 'Piers, will you be quiet, right now, or you'll go right up to your room.'

The bawl of command cracked across Joe's eardrum like a whip. 'Piers? Oh yes... Yes, I think so, Ursula.' He read it back to her.

'Correct, Joe. Well, what does it mean, Joe? I have to know quite urgently.' The privilege for Joe obviously lay in being asked to translate the line in the first place.

'I think it means "Who is now free to enjoy your gold",

Ursula, but I can't be absolutely certain. I can check it for you, if you like. I'm pretty sure that it comes from Virgil.'

Unkind thoughts chased through Joe's mind as the threat of imminent dissolution diminished, courtesy of Chaebol Trust. *Why can't she work the fucking line out for herself? So why should I give her the correct rendition? Time for a spot of fun with this buffoon.*

There was a brief pause and a slight intake of breath as Ursula digested the personal implications of the quotation. Then the breath came out again as more furious fighting broke out in the background. Ursula decided that it accorded well with her recent pillow talk with Tom. Yes, she decided, it was a beautiful compliment.

Then she came back to earth. 'Be quiet, will you, Piers, for the last time... No, no, Joe, that'll do and thank you very much. Pretty, isn't it? Virgil, you said? Good. I thought I recognised it as Virgil. I have to rush. I got so far as "enjoying your gold" but I got stuck after that. Very helpful. Are you coming to the bridge this morning?'

'I haven't a clue. I'll only be there if Liz has a hole to fill.'

'I think she's full up for this week, but you can never tell, Joe. I'll maybe see you later. But thanks again... Piers, will you stop doing that this instant. And Clea, stop pulling his hair...'

Joe put the phone down. It rang again immediately. It was Lady Charley. She was in a hurry, too.

'Joe, I've decided that we ought to go and play together at Tony Savage's. As partners, you know. What do you think?'

'I thought you never wanted to set foot in the place. A woman called Sybil—'

'Yes, well I didn't, and Sybil can go to hell. But did you know that Grace and Amanda came top there in the duplicate last week and that Lynn and Leslie were second? And Penny was top the week before, playing with Mags? We've got to do better than that. Apparently it's quite fun too.'

Lady Charley was feeling the breeze from the competition and her social position, although quite, quite invulnerable, needed restating in all its refulgent glory via a stunning and victorious appearance at Savage's. Her picture in the *Daily Mail* was no more than fitting, but something more was required now that her acolytes were doing so well at Savage's.

Quite naturally, Joe was now in demand since he had an unexpected use. He had to play with Lady C and arrange for her to come top at Savage's. But Lady C's terms of trade were quite inflexible. She made it clear that it was her time that she was renting out.

'When would you be free, Joe, to play there? I can make next Tuesday, which is a good afternoon, I understand, and best for me. That's when all the girls will be there. Could you make that time?'

And Sybil as well, presumably, arriving by broomstick no less. It meant Joe giving up Joxer for a session. But Chaebol Trust should bring home the bacon, hopefully. Lady C would not be denied. Joe assented, weakly he thought and certainly without enthusiasm. 'I imagine so. Incidentally, Lady C, a nice picture of you in the *Mail* this morning.'

'Oh, you liked it, I'm so glad. David was very pleased, of course.'

'And the government job?'

Lady Charley said that she couldn't possibly comment on that and rang off almost immediately. She knew how to deal with snoopers. The shutters had been raised for a brief instant before slamming down with a crash.

Another phone call.

'Joe, it's Liz…'

'I'll be there, Liz. Ten thirty, is it not? Yes?'

'Thank you, Joe. That is very sweet of you, thank you. It is much appreciated. Another bypass incident.'

'But M-way, not heart-way?'

'Correct. Junction 12 again, or whatever it is.' Liz sounded tired and cross. She hadn't laughed at Joe's joke. There was irritation and anger in her tone. And a thickness to her voice that was unusual.

'Liz, are you okay?'

'Yes, Joe, but I'm just a tiny bit down.'

Joe was shocked at the thought. At six feet and blonde and gracefully muscular, Liz always struck Joe as invulnerable. She was a body that moved well every time he saw her. He grieved for her. Liz had always been good to him and vice versa as their paths criss-crossed in the random whirl of SW3. He didn't like to think of her in any kind of trouble.

'Liz, can I help?'

'No, Joe, I'll get over it. You know how it is. The word begins with h and has seven letters, every one obscene.'

'I can guess. I'm very sorry.'

Liz was faltering. Husband trouble, thought Joe, that's what it is. She wants to spend more time on her bridge and really do well on the circuit and he wants her to spend more time at home under his keen and vigilant eye. And they're clashing. She's quite caught and trapped between the two requirements. Poor Liz – such problems and such a fine player to boot.

'Liz, I'll be as good as gold if only…'

'I pay you in kind. Joe, I know that joke and it was old when you first told it to me.' But still she didn't laugh, before ringing off. She always laughed at Joe's jokes. She sounded desolate.

Still thinking about Liz and keeping an eye on the time, with an odd sense of joy in his heart, very cautiously, Joe phoned Sid. It was nine thirty. The markets had been open for an hour.

'Campbell.'

'Sid, it's Joe here. What—'

'185p, Joe. That's your question, isn't it?'

'Sell, Sid, immediately.'

'I already did, Joe.'

'What? You didn't ask me. What price did you get?'

'Opening price, Joe.'

'Which was? For Christ's sake, Sid, what price did we sell at? If you've fucked me…'

'Now, Joe, come on. What about those transitive verbs of yours? Still having trouble, are we?'

'Don't toy with me, Sid. What was the fucking price?'

'192p a share.'

'I don't believe it. 192p. Christ Jesus Almighty, say that again.'

'192p.'

'You're not bullshitting me, Sid, are you?'

'Would I do a thing like that? You've seen the *Chron* of course,

Joe?'

It was a trick question. Insider trading, especially of shares recommended in City pages, was banned in the City of London. But Joe didn't pause. Nor did he rise to the bait. He knew full well that all calls from broker to client were recorded. Joe boxed clever. He prevaricated.

'For Christ's sake, Sid, I've only just woken up. The *Chron* comes much later in my day. Give me a huge break. I'll read it when I've woken up. But 192p. That is fucking fantastic. How much is that I've made?'

'Enough to go easy for a month or so. Relax now, Joe. But are you sure you haven't read the *Chron*?'

A heavy change in tone for Sid. He was nervous about the implications of the puff for Chaebol in Tom Stone's column.

'Should I have done?'

'Stone's given a huge puff for Chaebol.'

'Well, bully for him. Great minds think alike. And you know what this means, don't you, Sid, before you try and make a citizen's arrest? One, that he's intelligent, part of the elite like you and me; and second, that he reads his own newspaper. I found all that stuff in the *Chron* for God's sake. So will he have done. Don't try and pin anything else on me, apart from Stone's intelligence.'

Sid sounded mollified. After all, he had Joe's words and denials on tape now. He could afford to relax.

'Only chaffing you, Joe. No, your profit's safe with me. Congratulations – a very profitable trade and a good idea well worked out.'

Joe pushed Sid a little more, just for the record.

'Sid, you've disturbed me with your allegations.'

'Not allegations, Joe. I didn't allege anything. Just suggestions, that's all.'

'Well, I hope you're satisfied. Anyway I don't care what you think. Right now, I'm going to have some breakfast and then, and only then, if I'm feeling brave, will I venture to read the *Chron*. And if it contains what you, er, suggest, right, then you should be prepared to hear a whoop of joy from here to the Stock Exchange. Okay? Is that okay, sir?'

'Perfectly, Joe and good morning to you.'

Swine, thought Joe as he replaced the receiver. Sid will be tops with all his clients after the Chaebol buy idea was followed by the puff; his Sherlock Holmes bit with me was just to cover his trim little rump. Crafty little tart of a broker.

As Joe left the flat, feeling richer, the phone rang again. He let it ring until the answerphone clicked in. It was Emma, a very chuffed Emma indeed.

'Joe, are you there, my little money-making friend? Joe, Joe, are you there? Damn you, Joe, why aren't you there? I want to congratulate you on your little Chaebol idea. Fantastic – they're through the roof. I've just had my broker on the phone eating out of my hand, which is not something he was brought up to do graciously, I can tell you. But what do I do now—'

Joe slammed the door on the rest of the message and hurried down the stairs of the block. He guessed it wouldn't change much in content from its preamble. He could afford to let the tape take the strain. He was running late.

He jumped on a sporty-looking 22 bus with a tired conductor sprawled on the back seat, and with the bus three-quarters empty they all careered down the King's Road at speed, Joe all the while reflecting on the boost to his minuscule hoard of gold from the Chaebol trade. Good, fat thoughts.

Ten twenty-nine exactly. Up the stairs, and then round a few corridors again at speed, to the Liz Playfair chambers, where the ladies of Sloane Square, in varying stages of wakefulness, jeans, jumpers and hair just a touch ruffled, were gathered together for their weekly fix of pillow fighting and midnight feasting bridge. As he eased his way round the door, he caught a snatch of gossip.

'And do you know, Arabella actually threw a glass of wine over her. Yes, Arabella Poole... Yes, it's true, but there was lots of provocation. You can't really blame Arabella, she's been chasing Teddy for years. The girl is just out for what she can get, and she's playing the field in a way that is unforgivable... She's too old to be doing that kind of thing for a start. I'm told she's some jumped-up tart from Norfolk, who's suddenly come into some money. There was a husband somewhere along the line. She's hotfooted it down to London to find a man for herself and she doesn't care who she upsets in the process.'

'Emma, I think she's called. Oh yes, I agree, it's rather a nice name, we toyed with Emma for Francesca... She went there hanging on Teddy's arm, and of course was completely insulting to poor Arabella who feels she's been completely jilted by Teddy. This Emma creature wouldn't even say good evening to her, she just swept on past her according to Arabella, who's completely hysterical about the whole business. Anyway, Ma Poole rang the creature up and they're going to have a long chat about ways and means in London. What one does and what one doesn't do...'

Murmurs of sympathy, approval and understanding from the listening chorus for Arabella. The fort was hard enough to hold together at the best of times without trollops getting in the way of the machinery of government. Joe realised that they were talking about Emma's epic encounter with Teddy's ex-girlfriend, reported in this case from wholly another angle. But it was not Joe's place to intervene and set the record straight by pleading for Emma.

How stories got garbled! Poor Emma, he thought, as the general conversation moved across her reputation like a Serb army, destroying everything in its path. Joe kept silent and avoided the brief glance of Lady C and Ursula, who were both knee-deep in the revelations. All coffee cups were held high, just below the chin, and heads were cocked well back, assessing the social strength, in this case profound, of the revelations. Black spot time for Emma without a doubt.

Then it was time for the bridge. Lots were drawn in stately measure for partners and Joe fell to Ursula. They all sat down to tussle with the pre-dealt hands. Ursula looked slightly more composed than she had sounded earlier that morning. A touch smarter dressed too.

So Thursday morning had become the date of the tryst – how civilised. And the children? Presumably the children's nanny was even now gassing them into submission, Joe thought. Ursula was far away from the whole scene. Alone among the women she was set for a hot date that day and she could afford to look contented. But not too pleased with herself.

It was a Thursday morning like any other Thursday morning in Sloane Square.

After about thirty minutes' play, the phone rang in Liz's office next door. Ursula moved with calm to take the call. Nobody else moved. The chorus was unfazed. It had been informed in so far as was necessary about Ursula's joyful encounter with her ex-beau. The chorus could guess that nothing drastic would happen without a long period of inter-female consultancy and discussion. Ursula was still in their frame. To the extent that Ursula's indiscretion was public knowledge shared among the women, it was sanctioned, albeit, Joe suspected, only up to a very definite point. Society would take so much but no more.

The call was from Tom. Ursula was quite relaxed about it all and the chorus smiled at the obvious pleasure she derived from the call. She grinned as she talked to him and then waggled the receiver up and down as she cooed into it. Joe was appalled. The cards trembled in his hand. He had a sudden ghastly presentiment about what was going to happen. Like Lady Pugh, he had future knowledge – and very painful it was too.

As if in a dream, Ursula drew a sheet of paper from her jacket pocket and began to read from it. She was almost chuckling. Joe could guess what was coming. Gradually her expression changed from a smile to a frown to a look of fury. There was a pause as she stopped talking to listen.

'But, I was sure it was Virgil...'

It transpired that the line was not written by Virgil. Emphatically not. 'It was by Horace, my dear.' Joe could practically hear Tom pointing this out. Ursula was not the woman to take kindly to such pedagogy. She read it as a put-down from an unworthy hack. Shades of their previous relationship.

Down went the phone and Ursula stalked back in silence to the table like one of the Furies. The lunch, of course, was still on. That was set in stone – or Stone. But she had been made to look a complete fool by that blithering idiot Joe! How stupid she'd been to trust him with anything at all, still less a Latin quotation. As for bridge...

There followed a difficult hour or so for Joe. Every bid he made became the occasion for Ursula's pursed lips and darting glances, accompanied by the occasional blistering comment. The cards ran badly for him; none of the finesses worked. The god of bridge was asleep on the job so far as Joe was concerned. Joe and

Ursula scored badly. By the time the session was over, Joe felt about two feet tall and a total social inadequate. Nor did the other women fly to his aid, even though his bridge was fundamentally impeccable. If Ursula was upset by him, then that was his business. They weren't going to take sides on his behalf. Liz Playfair looked on without comment. She held the non-voting stock on this occasion. Bad hair day all round, suggested her glum look.

He left the Playfair establishment feeling as if he'd been chewed over by a herd of cows, plus a meat mangler. Very few goodbyes from the women, and those that did come sounded merely dutiful. Then right on cue, just before the door closed behind him, Lady C managed to slide her wretched envelope across the table at him, nodding at him in silence but most meaningfully. To be about his chores, and *subito* – it was ostler time. Don't forget, Joe!

Joe wandered down the King's Road realising that jokes had their limitations. Tweaking society's nose was not encouraged and would be punished accordingly. Heavily. Jubilation over the Chaebol coup had been briefly suspended. The Till Eulenspiegel of Liz Playfair's was in severe disgrace.

His mood darkened still further when he reached the old town hall. It was a poignant, dramatic and baleful moment for him. Effectively a turning point in his life. He had never felt such pain before. He just couldn't believe his eyes. It had to be her, didn't it. She always turned up, right on cue like Lady C!

Standing there on the steps as a radiant bride was Lucy-Miranda, his long-term ex-girlfriend, the woman who had shared his university days with him, who then had ditched him, whom he had bumped into by accident, years later, when a rising star at Martins Bank, and whom he had lost to another man at the peak of his fame and power in the City.

Now here she was with the world at her feet and married, so it seemed, to that same man, Charles, who had claimed her some years previously. She stood waving on the steps, flanked by Charles's friends, on Charles's arm, at peace with the world, as the confetti whirled about her veil. The cameras clicked. Her eyes said it all – home at last to the deep bliss of the double bed, after the hurly-burly of the chaise longue. Home at last. Meanwhile her ex-lover trudged along drearily on the pavement below, practically in bum freezer and trainers. Lucy-Miranda did not see Joe. She was gazing at the stars in gratitude. Widowed, destitute, beaten and then imprisoned – at one point to her it had all seemed to be over. And now…

Joe stared at her open-mouthed. The shock of Lucy-Miranda's radiant happiness was almost unbearable. It cut Joe to the heart. Life almost stopped for him there and then. And she looked so contented! And her daughter as well! Lucia, whom Joe had rescued from the flames years ago was standing there beside her mother, looking smart and cool in her City suit, a Maitland on the fast track in the Square Mile. Oh, it was unbearable for Joe.

Joe stood there immobile in his grief as Lucy-Miranda prepared to descend the steps. Joe realised to his horror that she was approaching him and that, unless he moved rapidly, he would find himself face to face with her. That would have been intolerable. She in her bridal veil, laughing and open, and he in his jeans and shirt. Impossible. Joe felt quite sick at the prospect.

He turned fast on his heel and headed down the street beside the town hall and then accelerated as he realised the whole wedding crowd were following him in hot pursuit to their cars. Toppers, cameras, laughter, excitement and much running about in high spirits. Charles and Lucy-Miranda were heading towards their carriage; Joe could see the nag standing twenty yards in front of him with its head down. Charles had laid on a traditional wedding. Unless Joe found a diversion, he would find himself seated on the back seat of the carriage with the two newly-weds. Oh God, he thought, not that. Anything but that. I couldn't stand that for one second. Talk about gooseberry.

He spied a door to his right and shot through it. He found himself in some sort of gym or sports club. He gazed about him in total dire confusion as the crowd surged by outside, a frieze of happy jowly faces, glimpsed through the door windows. Something registered with him, perhaps a sound or a comment. Joe looked up. A light broke in upon him. Music played. He had just had another, perhaps even bigger, shock.

Joe had found Marcello.

No question. It was the photograph come to life.

There he stood in front of Joe, not two feet away from him, lightly clad in leotard and trainers. Well tanned. Marcello was an aerobics teacher in the King's Road. So much for the huddled waif theory.

Joe felt as if he'd stepped through a fold in time, as indeed he very nearly had. Another second either way and Joe would have missed him. Marcello was on his way to give a class, judging by the gear he was carrying. Head up, highly relaxed, moving easily from the hips, he had emerged from the changing room en route for the class at exactly the moment when Joe had bundled through the sports club door. Evidently Marcello had then stopped to exchange some friendly comment with reception. A split second later and he would have disappeared, like a quark, into the ether.

Joe continued to gawp at him from his spot next to the front door, comparing the impressive and well-moulded cubits of flesh and blood before him with the photos which even at that moment he carried with him. Joe felt old before this vision of springtime youth.

Marcello at that moment was bent over reception's desk, burrowing away for something in the rubbish underneath the desk. Joe could see the graceful taut line of his back running in a smooth curve from nape to rump, and the muscles bulging slightly behind the shoulder as he reached for some keys. Yes, the height was right too, and so too was the trim, basic build.

Marcello straightened up and saw Joe standing there and smiled at him. 'Are you coming to the class?'

Joe smiled back at him, and shook his head. 'I'd be too frightened. All those tough girls.'

'Nonsense, come along. Give it a try. Aerobics is easy when you get the hang of it. A posse of half-naked women going for it must be an encouragement for anyone.'

Joe was fascinated. Marcello spoke very softly but with great assurance. The words seemed to wander out from his mouth, but they were nonetheless uttered with panache. Joe could see Betty, Marcello's mother, in the line of the jaw and the flicker of the eyes as Marcello spoke. But he could also see something more dour and more dogged in the set of the head, something almost conformist and authoritarian, which surprised him. That had not been in the photographs. A desire for stability? To be in charge? Not a mummy's boy at all, thought Joe. He takes after his father. That's a masculine trait, that dourness. Yet it was his father who drove him out with the beatings and the privations.

Joe could see the problem in all this straight away. Massive unrequited affection both ways between father and son, from what Joe knew of the background to Marcello's escape. It was highly unlikely that Marcello would want to come home to Betty unless he made peace with his father. Marcello had made his own way in the world so far. It would cost him a lot, perhaps too much, to return home.

Marcello waved a casual hand at him as he turned to ascend the stairs up to the studio. 'Whenever you change your mind...'

Then he was gone. Joe, recapturing his presence of mind, turned to reception, and apologised. 'I've been told that his class is very good. The best on the street, so I'm assured. I was coming just to check it out. I didn't expect to meet the maestro himself. That was quite a shock. I took fright at the thought of actually doing the class. You know, actually getting down to it.'

Reception was chatty. 'I know just how you feel, dear. As you can see, I've got the best of intentions but they never quite work out on the follow-through.'

Reception was more than just plump. Almost a heaving mass of uncoordinated flesh, although not quite in the class of Norman the tramp.

'You'd enjoy his class though, dear. He works them very hard but they all keep coming back for more. Him and Jean-Paul, they do it together.'

'Jean-Paul?'

'They work together. They're very close. Jean-Paul's lovely. He's really smashing-looking. Just like a little doll, he's so beautiful. So today they'll start the class together, working off each other like and then Marcello will take over on his own. It's very popular. The girls love it. You should go up and look into the studio and see for yourself.'

'I might just do that. With your permission?'

'You'd better get one of the instructors to take you up there.

Wait a second.'

Reception mumbled down a phone and in a few moments another bright limber fresh-faced lad appeared, ready to show Joe around. Joe felt like Alice; in a few odd moments he had fallen into a total wonderland.

'Thinking of joining?'

'Don't rush me. I'm just thinking of taking exercise. That's as far as it goes for the time being.'

'We'll see about that. Wait until you see Marcello's class.'

Joe gawped for the second time that hour. They were gazing at Marcello's class. About fifty or so girls in varying stages of undress, or so it seemed to Joe, were punching the air with vigour in coordinated unison as the music blasted out, all the while grunting 'Ugh!' as they punched. As a vision of woman militant in the future it was impressive and terrifying. In front of the army stood two young men, Marcello and presumably Jean-Paul. Obviously they were friends. They encouraged each other and smiled at the class at the same time as they went through the routine.

Reception had been right. Whereas Marcello was impressive in his own right, as a young man trained to the peak of fitness and doing it his way, Jean-Paul was beautiful in a quite different way. He was a cherub. Brown skin, a smile that split his face in two like a ripe apple, blue eyes, unusually, a way of moving that was almost feminine in its delicate intuitive stealthiness, and a shock of black hair.

Joe could see that the women in the class wanted to eat him up in sheer lust every time he moved a hip or an arm. Mass fucking of this young man. Marcello was there to offer him protection because, as the class warmed up, it was obvious that it teetered just on the edge of sexual hysteria. Pure African tribalism. Jean-Paul provoked the women. So it had been from the very moment of Jean-Paul's birth in some North African ghetto. And so it would always be, Joe guessed. Jean-Paul was a darling, always held close to the women, with every inch of his smooth dark skin always cherished. No chance for him ever at any time of breaking away and becoming a man, a tough hombre, as Marcello obviously had done. The women were always there to drag him into the tent and the bed. He had been raped to oblivion by the time he was five years old, Joe reckoned.

Looking at the two of them go through their well-practised routine, followed obediently by the women in slave-like imitation, Joe wondered whether he would have to report a few problems when he telephoned Betty with the good news. 'Yes, Betty, I've found Marcello, the Lord be praised, but you should know that he has a friend... No, not a girl, Betty, a young man... Well, I don't know, Betty, I didn't stop to ask... I know it seems unlikely but it does happen.' Indeed it does.

'Seen enough, mate,' asked the young trainer at Joe's side.

'Yes, I'm looking at the future and it's terrifying.'

'You've seen nothing. You should come on Tuesday evening. Eight o'clock. They actually give the class all the way through together. It's amazing. It's like a battlefield. That Jean-Paul really knows how to work those women up to a frenzy.'

'So they actually get to eat the Christians?'

'Not quite but we live in hope. We've got the videos ready for the day it happens. There won't be much left of those two when it happens, I can tell you. The women will devour them.'

'I'd better buy a ticket. This is better than the opera.'

'Half an hour before, mate. Not before then. Seven thirty at the earliest. But come early. It's a sell-out every Tuesday. Best show in town, I reckon. Even the other instructors do the class, it's so good.'

Joe was escorted back down the stairs, past reception who grinned at him, and then he left the building after shaking hands with the young trainer.

'See you Tuesday then. What did you say your name was?'

'Joe. And yours?'

'Ned. Look forward to Tuesday, Joe.'

'Thanks, Ned. I might just turn up.'

Joe knew full well that come hell or high water he would be there promptly on Tuesday evening shortly. The problem was clear. Would he be squiring Betty to her first aerobics class? Now Betty was a player, but even so... Time perhaps to check out some training kit for his momentous experience on Tuesday. Shoes, yes, shoes. He definitely needed some of those. Exercise was not a high ranker on Joe's list of priorities. He preferred to let the body look after itself, undisturbed by a rise in the heart rate.

Meanwhile he wandered down the King's Road, wondering just how he should approach Betty with the great news. She would be shocked, excited and eager to rocket down to London and scoop up her long-lost beloved son. Within five minutes. Which she mustn't on any account do. How to put that to her in such a way... Best play it by ear, he decided after a few hundred yards of dawdling rumination. I'll call her now, before I think about it too much and become over-elaborate.

He fished in his pocket for his wallet, and pulled out the small notebook where he kept his phone numbers. He found a call box, took some money from his pocket and dialled Betty's number. The traffic rumbled past noisily outside.

Such a mundane operation, he thought as the numbers punched out their code, but such a huge payload to the heart from the simple act of putting coins in a slot and pushing a few buttons. The leverage of modern life – terrifying. For forty pence you can get a shock that fucks you rigid.

The sound of a phone ringing. Briefly. A voice answered. It was Betty. Gotcha! Now for some serious talking.

'Betty, it's Joe here.'

'Joe, such an age since you phoned. Have you got any news?' She was anxious but craven in her hopes. The voice faltered. All hope had clearly fled. Betty, a strong woman, had been weakened over time by the fruitless quest for Marcello.

'What are you doing at this very moment, Betty?'

'Two of the girls are here at home for the week and we're having a good time just lounging around. I'm in the kitchen. I'm just about to make them some lunch. Why do you ask, Joe? Is there something wrong. Tell me quickly, Joe. Is it bad news?' A terrifying note of fear in her voice. It croaked on the high note.

'Betty, don't ask me any questions. That's why I'm telephoning. Where are the girls right now?'

'One is right here beside me, wondering what this conversation is all about. And the other is still in bed, I think. What time is it? Heavens, it's high time she got up.'

'Betty, don't ask me any questions. Not just now. Just send

daughter number one to dig daughter number two out of bed. Do it now.' Joe was not to be disobeyed.

Joe heard some mumbling, some expostulation, the tramp of dragging steps and then a door slammed in the high dudgeon of protest.

'Yes, Joe, I'm alone now. What is it?'

'I've found Marcello. He's well.' It didn't take long to say. Joe's voice was flat.

It didn't take long to register either. She gasped. The tears leaped into Betty's voice at once. 'Oh God, Joe, that's just incredible. But where is he? When can I see him? I want to bring him home. I'm coming down to London at once. Where are you now? Tell me. I can be there this afternoon. Oh God, this is just fantastic. Just wait till I tell the girls. Oh, I just want to scream this from the rooftops. Even his father might be pleased. Yes, even his father. Oh, Joe, thank you so much, thank you so much. You have given me such happiness with your call.' All this was delivered haltingly through the choking tears in her throat.

Joe was measured in his reply. Not cruel but decisive in his crisp tone. It was important to get a complex message across to her as quickly as possible. Nothing was as simple as she thought. Betty could only glimpse the hugger-mugger of the hearth and the home. But there was more to it than that.

'Betty you have to trust me, but it may take some time before—'

Joe was interrupted by the sleepy and quite cross entry into the kitchen of daughters one and two. Tramp, tramp. More door slamming. Joe heard Betty give them the news. Her voice quavered. She was very close to breaking down into uncontrolled grief and joy. A great primal shout of exultation from all three women in unison. Then a new voice on the phone. Daughter one or two. 'Where is he? Where is he? Where is Marcello?'

Then Betty was back on the line. She was half sobbing, half laughing and her voice kept breaking up in mid-sentence. 'Joe, will you ring us back in five minutes? We can't speak. We're just going to have a quick dance on the table together. You're sure about all this? You're absolutely sure?'

'I was talking to him not five minutes ago. No shadow of

doubt, not a flicker. I've found him.'

'Girls, it's true. It's true. Joe was talking to him not five minutes ago.'

'Hurrah, hurrah, hurrah for Marcello!' came down the line. Then more sobbing, this time en masse.

'Betty, I'll ring you back in five minutes.'

Joe replaced the receiver and left his phone booth in the King's Road, while in deepest Hertfordshire three women cavorted together in crude dance across their stone-flagged kitchen floor, shouting in raucous joy.

And somewhere else in Chelsea the groom was just making his soft-voiced address to a sea of smiling faces as Lucy-Miranda sat in calm smiling splendour at the top table beside her husband, dear sweet and kind Charles, Lucia beside her. What was lost had been found, and would not be let go of again in a hurry, that was for sure.

Joe rang Betty back from another phone booth and found her calmer and more controlled. But anxious.

'So what is the matter, Joe? Why can't I see him?'

'Betty, you have to trust me on this. I think I have to find out the lie of the land before returning him to his family.'

'Joe, this is rubbish. His place is with his family.'

'Betty, don't be so sure. Ask yourself why he left home in the first place.' Suddenly Joe could see the line to take.

'I never stop asking myself that very self same question. So why did he leave home?'

'Because his father beat him. That's what you told me.'

'I suppose that must be the true reason, Joe. But don't sidetrack me, just bring him back to me.'

'Well then, Betty, ask yourself this next question. If that was the reason why he left home, and if he's managed to set himself up in London in a small business, say, then he has no reason to want to come home. Or rather, if he does come home, it will be by negotiation. He's a proud young man from what I can see, and his pride has been hurt by his father's brutality. He won't tolerate just being scooped up again, even though I guess he misses his family.'

'Oh Joe, this is painful for me. I feel such a fool. You mean you've actually seen him this morning? You were close to him, physically, I mean physically?' Betty sounded crestfallen after the joy and tears of five minutes previously.

'Yes, and he looked magnificent. You need have no fears on that score. He is in the rudest of health. He is a credit to his mother. Have no fears on the physical side, that's perfectly okay. But I think – or rather I fear – there may be a diplomatic angle to all this which needs careful treatment. That's all I'm saying. I think we have to tread carefully. If you go in too hard initially, you risk making the breach permanent. You must leave it to time, and a spot of diplomacy. I mean only a couple of weeks, just to give me time to get close to him and sound him out about his mother Betty – that's you, remember – and his sisters. To see how he feels about home. We've done brilliantly just to find him in the London haystack. Let's not mess it all up by an excess of zeal.'

Betty could see the sense of this. She had taken Joe's views on board. 'Joe, you're being very good to me about this. After all, we are very nearly strangers to each other. It is very kind of you.'

'No more of that, Betty. We are in this together, even though you are operating at long distance from the scene of the crime. But I have to tell you that he did look very well. Absolutely in top form.'

Betty sounded humble. Almost beseeching. 'But you won't tell me any more about the way you met him?'

'Absolutely not, Betty. It would give the whole game away. You'd rush down immediately to London and shanghai him. And maybe put him off his stroke by so doing. And ruin all our efforts. It would be only human to do that but I don't think it would be a good idea. That's why I'm telling you nothing. But the whole adventure makes a good story and worth waiting for. Never fear – you'll be told.'

Groan from Betty. She wanted it all now, at that moment, and served with Béarnaise sauce, preferably.

'Yes, but, Betty, I ran into him purely by accident. It was a freak of fate. Let's not tempt fate any more by asking too much of it. Let's walk warily. All I ask is a week or so's grace and then you can see him. Or at least, I'll give you all the details so that you can descend on him yourself.'

More misery from Betty but admission that caution might be best. An admission given very grudgingly, but given nevertheless.

'Is he all right? Does he need money?'

'I don't think so. I think he's okay for folding stuff.' Joe banished the thought of his own dire lack of said folding stuff from his mind as he negotiated a peace settlement with Betty.

'Hmm.' She sniffed. 'Hmm. Well, perhaps you know best, Joe, but tell me, when are you going to ring again and keep us all informed?'

Joe could answer that question. He was happy to be able to say something positive. 'We can talk over the phone during the next couple of days and I can give you reassurance, but nothing positive will happen before Tuesday after next. And the reason that I can be so certain of that date is that I've fixed an interview with him for that day, in the evening.'

An interview with him and about fifty rabid females into the bargain, plus a male friend of questionable sexual orientation. But those were just details. There would be an interview. Joe felt that he was winning the battle for Betty's support.

'So he's in business? That's what it is, is it?'

'Don't try and crack it, Betty. Be content with what I've told you and that should suffice. What I will tell you by way of confirmation is that he's very well set up. Beyond that, I don't know myself. I will find out as much as I can so that on the Tuesday evening I can give you a full report. But feel free to ring me any time before that and we can talk. To fix a time for Tuesday, I guess I'll be ringing you with news around ten in the evening. Can I call you at that time? Will it cause problems for you at home?'

'You mean with my husband?'

'Exactly.'

'I'm going to have to tell him, aren't I? I hadn't thought about all of that.'

'You begin to see my point about diplomacy.'

'Damn you, Joe, why are you always so clever? You're quite right. It does need careful handling. He'll guess from the way the girls are cavorting around that something is up. So he'll have to be told something. But what? What do I say to him? I can see the whole problem starting all over again, if I'm not careful.'

Joe paused as the chatelaine of Betty Towers carefully mulled her next move.

'Betty, I have an idea. Why don't you give him my number, say to him what I've said to you, and get him to give me a call? I'll talk to him direct. That way I can soften him up for the next big moment, the return of Marcello.'

Which might be hard to arrange. Joe had a brief glimpse of the Chernobyl effect that Marcello and Jean-Paul turning up together might have on Betty and her family. He shuddered. He could hear the words and the abuse. And could see a whole range of possibilities. These situations were incalculable. Anything might happen, apart from the preferred outcome. The mind might well have to boggle hard.

Fortunately Betty agreed with Joe's suggestion. And that was how they left it. 'Roll on that Tuesday,' was Betty's parting shot.

Joe decided to take some lunch and plodded off towards the nearest greasy spoon in the King's Road.

There is always a moment when a mission starts. There is heavy spadework in the beginning getting the props into position, like setting up the reporting structure and organising the reporting flows and arranging the cover. All this comes after the key operatives have been selected and the basic elements put securely into place. Relative to the real thing, to the moment when the starting pistol is actually fired, this is just vamping till ready. Reality and danger start when the agent gets his first set of instructions. Then the mission is launched. There is no turning back after that. Everything until then has been set in pre-time mode. But now it is go time, as the agent starts to rock towards his target over the windy uncertainties of space and time. And everything is timed almost to the last second. A flash out of time beyond the parameters and the mission can be lost entirely. After go, nothing major or vital can be allowed to go wrong.

These were Annie's thoughts as she prepared to press the detonator. She was alone in her office. Bootface had disappeared, as he had warned her, in a fit of temperament. She was meeting him tonight for their drink and whatever else that might turn up in their conversation. But in the meantime the show and the mission went on.

She had carried on working after Bootface had flounced out on her. She didn't think Bootface would have a lot to say beyond bluster that evening. Her mind retuned to the mission. Time, circumstance and the precise location of proximity to the flow of events had crawled towards the natural limit point and reached it exactly now, right on target. It was time to get serious.

Annie paced about the office for a few seconds, reflecting on the successful way that various individuals had been pushed and pulled and tugged into their correct vantage points – Joe had been reactivated and was not desisting; Joachim was there to do the briefing and was doing it well; and dear old Tom Stone, after many years' silence, had been contacted and had reacted well to Annie's suggestions that he pass on the odd message or so. So far, so good. To her surprise, there was a smoothness to it all which defied her earlier pessimistic predictions and expectations. If only Bootface…

She dismissed the thought from her mind. She would deal with that later. But now for the big moment. Now for the moment when structure joined up and completed the circle, Joe at one point, she at the opposite point along the circle, and Joachim and Tom standing pat in their positions to assist the circular flow of communication. Five seconds to zero hour…

This was the moment when she came into the ring. To her, on that overcast, gusty late morning, it felt fine. The vibes were agreeable and not too threatening. It all had a reasonable feel to it. She guessed that Joe was at lunch. If he wasn't, well then, he should be. A man needs his lunch. But Joe was a man of regular habits. She was safe to call him and leave a message. Now for it!

She phoned his number, listened for the ring, waited for the answerphone to click in with its familiar greeting and then left the following message: 'Joe, the Fat Man is back in town. Time to get up and go. More instructions to follow. We'll get back to you.'

The Fat Man was Joe's call sign. Joe would know full well what iteration of the call sign meant – it meant he was fully operational again. Annie knew that Joe would not be entirely overjoyed to hear his call sign on his answerphone. But it would not be for long; just for the time it took to complete the mission. Then he could go back to being Joe, the force in the City again. But not until the mission was over – always provided, of course, that he survived the mission. Until then he was Annie's prisoner.

Annie knew Joe very well. She had worked with him before as a front-line agent. She had no doubts about his ability. Joe had been chosen for his survival capacity. Even so, it would be very difficult. The mission fell into three stages, all of which naturally telescoped into each other very fast, with fail-safe breaks from one to the other. Timing was crucial.

The first stage was easy and had very nearly been accomplished, the second was practically impossible and the third stage looked even more difficult. Well-nigh terminal. Very, very dangerous. That was where Joe would come to grief, if he failed at all. And what was the glitch in stage three? Why Rivers Pugh, of course, and the complications that he represented.

That young man had become a real problem for Annie and showed no signs of going away or reducing his impact on the assignment. That introduction to Perdita for Joe posed almost insurmountable problems. It was next to impossible to warn an agent off emotional succour when it was offered, even though it might be a honey trap. And Perdita was certainly all of that! Just a chance meeting late at night in a bar between Joe and Rivers and years of careful planning risked instantaneous destruction. But then again, so far so good. And Joe was still playing the part to perfection. Perhaps they would enjoy good fortune after all.

Annie waited another five minutes and then dialled Joe's number again. She waited again for the answerphone to click on and then she sent across to Joe the following message: 'Joe, this is a message from the Fat Man. Get very close to Lady Charley and stay very close to Lady Charley. Get as close as you dare.'

Then she put the phone down on her desk and went out for a slow walk beside the Thames. Time to think about Bootface and her drink that evening with him. Bootface would not be easy. But the die was cast and the mission was under way. Annie, like Caesar, had crossed the Rubicon. No turning back now. The shooting had started.

Joe ate a reasonable lunch for a greasy spoon and then returned to his flat. Bridge with Joxer? It was a temptation, especially since Joxer was on a good roll. Some tough bridge would efface the memory of his savaging that morning at the hands of Ursula. Yes, why not a frisk with Joxer?

He eyed the crack on his way into the flat. It had stabilised at its norm of the morning. So the building was not about to collapse about his ears. So far so good. And he had, after all, just found Marcello. Now that in itself was a tiny little coup-ette of a coup.

Many messages on the answerphone. He scrolled the tape back. A second call from Emma, telling him ecstatically that she had taken her profit and wasn't that grand and did he have any further ideas and could they meet for lunch and had he made that telephone call yet to the Confederation of Authors? All a bit breathless. A call, surprisingly, from Ursula, who sounded oddly sleepy and relaxed. The call went some way, it seemed to Joe, towards making amends for her appalling bad temper of the morning; apparently there'd been a misprint of her Latin quotation which completely altered the sense of the phrase. Anyone could have made that mistake in translating the line; and as for the Virgil gaffe, well, wasn't it time Joe did some swotting on the difference between Horace and Virgil?

And why not, Ursula, thought Joe, as he listened to the next message, thinking of the rictus of dismay that would smash its way across her face at the very thought of doing some harsh close work on a Latin unseen.

A call from Joachim, demanding to know whether Joe had read the papers which Joachim had given him – Joe was at that stage halfway through the numbers – and then a call from Tom, asking him to ring early next week for a chat. So far, so procedural.

That man Tom's a professional, thought Joe. He knows how to blend it beautifully. I'm impressed. I have time to work out a new idea for him, and I think I may have just the one which will delight him. I'll call him Monday. This is like writing his column for him, without the hard work. I've always fancied myself as a journalist, except that I couldn't actually tolerate the writey-writey bit. Next call.

The next call on the answerphone carolled out its message of doom. Time to meet the Fat Man – again. Joe froze. He had dreaded this moment although he knew it was coming. Always the Fat Man coming to call, coming to call, coming to call. Had known it for some time. Like a knife in the wind swinging towards him. It was the formalism of the Gents that was so impressive. They manoeuvred you into a position of their choosing and then politely informed you that hell on wheels was about to dine that night with you. And etiquette was important. There was a dress code. Be sure to wear a black tie – ha, ha, ha.

'Time to get up and go... We'll get back to you.' Click.

Joe pondered his chances of survival. Nerves were tightening and stomach muscles were clenching already. The cringe of fear before the expected bullet. Always there at the back of his mind, always, always. But at least he had some deep cover and that was worth something. Berlin and the empty squares with the snipers in position glided across his mind's eye. The uneasy movement around the pillars of the high buildings, waiting for the rifle to crack. Surely all that was over now? Not just yet, he told himself, and didn't you know it was coming anyway? Get serious, Joe, for Christ's sake. Get fucking real for once. You're too far from home to play the fool now.

One final message to come. He'd like a nice call from Sharon Stone now, Tom's big sister, ha, ha, asking him, no, better, begging him, for a date. Wouldn't that be just fabulous?

New message of doom. Very insistent and very tightly worded. He knew that tone. It brooked no argument and no discussion. They were in a hurry. They were on their way. It was starting now. Big time. No quarter, given or asked. And he was the front man. As ever. In the front line. Going to meet the man. As ever.

'...stay very close to Lady Charley. Get as close as you dare.' Click. End of message. End of messages.

End of life? Could be – you never know these days what a life is worth. Cheap or dear. And what's the exchange rate on a life, then? Tell me that after you've given me the price of fish. Joe's thoughts were in turmoil. No takers on this trade because the party on the other side of the bargain is none other than death himself, whose terms of trade are harsh in the extreme.

Joe sat there on the floor for a long time, thinking about death. His old friend come to call again. To do a little trade with him.

Joe, I've missed you.

Yeah, long time no see.

Yeah, we missed in Berlin. Such a shame too. I was certain we were going to socialise. But there was such a crush in Berlin, we never had a chance to meet. Just so many people crowding me. Too bad then, but now it's simply a pleasure. We're certain to meet.

Keeping well, I see death babe.

Oh, passing fair, mustn't grumble.

You're looking spruce beneath the hat, death babe. Carrying the scythe well, indeed impressively. Somehow the holes in the skull look quite fashionable, almost designer bored.

Thank you, Joe, you were always so observant. I had the holes freshly done only the other day. But Joe, what's wrong? You don't seem pleased to see me, and you always the life and soul of any party. I was counting on you. The light fantastic, you know you do that so well, Joe.

No, death babe, I'm not overjoyed to make a date with you. To tell you the truth, it's a trifle inconvenient right now. You see, I'm a bit busy...

But you'll make the time, won't you, Joe?

Joe thought about Perdita and life and hopes and aspirations and ambitions and gradually started to feel like vomiting. It all seemed so ugly and perspiring all of a sudden. The room closed in on him. He knew he'd make the time. Any time at all.

Then he started to stare at the wall as the safest place to find shelter and sanctuary. A little feeling tightened in his throat. He thought of the dead Viking chieftains going to meet their gods in the flaming longboats, laid out serenely by the helm, treasure alongside, while the swords and spears of fighting comrades clashed out their message of triumph across the vacant swirling seas, as the boat drifted to its own eternity. He wished he could be as brave or as flamboyant.

Joe stayed for a long time seated beside the phone staring at the wall. Somehow he lacked the incentive to rise to his feet and get on with the frantic business of staying alive. He seemed to curl in on himself physically, but mentally he found he was relaxed, even slightly joyous. Certainly clear-sighted and balanced. He found himself, as ever, plotting the steps needed to stay alive, taking as ever the basic precautions in his mind, getting the feel of the darkness and the fear ahead, teaching his mind to stay above the battle.

The long afternoon declined into a blaze of sunset and Joe sat still beside the phone and in front of the wall. Nothing moved in the flat around him. No telephones rang as darkness fell from the sky and the wind began to sing. He was alone with his fears – and his strength.

This surprised him, as did the secret exultation which kept licking at his mind, giving it tiny uplifts from moment to moment. So why these good feelings? Why this feeling of release? Eventually, after much soul-searching, he tumbled to the truth of the matter. For him this was the end of the business. This was the final mission for him. One more and he was out. Far far away from the Gents. It was that sensation which gave him such colossal feelings of release. So this was what they meant when they talked about the trapdoor mission. He could see what it meant. The future held enormous riches for him, on one side of the balance sheet. Survival meant restitution of his dollars held God knows where in some secret cache. And a failure to survive? Well, you can't eat the dollars, now, can you? So what the hell, he thought. *Toujours gai, toujours gai.*

His blitheness of spirit shocked him into flesh-creeping terror. That was what killed – the sense of devil-may-care. Long-term prisoners went mad, paradoxically, as soon as they learned the date of their release. Man could only stand so much reality. Joe told himself to beware of easy triumphs and facile joys. Hence he was at pains at once to stamp down any feelings of joy at his imminent release. I see now, he kept telling himself, how it may go. Too much *joie de vivre* and that's it. I'm dead meat. I have to take extra care. This is the time for total ring craft. I don't want to go down the trapdoor. Into Hades? And across the Styx? No way, pal. And no way that Charon would take me for a moment, not even with a Visa card.

Joe carried on thinking about death, telling himself how much he still wanted to live. The image of a boisterous Perdita kept flitting through his mind. Terms of trade, terms of trade, he kept telling himself. That's where I want to be and that's the bosom against which I want to nestle my head. That will make it all worthwhile. And so saying, talking himself into careful oblivion of danger but focusing on survival and giving himself something to live for, Joe stayed where he was for many more hours. It seemed to be too dangerous to attempt anything more positive. Besides he was quite comfortable down there on the floor.

Eventually, for want of anything more constructive and because he had to do it at some point, Joe dialled the Confederation of Authors' number and left a message on the answerphone. Sufficiently circumlocutory to sound genuine. He carefully repeated himself a number of times.

Annie went to keep her date with Bootface with mixed feelings and a divided attention. Part of her mind kept straying back to Joe. She had acted with deliberate calculated brutality by sending two messages in order to shock him into a realisation that he was in danger and to keep him on his guard. That seemed to her to be the only way she could try to preserve him from an excess of affection and humanity in certain specific directions, most notably Pugh Park in general and Perdita Pugh in particular.

Her mind was almost wholly focused on the mission, now that she had started the ball rolling. Bootface was a kind of footnote. Now that they were into go country, which Joe knew about, then sooner or later Joe would come back to her and communicate with her directly. That was the next phase. It had to happen and it would happen; Joe was too good an agent to risk staying out of communication in the middle of a mission. Joe knew the numbers and the codes and the call signs; it was only a matter of time. And as soon as he came back into orbit, say quite shortly, then she could start to push him again in a more sharply angled direction. And she was optimistic. She knew now where he had to be at in a month's time. And could she get him to that point? Chances were that she could, provided Lady Charley came into the equation. But that would be delicate. She needed direct contact with Joe to ensure that took place smoothly.

By the time she found the bar, Bootface's 'neutral territory' drinking hole at the back of Victoria, she had almost forgotten why she was taking a drink with him. Bootface forced her to refocus her attention pretty sharply. He greeted her warmly as a man greets a woman, not as colleague to colleague, and that upset her. He was obviously going to transgress any number of boundary lines that evening. He was nattily dressed, expansive at the bar as he ordered the drinks, and he played the man about town role with excessive bonhomie. Annie thought he behaved like a man who'd just left his job. Suddenly this did not look good to her. Perhaps she should have brought a colleague along with her. But now it was too late.

'Annie, how long have you been in the service?'

'Oh, quite a few years now.'

Bootface's brow furrowed and his jaw stuck out like a spade. 'I see you're going to be as open with me tonight as you normally are in the office. Well, I can live with that. Tonight will be just like working in the office, apart from the drinks. Communication lines as normal.'

He took a good steady pull of his whisky then replaced the glass a touch heavily on the table, eyeing it fondly.

'So, to proceed. Let me tell you where I'm coming from. I've been in the service now for about twenty-five years and I've seen it come and I've seen it go, but mostly I've seen it bumble along in its own sweet way. Spying is a very odd business indeed. Most of it is futile in my opinion and most of the missions fuck up huge. The human factor just cannot function nowadays against the enormous tide of randomness. The world has changed. El Niño is a negative factor in espionage as much as in weather forecasting. Now my point in saying all this to you is not to challenge you. I know you love your job and you're good at it – don't get me wrong, you're very good at it – but for me the sweet sensation of excellence is no longer enough. I have to have more. I have to have more by way of recompense for all the long years of snooping, watching, betraying, opening confidential files, tracking people down and what have you. It's called abuse of humanity. Largely by me. Do you follow that? I need recompense for my persistent abuse of humanity, mine and other people's. Do you understand that?'

Gambling debts, thought Annie, it must be about money. Lots of money. This is going to get very nasty indeed. 'Go on, Bootface,' she said. 'I'm listening.'

'So the question is, where do I go for the honey? Not the service that's for sure. The service isn't what it was. Never will be. It's been struck a terminal blow. As soon as you get confidential files stuck on the Internet, then you know that's the end. The whole of the spying game has to change; as soon as the Wall came down, that maybe marked the end of a whole way of life and procedure for us all. No, I'm not going to find my salvation in the service. That is totally certain, as sure I'm drinking this drink.' And so saying he quaffed back some more whisky.

'So where do I go? Now before I answer that question, can I ask you a question, Annie?'

'Certainly, go ahead.'

She felt prim but poised as he leered at her. She felt like a clever, well-prepared student ready to take a tricky question in her viva, but harassed by maleness, with all its disconcerting, tawny smells.

'What is this mission all about, Annie? Just tell me in your own words.'

'You know, Bootface, these things can't be discussed outside the office. It's absolutely forbidden.'

'Yes, I know that, but do you think anyone here is listening?'

They were seated in the far corner of the bar at a table, quite alone and separated from the other tables. Elsewhere in the pub whoopee was being made with great enthusiasm. Impossible for anyone else to overhear their conversation. Annie felt beneath the table and Bootface jeered at her.

'I've already done that. I can assure you there are no mikes.'

'Okay, you win, and I'll talk. It's about getting close to Lady Charley.'

Bootface looked at her hard. This time his reactions were genuine. 'No it's not. It goes further than that. It goes a lot further than that. It's about Sir David, Lady Charley's husband. It's about getting close to him. Isn't that correct?'

'It might be. On the other hand…'

'It might not. You amuse me, Annie, with your studied replies. I know the form too, you know, just as well as you do. Okay, since you're not going to talk much, let me continue. I think the whole mission is about getting close to Sir David through Lady Charley, which is very subtle. That's what Joe is about, isn't it? Attack through the weak link. The weak link is the wives. That's why Joe has been pushed into all that bridge-playing malarkey in Sloane Square, isn't it?'

Annie shook her head. She wasn't going to say an extra word beyond the dictates of politeness. This was sounding very dangerous. She felt increasingly concerned. Yet it had its own overstated aspect. This distracted her. Part of her kept imagining that she'd strayed into some film about spying, where the characters spoke in clichés and adopted aggressive attitudes, along with guns, molls, and fast cars. Bootface sounded more and more like Eddie Constantine with his Kennedy heavy jaw and his crashing clichés. It was all oddly surreal. None of it added up. Was he simply mad?

But Bootface was not to be denied his speech. He ploughed ahead. Years of resentment were coming to the surface. For him it was all too, too real.

'Okay Annie, let's cut to the chase. Let's pursue my line of reasoning. I'll give you a clue to start off with – I went to Sloane School.'

Annie looked staggered. That she had not known.

'You didn't know that, did you? I never put it on my CV; I think I put Harrow or something. To confuse everyone and to prevent myself getting bracketed with all the other old boys. Nobody checked and I got away with it. But over the years I've come to realise exactly what Sloane School meant – and means – to me. The answer is a lot. It runs the country and it is the backbone of the country and I won't have anything about it, or its traditions, fucked about by the likes of you. I'm proud to have been there. And I say all that because in some subtle, cunning way that I can't quite fathom as yet, I think this whole mission is an assault on Sloane School. You want to frame Sir David and you want to bring the school and its reputation into the mud somehow at the same time. Well, you never went there and you haven't a clue about it and you don't know anything about how important its traditions really are. But I can tell you this – it'll take a good deal more than you're capable of achieving to torch the reputation of Sloane School.'

Bootface didn't quite say 'And also you're a girl', but he was getting close enough. Annie said nothing and listened to the tortured dialogue. He was a sad man. Disloyalty was a terrible thing to observe in a disenchanted forty-five-year-old.

'Anyway, enough of that. That's what I think you're up to and I don't want any part of it. Is that clear?'

'You could always ask for a transfer.'

'No, I've gone one better. I've worked out a game plan. There is a transfer, but not in the sense that you imagine it. I'll tell you more by degrees. It concerns you in the sense that I can offer you some choices. D'you want to hear them?'

Bootface leaned forward towards Annie. His face was sweating hard from the whisky. More Eddie Constantine, she thought.

'If you want to tell them to me, Bootface, then I'll listen. But don't think it goes any further than that with me. I disagree with what you're saying utterly.'

'Disagree away, Miss Muffet, I'm indifferent to your disdain. I don't have your luxury of choice. Time is not on my side. I'm in a hurry.'

'Debts, Bootface?'

He looked startled for a second. 'Could be. How did you know that?'

'I see we're both being coy now about our revelations.'

'Not bad, Miss Muffet, and quite a good hit, but we'll see how you're scoring in a second when I've finished talking about the game plan.'

'Game plan away, then, Bootface.'

'You think I'm a disgusting old fart, don't you? Well, you may be right but we'll see. Every fart has his day, what? Anyway, ready for this? You'll love it when I tell you. Sitting comfortably? Okay, let me begin. Once upon a time there was a man called Joe who had amassed a large fortune. But we needed him for a job, so we distrained his assets from him. Right?'

'Right.'

'About two million or more?'

'Probably more by now, what with the interest accumulating and the rise in world stock markets.'

Annie knew now what was coming, not in specific shape but in broad outline. It was horrible.

'The assets are held in escrow in a certain bank's accounts and they can be unlocked by two mutually matching computer keys.'

Annie was right in her suppositions. It was as she had surmised. What a dung beetle Bootface was! What a total shit!

'Correct, Annie?'

'Correct, Bootface.'

'I know the bank, Annie. I found it out. I know I wasn't supposed to know but I do now. As you would say in your careful methodical way, that is fact. But not only that. I know more, much more. I discovered not by chance but by diligent digging away in the files exactly where half of the computer code was located. I found it and I have it in safe keeping. So in theory I now have access to half Joe's fortune.'

'In theory, Bootface.'

'But Annie, you have the other half of the code. So without your help I cannot plunder Joe's fortune and make my escape.'

'That is true, Bootface.'

'So will you give me the code, Annie? It's so easy as I see it. If my suppositions are right, we can take the money and top Joe by turning him over to the tender mercies of Sloane School. It's beautiful and it all fits and it's so easy. We make a fortune in the process.'

'You mean shop him and abort the mission? Isn't there something here about the steward being worthy of his hire?'

Bootface ignored her interruption. He had too much on his mind to pay heed to her thoughts. This gave her a tiny sense of inspiration. If she could only just squeeze… he maybe wouldn't notice. But it was important to be smooth in the transition. No give-aways.

'Of course, that wouldn't be too difficult, aborting the mission. Just breathe a word here and there in the right quarters. Joe's an outsider anyway. They'd spot in a flash just what he's up to with Sir David and they would carry out the appropriate response.'

'Like?'

'Some dark alley could be arranged. Joe is particularly vulnerable at the moment. He is out on a limb and not easily protected. As I say, he's an outsider. It wouldn't take long to knock him off for good. He wouldn't be missed. And then we—'

'Collect his fortune. And scarper.'

'Exactly. You catch on quick, Annie. You're truly very smart.'

'So we share about three million pounds between us.'

'You've got it. And listen, Annie, this is Joe's trapdoor mission.'

Bootface was talking from his obsessions now. Annie remained tight-lipped, hoping he'd register her silence favourably.

'Annie, agents never come back from this, because they get too cocky and they foul up somewhere along the line.'

'To be honest, Bootface, I'd never seen things in that light before. But now you put it in the way you do…'

'So are you interested? We don't have too much time. I know about these things. The whole thing is starting to move now. If we're going to make our move, we have to do it now.'

'You know, I think I might be tempted. No, that's the wrong word. Too strong. I could get interested. Let's put it that way. More oblique. It's a neat little scheme. It needs thinking about.'

Bootface was immediately suspicious. But also desperately hopeful.

'I'm very surprised to hear you talk like this, Annie. I didn't think you were the type to be tempted.'

'What you just said about the service touched a slight chord with me too. Suddenly I can see work on one side and lots of sunshine on the other. It's quite a shock. It needs thinking about, as I said.'

'How long do you need?'

'Maybe a week.'

'No more. We have to move very quickly in my view. How will you tell me.'

Again the sense of something bizarre, something pre-scripted and cinematic. At this point, Annie thought, Bootface should pull out a huge cigar, light it and say 'All you have to do is whistle, kid' or something equally fatuous. But it was no joke. Annie knew this. It was all for real. She also knew just how vulnerable

Bootface's offer had made her. Talk to her bosses about this? Impossible. She was her own boss on this mission. Referral went right to the Top because it was so sensitive. And the Top was abroad right now and uncontactable by her. Bootface had chosen his time well. No one else in the organisation to turn to; no one else had the faintest idea of what she was up to.

And then there was the further complication which always surrounded the bent employee to consider. Anyone who was offered a crooked deal – and this applied across the board – is automatically suspect in a mild but distinct way, by very virtue of the deal being offered in the first place. Otherwise, so the perverse logic of the marketplace went, there would have been no approach in the first place. And was the plea for help now a double bluff? And so it went on. But meanwhile integrity had slipped a tiny vital notch. The declension from par was absolute, like the difference between nought and one.

She found herself saying that they could meet here in this same bar in a week's time. She would give her decision then. Bootface was just about willing to accept that.

Annie could see he was in a hurry. Seven days' wait would be torture for him. He was making his getaway plans even now. Plane booking, new bank account somewhere in the US, perhaps fresh passport and change of name and identity, maybe even the full works, with plastic surgery and a hip replacement. And the debts? Perhaps left unpaid, who knew? With a new identity, why worry about the debts? Best left behind and undisturbed, old boy, would be the soothing self-counsel.

His tone was roughening towards Annie the more he grappled with the idea that she might be coming on board with him over the scam. Relative authority was changing between them. This was his show and she might as well get used to the idea right away was what he implied by his tough words. Expletives pebble-dashed his speech. He was very agitated.

'You see, my dear Annie, we're in this together now. I can't move without the other half of the computer lock and you can't do anything to save Joe by tipping anyone – and I mean anyone – off as to what I intend. You do that and I'll tell you what will happen. The slightest hint that you've shopped me – and I mean the merest suspicion on my part, no more – and I turn him over to Sloane School. And that, as you know is easy. I ring up Sir David and I say to him, "Sir David, you know that rough fellow that plays bridge with your wife? Well, he's there for a purpose and the purpose is not to make three no trumps every second hand. It's to get into the pants of your business through your wife. Got that. Sorry about the anonymous tip-off, but the chap was indiscreet over a drink and I thought you ought to know." And I ring off.

'Now what d'you think Sir David's reaction to that will be? One of acceptance? Not on your life. That man is as sharp as a razor. He's used to the killing game. I know. He's done it all his life. That's how he's risen so far and so fast. I checked him out through Sloane School. He was famous at Sloane's for surrounding himself with all the school's undesirables and extracting money from all and sundry. There was an incident when one kid couldn't pay, or so the school's authorities thought, and the child was found hanged in the lavatories. Not a mark on him, but he was well and truly dead with a terrible look of reproach on his face. It was all hushed up, but the school still turns white if you so much as mention the incident. Sir David, of course, had a perfect alibi because his boys had carried out the hanging. No one could touch him. He was just sixteen at the time. Apparently the collections improved a lot after the hanging because everyone was scared stiff.

'So thirty or so years on from that, Sir David's a lot older, with a lot more killing under his belt. Or corporate disposals, as he would call it. And he's got a lot more to lose, now that he's being tipped for a seat in the cabinet and a peerage. He wants no trouble at all for the time being. If he so much as hears a word of what I will say to him, he'll have a contract out on Joe within three minutes. And within a day or so, Joe will be joining someone else we know dancing the Newgate jig beneath Blackfriars Bridge. Savvy, Annie?'

Annie nodded her understanding of Bootface's words. 'But if you kill Joe, then I don't give you the computer lock…'

'Yes, but you lose the entire mission and that means a lot to you. A huge amount and all the usual et ceteras so far as your career is concerned. Because I then shop you to the Top and say that you offered me the deal. No one will believe me, but if I get my blow in first at the woman in white, that will hurt you. There's no smoke without fire, is there?'

After Bootface had delivered his final and highly elaborate threat, there wasn't a great deal more to say between them. Annie finished her drink slowly and then rose to her feet and nodded at him. For his part, Bootface stayed where he was, suddenly silent, and ordered a fresh whisky from the wine waiter who had been hovering for some time. He looked up at her with the fairly blank expression of a man whose career is now shot.

'Until this time next week then. Same time and same place. Don't expect to see me in the office in the meantime. But I'll be here for our tryst and I'll be expecting that computer lock. No funny business, and we'll both be fine.' His words had a tone of complete finality.

Annie stumbled out of the bar and into the darkness of the street. Bootface remained slumped in hunched pose in front of his whisky, across in the far darkened corner of the bar. In the street Annie called a cab and very deliberately placed her bag on the back seat beside her, opened the window to let in the night air and sat quiet and motionless as she let her thoughts run on. Thinking of nothing in particular, just trying to absorb the shock of the discussion with Bootface. Trying to put the pieces of normality back together again. Oh yes, it all made very good sense now, including Bootface's odd behaviour from the start of their work together.

Struck by an impulse, she told the cab driver to drive to Hyde Park, a slight change in the planned route back home, and once there told him to wait for her as she strolled along the Serpentine. Off went the engine, out came the *Sun*, and one grateful cab driver relaxed on the job. The meter carried on ticking. Fortified by his lack of urgency, Annie walked slowly alone along the towpath.

She knew there was an idea, she could feel it forming in her mind. She knew there was a solution. Just let it come, she thought, just let it develop of its own accord in the back of my mind. The idea had started germinating even as Bootface was going through his terrifying hoops, running in seeming counter-rhythm to his words. As Bootface had been proclaiming his invincibility and his hold over her, the idea, like the little musical phrase of Vinteuil in Proust, had been starting its little gigue and saraband away there in the outer space of her imagination. How it wriggled and jigged…

She felt very cool and detached as she strolled along the tow-path. Just like any other young professional woman out for a short break before partying the night away. The sun played on the leaves in the trees. She could see the Hilton tower away in the distance. To her left, far away, by Marble Arch, was where Tyburn had stood. That was where the mass hangings had taken place in the eighteenth century. A day out for the whole family.

There! She'd got something. As she looked at the waves, gently ebbing and flowing on the Serpentine, something about Hedda Gabler swam to the surface of her thoughts. Hedda Gabler? Yes, Hedda. She relaxed very gently into the thought process. Yes, that was it, something that Judge Brack said to Hedda in the final scene. What was it now? She'd seen the play at the National years ago with her sister; she recalled it all clearly. And what was it Judge Brack said to Hedda? Yes, she had it now; she had it nearly exactly. He had said to her something like, 'Every day, Hedda, Every day.' Something like that because he thought he'd got her just exactly where he wanted her, so that he could come round to see her every day at his own choosing and screw her stupid and… And then what did Hedda say? She said, 'We'll see about that, Judge Brack,' or words to that effect, and then she went upstairs and all that was heard afterwards was a loud explosion as she blew her brains out with her silver pistol. And vine leaves through his hair… No that's not it, that's not the continuation. Stop… She walked on slowly beside the lake, oblivious now to the setting.

The idea began to fade a little in her mind and she walked some more, still trying to coax the thought into articulation. She stared at the boats for a while unseeing. What was it about the setting that had so impressed her? Gently she tried to ease her way back into the reactions she had had at the moment of the explosion and just immediately before that, when Judge Brack was talking to Hedda. Yes, it was something about a mirror. Yes, she had been nervous about the thought of Hedda's brains being blown over the mirror because of the mess. The thought of all that matter sliding down the mirror had…

Suddenly she had the idea. Yes, that was it. No question. She was walking back briskly to the cab. She had it now. She knew what to do. Calm and the universe were restored. Like a little fish, the idea had come to the surface. Very delicately, she now held it wriggling in space. It was her only hope. It might not work, but then, on the other hand, it just might. But it was a good idea and one that squared the circle of Bootface's hold over her. It certainly did that, geometric impossibility though it might be.

We'll see about Bootface, she thought with no malice. Just the directness of accepting that what had to be done might as well be done swiftly inspired her now. The cab driver looked up with a smile as she returned and put away his paper.

'I was just starting to get worried about you,' he said, starting the engine. 'Now where to, young lady?'

'King's Road,' she said.

'You didn't look the type to dive into the Serpentine, but you never know these days. Some of these young girls work awful hours and get very het up. I see it every day. I see we're going the panoramic route back home tonight.'

'Boyfriend trouble, you know how it is. That's what I had to think about.'

The cab driver shut up at that. Boyfriend trouble ranked in his mind with women's troubles. Best avoided as a topic of discussion and left to the wife. In merciful silence now, they bowled along past South Kensington tube station and hung a few lefts and rights before debouching into the King's Road via Old Church Street.

'Where now exactly?'

'World's End. I'll tell you where to go when we get there. We may have to stop again for a while. Have you got plenty of reading matter?'

'I've nearly read the *Sun* for today, but that's fine by me. I don't mind waiting. You're going to see him now, are you? Bit late, isn't it? He'll be in the pub or out with his mates. You won't get no joy out of stopping at his place.'

'We'll see... Now we're just about there. Just wait here for a couple of minutes, will you, and I'll see if he's in.'

Annie felt cool and calm and detached. The more she thought about it, the more this seemed like a winning line. She couldn't be sure but she had to try it. Nothing else looked remotely favourable.

Joe's flat was at the top of the building. Annie climbed out of the cab and disappeared into the building which had no security check on it whatsoever. She climbed the steps and then stood on the first floor, about eighteen floors below Joe's flat. Timing her ascent, she reached the second floor and then the third. Again she checked the time. She waited. Then she descended the steps and returned to the cab.

'Not there? I told you, didn't I. Want me to try the Goat in Boots for you?'

'No, I'll go home now but I want you to wait outside for me again. Only for a little while. I think I know where he might be and I want to check the answerphone.'

Off they drove again, reaching Annie's flat in about ten minutes or so of driving.

'You'll be wanting a receipt for this, won't you?'

'Of course,' said Annie, trying to allay his fears and calm her bounding excitement at the same time. It was not easy.

She turned the key in the lock of the flat and found the place quite undisturbed. Good, she thought. Now to work. First she changed, ready to go out again immediately for dinner. Then she sat down at her desk and wrote a full description of what Bootface had offered to her in the pub that evening. Standing up, she walked to the mantelpiece and pushed the two clocks together. She then folded the sheet of paper between the clocks so that it was unmissable.

Two can play at this game, she thought. Now let's see how smart they all are. And let's hope they're as smart as they think they are. Because otherwise, if they're not, then we're all in trouble.

Then, taking a book with her to read over dinner, she left the flat and found her cab again for the third time.

'No, no sign of the bastard, but too bad. Take me round the

corner, will you now? Just wait until I catch up with that louse tomorrow.'

The cab driver was all commiseration and said that he would have stayed to have a drink with her but he had to get back to East Ham to meet some of the lads and that was going to take him all of an hour at least. He was running late now. But he was sorry she had a messed-up evening. Annie thanked him sweetly for his sympathy, as her heart pounded away with apprehension. Certainly time for dinner. She was hungry.

She paid the cab driver, refused his offer of his telephone number – 'Just the mobile number, you understand, just so's the wife doesn't get upset' – and wandered into the restaurant, asked for a quiet table, got a quiet table, and then suffered the attentions of the wine waiter and the maître d' for the next hour and a half. Too bad she couldn't read her book. But the food at least was welcome.

Around about eleven o'clock it was time to go. Now the dreamlike substance which seemed to have enveloped her for the whole evening began slipping from her. She felt nervous. Would her ploy have been picked up, the pretend visit to Joe's, which had involved clock switching on her part in the past? Because her clocks had also been switched on that occasion. That was what she had remembered in the park through Hedda and the mirror. Would the hint have registered?

She knew it was a subtle steer, but also – and here she only had supposition to go on but it seemed firm enough – the mission was so important that perhaps highly trained operatives, whoever they might be, were functioning behind the scenes on her behalf as well. She had to hope for that. It was her only hope and she had to get the message across quickly. There was no time to lose at all.

Calmly enough, she stood outside her flat and paused for a few seconds. This was hazardous in the extreme. If she'd misjudged the algebra of the whole thing, she had real problems to contend with now. Insuperable problems. She pushed the key into the lock and opened the door. With her eyes half closed, she marched down the tiny hall and into the sitting room. Then she opened her eyes and took in the mantelpiece.

Nothing had changed. The clocks still stood together like the

Red Sea. Her heart sank and she felt sick. Her stomach was in knots. Oh God, what to do now, for Christ's sake? The image of Bootface loomed in her mind. What can I do about Bootface? It's impossible.

Then she looked again to be sure. A great whoosh went through her. Yes, it had changed. Something was different. A vital change. She'd been too terrified to look accurately. The clocks were still together, but the sheet of paper had gone!

Nowhere to be seen. The sheet of paper with her full description of Bootface's perfidy was missing from its spot on the mantelpiece – and in the universe.

Had they, whoever they were, taken the hint? Had she guessed right? And was she being shadowed too, the hunter hunted? Too soon to be absolutely sure. To be certain she scrabbled around in the hearth to see whether it had fallen down from the mantelpiece. But there was no sign of any paper.

She knew now that she had guessed right. It was a frightening realisation. She knew nothing of what lay outside watching her. Suddenly her stomach felt enormous as she took in some air and the muscles ceased to distend. Home again, intact and alive and in one piece and functioning... all those sensations overwhelmed her at that moment. That was all that counted.

# Chapter Eleven

Only a week to go now before Joe's epic encounter with Marcello. The event came ever closer He was nervous about kit, and distinctly queasy about appearing half dressed in front of fifty or so half-naked women – all that kind of thing. Aerobics could be a daunting and salutary experience for the older male. Women, as he might discover, had alternative, clearly defined priorities.

But in the meantime Joe had some duty manoeuvres to make, like lunch with Lady Pugh and Perdita, to be followed immediately afterwards the same afternoon by bridge with Lady Charley at Savage's.

Negotiations with the Confederation of Authors were proceeding very satisfactorily. Lines of communication had been established. The offer of money for a long poem had been made to Gregory – or rather Mr Gregory Priest – and some reply was expected shortly.

Joe had recovered from his partial eclipse over Annie's phone messages. Real life and espionage reality were now so tightly interwoven in his imagination that he accepted the duality as a commonplace. He felt tight-lipped and he felt better for that sense of instinctive reticence which the eclipse had generated. He was going to enjoy himself but he was going to say as little as possible. That was the game plan.

Bridge with Lady Charley, he reckoned, would be a true tightrope walking act, but he could justify playing with her on the grounds that he had been instructed, in fact ordered, to do just that. Forget the bridge, he told himself; this would not be Joxer territory, not by any stretch of thinking. But whatever wobblies she cared to manifest, he had a safe enough line to follow – just go with the flow and keep her sweet. Smile nicely. He had enough experience of playing with Lady Charley to realise that retaining his sangfroid might pose problems. She might blow up at any moment like some Krakatoa, as he had seen her explode through wounded *amour-propre* in the past. He guessed the entire experience could be dreadful. But he would grin and bear it. Those were his instructions. But he would be fortified by his lunch with the Pughs immediately prior to the bridge.

As for the Pughs, he was fooling himself, he knew, if he described the lunch date as a piece of dutiful socialising. Not for him it wasn't. More or less his entire being strained ahead in its eagerness to be there and enjoy fresh fisticuffs with Perdita, as her mother held the ring. Battledore and shuttlecock SW3 style was how he depicted it to himself. Joe resented the sequestration of his assets keenly when he thought about Perdita. So much time lost...

There had been a fresh telephonic exchange between the house of Joe and the house of Pugh detailing the terms and times of the joust. Lunch was scheduled for twelve thirty, which was convenient. Savage's started play just after two so this gave him sufficient time to have fun, eat, be witty, hopefully at Perdita's expense, make a few more jokes and bring a smile to Lady Pugh's face, and then escape, leaving mother and daughter to London's tender embrace.

Rivers would cover his escape. Lady Pugh informed Joe that they expected to be joined over lunch by Rivers who was due back in the country that morning via Heathrow and a flight from somewhere. Somewhere eastern European, by the sound of it. Joe made no further enquiries.

Lunch was at Ziani, an ultra-chic Italian restaurant tucked away down Radnor Walk, an obscure-looking side street off the King's Road. Joe had decided that his financier could stand the strain, just this once. It was definitely his shout. Ziani was all yellows and whites. Sunshine burst through the windows, and steel tables and chairs clattered here and there as the food emerged at top speed from the serving hatches and the lunchers moved hither and thither, talking here, greeting there, and exploding in amazement at seeing Tommy So-and-So over in the far corner, so tanned and well and back from holidays with his new wife. It was practically a family restaurant in some ways.

Joe arrived five minutes early, but the two Pughs had beaten him to the spot, a table for four over by the window. Lady Pugh was sensibly dressed in something light and frothy, but Perdita was sensational in a white trouser suit. With her blonde hair and tanned skin she looked quite simply ravishing, like a fruit starting to open up in springtime. The waiters hovered in a group hoping for a glance of acknowledgement from her as the restaurant filled up for lunch. The spectacle of Perdita took Joe's breath away. He stopped momentarily in wonderment as he made his way across the restaurant towards them. She enjoyed observing the effect she had produced on Joe and she grinned and then prinked herself a little in affectation as he faltered in his approach.

Lady Pugh looked a touch helpless beside her daughter who sat there just radiating goodwill and excitement and bursting with the pleasure of being there. 'What do you think, Joe? Doesn't she look beautiful?' She gestured at her daughter as she might have indicated a piece of gorgeous horseflesh up for sale in the paddock or a beautiful hand-woven quilt. It was the inexplicable surprise of the beautiful mother gazing in adoration at the beauty of the daughter. Something unbelievable, like a rainbow after the storm.

Joe bent to kiss both their hands. 'Words fail me,' he mumbled, genuinely moved. Some Latin sprang into his mind – *matre pulchra filia pulchrior* – but he suppressed it savagely. For Christ's sake, no larking about, Joe, it's too dangerous, he told himself. No fucking exhibitionism here. But the self-discipline was hard. It was against nature. He wanted to recline in their bower.

He sat down beside Perdita and opposite Lady Pugh, so that Perdita had the commanding view of the room. Lady Pugh apologised for her daughter's possession of the pole position in the restaurant.

'Perdita has to sit like that. Always at the angle. She's not happy sitting in any other spot. She really can't bear it. She has to have a glass of water with her every night, too. Such a demanding child.'

Perdita for her part ignored her mother's comments and gazed round the room with perfect composure, her blonde and white blending perfectly into the setting. She looked like a great hostess in the making who was pacing the banquet, working the room and biding her time before bringing that couple over there, who looked just a tiny bit spare, into discussion with this couple immediately to her left – 'Yes, that couple there, can't you see?' –

who were far too self-absorbed, because both couples would be so much happier talking to each other than mooning about and disregarding the other guests. 'Of course, darling,' she would then say to the happy man who had married her, 'it's obvious... Can't you see it? I'm so surprised.'

Joe could read it all from her expression. Perdita was set fair on her existence. Both Lady Pugh and Joe could see that. She was staking out her territory. Joe felt rays of contentment spread all over him. He felt himself sinking with graceful acceptance into the warm embrace of the Pughs. The atmosphere at the table was full of excitement at just being there on this great occasion of the bursting forth of Perdita.

Then Perdita moved a fraction and the vision took on a different dimension, like another sketch instantly on offer by Fra Angelico.

Lady Pugh continued. 'You see, we don't come up to town very often.'

'Never, Mummy.'

'So we don't—'

'Ever go to good things like concerts.'

'Now Perdita...'

But the stress did not fall on the 'now', which would have made the interjection very menacing. The table relaxed. The stress fell instead on the first syllable of Perdita, which made it sound just like a warning. Far less dangerous. Almost benign. Perdita spoke on undeterred.

'Joe is musical, aren't you, Joe? Who's your favourite composer, Joe?'

'It's—"

'Vivaldi, I thought so.'

'Actually, no. It's Joe Green.'

That stumped her for a second. She paused. Lady Pugh smiled at the brief discountenancing of her daughter. The restaurant heaved with people lunching all around them and the din was rising exponentially.

Joe helped her along. 'Giuseppe...?'

'Oh, Verdi, of course. How clever of you. Fancy Italy's greatest composer being called Joe Green.' She made a moue. 'Such a low common name, don't you think?'

She paused again. She was searching for a riposte. She ventured it tentatively against Joe, waiting there with a grin and grizzled by comparison after a hundred street fights of no quarter repartee.

'Personally, Joe, I always prefer Persil. He's got such a clean sound, don't you find?'

'But it's got a Hidden quality, hasn't it. Don't you List to it? No, my personal preference is for Sibeelius.'

Perdita started to giggle at the explosion of plays on words.

'I'd never have thought of that. Sibeelius is good. What about Shosters? What d'you think of Shosters? And what about Proust's Second Symphony? That's my whole repertoire gone now. Shot away in the first five minutes, would you believe? Joe, you're a swine and you've been around too much for a young innocent like me to cope. I was counting on Proust's Second Symphony and now it's a no show. Oh no, I'm forgetting that old stand-by Ravell, but you'd have a counter to that, I just know.'

Lady Pugh was also giggling at Joe, as he and Perdita went at each other without restraint, first a thrust and then a parry and then an elegant pasado.

'Perdita, I prefer it all in Batches.'

*Coup de grâce*! Perdita was out for the count. No more plays on words. She gave in, waving her hands in the air and then framing a prophylactic cross at Joe with two fingers of her hand joined at right angles. She laughed and Lady Pugh laughed. The whole table started screeching at the same time and all three of them sat there helplessly, shoulders heaving with merriment at their absurdity.

Food arrived and they fell to, eating in fast rhythm all together. No time to talk now. Lady Pugh ate neatly with dexterity. Joe noted that Perdita's table manners were very nearly non-existent. She practically stuffed the food into her mouth with her hands she was so clumsy with the knife and fork. That's another thing I'm going to have to teach you, thought Joe as he ate. Perdita was barely capable of using the table implements. Goddess to all the world outside and a five-year-old child to her nearest and dearest – such an amazing contrast.

After some intensive chewing, Lady Pugh wiped her mouth with her napkin, drank some water, coughed slightly and then reached down under the table to fish some papers out of her bag.

Perdita groaned. 'This is the death camp stuff. I warned you about this, Joe. Don't say you haven't been told.'

Lady Pugh glared at her daughter who for once was sufficiently impressed to remain silent. Perdita stared round the room like a great huntress.

'Thank you, Perdita. That's quite enough now. It's my work and I want to show it to Joe to find out his reactions so you mustn't mock. I've told you before that you'll finish up on the gallows one of these days if you don't learn to...' Perdita pouted a pair of huge cherry lips at her mother who could not help herself from smiling back at her outrageous and outspoken daughter.

'Now, Joe, I promised you that I would bring up some of my translations to show you. They are very striking. These are letters from French soldiers during World War I that I stumbled across and I intend to use them to complement my edition of the family's letters during the same period. Now look at this one, Joe; this letter is truly harrowing. It's maybe inappropriate for the lunch party but I think this is as good a time as any. If you read this late at night, you will surely weep. It's beautifully written.'

Joe took the proffered sheet neatly typed in English, double spaced throughout. No corrections. Evidence of lots of hard work here.

'It is from a certain Jean Castel, thirty-four years old, who was shot for cowardice in front of the enemy – falsely, it turns out – on 4 December, 1914. The letter is dated eleven thirty in the evening on 3 December, and addressed to his wife, so it was written about six hours before he was shot. Read my translation. I was hoping that you could check it for accuracy but Perdita tells me that you have no French. I do hope I haven't made any mistakes. I would hate not to do justice to Monsieur Castel.'

'Just a tiny bit of French, Lady Pugh. Useless for this kind of work.'

'Read it anyway. See what you think of it.'

She sat and watched him anxiously. Joe wondered whether she gloried in this celebration of the dead and decided that she didn't.

She was slightly fey and that placed her at a disadvantage amongst the confident hustle and bustle to get ahead of her class. Diligently she was following her clan, he decided, and trying to make sense of a tumultuous and catastrophic century during which they'd lost more or less everything – the land, the empire, the authority, and finally themselves. A stunning reversal after five centuries of fantastic pre-eminence on the wrong side of Europe. No wonder England was confused. Like everyone else, Lady Pugh was just picking up the pieces and trying to fit them together again in her honest, humble, rather understated and groping way. No more than anyone else did she know the correct way home.

The letter, as translated, read as follows:

*My dear darling,*

*It is in a great distress that I begin writing to you and unless God and the Blessed Virgin come to help me it will be for the last time; I am in such distress and such pain that I do not think I can gather everything together that I wished to say to you and I can see from here when you start reading what I have written everything that you will suffer, my poor beloved who is so dear to me; please forgive me for everything that you are going to suffer. I would be in complete despair if I did not have my faith and religion to sustain me in such a terrible moment. For I am in the most terrible position that could be imagined, for I no longer have very much time to live unless God by a miracle of his goodness comes to my aid. I am going to try in a few words to tell you what has happened but I do not know if I will be able to. I hardly feel that I have the courage to do so.*

*On the night of 27 November we were in a trench facing the Germans, who took us by surprise and sowed panic amongst us in our trench, so that we retreated to the trench behind, and almost immediately we regrouped and returned to recapture our positions. Result: a dozen prisoners for the company and one for my section, but for this fault, we, the whole platoon, namely twenty-four men, went to the war tribunal and alas there are six of us to pay the penalty for all the rest. I cannot explain any more of this to you, my beloved, I am suffering too much; my friend Dallet will be better able to explain it to you. My conscience is clear and I submit myself entirely to the will of God who wishes everything to be as it is; it is that which gives me the strength to write these words to you, my beloved, who has made me so happy in the time that I have spent together with you and whom I had so much hope of meeting again after the war was over.*

*On 1 December in the morning, the charges were read out against us and when I saw the charge which was levied against us which could not be misunderstood, I wept for part of the day and had no strength to write to you, and on the morrow I could only send you a card; this morning, when it was generally assumed that nothing would happen, I regained my courage and I wrote to you as usual but this evening I can find no words to describe my suffering to you. Anything would be preferable to my present situation but like God on the Cross I will drink the chalice of pain unto the lees.*

*Farewell, my Sophie, farewell, my beloved, since it is the will of God to separate us on this earth, I hope that he will reunite us in heaven. The last rites will not be refused me and I will confess myself very sincerely. What makes me suffer most of all is the dishonour for you for our parents and family, but believe me on our love, my dearly beloved, I do not think I have deserved this chastisement any more than my unhappy comrades who are with me in this have deserved it either, and it will be with my conscience at peace that I will appear before the Lord to whom I offer all my pains and sufferings and to whose will I submit myself entirely. I have still a tiny hope that I will be reprieved – oh, a very tiny hope – but the Holy Virgin is so good and powerful and I have such trust in her that I cannot despair entirely.*

*Our Lady of Chartres to whom I had promised that we would both go in pilgrimage, that we would take Communion in her church and that we would give five francs for the completion of her statue, will not abandon us and if I am not forgiven in this life I hope that I will be forgiven in the next...*

Joe looked up in wonderment at such total hysteria and abjection of spirit. Lady Pugh and Perdita looked at him like ghosts. Perdita was very quiet. Lady Pugh broke the silence.

'That's the effect it had on me. And Perdita as well when she read it. It's shattering, isn't it? I just had to show it to you and I just had to translate it.' Lady Pugh was very apologetic and Perdita nodded as her mother spoke.

The party mood of the lunch had not been shattered. Far from it. The letter had introduced a different more robust note which strengthened the texture of their intercourse and brought them all closer together. The sighing wind of Pugh Park blew around them all from the cypresses to the house.

Secretly Joe was relieved. He was getting far too fond of Perdita during this lunch. The letter sounded a cautionary, and diversionary, note of reality.

'How can you translate something like that, Lady Pugh? It is very strong.'

'Stronger than anything written in English about the war. I found it quite by accident. As I said, as soon as I read it I had to get it into English. I know I take any excuse I can find to do some translations but this one was different. I think it will fit very well into the family album. Now read this. This is from another of the soldiers who had been condemned. The tone of the man comes straight off the page. I grieve for him just as much as for Castel. This man was called Henry Blanc. He writes about the same incident.'

Joe took the letter. It read:

*My darling Michelle,*

*By the time this letter reaches you, I will have been shot dead by a firing squad. On 27 November, towards five o'clock in the evening, after a two-hour bombardment of incredible violence, in one of the front-line trenches and just when we were finishing our soup, Germans launched themselves into the trench and captured me and two others. I was able to escape from the Germans in a moment of confusion. I followed my comrades and then I found I was accused of abandoning my post in the presence of the enemy.*

*Twenty-four of us went in front of the war tribunal yesterday evening. Six have been condemned to death, including myself. I am no more guilty than the others but an example is needed. My wallet and what is in it will be sent to you.*

*I send my last farewells to you in haste, tears in my eyes, my soul in torment. Humbly on my knees I beg your pardon for all the pain I am about to cause you and all the embarrassment which I am about to give you. My dear darling Michelle, once again I am very sorry. I am going now to confession and I hope to meet you again in a better world. I die innocent of the crime imputed to me of abandoning my post. If, instead of fleeing the Germans, I had remained a prisoner, I would now be safe and sound. It is fate. My last thoughts will be of you, my darling, right to the end.*

Joe could feel Berlin breaking through into his thoughts as he read Blanc's testament. He'd been there and he knew about the simple heroism of Monsieur Blanc's sentiments. When you think you're going to die, and there's no way out, then you have to steel yourself, he thought.

Once again, the atmosphere of death and carnage which Lady Pugh had conjured up by her translation did not serve to alter the holiday atmosphere at the table, rather it reinforced the sense of carnival. But it did more. The reading seemed to bind Joe more closely to mother and daughter, as if he had been privileged to glimpse some of the family's most intimate preoccupations, offered to him as an honoured guest.

Yes, there were jokes and japes at Pugh Park, seemed to be the inference, but there was also the responsibility of keeping the vigil, holding the memory of a dreadful shattering event, the Great War, when the family was broken and decimated, an event which had never been forgotten and which Joe must understand if he was to come amongst them. Because they still grieved for their fallen, with them no more, dead and departed in the flower of their manhood. Beauty and death – now indivisible. And the wind blew from the cypresses in Pugh Park.

Joe knew about both beauty and death. The image of the Fat Man rose unbidden in his mind as well as a specific setting in Fleet Street one bright morning. Joe resisted the chimera. Lady Pugh watched him closely as he riffled through the sheets of paper. She knew about Joe and death. Maybe that was another reason why she had shown him the translations, just to confirm from his reactions her original intuitions.

Joe opted to ignore those memories and concentrate on the present. No more snipers at five o'clock, thank you very much.

No more Fat Man either. But lots of Perdita, please. He gave a great sigh as he finished reading the two letters and handed them back to Lady Pugh. But otherwise he failed to react in any obvious way. Not easy but Joe managed it.

A brief silence fell between them all, as the wine waiter bustled up to recharge empty glasses. The wine splashed into the glasses. Then a presence appeared at the table, looking travel-weary and harassed. Rivers Pugh stood before them; he was back from his trip. But it was not the same Rivers Pugh they had all known before. Joe saw that at once. The others did not notice. Joe had not seen him for over a week now. He was changed. He held his head in a different way, and there was a light in his eye which was odd, almost intense. He looked upset.

Lady Pugh and Perdita stood up and they all embraced across the table. Rivers dropped his bags with a clatter on the floor and people at the next table smiled and made way for him. The prodigal returneth...

Joe felt strongly de trop. Rivers looked very very different. He could see that. Far less boyish, but not so much of a man either. That strange intense light in his eye was striking to an outsider and made him appear mortally dangerous. Even violent. He had been under great strain. Joe would vouch for that at least. Joe did not want to appear to be a hostile presence. Time to make himself scarce. He knew that look of old. It was the brooding look. Something had happened to Rivers, something probably irreversible. Joe had half expected this all the time he had been meeting him, because Rivers had always struck him as being too young, too spontaneous and too uncommitted as yet to the concepts of authority and control, the crucial hallmarks of a person with his background. Now it had happened. The brooding look was there, the gloomy look of the Caesars, thought Joe. Time not to be there, briefly. He went in search of the loo.

Annie went back to her work with mixed feelings. It was odd for her to feel that she was being shadowed – that was the job she did on other people. It was a weird feeling but in the end she found she didn't care one way or the other. That was her world and so it was tough for her but tolerable even if she had to put up with some of its wrinkles. Annie, the supreme rationalist, came to terms with that one. Part of the job maybe. Meanwhile, on the other hand, she felt protected. That was good. She felt better. It enabled her to put Bootface out of her mind. Annie put it all together in terms of percentages. She'd taken a risk and gambled that she was being watched. It now turned out that the gamble had been correct; she was under surveillance. She assumed the scrutiny was friendly, because otherwise the whole thing became a dangerous farce. They might as well all give up at that point if the shadowing was hostile. But if it was friendly, however, she'd be protected in some way from Bootface. And so would Joe, with all his assets held under lock and key.

In the meantime she could get on with the job of planning the mission. In this instance that meant getting some watchers on to Joe. During the whole time she'd been working with Bootface she'd been in information deficit. The mercurial Bootface, for reasons which were now clear, had disagreed with her use of watchers, deeming it first vital and then later unnecessary and over-control, whatever that might mean. But latterly no watchers had meant no information feedback as things had been happening. There were data lags all the way down the chain. The net result had been that she never quite knew to the minute exactly what was going on. She could change all that now. Mercifully, now that Bootface was out of the room and out of the loop, she could yank everything back into information focus.

So Annie had a watcher at the table right next to the Pughs as they lunched with Joe. The message came over to Annie as Joe went to the loo.

'Yes, Annie, I've just popped outside the restaurant while Joe takes a leak. They're all very pally and friendly and his eyes are out on stalks at Perdita, but what man's wouldn't be? She looks gorgeous. But apart from that, nothing until Rivers turned up. Rivers looks very wild. Yes, odd. Ah, Joe's coming back... I'll call you soon. Out.'

Rivers did not want to be with his family. That was the first indication that something had changed for him. He was not at ease in their company. Joe thought back to his first meeting with the Pughs and how Rivers had suffered Perdita to comb his hair for him as he reclined gently on the sofa. There would be none of that now. She couldn't get near him and that distressed her. All he did was glare at her as she made her overtures, overtures which in the past had made him relaxed but which now provoked an angry glare. Baffled, she retreated into silence. Joe said nothing but made himself as inconspicuous as possible. His mother fared no better. Rivers snapped at her when she asked for details of the trip and questioned him about minor details such as his hotel and the food. The eyes were angry behind the spectacles and the fingers on his left hand were working away at their own rhythm, drumming out a beat on the table. The collar was too tight and the neck kept straining to be released. Joe saw and recognised all the classic signs of tension and a bad conscience.

Finally, and sadly, the women retired to the loo to fix their faces and rebuild morale which Rivers's arrival had briefly shattered. They trooped off through the tables with many excuses. Joe watched the vision in the white trouser suit depart with much regret.

Rivers talked to him eagerly but very intensely as soon as the women had left the table. 'Joe, this job is quite extraordinary. What do you think?'

'Don't tell me anything you might regret, Rivers. I'm not that important for you to take any risks.'

'No, but Joe, let me tell you this. Where I was – well, I won't tell you exactly but it was in eastern Europe – I had the Foreign Office just eating out of my hand. I was astonished. Now you know that I was thrown out in disgrace. The report and all that kind of thing. You remember, don't you? The naming, yes?'

'How could I forget? You nearly got yourself killed over that. The bridge of sighs, remember.'

That was ancient history now for Rivers. He was very excited. Almost about to yell, Joe thought.

'Yes, but all that has changed now. Let me tell you how it went. I was ordered by my new boss to go and see the ambassador in order to get some briefing on the local bigwigs. Apparently we're in very good odour out there, that's my company, I mean, and the FO looks on us favourably too as a good export bet. Well, you can imagine how I felt as I went up to the embassy. Not exactly overjoyed, I can tell you. I was expecting very cold shoulder treatment because that's how the FO will always play it with someone who's got out of line. But not a bit of it. Guess what happened. Yes, go on, guess what happened. I couldn't believe it. Every door was flung wide for me, I was treated like a maharaja and the FO did exactly what I told it to do. Can you imagine that? The FO did exactly what it was told. It's never done that, at least not in my experience, since the Creation. It was like finding a secret door and an alternative universe. They were obedient to me, the unclean one who had just been kicked out. I even ticked the ambassador off on one occasion and he just crumpled. I was the lord of the manor. I couldn't get over it. They were bowing and scraping to me as if the report had never happened. Nothing was too much trouble.

'To cap it all, there was someone in the embassy I knew from the early days in the FO because we started together. I thought he'd really go for me. And do you know, he simply fawned on me. I was astonished. I really played God there, I can tell you.'

This was part of the blooding process. But not the full story. Joe looked round for the women. He saw them hemmed in at the bar by some friends. He had time to ask his question. 'But was that all that happened?'

A shadow passed across Rivers's face. There was a lot more to it all than just swanking around the embassy. Now for the revelations.

'Well, yes, as a matter of fact, some other things did happen. Pretty horrifying for me, and I wouldn't normally care to talk about them, but I suppose I can tell you of all people. It's not as if you're in the Pugh loop, so there aren't any comebacks. No offence, but that's the truth of it, isn't it?'

Joe nodded his understanding of all this.

'Some of the stuff I'm selling is pretty lethal. I won't go into the details but... Anyway, I finish up in the hills talking to these chaps who are all frightfully impressed with what I'm offering, but still a trifle sceptical. Now I've been told by my boss in London that everything will be laid on but that I have to clinch the deal that trip. Very important to get that deal through. My chaps in the hills are nervous about how good it all is, so they—'

'Ask you to test it out?'

'Exactly. You've hit the nail on the head, Joe.'

'But they really wanted you to test it out. Not a dress rehearsal. For real. So you were on the square.'

'That's right. I...' Rivers paused. He was looking for the words. He found them. 'Did rather more than just supervise.'

Joe helped him along the path of revelation. 'Well, I suppose if you're going to clinch the deal you have to give a demonstration.' Action and reaction in the dialogue. Joe knew what was coming full well. He made it easier again for Rivers.

'Someone has to pull the trigger in the last event.'

More shadows across Rivers's face. But he leaped at the bland-ness of Joe's words. But still the words did not come easily.

'I'm being very well paid for what I do,' Rivers said very defensively. Joe was still some help to him.

'I can imagine. I suppose they were just prisoners.' Joe was noncommittal.

Rivers recovered some of his poise. 'They were going to kill them anyway. You're right, they were prisoners. I just hurried the process along a little. It didn't last for very long, not for them anyway. The stuff I'm selling is lethal. Very fast acting.'

It sounded to Joe as if Rivers had half-burned them to death, before the shooting, with the new kit. The women were coming back to the table again, threading a way through the conviviality.

'You're quite right. Many deaths, Rivers?'

An expression of forked lightning which seemed to blast his eyes in their sockets broke across his features. But his composure was returning with the confession.

'About a score, no more than that. It was all over very quickly.' He spoke lightly and then recovered himself. 'Not a word to my mother. She wouldn't understand a bit. It was a very special thing for me. It won't happen again. But I don't want her to know. As for Perdita...'

Joe nodded and Rivers fell to talking about something else. He was more relaxed now that he'd blurted it all out about what he'd done to somebody else, especially since that somebody else occupied no position of judgement on his behaviour. The women were sitting down now at the table feeling pleased that Rivers was looking happier. As indeed he was. Lady Pugh's brow cleared. The tactical withdrawal had been a success. The women were pleased now that the men looked more human.

Rivers remarked brightly, 'But we got the contract. And my boss was very very happy with me. He said they'd been after that contract for years.'

Lady Pugh was delighted. 'Oh, Rivers, I'm so pleased. You'll be getting a promotion very shortly, you're doing so well. You see, it's as I told you; it hasn't made any difference to you, that awful nasty report.'

All acquiesced in the general acclaim for Rivers. Rivers then told the story again about the embassy kowtowing to him, and both Perdita and Lady Pugh were astonished and delighted. It was as if some family curse was being lifted. Head held high, the Pughs could ride again. General merriment all round. The lunch party had been a great success. Gradually, as Rivers reasserted himself as the head of the family, Joe was readmitted to the circle from the outer extremities on terms of silence and subservience which suited him fine. The less visible he became in this set-up the better. Joe knew very well what the gullible and trusting Rivers had stumbled into after his dismissal from the FO.

Joe could see the transformation of Rivers taking place before his eyes. Whatever dreadful things he'd done in the past week had taken place far away in another country. They didn't count and they could be forgotten. Here, back in the UK, he could bask in the glory of achievement and ignore the terrifying collateral damage. And wasn't that what Sloane School counselled its alumni to do above all else – get ahead and don't count the cost? Let the other man pick up the tab?

Glancing sideways at Rivers, who had brusquely elbowed his sister out of the window seat, much to her annoyance, Joe could see him resuming and regaining control – of himself, of his surroundings, of his self-esteem, of his family, and finally, in due course, of his group of friends. A process of personality crystalli-sation was at work. The eye was hard and tight now and the expression quite aggressive. Nor was that aggression feigned. The attractive delicacy in him was being savagely suppressed. No quarter could be expected. Rivers was back. He was not wholly altered one hundred per cent but the process was in train and moving towards its inevitable conclusion. He had decided to be a leader and he was going to be in charge, no matter what the cost. The fusillade of shots that had rung out in the hills, murdering God knows what group of suspects, was a fanfare of accolade to his decision. Rivers had pledged his humanity now in his Faustian pact – a heavy pledge. Not a contract to be broken this side of the Styx. But the die was cast and Rivers could not allow himself to care.

And why not? He was fulfilling his destiny. He had been born to lead; he had been brought up to lead; his family would always be supportive of his decision to become a leader and so too would be his friends. If any one of them happened to walk through the restaurant door at this moment, they would not see Rivers the fallen sobbing at the table, but Rivers the resurgent, newly arisen and resplendent. Rivers was the man who could kick the FO in the slats as soon as look at it – and be admired by the FO for doing so. And friends would congratulate him on his resurrection as no more than richly deserved. And finally Rivers was the man who could cut the mustard and bring home the bacon when it came to the deals. Success all round and hats off, gentlemen, to the tyro!

Joe didn't know how all the chemistry worked so accurately because that was not his background – far from it – but he marvelled at its unerring precision as he traced the effects of the transformation. Sloane School must be a very good school in itself, he thought, for all of this dynamic conversion to have taken place so smoothly. Truly did it teach grace under pressure. Maybe it was the cocooning aspect of it all, so that morality became a local, relative factor, not some overarching absolute. Almost an option, like a menu at a restaurant. Joe could not gauge it all so precisely. But he was impressed. Whatever it did, the effect was marvellous to behold. Maybe I should have gone to Sloane School after all…

Joe found himself thinking about Joachim and pondering the importance of the impromptu lectures he was receiving in the drug dealers' den from his little German savant. Perhaps he hadn't paid quite enough attention to the words of wisdom, and perhaps now he should start getting to grips with them. He had a lot to start to try to understand. There was more for him to grasp than he had imagined. The perspective was very large.

Rivers was in full swing as he recounted the embassy anecdotes, recalling suddenly that Sir Frank, an ex-colleague of his father, had sent his best regards to Lady Pugh. He would be in touch as soon as his leave allowed him to return to London. He had some good stories to tell the Pughs; that was the message Rivers brought back. The merriment at the table continued unabated and Perdita was grinning from ear to ear at a revitalised Rivers. It gave her such pleasure to see her brother restored to top form.

In an obvious way, the table had regrouped so that the focus of attention had swung right away from Joe. But Joe was content with this. He was still pondering the logic of his perceptions of Rivers. Meanwhile the mission was getting bigger and bigger in Joe's mind. He swam in the flow of the conversation without making any significant contribution beyond a bright smile.

Shortly it was time for Joe to depart. Time also for the Pughs to return to Pugh Park and shake Rivers down from his long trip. Joe paid the bill without any tremors – it was reasonable – and they gathered outside the restaurant in relaxed mode, discussing which way to go. Perhaps out of politeness, Perdita remembered Joe sufficiently to ask him where he was playing bridge. Joe, by a reflex action of evasion, told her that he was playing in Earl's Court. He felt concerned to distance himself from the Pughs, again by an animal sense of camouflage. Rivers had alerted his senses. Perdita said she wanted to accompany him to the club and watch how real bridge players acted. She seemed quite sincere in her expression of interest. But Joe dissuaded her. He promised to take her there another time. He promised faithfully and she looked disappointed that he was leaving her. Rivers was not disappointed at this. That marked another very distinct change in attitude.

Joe felt his heart starting to crack under the weight of his insincerities. The white trouser suit and its blonde inhabitant were very powerful arguments in favour of the truth. They debated the bridge for a few seconds apart from Lady Pugh and Rivers.

'Annie, they're standing just outside the restaurant now and just talking. Joe, dear Joe, is having the time of his little life with Perdita, but they don't seem to be able to agree on anything. Like where they're going. Lots of jokes. Call you.'

Annie stomped about her office. She did not want Joe to linger in the Pughs' company. She knew very well that Joe was playing bridge that afternoon with Lady Charley and she did not want those two circles of people – the Pughs and Joe's bridge-playing crowd from Liz Playfair's – to merge. Too much fusion of groups meant too much information was shared in common. That made it far more difficult to manipulate the groups. In particular, she did not want Rivers getting into communication with Lady C. That would pose a horrendous threat to Joe's survival chances. She wanted Joe to leave the Pughs now this instant. She wanted him to shake off Perdita.

'Just walk up the road, Joe, just walk up the fucking road,' she found herself muttering quietly to herself as she walked about the office, kicking the furniture in exasperation. Joe should have been warned. That was obvious. She should have a direct line to him. Very shortly she was going to call Joe direct, unless he called her first, and she was going to dish out some home truths about what was off limits. She promised herself that. Yes, soon, very soon. That way he'd get the message.

Her phone rang again. She snatched at it. 'And…'

'Relax, Annie, they've all gone now but in separate taxis. Joe in one and the Pughs in the other. But I have to tell you, Joe and Perdita did not want to part. I think her brother disapproves but she's very keen on him. Kept clutching him by the lapels, and that's always an obvious sign in a young girl. I can remember doing it myself. As for him, I leave that to your imagination, Annie. Eyes out on stalks. Call you, bye.'

Annie sat at her desk staring at the waves, speechless. She was in heaven. It was going to be fine. Her fears had been groundless and she was relieved by that. Rivers and Lady C had been kept apart. That was marvellous. It was all starting to have a lucky feel to it, at last. Now for the real business of the afternoon: Joe and Lady Charley. She refocused. Yes, Joe and Lady Charley. That was where and when her real business got going. That was what the mission was all about. She left her office feeling cooler and more confident about the whole business than she'd done since the start.

Joe reached the entrance to Savage's, still above the grocer's in the Fulham Road, feeling blithe about lunch and Perdita. He got out of the cab and was reaching for cash to pay the fare when a truly terrible pang of fear hit him deep in the pit of his stomach, practically knocking him sideways. His whole intestines appeared to seize up.

What if Emma was there this afternoon? Oh Christ, yes, he'd forgotten about her. What if she came gambolling up and started talking about Chaebol Trust? Oh God, that would put the cat among the pigeons, well and truly. Lady C would have to do a sudden reality check on the spot. So Joe, this dumb bridge player she was patronising, was in reality a red-hot City trader. A big, big trader with a following. And Emma dealt with Brasenose. Lady C would be impressed by that. Worse, he seemed to be trading off advice and recommendations made in the *Financial Chronicle*, recommendations given by none other than Tom Stone, with whom Ursula… The platform was getting crowded.

Joe ignored his fears. It just didn't bear thinking about. Maybe she wouldn't be there. In fact, didn't he recall her saying something about Norwich and a duty visit? Wasn't that why he'd selected this particular afternoon? Who knew? Who cared? He didn't. He'd fix it anyway if he had to. He squared his shoulders and climbed up the stairs to the bridge rooms at the top of the block. Same impression of hundreds of women milling about in an army, all pushing here and there very quietly and politely but equally quite firmly. It was like a brightly coloured quiet sea in swell as it moved in currents and eddies.

One of the professionals in the club came up to him. 'You're Joe, right?'

'Right.'

'Got a message here for you from Mrs Winterthorn. She's away in Norwich today and said that she couldn't play with you. But she wants to play with you next week when she'll be back. Here's the number to call her on to make a date. She told me to tell you in particular, Joe, that you're a toad. Got that, Joe? Toad, yes?'

'Doesn't surprise me. Could have been worse.'

'She also told me to remind you about your latest tip. She wants to know, she does.'

Joe shrugged.

'What kind of tip is this, Joe? Stock market tips. D'you trade the market, Joe?'

Joe could see Lady Charley approaching from his left. She was closing in fast.

'No, horses. I gave her a good idea and she backed it. Made some good money on an accumulator.'

'Such a dark horse you are, Joe. Any time you want to spread those tips around you know where to come.'

'Sure do.'

'Tell me, Joe, just before I go, didn't I see you at the Jack of Hearts last week, with that guy, what's his name, Joxer...'

'Treadwell-Biddulph.'

'That's the one. I heard he injected himself at the table.'

'Yes, it was pure cocaine. The finest stuff. That's all he uses. He's a doctor, so he should know. I think the Jack is going to bring in compulsory drug testing at the fifty-pound tables as a result.'

Lady C was upon them. The professional gave Joe a funny look and departed, his message having been imparted. The professional's line of thinking was obvious. So Joe was into coke, eh? That was good to know. The pro knew where to go for a line then, didn't he? Table six East–West before the move was called. That was where the nose candy was stored.

'Well, Joe, so you finally made it here. Now what are we playing?'

Joe could see the rest of the Playfair crowd gathered together at the bar, poised to take their places at the tables. He glimpsed Penny and Mags, normally a winning team; Lynn and Stella, who'd done well the previous week; and further off, heads together earnestly, Trish and Nancy, who'd been second on Monday past. Despite the bangles and beads effect of the ensemble, Joe knew full well that these women wanted to win, if only to be able to tell their husbands they'd achieved something during the hours of daylight when the men were getting carved up in the City boardrooms. They were armed to the teeth with aggression.

This was Lady C's first outing at competitive duplicate. She sounded nervous, but full of self-control. The competitive bug was biting her as well. She was determined to get a good score. She had to keep up with the girls. Social standing, briefly, in her group was governed not only by cash but also by bridge pre-eminence. It would pass in due course and the true values of money and breeding would reassert themselves. But for the time being success at bridge – and that meant success at Savage's – was the new element in the social equation. A bad result this afternoon, plus a good result say for Penny and Mags, or unthinkably Penny and Mags and Lynn and Stella and Trish and Nancy but not Lady C, would mean her ladyship would find difficulty in bossing the rest of them over anything else that happened to crop up. Thus were the terms of trade altering *chez* Playfair's mob. They were breaking out into tommy guns and bidding boxes.

Joe could gather from Lady C's tone of voice that she had worked out part of her game plan that afternoon, the prime component of which was to get her partner well under tight control so that he knew his place. To heel, Joe, was what she was saying to him. After that she would dominate the table. Joe had seen her in this mood before. It normally led to a pretty spectacular blow-off, round about the sixth hand. This time it might be worse. There was no Liz Playfair hanging about in the background ready to give the soothing and constructive advice which made the contract.

Joe ran lightly through the conventions they normally played at Liz Playfair's. His heart was full of foreboding. Lady C wanted to add some extra knobs to the portfolio. It was futile. Joe knew full well that Lady C had the greatest difficulty under pressure in counting up to twelve, let alone thirteen. More conventions just made it all more complicated. They could go one hundred ways wrong now instead of just ten. But Lady C was adamant, so Joe whacked in some more conventions. Like Don Quixote and Sancho Panza, they staggered to the first table, equipped to cope with every eventuality, apart from playing a good game of bridge.

Their first opponents were American. One of them claimed to recognise Lady C. Lady C was flattered.

'I'm sure I've seen you somewhere before. Deirdre, you know this face as well, don't you?'

'Sure, I do. I'm trying to remember which game show she was on.'

Lady C was not amused and snapped out her name quite sharply. The Americans were impressed. Joe introduced himself quietly. Lady C informed the opposition she was playing a weak no trump.

'We're playing Standard American.'

Lady C goggled. She'd never heard of Standard American. She played Acol, that was all. She remained silent and gave Joe a beseeching look. She was in hell already. But Joe said nothing. The sooner his chalice of pain might pass from him the better.

Lady C had a sadly forlorn look to her as she sat at the table waiting for the cards and shorn of her protective entourage. She looked as if she was missing her mummy of a long time ago. She looked very human. Joe had never seen her look like that before. The protective shards of her life had fallen away. It was a revelation. Jerked out of her theme park life and stuck in the real world she looked like a waif. The shoulders were thinner and the auburn ringlets drooped a touch. Her plump and indulged face was quite pinched.

The cards were snatched from their spots in the case by each player and the play began. The American woman on Joe's right – Yank one – opened a spade and Joe with fifteen points, and five spades with her bid one no trump. He had a stiff king of hearts, which might cause problems but one no trump looked about right. Yank two passed as did Lady Charley and Yank one came back into the bidding with two diamonds. Joe passed and Yank two gave suit preference, bidding two spades. Joe, forgetting that he was not playing at the Jack of Hearts with Joxer, and thinking about his two diamond stoppers, doubled as matter of course. It could be a good score for them, if the contract went two off.

Lady Charley looked frightened. She was thinking about the social implications of Joe's harsh and aggressive play – in public! Her eyebrows had risen to the top of her forehead in manifest rebuke. The American women, well used to this kind of feistiness, shrugged with a smile; Joe led a club from four to the king and down went dummy.

Dummy had three spades, and very little else. Two off looked cold and so it proved. Joe was sitting over declarer the whole time. He made three spade tricks, two diamond tricks, a club trick, and a heart trick. The last trick was basically a steal. Declarer played Joe for two hearts, and finessed the queen of hearts from her hand, leaving Joe's stiffy to win. Rueful smile from Yank one. These cheating perfidious, bastard Brits or something like that was running through her head, as the king of hearts made.

Afterwards, as they filled in the traveller, Yank one opined about the hearts, 'I thought for one moment that you'd done something unethical with that heart play, after you'd called one no trump.'

No more than a gambit from the Americans. The suggestion was rubbish. They were trying it on. But Lady C, who had watched the play with openly disapproving eyes and was eager to appease, chimed in immediately, 'Yes, I thought so too. I'm sure your call was illegal, Joe.'

Joe was astounded. You idiot, you're supposed to be with me, not the opposition, he thought to himself, as the American women, fortified by Lady C's support, called the director for a second opinion.

Lady C seized the opportunity offered by the director's belated arrival to do some more socialising. Ascot Week and Sir David got a mention. The Americans were polite. The director arrived. He looked at the cards, looked at Joe, looked at the traveller, laughed, told Joe that he was more than somewhat sharp in his bidding and that he, the director, wouldn't have made that bid; then he told them all to get on with the next board. No penalty. Lady C looked chagrined at the imagined slight. The Americans dived for the cards as Lady C rumbled away opposite Joe.

The next two boards passed without incident. Joe felt certain that he was going to receive a monumental ticking-off when the move was called, but no – he suffered a reprieve. Lady C made a point of nipping across to one of the other tables and gossiping for two seconds with Mags. Mags and Penny chatted away loyally to her. Then it was time to play again.

The Playfair spirit of inattention was alive and well at Savage's, thought Joe, as Lady C returned in manifestly handbaggy mode to their next table.

'Hello, I'm Lady C,' she said gaily to the two women, both of whom had mobile phones stationed at their elbows. They were polite in their replies. The cards were taken from their slots and the bidding began.

Everything went smoothly for two hands and Krakatoa opposite Joe was in non-erupt mode. They were scoring quite reasonably as well. Some notches for the good guys on the traveller. Joe started to relax. Then catastrophe. Just as the bidding ended, with three no trumps bid on Joe's right, a bid which bought the contract, one of the mobile phones rang. But which one? Perhaps both of them? Impossible to tell, because the shrilling was so loud. Consternation as both players dived and scrabbled for their phones. Lady C lost the plot completely. Dummy started jabbering into her mobile, which unnerved the noble lady still further. She led a card out of turn.

Oh, heinous crime, wicked Lady C. The director was called again and this time there was no get-out option. Declarer had five options, or was it six? As he detailed the options, Lady C looked about four years old, as if she'd been caught raiding the larder, the very picture of guilt. She actually blushed to the roots of her hair and looked ready for the spanking, as Declarer pondered her options.

Joe sat there and waited for her to make up her mind. It was no big deal, even though Lady C clearly wanted the earth to swallow her up. Leads out of turn happened all the time. Just keep cool, Lady C, and we'll be fine. Just keep cool, he found himself transmitting to her as a matter of urgency on the psychic airwaves in a bid to calm her down. She fingered her cards as if she was about to throw them in the air and walk out. She looked very rattled.

In the event it worked out rather well for the Joe and Lady C dynamic duo. Declarer had so many options to choose from, she quailed before the decision, made the wrong choice and a cold three no trumps contract went one off. This gave Lady C a clear top. She looked radiant as she saw how the score compared with the opposition. She almost started to join in with her partner in the exultation of feeling good but then stopped herself from making common cause with Joe opposite her and shut up abruptly. He was just so obviously the boy from the village with whom she'd always been forbidden to play as a child, she could not bring herself to invite him to join in. Best to leave these things unsaid. So silence between them. Joe could see Britain's entire social history writ small in that fleeting moment. He thought as ever of imminent escape to distant shores.

They left the Mobiles and passed to the next table. Joe raised his head a fraction and saw something which gave even him a start. It was Sybil. Oh God, not Sybil, anything but her. He'd quite forgotten about her and the tie-up with Savage's. She was at the table immediately after the one they were seated at, and she had seen them and she was looking forward to the meeting. Joe could see her almost licking her chops at the thought of carving up Lady C. She waved at him; Joe smiled a greeting. It was going to be very tricky. Hell corner at table four.

Joe glanced some more at her table and realised that it was an even worse set-up than he'd imagined. Sybil was playing with someone who was obviously quite good. Joe could see that clearly from the way Sybil's partner sat at the table. She was quiet, very self-contained and gave nothing away. Like all the good professionals. Young, say about twenty-five, rather Slavic in appearance, but dark skinned, with the static look of someone who'd been at the tables since birth or thereabouts. Violently blonde hair but apart from that no obvious eccentricities. And no handbag to be seen. She'd perhaps slung it in a corner, if she'd brought one at all. By the looks of things, Sybil, very sensibly, had acquired a youth international to take her round the tables, in a bid to improve her game and her score; it was a commonplace in bridge clubs although Joe was surprised that Savage's allowed that kind of thing. Maybe Sybil had been less than frank about her young friend's status in a bid to boost her rating. After cheating on the Liverpool ration books after the war, Joe doubted whether Sybil could ever be over-scrupulous. She just wasn't that kind of person. Sybil the short measure most likely, although she had a sort of animal ferocity that compelled respect.

The hands at the current table were slightly uninspiring. Dreary part scores, nothing more. No excitement. Between the second and third boards, Joe was able to lean across and mumble to Lady C something about an old friend waiting for her at the next table. Lady C seemed surprised at Joe's comment, but looked up and towards her right. She recognised her and a hard look came into her eyes, accompanied by an upward angry tilt of the jaw. What on earth was she doing here? This was followed by a rather different, more abject expression, expressing something approaching fear, or at least apprehension. Lady C was about to meet Sybil on open ground and it was not immediately obvious that she relished such an encounter. But she looked angry enough to tough it out. Joe resolved to stick by her.

As they changed tables, Joe tried to mumble some counsel to Lady C but he was forestalled. Sybil was on her feet, and she greeted Joe with a fulsome kiss on the lips as though they had recently become lovers. Then she introduced her partner whose name Joe found truly unpronounceable. It seemed to begin with an O. Reaching for the cards, O grinned and then her face resolved itself back into a mask of concentration. Lady C was not introduced at all by Sybil who treated her like a scullion. Lady C had gone dead white in the face at the intended rudeness. Joe did the honours with the O girl, whom he called Morka, for want of anything better. Morka's head nodded briefly.

They all sat down to play and then Sybil leaned across and stroked Joe's hand like a lover. It was totally unexpected and almost wholly proprietorial. Joe affected to disregard it all but he thought that Lady C was about to have some form of seizure at the point of grope. Sybil was like a wild beast trying to communicate its savagery. Morka looked startled, as if she'd discovered a fresh English bridge convention. Sybil was delighted at the havoc she'd caused. They all started looking at their cards – grudge bridge, Fulham Road style. Joe noted that the hands of both Sybil and Lady C were shaking with rage.

The first board took Lady C and Joe to three no trumps with Lady C as declarer. She was concentrating wholly on the play now and she was determined to make her contract. Joe could tell from the huffing and puffing that went with her scrutiny of dummy that she wasn't at all sure about it. She thought for some time. Then she played, and with some verve. Finally, she made her contract in style by taking a slightly risky finesse that paid off. That was something of a triumph for her. Lady C looked like a human being again and Sybil resembled a rather testy bird of prey. First blood to Lady C, as the temperature at the table edged up by a notch. She smiled at Joe and Joe equally felt that they were actually playing together as a partnership for the first time that session. Perish the thought, but maybe Sybil was good for Lady C's bridge!

The second board was fairly uneventful and again Sybil was unable to get her talons into the delicate flesh of Lady C. It would all hinge on the final board to see which of the women became carrion.

Sybil opened a spade and Joe bid five diamonds, with a spade void and nine diamonds. Morka doubled, Lady C passed, and Sybil, to her partner's horror, took out into five spades. Pass, pass, and Lady C doubled, having presumably some spades and some values. Joe had nothing behind his bid. Then, oh act of folly punished by the gods, Sybil redoubled!

It was the gesture of a woman enraged beyond measure who just has to seek and take blind revenge. Almost Shakespearean in its overweening jealousy and quite incomprehensible to anyone outside of the Sybil–Lady C axis of hate. Sybil's partner certainly thought so. She was nonplussed. She jabbered away in broken English and some obscure Slavic lingo as Joe played the ace of diamonds and dummy went down.

Three diamonds on the table! One of the others had to be void. As luck would have it, Sybil had the extra diamond. Lady C appeared to signal for a club, which Joe led to her, and the switch was correct. And so the long play of the hand dragged on. And so out came the spades and Lady C had a couple of winners there as well; Sybil hadn't been able to chuck her losing clubs on the hearts because of Lady C's switch. It all worked out rather well. Eventually Sybil went off three, redoubled and vulnerable and looked like Medusa on a very bad hair day indeed. She was uncontrollable with rage. Her fingers, sadly for her not running with Lady C's blood, tapped away on the green of the table.

To create a diversion, because Joe truly thought that Sybil's bulging eyeballs indicated she was about to strike Lady C, Joe called the director, and when he bustled up, expecting more trouble from the old firm of Joe and Lady C, he received instead a polite enquiry as to the availability of the hands after the session, just so that Lady C and he could check how the bidding might have gone on the famous hand. He was mollified and impressed. Joe's circumlocutory tactics helped to hold the fort for a few seconds before World War III broke out; the move was called and they were able to wander away without violence breaking out at hell corner.

Joe had never seen women enraged to such an extent before in his life. Both could scarcely breathe. They were both white with anger. In the absence of men's safety valve of mock fighting rituals, evolved over millions of years in the cramped and narrow caves, both women were quite incapable of externalising their rage by parody. They had no way to diffuse it. Their feelings were straightforward. They wanted to kill each other and would do, given half a chance. Their rage was epic, not least because of the add-on scorpion of the social dimension. Both their relative social positions vis-à-vis each other were now confirmed. Lady C hated Sybil as a jumped-up vulgar guttersnipe from Merseyside, who stained where she walked and who should be excluded at all costs and whatever the cost; while Sybil for her part thought that Lady C was a snob of the worst kind, who should be tortured to death on television and then dragged through the streets naked on a hurdle, spat upon by jeering crowds. Joe was just a walk-on part in this feud. Savage's very nearly lived up to its name that afternoon.

Heaving quite deep sighs of relief, but for different reasons, Lady C and Joe moved on towards the fresh pastures of new tables. Nothing else quite matched in spirit the open warfare of hell corner table. But the drama of Lady C's encounter with Sybil had a galvanising and beneficial effect on the partnership for the rest of the afternoon. After surviving her trial by Sybil, Lady C started to settle down to her play. She grabbed some self-assurance from somewhere and started to bid her hand with some confidence, without perpetually looking over her shoulder to see if either Sybil was lying in wait for her or Liz Playfair was ready to hand with soothing advice.

Rapport of a sort was established between them. Bridge was a great leveller. As she started to play normally, Joe was able to observe her in more detail, most likely for the first time in isolation. He began to reach quite odd and unexpected conclusions. Lady C was not quite what the advance billing had suggested. She turned out to be very complex.

Bridge is a form of social x-ray. No one can escape truth in bridge. In ordinary society people are protected from the prying eyes of the curious and the ill-informed by convention's camouflage. Thus they can shroud their peculiarities and delinquencies. Make-up covers the warts. But not so in bridge; there is nowhere to hide at the bridge table. It is open ground. The truth comes out, fully exposed for all to contemplate, forced into the light under the stress of competition between three other people in a highly combustible crucible. Not a game for the squeamish or the furtive.

In Sybil's case, all polite social convention was thrown to the winds in the urge and desire to win. So much was transparently clear. She was a fundamentally dishonest rogue who would stop at nothing. She gave that away completely. Out of the three boards that Joe and Lady C had played at hell corner, Sybil, who was North and responsible for the scoring, had actually filled in the score twice incorrectly and on both occasions in her favour. Either involuntarily or otherwise was immaterial. Her partner was visibly discountenanced by such shenanigans. The desire to win, by cheating if necessary, and, by extension of the x-ray syndrome, her profound ignorance of correct social behaviour, seemed so obvious it was almost laughable. So much and so manifest. Presumably she'd had a deprived childhood of some sort. She needed help.

None of that held any surprises for Joe. It was of the same ilk, though more menacing, as the housekeeping wobble, which was much in evidence that afternoon. Joe noted that one player had taken the wobble convention so far as to refuse to play off her trumps at all. And in a small triumph for contrarians, she made her contract too, using completely the wrong line in the contract!

But Lady C was different again. It took Joe some time to nail the interpretation down but he succeeded in the end. Quite gradually he realised that he was playing with two people, not just one – Lady C and her well-concealed alternative persona. First, there was the obvious Lady C, a stickler for rules, correct conventions and prickly. She was for ever on the qui vive to tick Joe off for a minor breach of convention, to the consternation and then delight of the opposition. In an unusual, to say the least, approach to bridge, she played against Joe and with the opposition, as a form of control.

This was Lady C the monster, a woman incapable of entertaining the dialogue necessary to play in a partnership. This was the treacherous snake of a deeply privileged woman, wedded to double standards, to whom Joe had played second fiddle for many moons at Liz Playfair's, the Lady C who was always supportive of the gang, exclusive to them and conspiratorial against her partner, the epitome of fidelity to her gang's social mores, their conventions, their trysts and trusts and secret jokes. In short, a purely blimpish and deeply unattractive individual.

Joe could sympathise a little with Sybil's hatred of this side of Lady C. It didn't matter how good Joe's bridge might be, that secured him no incremental gains in the eyes of Lady C's exacting and predetermined social standards, although of course when her bridge was good, that constituted a win for her and her side. Hurrah, hurrah! The playing field was so lopsided, it was like a see-saw.

But as the afternoon went on, Joe glimpsed another side to Lady C. It was just barely perceptible, like the white scut of a hare as it hurtled into its burrow of a late September afternoon. This new Lady C was quite relaxed and quite genial and fairly forgiving. Almost expansive. And in turn the alternative persona suggested that the first Lady C was no more than a synthetic construct, born out of self-will and a fearsome set of defensive mechanisms.

The new Lady C was quite a bold creature on occasion who could afford to laugh at her mistakes and who played the cards with an odd touch of elegance. More striking, perhaps, the new Lady C showed a willingness to disregard convention, even to the extent of shouting 'Bugger' at the dummy when it hadn't come out quite as she had expected, much to the amusement of the table. There seemed lots of geniality, a bounce and spirit to her personality, and she had a graceful way of leaving a table after the boards were played which was quite enchanting. The new Lady C also had a nice line in self-mockery. By the end of the afternoon, after about twenty-four boards of thrills and spills, she looked more like a happy and carefree eighteen-year-old than the wife of the famous Sir David, one of the UK's leading entrepreneurs.

There was a different laugh too, he noted, a deep sonorous gurgle which suggested real enjoyment, not the usual trilled approval. Once or twice, the laugh bordered on the vulgar, something Joe found quite breathtaking. So why the double act? Was Lady C actually terrified of herself and her own spontaneity? Or of her husband perhaps?

Joe pondered these transformations as they played. He could handle the concept; indeed, it was second nature to him to seek and find the splits in other personalities. But this one was so well hidden and then so translucent once revealed… He even succeeded in coming up with an image of the Lady C duality. She was, he thought, like a piece of quantum matter, capable of being in two places simultaneously. The first Lady C was the queen-pin in the chateau, giving the knights hell for lying in bed, striding about the parapets and roaring at the servants for their sloth and running the entire place with maximum efficiency. Everything went like clockwork under that Lady C. Forget above all about humanity. But coexistent with the first Lady C was the second Lady C, a rather sluttish and irresponsible creature who lived in a huddled squat outside the chateau, consorted with the peasants and had a good time generally. Had known in short some Rabelaisian times too. Was a bit of a laddish girl, all told.

Most remarkable of all, everything in the first Lady C found its opposite counterpart in the second Lady C, like a reflection in a mirror. It was all still there but reversed. But which one was the reality? Or was there a third unifying persona? Joe pondered this as the bridge ended with all the hands played and the scores were then fed into the computer.

Even more crucial, had the second Lady C ever had an airing?

Was this sluttish counterpart to the great duchess of style anything more than just a living fantasy, such as many people construct to get through their lives? Had there been a dawn swoop by the parents to rescue a depraved Lady C as a youngster living in all the hell of a Notting Hill squat? Or worse? Had this delicate piece of porcelain ever actually cut loose for itself?

Joe could not be sure. He needed fresh information. He would bide his time. Perhaps another session at the duplicate table would reveal more. Meanwhile it was time to learn the results of the afternoon's endeavours. All the partnerships assembled at one end of the room to hear the results. Much well-bred pawing of the ground and controlled head-tossing. Handbags were very much in evidence. Penny and Mags were there, and Trish and Nancy, and Lynn and Stella, like an army poised to bivouac; a great sense of fun, occasion and excitement ran through them all ahead of the results. All had taken part and so all wanted to be first. Or second. Or third, at least! Anything worse would be a catastrophe, no less! Wouldn't it?

Much jumping and hopping and waving of scorecards and discussion of hands from Liz Playfair's gang. Sybil was nowhere to be seen, but her partner was hovering around, eager like everyone else to learn the scores.

Lady C was slightly split over Joe and her group. She had reverted almost totally to the first Lady C's persona, but not completely. There was still a residue of the second Lady C around, clinging to her like a penumbra, for those who had eyes to see. So she told Penny and Mags, who looked vaguely interested, that Joe had played well, but she also rubbed his arm in a friendly blokeish sort of way as they all milled around. She was pretty much part of the old group nevertheless.

Then it was time for the placings. They all stood together casual but tense as the results were read out. Penny and Mags second. Trish and Nancy third, and Lady C and Joe a mere sixth! Lady C had gripped Joe's arm tight as the figures came out and it was simply subterfuge for her to pretend anything but disappointment at the lowly placing. She carried on gripping his arm. Sybil and her swarthy blonde friend had come joint third, with Trish and Nancy. That was very bad news all round. Lady C was not happy with those results.

'We'll have to do better than that next time, Joe,' she said after wincing at the news and tearing Joe's arm to pieces in the process. 'We're going to have to practise more. You're going to have to become a permanent fixture at the Thursday mornings. That way we'll get all the coaching we need. We can't let Penny and Mags beat us like this. It's just too humiliating for words. Penny's only been playing for a short while and I've been playing nearly twice as long as her. As for Sybil, well I just can't stand it. Can you?'

'Sixth is not bad, Lady C, for our first outing,' said Joe dutifully and diplomatically, thinking dolefully of the spade finesses that Lady C had not needed to take but which in her enthusiasm she had taken and which had not come off. Squeeze play? She'd get that one wrong immediately. Joe also was thinking about the partial accomplishment of his mission. He had been told to get closer to Lady C and he had done as ordered. Regular play with her on Thursday morning. Eh up, lad, that's progress. You can't get closer than that, he thought, short of stripping her down. The results were immaterial relative to his instructions.

A well-known voice could be heard just behind them. It was Sybil. And Sybil at her most treacherous as well as her most triumphant. She was out to cause trouble. She was talking to Morka in a loud voice. 'No, you must play with Emma next week, I'm out of town.'

Ah, thought Joe, so Emma is part of the Sybil circus. How interesting. She too has blundered into the menagerie, which doesn't say much for her common sense.

Sybil carried on talking. 'You won't be able to play with her all the time. I know that she's playing with young Joe here at some point next week.'

Joe felt Lady C grip his arm very hard indeed. It was involuntary. She was off to rejoin Penny and Mags. She had no time to conceal her reaction. But she was not happy at the idea of Joe playing with anyone else, he could tell that. In fact she disapproved violently. But she made no comment at all. That was all the more worrying. Joe wondered speculatively if she would connect the Emma of Savage's with the Emma of wine glass fame. That would make things very interesting indeed. He might incur the wrath of both Lady Cs at that point! Maybe, if that happened, Lady C should arrange to partner herself – now that would be interesting!

'Thank you for the game, Joe. I'm going to see what can be arranged with Liz over Thursday morning. I can't do better than that, I'm afraid.' She sounded tight-lipped.

'Fair enough, Lady C. And thank you for the game too.'

They shook hands solemnly. Joe had the sudden impression that for two pins Lady C was ready to throw herself sobbing into his arms; that she didn't want to go with the gang at all; that she wanted to do something utterly different like fall asleep in a bus shelter; that she wanted to flee. It was something in her look, some residue of the unguarded revelations of self which had carried across from the bridge and which then, still abroad and wakeful, had been shocked into response by the duplicate results and Sybil's malice.

Then Joe looked again. The look had gone. Likewise the potential for the dramatic moment which had evaporated amid the busy chat of the session breaking up and the women dispersing to their duties and chores and shopping for the evening meal. Lady C departed with her friends, enigmatic as ever.

Annie got some good news at the end of the afternoon. Joe telephoned. He called in. Another good omen. He was coming back into line of his own accord. That gave everything a touch of gloss. Joe called less as a pressed man, which was what he was, but more as an involved operative, dutifully reporting in. Annie was jubilant. The psychology was working and the textbook, again, had been proven to be correct. She kept the bubble of pleasure out of her voice as she took the call. It was the first direct contact between them for over two years, since Joe had last worked for her.

'I thought you'd like to know that I got very close to Lady C this afternoon. We played bridge together.'

'Congratulations. Good bridge?'

Both played it very cool as if a quiet conversation between them was the most natural thing in the world.

'So-so. Grunge bridge really. She doesn't actually know what she's doing too well, but she tries. Not bad given her background and the fact that she can't count much beyond eleven in a crisis. But she tried very hard this afternoon.' Joe spoke deliberately slowly. He was still turning the whole thing over in his mind.

'There are really two people there, coexisting within one Lady C. We'll talk about it some more in due course, but the existence of the alternative Lady C, who is the diametric opposite to the Lady C that I know, makes for some intriguing communication problems.'

'We know about all that. Well spotted, Joe. You did well to see that far. You'll find out more, the closer you get.'

'So there is a story there?'

'Most definitely. It's a living tragedy.'

'That makes her very tough indeed. A bit crazy but tough. But quite impressive.'

'Resilient, I'd say, Joe.'

'I carry on getting close?'

'Just play down the line as you have been doing. It's going fine. And stay in touch. Nice to hear from you.' That was the only acknowledgement given, or permitted, of the momentous step forward for the mission.

After he put the phone down, Annie gave a great whoop of joy. He was back on the line. Communication restored with Joe, and at no cost whatsoever to the command structure. She had not been obliged to give anything away at all! Oh frabjous day… Many more bits were now in place. All she had to deal with was that wretched Bootface. And preserve Joe's millions.

For one rapturous moment, Annie thought to ring Adrian, still plodding through his thesis in the USA, but she refrained. They had a pact and they had both stuck to it – no contact until after the mission was over. If she called him now, he would think it was all over and they could have some free time together. Which was far from the case. After the mission was over was the time for frolicking; his tousled head and beautiful kissable lips would have to wait. She kept her hands well clear of the phone for a full half-hour, pacing the office in a strong effort to regain self-control. She used the thought of Bootface and her utter helplessness in the face of his offer to cool down. That helped a lot. If the unknown guys who took her sheet of information didn't come up with the goods when she met Bootface, then no amount of exulting would help her. She and Joe and the whole mission were sunk beyond recall, if Bootface got what he wanted. That sobering thought helped her focus on the constant risk and danger of the mission.

More days passed for Joe with fewer dollars. Then more messages for him when he reached his flat, after skirting the crack in the wall, which in truth looked slightly shorter for once. There was some sunshine about among the clouds that made him feel more cheerful.

Emma said she hoped he'd got his rude message at Savage's and when were they going to play together? She had an idea for the stock market. Had he heard from the Confederation of Authors? That was Emma. Joachim had rung to confirm the next dinner date, which was shortly. Lady Pugh sent her thanks for lunch, and said she and Perdita would have written but they didn't have his address; meanwhile Rivers was still in town and would be contacting him shortly. A message from Rivers to ring him. The Confederation of Authors had left a message suggesting a definite time and place for him to meet Gregory Priest and make his offer in person. Mr Priest was very definitely interested to hear the proposition. I'll bet he is, thought Joe, reading between the lines of the rambling but excited communication.

One final message. It was some time in emerging from the ether. A click and then a whirr and then silence and then a much cherished voice came through that he had not expected to hear at all on his answerphone.

'Joe, is that you, Joe? Oh, bugger, why aren't you there when I call. This is just so boring, the fact that you're not there. Look, Joe, it's Perdita here, as I expect you've gathered, and I'm ringing to say that we're both very concerned. Mummy and me. Oh, thank you in the meantime for lunch; that was just glorious, as I'm sure you'll agree. But I'm not ringing about that, I'm ringing about Rivers. Mummy is very worried and so am I. I'll tell you more if you call me on my mobile. Here's the number, and if you ring me between six and quarter past I can guarantee that I'll be standing somewhere discreet so that we can talk together. Will you do that? Mummy's worried stiff. Don't tell her that I rang you, please. Nor Rivers. They're not to know. This is between you and me.'

Joe rang Rivers, hoping to get some intelligence on the situation. And trying to sound obtuse.

'Rivers? Joe here. I got your call.'

'Joe, yes, thanks for calling. Now you're not doing anything tonight are you?'

All I can steal from you is your time, thought Joe.

'No, of course not Rivers. What did you have in mind?'

'A little drink at Zorba's? I've had some good news. I'd like to share it with you.'

'I'd be delighted, Rivers. Until seven thirty then?'

'Until then.'

Rivers clicked off abruptly. Quite abruptly, in fact. Joe thought about the chat and then the click and dismissed them both. Nothing of any significance in any of that. Chief executive in the making, that was all. Then he looked at the time and started scrabbling at the phone – it was 6.14. My God, this is cutting it fine. Another minute and there'll be a very angry Perdita marching around some heath somewhere slashing at the ground.

He dialled the number and then, to sidetrack her, when the mobile was answered instantly, asked the sad voice at the other end in a high-pitched voice if Sean was there. 'Is that you, Sean?'

With great tears almost billowing through her tone, Perdita replied in the negative, and then squealed in rage as Joe reverted to his normal voice and introduced himself.

'Joe, you are the limit. I'd almost given up on you and it's cold out here on the heath.'

'I only just got back from—'

'From your bridge?' She sniffed in disapproval.

'That's the fella. Now, Perdita, what has happened? What is wrong with Rivers? I must tell you that I am down to have a drink in town with him tonight so I can tell you later if he starts biting the carpet or attacking the barmaid.'

'Joe, be serious, it's very important. We had a terrible night last night with him. I'll tell you – he's always been very close to Mummy and she always reckons to be able to talk him out of any mood that he has. But he's very angry with her for some reason, to such an extent that I thought he would actually strike her last night. Mummy thought so too. They had high words and all about nothing. He was screaming at her as if he had gone mad. That is just quite unlike Rivers. He is always very placid at home, like a big dog really. He just pads around. We know there are things on his mind, because he's just got – or is about to get – a big promotion and his boss is planning a big deal in the US and he wants Rivers to get involved in the deal with him. That's just between ourselves, right. So everything is going well for him, but he is not happy.'

Something to do with Faust and Mephistopheles, thought Joe. It doesn't come up very often but when it does…

'Do you think it's some sort of delayed reaction to the FO? To his getting chucked out from there? Joe, I don't want to sound terribly girly about all this but it is very worrying. His face was nearly purple last night with rage and we were both very frightened.'

'Perdita, I don't think you're sounding girly at all. I'd tell you if you were. No, let's be sensible and let's be practical. Just tell me what time I can call you tomorrow and I'll do that. I'll tell you how he seemed to me tonight and we can take it from there. How does that sound?'

'Brilliant, Joe. You're a real pal. Thanks a bunch. Joe, can I say something else now?'

'Go right ahead, Perdita.'

'You know we had that lunch at Ziani's?'

'I do indeed. My eyes have not yet returned to their sockets.'

'Well, we're going to have another lunch there shortly. Mummy's going to set it all up. She thought you were very impressive. She wants to socialise some more with you. Now how about that?'

'I thought you said that Rivers was barmy. Now I find it's your mother who's insane.'

'Joe, she's convinced you've got a secret. She says you're far too intelligent to be just a bridge player. She thinks you're actually very rich and that something has happened to you. So she's going to set up a lunch and invite some friends along and see what they think.'

Clammy hands of fear wrapped themselves round Joe's heart. Perdita continued. 'And do you know why she's doing this?'

'She's nervous about the tab?'

'No, guess again?'

'I don't know.'

'Well then, clever clogs, think about it and I'll tell you tomorrow. It's a very simple answer. I'll give you a clue to be going on with. You're about to be introduced to our circle.'

Click. She rang off in just the same way as her brother. The Pugh click. Joe wondered if he'd actually hear the revolver hammer going back before the bullet went into his brains. It wouldn't take long for all and sundry to get going once it became known that he was a lot more than just Joe the bridge player. Most likely he wouldn't hear the click of the revolver hammer.

It was academic anyway. A riddle of circumstances where he finished up as the solution. In a coffin, if he was lucky. And Lady Pugh would bring it about through good intentions. Who would have thought that Lady Pugh could be the agent of death? But then who, per contra, could have thought otherwise? Didn't she idolise death? Wasn't she fascinated by it? And didn't she think Joe, quite rightly, was half in love with the same? So why should he be surprised that she'd connived this incredibly pleasant conclusion for him, all on her own? So much material here for analysis, he thought.

Joe left the flat at a run. Time to meet Rivers. Not much time to spare, he'd dawdled so much. He passed the crack in the wall which seemed to stretch to the ground. And that's just the start of it, he thought. Wait until after the Pugh lunch – it'll reach Australia.

Joe came round the curve of the King's Road and pushed past the café on the corner at some speed. Not so fast, however, that he missed a curious sight. Out there on the pavement, and surrounded by what looked like five very tough hombres indeed, all most likely from the eastern European redoubts, was Morka, or whatever her real name was, yes, Morka, Sybil's bridge partner. Joe captured a glimpse of her as he swung past. She didn't see him. But Joe noted how tough she looked, as well as a blonde babe, and how much in control of the guys she seemed. She was the one seated in the middle of the table laying down the law. Joe clocked her on the instant of her banging the table with her fist, employing a demeanour that was the reverse of her withdrawn and demure appearance at Savage's.

All she needs is a shave and she'd be indistinguishable from the blokes, thought Joe as he forgot about her in the rush to arrive on time.

Joe went up Park Walk from the King's Road to get to Zorba's. He calculated he should get to Zorba's just about on time. Towards the top of Park Walk, as the shopping complex started, he looked for a bearded black face among the pillars – his other beggar. He hadn't given to him for some time. He could see the massive figure of Norman on his pitch outside the grocer's, snarling at all and sundry as he begged, a figure in the local landscape. But Joe was not interested in Norman that night. He wanted to have just a snatch of quietness with the other beggar on the strip, a sad, quiet, withdrawn, highly intelligent man who'd managed to get on the wrong side of power and money and found himself busted. Joe gave to him whenever he could. Joe fished in his pocket and pulled out a coin. The hand came out in silence and went back, taking the coin without deference on the one hand or patronage on the other. It was begging of the highest degree, begging elevated to an art form, with dignity and style.

'Have a pound my friend,' said Joe.

'Thank you, my friend.'

Joe passed on. Neither knew the other's name. Hardly necessary. Both of them knew the contract – to take was to give and vice versa, but only under optimal conditions. Such is the morality of the very poor. Nothing else mattered.

Joe entered Zorba's to find Rivers seated at the table where he had first encountered him. But no longer sobbing out his heart. He encountered a changed Rivers and a Rivers, so far as Joe could judge, in full control. Joe noted the new suit, the fresh shirt, the bright cufflinks, the alert no nonsense manner, and wondered at the British potential for painless transformation, its effortless chameleon capabilities. One moment, Rivers was down and out, and the next… Was he running the country already?

Rivers interrupted the reverie. 'A drink, Joe?'

'Why not, Rivers? I'll have a glass of retsina, if I may.'

Charley bustled over and took the order with the exaggerated and contemptuous deference he kept for the rich upstarts patronising the café. Rivers ordered a retsina as well.

'Well, Joe, this is a big moment for me. I got a promotion yesterday and today I got another leg-up. I'm running quite close to the board already. Any time you feel like giving up, just use my experience as a comfort. It's happening fast but it's happening on schedule.'

He raised his glass, as did Joe, and they clinked in mid-air.

'Happy days.'

'Happy days.'

'Rivers, you're moving at great speed. Aren't you afraid of...'

'Hubris? Oh, I'm sorry, you wouldn't know what that means. Let's say... over reaching myself? No, not at all. The chairman likes me and I like him. We see eye to eye. That's good enough for me.'

A brief pause as Rivers let the conversation die. Joe could see that the wild look was still there, dancing at the back of the eyes. He wondered where the other possessor of that look, the mad blonde, was to be found at that moment. On the pavement at King's Cross, hustling? Or lying quietly in her room at The Priory, heavily tranquillised? Or just a bag of bones in some mortuary? It's a long way to fall in London when things go badly, he mused.

'How do you feel about my sister, Joe?'

Joe was alert to the implications of the questions. The undertone of Rivers's voice carried a hint of menace. Joe kept his face straight. He was evasive.

'It was a great lunch and it was great to see her. And your mother of course. She let me read some of her translations. Did she tell you?'

'No, she didn't. But then she doesn't tell me everything at all. I think she should discuss things with me more. Especially you and Perdita.'

Had Joe's attempts to distract Rivers's train of thought succeeded? Joe couldn't be sure. Rivers was in a brooding mood of deep melancholy. The slight of the FO report was still troubling him heavily, Joe guessed. More retsina might or might not fix the mood.

Rivers swallowed his retsina. 'Time to go, Joe.'

'Where to, Rivers?'

'You'll see. I'm going to show you something, something that will alter your original view of me as a snivelling idiot who'd just been kicked out of the FO. That's why I invited you here tonight for a drink. You'll notice that we sat at the same table as I did when the report came out.'

Joe carolled in an obedient kind of way that he had. Such meticulous attention to detail was inhuman.

'That was for a reason. This is day one of the fight back. That's why we sat at the table.'

Rivers stood up. As he did so, a shape moved in the half darkness at the back of the restaurant. An enormous heavily muscled man with a shaven head, in a dark suit, came into view. Rivers introduced him. 'This is Marty. He's my bodyguard. I have to have one after my promotion. I got him two days ago. Let's go.' Rivers might have been referring to some Nubian slave.

They left the restaurant and crossed the road immediately. Norman had his head twisted the other way and didn't see them coming. So he had no time to offer them some abuse.

Rivers stopped the three of them in front of Norman. Norman turned his head very slowly and looked uneasy. He said nothing but pulled a face at Joe. Just the three of them on the pavement. Very quietly, and ignoring Norman's eye-rolling grimaces, Rivers said to Joe and Marty, as if addressing them in private in a small back room, 'Last time I was here, Norman here was mortally offensive to me. He abused me. I think he should be taught a lesson. See what you think, Marty.'

Crisply, almost without thinking, in a controlled curve, Marty swung a quick foot and caught Norman on the side of the head. Norman gave a cry of pain and protest. Marty grunted. Norman glared at his most horrific. Marty then swung the other foot and caught Norman again on the head, full on the side, with a terrific crack. Norman's head flew first to one side then to the other, with his eyes rolled up with pain. Then his head went down, almost in slow motion. Taking a short run almost right up to him, and putting all his force and weight into the flying attack on the seated man, Marty then let fly with his foot again and this time caught Norman in the face. Bone crunching and teeth cracking could be heard as Norman grunted and then screamed and the blood spouted from his mouth. His head went down again as he tried to defend himself from Marty's boots. Casually, and choosing his spot, Marty then kicked him again, this time in the side. More cracking. Marty carried on kicking Norman on the ground, a black silhouette apparently wading through Norman's writhing body.

Joe felt Rivers's eyes upon him and he stood and watched impassively. Rivers is telling me that I'm next, thought Joe. Even now perhaps. No point in making any move at all. Just no point. Just wait until it's all over.

Marty stood back, breathing heavily. He adjusted his trousers which had ridden up slightly and then tugged his waistcoat straight. The frenzy in the street abated. In no more than ten seconds of controlled fury Marty had almost crushed the life out of a man. Norman's head was on the pavement. Blood was gushing towards the gutter across the flags and he was groaning and holding his head. His breath was heaving through his huge body.

Marty got his breath back. He spoke to Norman. 'Now say you're fucking sorry, you cunt, and say it proper, otherwise I really will fucking kill you. Say it nice and slow so that everyone can hear you and believe you. Repeat after me: I'm very sorry, Mr Rivers.'

A terrible moaning gurgling sound came out of Norman's battered mouth. More blood gouted from his lips.

'That's not saying it right, Norman. That's not saying it proper, and with the right respect. You know that, don't you? Don't you, you cunt? Right, am I going to start on you again?'

More awful sounds from Norman. Joe reckoned his entire jaw was broken. He couldn't say a word. In the logical order of things, Marty would now kick him to death. Joe had seen all this before, in another life.

Rivers intervened. 'That's enough, Marty. I think justice has been done. It's time to say goodnight. Goodnight Norman.'

'Goodnight, Norman,' sneered Marty.

'Coming, Joe?' Rivers did not press the point. The exhibition of violence had served its purpose. Marty towered over Joe by a full six inches.

Joe shook his head. He stood there in front of Norman as the tramp groaned and bled some more. Marty glanced at Joe. Rivers shrugged. He had a bright sound to his voice. He looked very pleased with himself. The Pugh honour had been restored. It was time for him to be on his way in nonchalant manner. After all, mugging Norman was small beer after wiping out a score of unarmed helpless prisoners in the mountains – and getting a promotion on the strength of it all. The old service maxim was true. Once you'd taken life away, on your account, everything else was relative.

It was clear what Rivers was after. He was evening up the score. He was rolling back the clock, undoing the various awkward postures that the adverse FO report had placed him in, and rewriting history in general. The people who had seen a sub-par Rivers Pugh and taken advantage of that were to be disciplined or silenced or eliminated.

All of which augured badly for Joe. Rivers had summoned him to bear witness to the punishment of Norman as a warning which was unmistakable. Stay clear of my sister.

Rivers and Marty walked away down the Fulham Road. They were invulnerable. The law couldn't even try to touch them. Impossible. They'd just say they were provoked and there'd been an altercation. Joe couldn't quite see Norman pressing charges against Marty in his current state. The two them climbed into a car, away by the lights, that just happened to stop for them.

Joe went slowly into the grocer's and asked them to call an ambulance. He got Norman some water and tried to make him comfortable. Norman was in a very bad way and in great pain. He was surrounded by a great pool of blood. He could hardly move. The Pakistani boys in the shop were shocked and silent. Norman was a great favourite on the street. He was one of the natural curiosities. Water was produced, amid murmurings. A cushion appeared.

Joe had only to put a foot wrong and he would find himself on the receiving end of Marty's boots just like Norman. That was obvious. Marty had very nearly started on him there and then. And now Joe saw why Rivers and his mother had had such a set-to. It was over him. Lady Pugh wanted to bring Joe into the family and Rivers was adamant that a mere bridge player should remain firmly on the correct side of the palisade. Way to solve it? Why, easy – just kick the said bridge player to death and the problem would disappear.

The ambulance arrived and Joe managed to tuck a twenty-pound note into the tramp's pocket. More groaning as he was hauled into the ambulance. It took five men to lift him from the ground onto the stretcher. His head lolled from side to side and his eyes were closed. He was in pain. Joe watched the ambulance speed off, its hooter at full blast. Music in Rivers's ears, no doubt!

As arranged, Joe called Perdita very early the next morning on her mobile. The phone was answered impatiently. Joe temporised. He said that in his opinion Rivers was absolutely fine, just a little bit stressed but that the worry should pass. He said that Rivers had talked about his promotion. It had been a fun evening. Nothing to worry about. Her mother should relax. Under the circumstances, he thought that was all he could say. Joe did not mention Marty and his footballing skills. Perdita and her mother would be none the happier for knowing their brother had turned into a psychopath.

Perdita sounded relieved and then told him, eagerly, to look out for his lunch invitation. It should be in the post shortly, she said. Joe should have been even more unhappy at that piece of news, except that he knew Perdita was overstating the whole business of the invitation. Impossible to send the invitation. None of the Pughs knew his address. And wouldn't. Joe did not want to play host to Marty on a day when he was feeling a touch temperamental.

Joe also went to the hospital and discovered that the tramp had a severely fractured skull. Heavy concussion. But they had to release him because of the bed shortage. Joe complained that he had nowhere to go, that he was homeless but the hospital said that it had no choice. No more beds, savvy. Joe left the hospital feeling bleak.

★

PART TWO
# DUMMY

Joachim started the briefing. He looked rapt.

'In order to understand the oddity of British finance, its sheer crazy and perilous custom and practice eccentricity, you really need to go far further back than the seventeen century, when it is all popularly supposed to have started. You have to go right back to the Middle Ages, to the wool trade, no less. The UK produced the best wool in Europe, very conveniently for the Flemish weavers on the other side of the North Sea. If therefore you fast rewind to that era, a number of familiar features stand out immediately. The wool trade was London based, that is to say City of London based, obviously, because of the proximity to the Thames. It was organised on a semi-monopolistic basis through the wool staple; it was conducted by a small group of merchants with a highly developed sense of group identity, so that a sense of cohesive kinship in the face of the enemy was very prevalent. The wool trade was very, very profitable and our small group of merchants was afraid of nobody. Just nobody. They reckoned they had a winning line and they stuck to it. Their ambition was cosmic.

'There was a prolonged struggle in the Middle Ages between the king and the merchants as to who should garner the lion's share of the wool profits and in the struggle the king came off worst. The merchants were not afraid to give the king a bloody nose and he in turn was forced to agree a compromise which left him in possession of a high permanent tax, parliament with the power to control it and the merchants able to pay the king's subsidy because of the monopoly control of the trade exercised through the English Company of the Staple. And the monopoly suited the king because he had found a body of men who could lend him money far more securely than his previous bankers, the Frescobaldi, the Bardi and the Peruzzi, all who had been bankrupted more or less because of their loans to the king. But a company with a monopoly of the wool trade of England and with the custom and subsidy on wool as a security – that would not fail. Joe, note that point about lending to the king; it is quite crucial in terms of our historical narrative, as you will see shortly.

'So now we have established the finance part of our basic equation. Now for the other factor: land. Again it is assumed that this relationship in the UK between finance and land is of quite recent genesis, but that is not so. Not correct at all. We go back to the time of the Reformation, with the king, the fearsome paranoid Stalinist Henry VIII, as ever short of money, this time because of the massive inflation of the sixteenth century. Much as the Thatcher administration did in the course of the 1980s, and for much the same reasons, the king disposed of assets, in this case land which he had expropriated from the monks following the dissolution of the monasteries. It was the UK's first, and highly accelerated, nationalisation and privatisation programme. And the buyers? Our merchants from the City of London, of course, who had grown very rich on three centuries of wool and other commodity trading and who were now eager to expand their power and influence away from the Square Mile and in the direction of Whitehall and parliament. They bought land from the king very heavily and with the property qualification were now eligible to enter parliament. Which they did in great numbers. Result? To be expected – over the next century or so they begin questioning the basic right of the king to operate in the despotic manner which is so familiar on the continent; that is to say, levying taxes without consent.'

Joachim paused and rolled another cigarette into the black holder. He looked at the ceiling for a second. Joe said nothing and waited for the briefing to continue. Which it would. Joachim was undoubtedly the business. He did finance as other people did breakfast.

Joachim drew on his cigarette and continued. 'So let us look at our basic equation for the model, which is finance and land, these two having joined together as England starts to emerge from the Middle Ages. I think – and I have to confess that I have not done all the work that I would like to have done on this topic, so my judgements are provisional – I think that this combination of factors is very unusual and contains many odd features. There is nothing, for example, in the way of assembly in this model; nothing has to be put together to last. The land is there, of course, but that in a sense is eternal and will wax and wane according to the quality of husbandry. Nothing new is being brought into existence by finance and land, I think by a sense of combined effort which involves wrestling with raw materials. This sounds impossibly abstract but it is, I think, a valid point.

'Forgive me, Joe, but I did some thinking about it all since our last meeting because I was slightly puzzled in my own head. I decided that the combination of finance and land was odd because the timeframes were not symmetric. Land has no time frame because it always has been and it always will be. Possession of land encourages a sense of timelessness which over time will harden into rigidity, perhaps through an excess sense of control. Finance on the other is more instantaneous, because it is a deal which requires resolution or redemption over a fixed period of time which can be quite short. So finance in a sense is more detached from the contingency of other factors. It is also more abstract in a very specific sense. Credit takes place between consenting adults, no more, no less, and anything, literally anything, will serve, even nylons and cigarettes, as the credit vehicle. Provided confidence endures, it may stretch out in its time frame across the horizon to meet the timelessness of land. But only if confidence endures. That is the crucial factor and our early merchants understood that all very well.'

Joe smiled.

'You look sceptical, my friend?'

'I was wondering how City dealers would react to your speculative fancies.'

'By blowing the usual raspberries, I imagine. They are focused elsewhere, your dealers, let us say. But no, Joe, this is a serious point. I can take the point about time horizons further, beyond the obvious idea that creating a piece of machinery like a motor car requires a very much more integrated concept of time so that the desired artefact will come into being at a guaranteed moment. That is something the Germans understand very well and equally is something which the English are incapable of grasping. No, I think that there are two points to be made here. On the one hand this disparity in timing horizons between finance and land in the UK has made over the centuries for both an excess inflexibility and an excess flexibility at one and the same time. There is always an unwillingness to change, followed by a moment when everything seems to change all at once. The sticking point is followed by the door blowing wide open. The unbearable lightness of being if you want, in odd shape. Britain in that sense is weightless. It always seems to move from one extreme to another without, surprisingly, a second backward glance at the prior set of conditions or a moment of intellectual remorse. You want an example?

'Please.'

'I give you one. In the late fifties, the UK had no intention of joining the Common Market, so much so that it was a taboo subject. That lasted for some years. Next thing, all change. It is on everyone's lips that Britain is going in. I was amazed as much by the mental agility of the country as by the decision.'

'And the other point?'

'Let me read this to you by way of reply. It is a description of the role of the Council of Ten in Venice. I looked at Venice, which I took as a proxy for the UK in many ways, not least for the purity of its trading profile and its ruthless colonising effort. I wanted to find out if the element I was looking for in the UK existed in the Venetian model. I was also very fascinated by the concept of proximity between Venice and Byzantium, which I took as another proxy this time for the UK and the US in the twentieth century.'

'And you found what you were looking for?'

'Patience is a virtue, Joe. Don't be so hasty. Let me read this to you. It is from John Julius Norwich's *History of Venice* and it reads as follows: "The Council of Ten... Important and yet somehow not quite integral: from the beginning, it had refused to fit tidily into the pattern of the constitution. This pattern took the usual form of a pyramid – the Doge at its apex, then the Signoria, then downward through the Collegio and the Senate to the Great Council. The Ten however had always remained apart – an illogical anomalous body with extraordinary powers which, in an emergency, it could use to cut red tape, to bypass the slow-moving decisions of the Senate, to take its own decisions and put them immediately into effect. Normal business... passed through normal channels... Urgent matters or those demanding extreme secrecy or delicacy of handling could be passed by the Collegio direct to the Ten which was authorised to act on its own initiative, to make payments out of clandestine funds and even to give covert instructions to Venetian diplomats proceeding abroad. Its field of competence covered, 'all things concerning the security of the state and the preservation of morals' – limits so nebulous as to be practically without meaning.'"

Joachim closed the book. Joe watched the covers slap together.

'So, Joe, who does the Council of Ten remind you of?'

Joe replied without hesitation. 'The Bank of England.'

'Correct. And the bank's role in the City has always been?'

'As a control agent, especially with its secret police and an army of informers.'

'Exactly. You are right, Joe. More right, in fact than you can possibly know. As a control agent. Likewise in Venice. In other words, the concept of land and finance allied together, with two different time horizons, requires—'

'A control agent designed to neutralise the disparity between the frames and bring them back into alignment. Otherwise it all goes smash because financial confidence is a delicate flower.'

'Very smart, Joe. I am very impressed.'

'I've been around, you know, Joachim. To a City man it is obvious.'

'That is very clear. I was forgetting that you were a City man. Foolish of me. Now let me read you this and see if you can still recognise the Bank of England. "In practice, Council of Ten abuses were largely avoided by built-in checks and balances. Election was for a single year, with no eligibility for re-election until another year had passed. Two members of the same family could never sit at the same time. Leadership of the Council was never vested in one person but in a triumvirate – the *Capi* – which changed every month and whose members during their period of office were forbidden all social intercourse with the outside world lest they be exposed to rumours or bribes. Venality or corruption was punishable by death. Finally… the Council, as well as its ten elected members, also included the Doge and the Signoria bringing its effective strength to seventeen." Still recognise the Bank of England, Joe?'

'I can't comment on any of that, Joachim. I never knew anything about the running arrangements of the bank.'

'You will learn them, Joe. And you will see that here the bank differs very radically from its Venetian proxy. It is so important. I will not go so far as to say that it is in this difference that the odd outcome for the UK in the twentieth century lies, but it does, I think, go some way towards explaining why the UK has finished up in the odd posture that it has developed as the new millennium opens.'

'That's a big claim, Joachim.'

'I think I can prove it, Joe. At the very least, those checks and balances which the Venetians built into structure have never existed in the UK. And this factor, almost alone, explains why London and the UK have developed as they have done. Now back to our muttons... We have our basic model, which is what, Joe?'

'A very tough set of guys, medieval men from a medieval place if you want, who are edging upwards through time as the world changes around them. They have edge and they think they have a winning line.'

'Correct. Anything else?'

'No limits? Is that the point? Limits or absence of same. They don't strike me as having any frontiers. They can deal with anyone and take a turn.'

'Better than that, Joe, this tough set of guys as you call them have invented, or taken on board, a religion, Lutheranism, which in its anti-Catholicism more or less rules out the concept of limits because of the importance of self-revelation.'

'And also gives them freedom to trade better because, if I recall it correctly, Lutheranism relaxes the Catholic prohibitions on charging interest.'

'That was the role of the Church in the Middle Ages. It lent to the king at disguised rates of interest because the Church ran a surplus and the king was in deficit.'

'But these guys have bought the Church out, so they have a more powerful trading profile, in addition to which they have bought the land as well.'

'Correct again. I see you are getting into the swing of all this, Joe. Now before we proceed further, one small thing. These guys as you call them, are on the brink of greatness. Can we give them a name? It will make our narrative easier if we can entitle them in some way.'

'Perhaps, Joachim. I'm normally quite good at this sort of thing. Just give me some more detail, Joachim, just feed me some more snippets. I can feel a name coming on somewhere, even as we speak.'

'Very, very resolute, Joe, are these men. Very hard. No compassion here. It is about land, money and dynasty. And they take risks in order to get ahead. They are traders whose horizons gradually encompass the globe. But proud, even arrogant, as they make their way westwards from the semi-swamps of Eastcheap in the City. No women feature much in any of this because there are none of what you might call the female virtues, such as caring and sharing, present in the story. It is single-minded and obsessional. They have fought their way—'

'Company? Society? Sect? Tryst? Conventicle? No, that's not it. None of them will do. Keep going.'

'They have fought their way by finance and greed out of one world picture, that of the Middle Ages, with its huge irrationalism, into another world picture, that of modern times with its stress on logical causality.'

'And, Joachim, they form a group, don't they? They are heavily intermarried, almost… I've almost got it now. It's coming to me. It's something like clique. But not quite. It's pejorative in a way, the word clique. It doesn't convey the sense of shared enterprise and slightly sinister menace which these men incorporate. Because they are arrogant as well, yes, Joachim?' Joachim nodded.

Then it came to Joe. In a flash. He saw the word he wanted and felt pleased. The reflexes were still there, on demand. He felt pleased at that too.

'I know what we call them. It's a very short word. We call them the cabal, Joachim. That will do for our story, won't it?'

Joachim was pleased. He puffed away at his cigarette. 'Better than you can imagine, Joe. That is a very good word. Cabal is excellent. It spans a lot of factors so far as our story is concerned. You see, it's a word that must be in use by the end of the seventeenth century, the point at which our story really gets going. The key dates for us are 1693, when the London club White's is founded, and 1694, when the Bank of England is set up. Land-owners in one club, and financiers in the other. Obviously, over time, the membership of one fuses with the other, embodying our finance and land concept in real bricks and mortar. But before that, we have the Committee for Foreign Affairs formed during the reign of Charles II, around 1670, and this committee is the forerunner of the modern cabinet. Now the names on the committee are Clifford, Arlington, Buckingham, Ashley, and Lauderdale, and their initials just happen to form the word...'

'Cabal, Joachim. I know how many beans make five, you know.'

'Sadly, Joe, I can only get up to four and a half. And that only on a good day. But there we go. Now back to our story. After some two centuries of struggle with the king, during which time they cut his head off, bring him back, and then send him away again, they decide on something quite revolutionary. They decide to have a constitutional monarch. A king, that is, who exists somehow *primus inter pares* with his court, if you can imagine such a thing. This is a model for royalty and royal power which is quite unique in Europe and is testimony, if you like, to the power of the cabal. History at that point teaches them that they have to have a king but they are damned if they're going to have one who escapes their vigilance. They install a king who can be controlled. This makes for a huge triumph for the cabal. From the Square Mile it has moved to Whitehall to parliament and after a century of bickering it has now overhauled the king as well.

'A key feature to note here is that in the process of radicalising its monarchy, which now comes from Holland, the cabal also manages to absorb the new financing techniques, especially involving banking, which the Dutch perfected in the early seventeenth century. This is why the foundation of the Bank of England is so important. It is established – and note that its initial capital is huge by contemporary standards – in order to lend to the king. Wool staple time again. So the royal finances are put on a secure footing by means of this extraordinary device whereby the King rules his citizens and taxes them, but at the same time his citizens finance the king by loans. This amounts to a total financial revolution which dwarfs in its impact the UK's industrial revolution of a century later by a wide margin.'

'Just amplify that point a little for me, Joachim. The concept of lending to the crown or to the state, which is what happens nowadays, is so familiar to me that I don't quite see the ramifications of it for the period.'

'Easy one, Joe. The Bank of England is banker to the crown. It is responsible for the royal finances. Agreed?'

'Agreed.'

'So what kind of an organisation do you think it will be? Now think very carefully before you reply...'

'No, you tell me, Joachim. I'll never get this one.'

'Fine. The bank functions on the one hand as an organiser of loans to the king, mainly from the City. So it has to have standing in the City, agreed?'

'Agreed.'

'But it is also banker to the king, so it has to have standing at court, so it is in effect...'

'Yes, I see it now. Suddenly it's so obvious. How fascinating. It's part of government, but in a way that is never stated. Is that the point, Joachim?'

'More or less completely. From the moment of its inception, the bank has a foot in both camps and it is, if you like, a kind of Janus operation.'

'Speaking for the crown to the City and to the crown from the City. And never wholly defined in both roles.'

'And this, in turn, accounts for the bank's obsessive secrecy and its passionate desire to protect its independence, even at the expense of all around it.'

'Presumably few people spot this duality, Joachim.'

'The bank goes to enormous lengths over the centuries to camouflage itself. With good reason, as we shall see. But the indispensable point to grasp is that from day one, the bank is an integral but ill-defined and vague part of UK government. It is the invisible part of an unwritten constitution.'

'You can't get better than that in a Bill of Rights. But like the Council of Ten in Venice?'

'Similar but very different as we shall see. I can give you a central image of the bank which will guide us through the narrative of the next few hundred years. When the bank's great building is constructed, it is built with windowless walls. No one can see in…'

'And no one can see out either. Ha, ha, ha! Has anyone else ever made that point? I'd often wondered about those walls as I toiled around Lothbury. Now you've explained it. Thank you, Joachim.'

'People have remarked on the bank's windowless walls many times and never to their advantage, in my experience. The bank is a sinister creature. When Denis Healey was chancellor the bank even forbade him to talk with senior executives of the clearing banks, unchaperoned. Imagine that – the chancellor himself ruled out of line! But back to our muttons again. We return to happier times of hope and optimism in the late seventeenth century. An easy question now for you, Joe. What happens now that the cabal has captured the king and set up a revolutionary method of financing?'

'They keep going. No limits as yet, that I can see.'

'Correct. But which way do they keep going?'

'Outwards?'

'Correct again. But in which direction?'

'Across the seas?'

'That is a cop-out, Joe. As you know. True, they move across the seas, but first they must remove an obstacle in their path, the most powerful country in Europe at the time, which is, Joe?'

'I think it was France, but I'm not sure.'

'It certainly was France. Your sense of history is vague but unerring. France was the United States of its day, certainly so far as Europe was concerned. Yet the cabal takes out France. It is awesome. England stood in the same relationship to France then as the Isle of Wight does to Great Britain now. But the cabal does it. It takes out France. It is absolutely monumental, similar in its impact on world history to a huge meteorite striking the earth. And how does the cabal take out France, apart from sheer brutal determination and the Royal Navy, Joe?'

'There you have me, Joachim. By divine will, perhaps? Prayer?'

'No, Joe, far more prosaic. By borrowing. And the sums

involved are enormous. Borrowing on this scale has never been seen before in the world's history. To continue our analogy, it is as if the Isle of Wight borrowed in New York to take out Great Britain – and bankrupted New York in the process. So we glimpse immediately the impact of this political and financial revolution in England. Savings can be mobilised on a massive scale by the crown to fight overseas wars which broadly look pain free because they are not apparently financed out of taxation. By borrowing the crown never suffers a loss of popularity. It is a winning formula which the cabal has stumbled upon in its onward march.'

'What do the numbers look like?'

'I dug them out for you. I thought you'd ask that question. Between 1688 and 1697, English war costs are £49 million, income is £33 million, and the balance, just over a third of expenditure, is raised by loans. During the century that follows, that expenditure figure rockets ahead, so that by the time of 1800, or 1793 to 1815 to be absolutely precise, it has reached £1.6 billion. But the loans keep coming. British credit never falters during the century. During the same period loans are £440 million, or twenty-six per cent of expenditure, slightly below the century's roughly constant percentage of loans equalling a third of expenditure. The overall figures are as follows: total war expenditure reaches £2.3 billion, of which about £0.7 billion is raised by way of loans.'

'So the Bank of England did its job, especially in the closing stages of the war?'

'It certainly did. The innovation paid off. Peerages started to fly from the court in the direction of the City. Quite understandably. After France had been taken out, the way lay open for the cabal to conquer the world in the nineteenth century – or at least to buy it by trading with it.'

'A subtle difference?'

'Too subtle by half, as I will explain. But first, some recap. British credit never falters in the eighteenth century essentially because Britain pays its debts promptly and the security is good – the land base of the aristocracy. The currency does suffer admittedly because the pound is forced off gold in the final closing stages of the war with France, at a time when the burden of the national debt equates to some eighty per cent of government revenue…'

'You're pausing, Joachim.'

'Yes, in order to emphasise just how astutely the cabal organises its affairs after the war is over. It is all very well done indeed. Its members act remarkably shrewdly in a way that indicates their complete self-confidence as an elite. In a nutshell, as soon as the war is over, they move heaven and earth in order to reassure investors and to reinforce the credit system. So, public expenditure is cut after 1815, the country returns to the gold standard in 1819, tariff rates are reduced in the 1820s, and government withdraws progressively from participation in the economic process. We see the first statement of the UK's basic mantra – sound money, cheap government, and free trade in all directions for goods and capital.'

'Translate those clichés for me into contemporary jargon, will you, Joachim, just so that I'm sure I understand them.'

'Tight fiscal and tight monetary policies backed by a currency with a triple A credit rating. But the free trade part is the real bit of dynamite in the equation. On the one hand it amounts to cheap food for the masses, because tariffs are reduced, while on the other it equals an overall expansion of the role of the Bank of England, that invisible part of the cabal's winning line. Putting it another way, the UK aims to collect on the empire it has won at the expense of the French by exporting capital in massive amounts in order to trade with the whole world. That justifies the reconstitution of the credit base and of course it enhances the role of the Bank of England because ultimately it starts to stand behind the whole of the City's overseas credit edifice as a lender of last resort. Don't forget at this point in our story that the Bank of England enjoys a monopoly position as banker to the crown, in much the same way that the wool staple operated as lender to the crown in the Middle Ages. In that sense the wheel has come full circle for the cabal in a practical sense that the textbooks ignore. After five centuries of kicking and gouging, it is now back in its original habitat, in the City, backed by a monopolistic credit engine, the Bank of England, supported by a compliant political structure and lending to the whole world. Now that is fact, Joe, which cannot be disputed. The key to it all, so far as the cabal is concerned, is the currency. Provided the pound holds up, then everything else fits into place. Hence the moves to restore confidence in the pound after the French wars are over. You follow me so far?'

'With fascination, Joachim.'

'I ask that because I want to build into our model of finance and land some extra factors. The cabal is even smarter at this juncture than we have given it credit for. Those post-war reformist measures that we discussed just now amount in a very far-reaching sense to the reassertion of the pre-eminence of the financial order over the political. Can you agree with that? There's an awfully large amount of interest to pay on all that debt. Things like that need attention.'

'No problem, Joachim, so far.'

'So the balance of emphasis swings back to the City within the overall body politic of the UK. The political process is effectively subordinate to financial interests.'

'Granted. I can see that in a way that perhaps I shouldn't.'

'Don't you believe it, Joe. You can see as far as you like. Now let's build some extra bits into structure. The cabal, realising that it has acquired the outline of a trading empire, based more or less on the confidence surrounding the currency and backed in turn by the one key remnant of the French wars to survive into the nineteenth century, the Royal Navy, begins to extend the franchise of its membership. It thinks globally for perhaps the first time in recorded history since the Romans. It is actually contemplating setting up a development programme – the world's first. Not so much in order to protect its position but to further its extension. The cabal wants to make its grasp equal to its reach. So, it sets about extending membership of the cabal, mainly via the English public schools which represent by and large the professional middle classes of the south-east of England. That way it can populate those wide open spaces which it has acquired with like-minded folk who know the rules of the game. It creates an elite in order to export it, to Australia, to India, to Egypt, indeed to anywhere where it can do business. In a trading empire it is very important to know that your opposite number at the other side of the deal thinks in exactly the same way that you do. With me so far, Joe?'

'All the way, Joachim. I imagine as well, Joachim, that the Foreign Office will be part of this hegemonic elite?'

'Very much so. In the City, in the FO, and in those far-flung places like Calcutta and Sydney, the language that is spoken is the language of Sloane School, Eton and Winchester. To that extent therefore it is a lingua franca which in turn represents a shared culture and pooled ambitions. But driving the whole thing along the entire time is credit, based on the solidity of the currency. I want to emphasise this point for two reasons. First, because at this stage, the City has no problems between its imperial centre and its periphery, because of the strength of the currency and the social stability consequent upon the cabal's perceptive enfranchisement. So those puzzling dynamics of the centre versus the periphery fatal to large organisations are largely absent, at least for the time being, in the British Empire. The currency holds the entire structure together, like a series of spokes on a wheel.

'Second, it is essentially a junk credit empire. There is no way, in a sense, that credit should have been extended in the way that it was to the whole world because of the risk factors. But the fact remains that the credit was made available, largely via the massive help that the Bank of England was able to extend to the London credit markets, help in turn that was backed by the stability of the currency. So the whole world almost takes off in a very dramatic way as London, and by that I mean the City of London, buys and sells, exports and imports, then re-exports, more or less anything that moves or is made under the sun. The cabal has fought for the world and won its battle. So it is entitled to trade the world. Which it does, and very nearly buys the entire world in the process. To grasp that you have to imagine just how many times a pound can be used and just what commissions can be earned on it, if you invoice for the goods in sterling, arrange the insurance in sterling, borrow the cash from the banks in sterling, and then pay for the freightage in—'

'Don't tell me – yen!'

'Almost right, Joe. Very funny. I'm glad to see that you're still awake.'

'Wide awake, Joachim. Never felt brighter.'

'There are a couple of extra features to all this. Around the mid-nineteenth century, part of the bank's monopoly in the City is challenged by an upstart broking house called Overend & Gurney. The bank destroys the house and allows it to go spectacularly bust as a warning to any other interlopers who might be tempted to offer some competition to the established structure. The bank is very definitely not standing behind this house as lender of last resort. Basic Mafioso stuff. But an indirect benefit accrues to overseas trade from this collapse. The London banks are now nervous that the Bank of England will withhold support from them at a given hour of crisis, as an exercise of its absolute power, and they restructure their balance sheets in order to emphasise and retain a high degree of liquidity. Just in case…

'This means that industry, which is now in the throes of the second industrial revolution cannot borrow long term from the banks even if it wanted to. Therefore by extension there are more funds available to invest abroad in the trading side of the empire, in securities that can be easily liquidated in the case of a panic. Britain's savings go flying overseas and not into industry as happens everywhere else – and quite rightly in a sense since the premium enjoyed by investment into the British empire is more or less risk free. London at this stage is a kind of teeming warren of business drawn from all four corners of the world into this deep rich market trading day and night in every conceivable commodity; and everything can be sold almost in a flash.

'Nobody is entirely certain how the mechanism works but it does, largely, I think, because the Bank of England helped to extend these very large and quite short-term credit lines into every conceivable worldwide market thus guaranteeing the trade and underwriting the liquidity. Now later in the century we see a very different state of affairs when Barings gets into trouble in the 1890s. Barings represents the very acme of respectability so far as the City is concerned. Not exactly cabal pedigree but very nearly. The Bank of England gathers its supporters around it, in much the same way that it acts a century later during the secondary banking crisis in the 1970s. The big clearing banks are threatened with the loss of their banking licences if they refuse to rally round, and the bank broadly instructs government to keep its cheque-book open and ready. Such at this point is the power of the cabal expressed through the medium of the Bank of England. And government does what it is instructed to do, such is the power of the City and the cabal.

'At this juncture, just as we pass into the twentieth century, there are a few observations that I need to make in order to clarify the exposition. First, the wealth of the cabal. It is colossal. It can be simply summed up. Something like just seven thousand families own approximately eighty per cent of the land in the British Isles. Making it all very specific and down to earth, it is the Cliffords, the Arlingtons and the Lauderdales etc. of the original cabal who own the whole show. That is an astonishing concentration of assets. But it is even so an underestimate of the value of the cabal's total portfolio. The close links we have established between land and finance mean that those land value figures need to be multiplied again many times to take into account the value of other investments worldwide in order to give you in turn, Joe, a rough idea of the magnitude of the wealth accumulated by these plutocrats during about half a millennium's trading. Nor do they own this land inconspicuously. Not only do they have wealth, they also have status and power. They are local government and they are national government. They have everything. The cabal enter the twentieth century as acknowledged masters of the universe.

'But oddly this universe is flawed in ways that we can identify very clearly with hindsight. The concentration on trading overseas and the returns which this generates, aptly named invisibles, have taken place to the detriment of industry which is always viewed through the cabal's perspective as an unfortunate presence. Industry has no voice in this traditional alliance within British politics. Not that this seems to matter. External deficits on the UK's manufacturing account are easily covered by investment returns from trading, that is the invisibles. Indeed, British industry can be penalised still further. When various countries in which the City has invested heavily get into difficulties and have problems repaying their loans, then in order to service those loans the local industry base has to be built up – which means in turn that British industry is denied export opportunities and British imports boom. The equation of the cabal as you can see, Joe, is both subtle and delicate.

'But meanwhile, danger begins to threaten from elsewhere. Both the United States and Europe, in particular Germany, have embarked with great skill and enthusiasm on the second industrial revolution, from about 1870 onwards. They overhaul Britain very fast indeed. In open world markets Britain is losing ground fast to the competition and is being obliged quite rapidly to retreat into the more secure markets of the empire. So what will happen if the long peace of Europe during the nineteenth century is shattered? Is this mighty trading empire of the cabal just a brief lull in the broader story of European growth and US full-bodied emergence onto the world stage? In short is the cabal just a historical accident which takes place because of a favourable and one-off conjunction of geographical location and the correct timing of financial innovation? We shall find this out shortly, you and I, Joe, but in the meantime let me read this paragraph to you from de Cecco, who sums up the position regarding Britain's external position quite admirably.'

Joachim pulled out a text from his briefcase and started reading. 'British capital exporters preferences… created additional problems for the British balance of payments. The solution to the British payments equation was found by creating and maintaining a trading surplus with the Empire, mainly with India. British imperialism was a complex phenomenon from the economic point of view. Britain lost to Germany and to the United States the race to produce and export new products. She remained tied to old products and found a sheltered market for them in the Empire. The Empire could pay for them because it sold primary commodities to the rest of the world. Thus Britain strove to keep her Empire industrially under-developed while she tried to bolster its ability to earn foreign exchange as an exporter of primary commodities. By so doing she managed to exist without having to restructure her industry and was able to invest her capital in the countries where it gave the highest returns. To an increasing degree British capital did not create a matching demand for British exports… This allowed Britain not to be pressured into putting her industrial house in order... British industry became geared to a static under-developed market which could not absorb more than a certain amount of industrial commodities...'

'In other words, Joe, Britain ran a deficit with the rest of the world and relied on the surpluses of the empire to balance the books. Simple but clever, don't you agree? Now, Joe, build into this changing picture two other key factors – the underlying weaknesses in the City of London, and the way that the UK social algebra was starting to change – and we are well placed to understand just how and why the cabal was forced to fight hard during the twentieth century. By 1907, Britain's gold reserves were very tiny in relation to the pulls from other countries. Meanwhile short-term debts were starting to grow very rapidly indeed. The liquidity position of London was beginning to worsen, perhaps because there was a constant outflow created by Britain's trading deficits and its insistence in exporting capital on a massive scale. As regards the second point, it is easily stated. The cabal's mantra in the nineteenth century of free trade, sound money, and cheap government equated to a few guns and no butter social and defence policy mix with the weakness in the external trading accounts balanced by the invisibles. But what if that structure was unbalanced by a switch in social priorities?

'We fast-forward now to 1919 and the end of World War I. To an extent the picture is familiar: the war has been financed by borrowing, and, just as in the 1820s, the cabal, spearheaded by the Bank of England, is about to put the familiar formula into operation. It kills the post-war boom by a savage tightening of monetary policy which stimulates possibly the worst recession the UK has ever seen. This pushes unemployment up, something the cabal is keen to see since over-full employment will stimulate domestic industry. After that it's back to gold at the pre-war parity of $4.86, and an overvaluation of perhaps ten per cent, achieved in 1925; a resumption of fiscal prudence; and a negotiated reduction in the coupon of War Loan in the early 1930s so that the cost of financing the war is reduced in peacetime to the benefit of the government accounts. Foreign lending resumes and everything in theory looks just about as good as it can get.

'We can take this point a stage further in order to gauge just how secure the cabal feels in this changed post-war climate. On balance the judgement must be that it feels highly secure, after it has reinforced structure at key points, notably at the Bank of England. Let me explain. During World War I, the governor is a man named Cunliffe, described as a bully even by the normally emollient Sayers in his history of the Bank of England. The war as I said is financed mainly by US borrowings, serviced as and when by British gold held mainly in the account of the bank in Canada. The administration of the UK's overseas finance position is supervised by the London Exchange Committee where the Treasury has a powerful presence. Here we can see immediately the potential for conflict – potential which duly matures. Cunliffe insists that Chalmers, certainly, and possibly Keynes should be sacked from the committee because of an excess of zeal as they get involved in City affairs and then in order to reinforce his point and his power, instructs Canada, on his own initiative, not to deliver any more gold to New York. Effectively the governor of the Bank of England has put a stop on the government's cheque and this at the height of the war when thousands are dying daily in the trenches on the Western Front and when the pound is very close to devaluation because of the strain on Britain's credit position! You can imagine just how bitter the recriminations between Treasury and bank will have been at this point.

'But now, Joe, from our vantage point the key element is not the row which ensues between Cunliffe and the then chancellor, Bonar Law. It is the fact that Cunliffe even at that point, when he has provoked what amounts to a constitutional crisis, when apologies are flying backwards and forwards, still manages to wriggle round the process of prostration so that his resignation is not placed in the pocket of the chancellor. The bank's independence from the encroachments from Whitehall of the professional men, led by Maynard Keynes, has been preserved by a whisker. We see subsequently just what steps the cabal takes in order to preserve its position. Up until 1920, for example, the governorship of the bank was a matter of rotation from within the court of the bank, a Buggins's turn appointment which lasted just a few years. Not after the Cunliffe debacle. Cunliffe is succeeded by Montagu Norman, who suspends the constitution, transforming the bank from an oligarchy into a despotism, and who remains as governor of the bank for twenty-four years until 1944. Total transformation of the operating structure, which now has no relationship with the political cycle. The bank can always play it very long indeed – and win. Now note, Joe, Norman's background – Eton, then King's College, Cambridge, which he leaves after one year to go into the City, eventually progressing to the bank. After a slight post-war intermission, Norman is succeeded by his dauphin, Cameron Cobbold, who reigns as governor from 1949 to 1961 and who was educated at Eton and—'

'I don't believe it. King's College, Cambridge.'

'Worse, Joe. Not only was Cobbold at King's, but he too left after a year to go into the City.'

'Amazing. The cabal in full cry, as you say, Joachim. Presumably subsequent governors bear the same stamp?'

'Precisely. It's either Eton or Cambridge and normally both, with special emphasis on particular colleges. Throughout the century, the bank is, as you might expect, a total fief of the cabal, which of course it has been all along.'

'A pattern is emerging, Joachim.'

'Indeed it is, but it behoves us merely to note these facts and then to compare them with our paradigm. That is the important perception.'

'You mean the Venice Council of Ten.'

'Precisely. The Council of Ten, with its wide powers, was set up in such a way as to prevent a rigidity of response setting in. The Bank of England, flagship of the oligarchy, inclines in the opposite direction.'

'With predictable results?'

'Not exactly, Joe. You must be like Asquith now and wait and see. The century has an unpredictable outcome for the cabal. Let us return first to Montagu Norman, the man who transformed central banking in the country and indeed in the world. First he was not a happy man, spending much of his time in sanatoriums during his long reign as governor; he was given to vendettas and his closest female friend described him once as the most vindictive man she had ever met.'

'And his enemies? What did they say?'

'Ask Churchill. Norman bamboozled him over the return to gold at \$4.86 and Churchill never forgave him – or the bank, especially since the General Strike followed pretty soon after. But then that clash was inevitable. Churchill, whatever else he might have been, was a great parliamentarian whereas Norman hated democracy.'

'Ah! Who would have thought it?'

'Of course, Joe. The cabal strikes back. Norman was a rigid ideologue, cast in much the same mould as Thatcher some seventy years later, and placed in his position with much the same ends in view. Norman's avowed aim was to take the Bank of England out of the political realm, make it independent, and locate it within an archipelago of other central banks across the world. Never complain and never explain was his motto and he maintained this to the letter. With great success.

'At the Macmillan Committee enquiry into finance and industry, 1929 to 1931, Norman's icy and uninformative replies to questioning border on the insolent, a pattern of behaviour which most governors have imitated ever since. Norman pulls it off on one level. He is determined not to participate in the democratic process and he is determined to restore to full working order the traditional cabal mantra of free trade in everything, including capital, sound money and cheap government. To the extent that he restores the pound to its pre-war parity he succeeds. At one point he was known as the most powerful man in the world. Hence, from our longer perspective, while modern British politics encroaches on the monetary realm and as society becomes more complex in its demands and its evolution, Norman aims to redefine the terms of the changing argument completely by abstracting the cabal's flagship from the debate, ring-fencing it with other central banks and restating the traditional argument. It works – for a time. The bank becomes an untouchable in the UK political conspectus but it is always capable through its manipulations in the markets of affecting the course of politics as we shall see. It evolves into a hostile restatement of the traditional status quo as the political dimension at the other end of town alters, a kind of transcendental statement of power without responsibility, or perhaps even an icon to a bygone age that requires deference at every turn. Norman is just the start of this process.

'But there are other factors at work too which we must now explore. Britain, for example, goes into the post-war period owing the US government some $5 billion, after liquidating a fair proportion of its overseas assets in order to pay for the war. By 1928, some forty per cent of the British budget goes towards repaying war debt of one form or another, putting a huge strain on government budgets. Worse, the locus of capital markets has shifted irrevocably during the war towards New York, which becomes and remains the major capital market in the world for the rest of the century. That is a huge blow to the cabal, because it reduces the insurance and shipping mandates that might be earned for the City in sterling. London is no longer a sun shining alone in the sky but a mere satellite of the USA. Worse, the loss of the overseas investments to pay for the war diminishes still further the returns from overseas, the invisibles, and hence leaves the external accounts looking still more exposed than before. Against this doleful background you have to admire in a sense the resolution displayed by the cabal in orchestrating that return to gold at an overvaluation. Or perhaps admiration is the wrong term...'

Joachim paused for a few rare moments in his briefing. He looked at the ceiling and then resumed. 'These are difficult points to make because at this stage, around the mid-1920s, so many things start happening at once in the UK and in the City, all with different timeframes. Let me make that point more strongly. On the one hand we see a return to the status quo immediately after the war, organised by what is effectively the doge of Threadneedle Street. He sits squarely at the centre of his domain in the Square Mile. But he is not the only power. I have also a strong feeling that behind this public doge sits another doge, an Ashley perhaps from the cabal, located very discreetly elsewhere, who was concerned with exploring other possibilities, other permutations, and who, in contrast to the sheer upfront unpleasantness of Norman, represents a throwback to the cabal's medieval roots, which amount in total to pragmatic survival.

'So there are two quite different strands running together, one of which is dogmatic and tough, while the other is tentative and experimental. One, the bank doge, deals in certainties forcefully expressed, while the other, the quiet doge, explores probabilities which are never wholly stated. Now if we accept this sense of fissure, we can fit a number of other more diverse strands into pattern. The quiet doge, for example, realises quite early on that he faces a seemingly insuperable paradox, notably that the machinery which has swept the cabal to this point in time over a period of half a millennium is both fucked beyond recall – if you'll forgive the phrase – but also too powerfully entrenched in the structure to dismantle without revolution. In other words, the system doesn't work in a modern context but can't be changed either.

'So Ashley the quiet doge seeks alternatives. We see this in the guns versus butter dilemma which is implicit in the cabal mantra. The UK cannot afford both. So, in the context of a return to an overvalued pound, the UK must increase its spending on social security in order to avoid complete civic breakdown as unemployment rockets, all the while cutting back sharply under cover of the League of Nations on its defence expenditure. This puts a premium on the diplomatic effort if the cabal is to hang on to its far-flung colonies. Hence the emergence of that mad ghastly triangle of Britain's negotiating stance: containment, followed by appeasement, followed by force. All bluff of course, in a context which includes political wizards like Gandhi and Hitler; it is a bluff which is gradually called as the twenties give way to the thirties. But the quiet doge, I think, expects this, and he can see immediately the limitations of the stance. But the bluff works for a time, as he explores other avenues and buys some more time. So the UK statement looks solid enough, but it is in fact full of movable possibilities, to be tested and discarded as the underlying survival formula of the cabal is overhauled.

'It is around this time, I think, that the quiet doge starts getting interested in that large former colony of the cabal, the United States, which has been growing steadily in the isolation of its Pacific orientation for over a century. The quiet doge likes the way that the cabal has been able to borrow from the United States during the war. And in English, too…

'Now, Joe, let me interrupt the narrative by asking you a question – what is your attitude towards borrowing money?'

Joe answered without hesitation, staring as he did bankruptcy in the face. 'Never been a problem.'

'Exactly. Do you worry about how much money you borrow?'

Joe again answered without hesitation, despite his heavy debts. 'I'm a City man. Credit is credit. To default, Joachim, is bad. Very bad. Gets you a poor name.'

'You see what I mean, Joe. You see what your reflex actions are. Now rewind to 1924 or so and the quiet doge in his ruminations. To borrow from the United States is the same for him as to lend to the Ottoman empire. And he likes the look of the US as a potential creditor. He's a trader by origin and instinct, is our quiet doge, and debt does not frighten him. To owe the US the billions which were borrowed during World War I is just a balance sheet item to be finessed, relative to all the other assets which the UK can still muster elsewhere in the world. Just a detail. Our quiet doge is sage. He can see lots of borrowing from the US looming in the future because, as he realises, the twentieth century is not going to be peaceful and untroubled by wars like the nineteenth and the UK with its long trading links across the world is particularly exposed. So he broods long and hard about the US as the Norman caravanserai at the Bank of England moves on to its inevitable disaster.

'Go back to our Venetian example. On the Rialto they thought long and hard about Byzantium across the water and finally invoked the help of the crusaders to sack it. But our quiet doge is not thinking along those lines. He is thinking of penetrating the US in such a way as to be able to manipulate its policies in line with those preferred by the cabal. It sounds a tall order and indeed a foolish one, but then the doge is a realist. He knows that the cabal has no future left in the UK, because of the paradoxical rigidity and success of the cabal's formula. Therefore it must move abroad in order to prosper and protect what is left of value in the UK – and that means moving to America, mainly by borrowing and hence burrowing deep into the American substratum. It is very far-sighted and it works. But it takes a very long time.'

'What happens to Norman?'

'He goes bust. The return to gold is a total failure. He is done in by a combination of French perfidy, the Wall Street boom and central European instability. Essentially, Norman pursues a policy in Europe of financial imperialism, trying to extend the sterling area by putting Germany on a gold and ultimately sterling standard. It doesn't work. The French spot what Norman is trying to do and determine to teach him a lesson because they think he has gone soft on German war debt reparation. Emile Moreau, governor of the Bank of France, pegs the franc at an undervaluation relative to the pound, so gold moves from London to Paris and Norman is highly embarrassed by these moves. Then the Wall Street boom accelerates and gold shifts to New York. Up go the British rates to preserve the parity. Finally, the central European banking system experiences a run and in the panic Britain is forced off the gold standard. The Bank of England loses all its money.'

'What happens to Norman?'

'He stays, of course. He remains at his post for a further thirteen years. This is an odd country.'

'And the mantra?'

'Discarded completely, at least for the time being. The UK as is its wont, heads in a completely opposite direction. It opts for a managed currency, administered by the Treasury in conjunction with the Bank of England, and a cheap money policy to help boost local industry and get unemployment down. This is a far cry from Norman's boast to the Macmillan Committee that the international position must take pre-eminence. The switch to low interest rates was to be followed in the late thirties by a burst of fiscal excess as a defence spending programme kicked in, worth some £440 million, nearly half of which was financed by borrowing. So from the few guns and no butter policies of the previous century, the UK was now well on the way to embracing guns and butter policies both at the same time by the late thirties. And of course this policy mix got far worse, as we shall see. Or better, depending on how you view that sort of thing.'

'I would have thought, Joachim, that by now the whole concept of the cabal would have been dead and buried after the onslaught of the 1931 fiasco.'

'You might have thought that but you would have been wrong.

Mind you, there are some very tough times ahead for the cabal, but let me remind you of its resilience. Its survival capacities are unrivalled. So let me ask you, does the regatta still take place at Henley? And is there honey still for tea? Are boaters worn at the Eton versus Harrow match still?'

'Indeed it does and indeed there is, Joachim, and indeed they are. But how come? How does the cabal recover from 1931?'

'The cabal retreats into the empire. A number of other countries, plus the whole Commonwealth more or less, follow Britain off the gold standard and together they form what came to be known as the sterling area. So this process that we noticed at the end of the nineteenth century, which brought Britain into closer relationship with its colonies, finds ultimate expression in the creation of the sterling area. Within the sterling area, the pound circulates freely, and all gold and foreign currency reserves are held jointly in common in London by the Bank of England. For a time the arrangement works very well.'

'This all sounds a trifle flippant, Joachim?'

'Not wholly. It is difficult to trace causality chains with complete certainty at this juncture because so much is going on. And in this instance, after such a mighty crash as the gold standard fiasco, lots of different things are going on at the same time all with their separate trajectories. The sterling area, for example, works quite well and the pound thrives in its sheltered environment. Norman starts setting up central banks throughout the area in order to coordinate monetary policy. Within this smaller trading area, it is clear that the writ of the cabal will run without question. But the diplomatic initiative fails completely, perhaps because of the split between Chamberlain and Eden and perhaps also because of the confusion behind the totality of foreign policy that I mentioned earlier. The UK speaks with two voices as Norman gets involved behind the scenes with Germany. He does this especially via his meetings with Schacht, his German opposite number at the Basle-based Bank for International Settlements, which evolves into a central bankers club. They are very cosy meetings. Norman offers various deals in much the same silver-tongued way that he beguiled Churchill. Month after month right up to the early part of 1939, all in a bid to extend the sterling area within the European confines and knock out the perfidious French. So the signals that go back to Germany and to Hitler are confusing. Hitler, one of the world's greatest political entrepreneurs, decides that both sides in the Munich talks and elsewhere are bluffing, concludes that he can ante up better than either Halifax or Chamberlain whose tough talk is belied by Norman's blandishments, and he calls the British bluff. The British are out-bluffed. They can neither put up nor shut up. So they have to go to war, perhaps the very worst eventuality which might befall them in the context of the altered financial position and the reliance for trade on the buttress of the empire. Britain finds itself by the end of the decade fighting a war on three fronts – in the Mediterranean against Italy, in Europe against Germany and in the Pacific against the Japanese.

'By 1940 Britain is effectively bankrupt because it has run out of reserves. Indeed, the balance of payments is giving cause for concern by 1938 as Britain rearms. And of course, the real beneficiary of the British accelerated arms programme is not the UK economy but the United States because the scale of the arms demand is so huge and so insistent. Ironically that is where the jobs are created.

'In the harsher world of the mid-twentieth century, the traditional British model – or rather what is perceived to be the British model because by now I think that the quiet doge is employing all forms of proxies to test out many forms of alternative directions – is seen to be hopelessly malfunctional. And this I think is where Keynes comes in. The Keynes that I want to give you here is the eager and outspoken polemicist raging through the twenties and thirties and railing against policy here and there and everywhere; the Keynes who writes *The Economic Consequences of the Peace*, condemning the scale of German war debt reparations; who writes *The Economic Consequences of Mr Churchill*; who pens *How to Pay for the War*; the Keynes who spots quite correctly that the pound is returning to the gold standard at a ten per cent overvaluation; the Keynes who is in America during the loan negotiations of World War I; who organises the financial setting for World War II; who speculates constantly in commodities; who tinkers with markets and economies in a bid to understand them in a new way because the old ways seem not to work any longer; whose mind according to Hicks never stays still but is always pushing on.

'The contrast with Norman, the other great financier of the age, is striking. The reclusive and mysterious Norman stays in his counting house in the middle of the City, bent over his gold, peddling and manipulating the ancient orthodoxies by a whisper here, a hint there, a string pulled elsewhere, like a medieval money changer with ears alert to the slightest change in the breezes. Keynes by contrast is out there on the world's highways raging and ranting, again like some medieval figure, but more of a St Bernard of Clairvaux or a Peter Abelard, more of a theologian or a schoolman, a man who is always looking forward to new solutions rather than Norman who is constantly defending the past. Both of course get their comeuppance, Norman as I have described and Keynes in a way that in some senses is more shocking, which I will describe shortly. But these two are linked in many more ways than you would imagine. I have described Norman's background for you. Now what do you think Keynes's was?'

'I don't believe this, Joachim.'

'But it's true. Both are products of the top cadre. Just like Norman, Keynes is a product of Eton and King's, Cambridge. They evolve in different ways but they share a common spiritual parentage. They share even more than that eventually. Keynes was certainly a very active homosexual up until the time of his marriage, whereas it looks as if Norman was a closet queen of some considerable and awesome regality. He certainly enjoyed the company of young Etonians, whom he recruited heavily into the bank, and his letters to Benjamin Strong of the New York Fed strike a cloying and very feminine note. The terms of endearment are very very odd indeed. And, of course, the two of them – Norman and Keynes – work together during the war at the bank, after Keynes is recruited to the court, even though they fall out heavily in the run-up to the Anglo-American loan negotiations.'

'So where does the quiet doge fit into all of this?'

'A good question. I like to think of him sitting alone or with a few very close friends somewhere quite apart from both Norman and Keynes, perhaps in his favourite chair at Boodle's, twisting the ring on his finger and watching both of them go through their paces, without comment, wondering which of them, the traditionalist or the innovator – or neither – holds the key to the future for the cabal as the twentieth century gets tougher and tougher and solutions last for a shorter and shorter period of time. The doge knows there is a solution because there always has been one in the past, but he doesn't quite know where it lies. He thinks it lies with America but again he cannot be quite sure of that either. So he watches and waits and scrutinises both Norman and Keynes, ever vigilant and ever silent, just turning things over in his mind and observing and experiencing the flow of events. Eventually he finds the key with Harold Macmillan, as we shall see, but it is not at all obvious at first, although later on it becomes far more straightforward. In the meantime, Britain stumbles into a war which it cannot finance let alone win, and stands alone in the 1940s against the hostile European continent, cutting a heroic but ultimately pathetic figure.

'I gloss over the war for obvious reasons. We have already discussed it in part. Only a few points are relevant to our story. First, the numbers. Of course, as we might have expected, the war was financed by borrowing. As one wag put it unkindly, the UK borrowed from the US to pay Russians to kill Germans – but that is merely a humorous comment and is taking an idea too far. Suffice it to say that the trend that we have observed from the eighteenth century onwards was preserved between 1939 and 1945. The UK drew on its credit to pay for the war. Taking authorities Hancock and Sayers together, Lend-Lease from the US amounted to $30 billion, liabilities to the sterling area and elsewhere totalled some $15 billion and net asset sales were worth some $4 billion. Reserves at the end of the war were worth some $2.4 billion and the immediate balance of payments position was horrendous. On a headline basis, the UK finished the war as the world's greatest debtor, but in a sense this is a mere bagatelle to such seasoned credit operators as the cabal. The Americans were persuaded to write off or forgive the Lend-Lease items and the debts to the sterling area were eroded by both time and devaluation. Ultimately it turned out to be quite a cheap little war for some people. Keynes's ideas meanwhile about deficit financing were certainly tested to the limit. In 1938, revenue as a percentage of central government expenditure was eighty-six per cent; by 1944 it had fallen to fifty-five per cent, after falling at one point as low as forty per cent. As Keynes said, "We threw good house-keeping to the winds." He spoke truer than he thought when he made that comment.

'Second, given the utterly parlous state of British finances immediately post war, the UK approached the US for a loan, a move which not all of Whitehall approved. But Keynes was insistent. He was confident that he would get a good deal from the Americans, say some $6 billion of grant with no strings attached. In the event the negotiations are a fiasco, viewed from one aspect. They go on too long; Keynes makes mistake after mistake in his approach, for reasons perhaps we discussed earlier, especially concerning the post-war role of the dollar; he also misjudges the tone of the US administration; wrangling takes place over petty details; finally, the UK finishes up with about $4 billion of loan on what with hindsight were good terms but which rankled at the time. Keynes dies of a heart attack shortly afterwards.

'But all these factors are subject to reinterpretation. The numbers can be run in almost any direction necessary to produce approximately a myriad of suggestive interpretations. Now the key point to make about these loan negotiations is not the amount, but the strings which the Americans try to attach to the loan – early convertibility of sterling across the world's exchanges and an end to the protective tariffs. The UK makes concessions here and there, but it fails to budge over much on the terms of the existing tariff arrangements. In other words it is fighting to hang on to the concept of the sterling area, which as we have seen is the absolute bulwark of the UK's financial and political system.

'Now the wonder of it all is that the Americans fail to protest much at the UK's vague promises to dismantle imperial preference at some point. This is quite crucial. The UK got more or less what it wanted in what again with hindsight appears to be a charade of a negotiating process. It had to be done and it had to be seen to be done, but the outcome had been logged in advance, long before the talking started. Whatever the US might say in public, it had implicitly underwritten by the terms of that Anglo-American loan the continued existence of what remained – and there still remained a substantial amount – of the British empire and its currency arrangements. A pattern emerged. It all happened in much the same way as the US had effectively via Lend-Lease underwritten the sterling area during the war when Britain was borrowing so heavily from the colonies.

'Our quiet doge will have noted all of this with great satisfaction. He was preparing his rainbow Bridge across which the cabal could ride in triumph to New York and Washington's Valhalla. That looks to have been his goal – recolonisation. As the US prepared to assume the mantle of world leader, it was clearly not prepared to junk entirely the prior structure of the previous hegemony. And this perception in turn enabled the quiet doge to begin building his long bridge into the US via the old colonies. A relationship was in the process of being forged, one which looked like one between master and governed but one in which essentially the serf was only play-acting.

'There now follows an amazing cat and mouse game between the US and the UK which lasts for some thirty years or so until Mrs Thatcher and Ronald Reagan become prime minister and president respectively – and crown the doge's quiet and deadly strategy. The UK pushes all the time to establish just how far it can go with the US in terms of independence within its overall subject and debtor status. To grasp the dimensions and the subtlety of the game, let me make my third point about the war – the legacy of the war debt to the colonies, the sterling balances. To recap, the UK starts the peace process with few reserves, huge liabilities to its colonies and a large loan from the US. There is a newly elected Labour government which has a radical agenda which includes nationalisation of the Bank of England and a large spending programme. The Bank of England is run by an unreconstructed old-style cabal representative in Cameron Cobbold, to all intents and purposes Norman's protégé. The sterling balances are unfunded, that is to say, no way has been established or even mooted as to how they should be paid off. So they sit in London. Moreover there are no constraints on capital movement within the sterling area.

'Well, Joe, it doesn't take a genius to work out what will happen, does it? Secretive and uncooperative at the best of times, the Bank of England is positively in its curmudgeonly element when it is offered such a chance to destabilise the Labour administration or, let us say, oblige it to modify its expansionist policies. Which it can do by the simple expedient of whispering it here and there in the City that the balance of payments figures look poor – in fact they held up remarkably well – and that there is a risk that exchange controls will be applied to the sterling area, and then delaying the figures – that kind of thing from time to time, when it suits the bank. Don't forget either that outside of London there are many loopholes to those sterling exchange controls. This is the Bank of England, as representative of the cabal, acting in opposition to the elected government in order to frustrate any attempts to alter the basic operating structure of the UK, with the added piquancy that both the chancellor and the governor of the bank have been educated at Eton – and hate each other.

'So there you have it – at a time when the world is acutely short of dollars and only the UK has guaranteed access to them via its loan, there is investor panic to get out of sterling, most notably in the great convertibility crisis of 1947. Threatened bad trade figures, low reserves and malicious rumours from a hostile central bank combine to make a very powerful and mischievous cocktail. The whole operation has the simultaneous and beneficial effect of providing the colonies with both dollars and extra spending power as the Anglo-American loan is recycled via Bank of England intervention in their direction. This rewards the sterling area for holding sterling – or rather selling it in time and then switching back into the pound after the 1949 devaluation from $4 to $2.8 – and also keeps it sweet in terms of the threatened communist world takeover while gratifying the US at the same time. Meanwhile the British tighten their belt and see a reduction in their bread ration as the Labour government's New Jerusalem agenda is modified in the light of poor trading figures. The British meanwhile must work harder at their much reduced industrial base.

'There is an extra almost diabolical kicker here which the Bank of England never hesitates to employ as a control instrument as time goes by. In the immediate post-war period the British pump capital into the sterling area to such an extent that the spending between 1946 and 1964 is equivalent to the pre-war British investment of the past one hundred years. Government spending and private lending – the whole shebang. A very large amount of capital is exported just as it was in the nineteenth century when the City was in its heyday. This I think now reflects part of the deal with the US whereby the UK can keep the empire, provided it spends to modernise it. This heavy investment is motivated partly, of course, by the attempt to boost the invisibles which took such a hammering during World War II. But this capital outflow puts great strain on the UK's balance of payments, not least because the normal presentation of the data tends to obscure the fact that capital which must ultimately earn some form of a return is being exported. The balance of payments figures are never as bad as they are initially depicted, at least on trade account, while the deficits on capital account are far larger than assumed because the sterling area is a very leaky ship.

'So there are periodic balance of payments fears and crises which are used as a stick by the Bank of England to beat the elected government into a more traditionally configurative policy stance. And, of course, the more that the economies of the colonies expand, the higher the risk grows of an expansion of demand in Australia and elsewhere. This in turn will threaten still more balance of payments problems this time on the periphery of the empire but which will impact on the centre since the UK stands as banker to the whole area through the pooling of reserves in London to the whole sterling area. In this sense, the flows in the sterling area reverse direction and instead of being centripetal become centrifugal. The latent dynamics of this are very hard to manage. London has somehow finished up in the outer circle of its empire as a power for influence, as its empire drifts inevitably towards the US, consequence of its strong gravitational pull, while of course remaining right at the centre of the empire as banker to the operation. It is as if the captain of the ship steers the boat by sitting on the rudder the whole time.

'Meanwhile the Bank of England, in an exercise of sustained post-war hypocrisy, hammers away, in public and in private, at the need to get back to some sort of fiscal orthodoxy in the UK, which basically means getting the level of unemployment up and the trend in wages and government spending on social account down. The Bank of England is true to itself, of course, but not helpful in terms of the overall UK body politic.

'This is not, as you might imagine, a harmonious exercise in the art of government. The Treasury is coping with all the problems consequent upon high levels of domestic demand and a reduced industrial base, while the Bank of England has a quite separate agenda – to restore operating conditions in the UK to what they were in the early nineteenth century. It is not, Joe, a recipe for success in a modern state.

'The pressure is all the more intense since some of those same sterling balances were used during the war to repay debt owed to the City of London; post war the colonies owe nothing to London and this makes them just that extra little bit more capable of cocking a snook as and when they feel like it – or when they are counselled to misbehave by the Foreign Office – by threatening to switch out of sterling.

'As you might imagine it, UK government for twenty or thirty years is conducted on a knife edge of uncertainty. Or again, Joe, I should qualify that by saying that the uncertainty is on at least one level, because on another level traditional long-term strategic business proceeds very smoothly as the US and the UK draw ever closer together via the intermediary of the colonies. Don't forget Eton still plays Harrow at cricket and the asset base of the UK is owned just as it was in the late nineteenth century despite one hundred years of agitation for social reform.

'Meanwhile the sterling balances, the ultimate frighteners, are used to keep interest rates higher on a precautionary basis than they would otherwise have been. This of course penalises UK industry which puts further stress on the need to rebuild the invisibles. Build into this scenario also the fact that after the Korean War the UK taxpayer starts to pick up some of the tab for the US global defence effort and it is clear that full employment carries some hidden drawbacks and many concealed costs. The British taxpayers' European counterparts are not exposed to these extra add-ons, by way of contrast, it should be noted. The Atlantic is full of unstated but clearly felt quid pro quos, flying back and forth between Washington and London.

'Meanwhile the Bank of England is edging back very, very slowly and gradually throughout the forties and the fifties into reopening markets for sterling. Finally, in 1958, sterling is made fully convertible for non-residents. Now granted that the years after sterling is made convertible are punctuated, throughout the 1960s, by almost yearly sterling crises, what, Joe, do you think was the sense of making the pound convertible? These crises, some of which are provoked by the Bank of England itself in its venomous campaign against Wilson in the 1960s, culminate in the 1967 devaluation, to be followed immediately afterwards by the Basle Agreement which humiliatingly promises to compensate sterling holders in dollars for any sterling depreciation. We have come a long way from the rock-solid pound of the nineteenth century, have we not?

'Yet, Joe, you must at the same time assume that there was some rationale to all of this. The US perceived the pound as being useful to the US as a regional currency in a non-dollar world, thereby absorbing some of the costs which might otherwise have accrued to the US in the dollar's transition to the world's top currency. Certainly the US attitude towards the UK during this period taken as a whole is incredibly tolerant. In flat defiance, for example, of the terms of the Anglo-American Financial Agreement, the UK allies itself with other sterling countries from 1947 onwards in a discriminatory trading club against the dollar. The US turns a blind eye. US support for the pound is shown in the European Payments Union set-up, whereby the US makes a large contribution in dollars which the UK is able to draw upon as a fresh source of credit. The UK draws hugely on the aid offered by the Marshall Plan when it becomes available in the late forties. There are many other American acts of favouritism shown to the UK through its dealings with the IMF, in the terms of the Marshall Plan, as I said, and via military aid under Nato agreements. The special relationship may look like an ugly form of public subordination in the political sphere – and I'm thinking here of Britain's craven "me too-ist" voting record at the UN – but in the financial sphere it contains many unusual and almost reciprocal resonances. In a treacherous post-war neo-communist world, Britain and the US create a massive tradition of mutual aid.

'Anyway, by the time of the Basle Agreement, this particular game between the US and the UK over the colonies is more or less played out. And not for quite the reasons you might have thought. The markets bring about its downfall. In the early stages of the post-war charade, the sterling area remains intact because the colonial rim is the dollar-earning bulwark and as such tends, as it did in the nineteenth century, to offset deficits at the centre because it moves in line with the US trade cycle. London of course moves asymmetrically to the US trade cycle. But over the years this asymmetry is reduced so that when deficits occur they occur by a far greater factor. The markets learn this over a period of years and learn just when and how to short sterling in huge amounts and in such a way as to make the Bank of England increasingly powerless to resist.

'The short point of all this is simple. The UK post-war strategy of opting for the colonies with their commodity-based dollar earnings source, as opposed to building up the industrial base, as Japan and Germany did, failed. It started to fail around the mid-fifties, at the time of the Messina Conference concerning Europe, when Germany began to emerge as an industrial power-house, and it was certainly dead and buried by the time of the Basle Agreement. The risks to the UK's long-term strategy of infiltrating the US are very considerable. If the US starts to focus its diplomatic attention directly on its two anti-communist buffer states – Japan and Germany – instead of routing its relationship with the world outside of America through London, then London will finish up as some form of insignificant European offshore Cuba, with all the revolutionary implications which that might connote.

'But fortunately for our cabal, although not so perhaps for the UK's much derided industrialists, the quiet doge, still twisting his signet ring in his favourite chair at Boodle's, saw all this coming. He saw it all as early as 1952 or thereabouts and positioned accordingly. So by the time the colonies gambit is played out, the UK has started moving in a fresh strategic direction and is already well advanced down that road.

'Oil holds the key to it all. The UK authorities know that post-war energy demand will rise very sharply. Therefore they must relocate the empire so that it is heavily focused around the Middle East, where the bulk of the world's cheap oil supplies is located. Therefore it makes good sense to build a diplomatic ring fence around the Middle East, a move which in turn leaves the UK in some sort of pole position relative to the US, some ten years hence. And the quiet doge also knows something else about oil, although he's not telling anyone about that particular snippet of data. Moreover, Churchill's ring concept, whereby the UK sits at the centre of a series of overlapping circles – the US, Europe and the empire – needs overhauling in the light of changing world politics. What is needed is a fixer.

'And the cabal finds the fixer. A fixer of genius, perhaps the most intelligent of all the UK's twentieth-century senior politicians, a man who arguably changes the UK's whole global strategy, while retaining everything seemingly unchanged. A fixer whose long-range bets just nearly – very nearly – come off over a period of thirty years.'

'And the name of the fixer?'

'Why, none other than our old friend Harold Macmillan.'

'Super Mac?'

'The very same.'

'I need some convincing on this one, Joachim.'

'Listen to me carefully, Joe, and I'll convince you. It won't take long either for me to unravel his stratagems for you. At bottom they are very simple once the code is cracked.'

'Joachim, I'm all ears.'

'You make a good listener, Joe. One minute, while I take a sip of water...' Joachim, eyes staring sightlessly at the wall as he concentrated on the next stage of his narrative, took a quick sip of water and then resumed the tale.

'Forget about the weary actor-manager of Mac's later years, Joe, and look at the early career of Harold during the war. That is where the brilliance and ruthlessness of the man can be glimpsed in their raw state. He's a hustler as you might expect from a man who is only one generation or so away from a Scottish croft and he is utterly adept at playing one side off against the other. Timing and presentation and a total flair for finessing a situation are the hallmarks of his trade. He basically runs the whole of the Mediterranean war for the British, liaising constantly with the Americans, the war cabinet, the Italians, the Greeks and the Yugoslavs and arrogating to himself in the process a considerable degree of operational independence. The US side of it all presents no difficulties for him since he has an American mother like Churchill before him. Mac is quite brilliant during the war, a success which is concealed by his return to the back benches after the war ends but which has not been overlooked by the cabal. In post-war politics, he starts his climb to the top, perhaps assisted perhaps making his own luck, but who knows? At Suez, he is the man who plunges the knife into Anthony's unprotected back, who gets the job and who can start the urgent job of shifting the goalposts of the empire. Anthony Eden was simply not up to the job of overhauling the British reorganisation of strategic imperatives so he had to go in one of those prismatic UK political events, like the Falkland Islands imbroglio in the 1980s. The cabal does not hesitate for long – ever. Thatcher was saved by the Falklands and Eden was dispatched via Colonel Nasser, with whom incidentally Britain found no problem at all in doing business after Eden had been defenestrated.

'And so the repositioning starts. Africa is closed down, helped by a number of bribes from the British government which are handed over courtesy of the Export Credit's Guarantee Department, so that adherence to the concept of sterling is preserved. A new deal with Russia is hammered out, in one way or another, perhaps even with the timely dispatch of a few spies to Moscow, and this incidentally bears fruit thirty years later when the West-loving Gorbachev pops up as Russia's president. As for the US, Mac plays it all utterly coolly, finessing Eisenhower, Kennedy and de Gaulle in the process in order to reach his ultimate goal: repeal of the MacMahon Act of 1946 so that the UK can get its hands on the US nuclear weapons. This alone will guarantee the UK continued access to the top table. And this is what Mac secures in 1958 coincidentally the year sterling achieves convertibility. The first leg of the quiet doge's new strategy is in place; the special relationship with the US has been restated and in such a way that it reposes on very firm foundations. Once the nuclear weapons have been promised, in whatever shape or form, they cannot be taken back, because of the repercussions in terms of world opinion. If the cost of the deal is a continued high level of defence expenditure by the British taxpayer, then that must be a price worth paying to secure the cabal's continued presence at a very high level in the US. Such is the way the logic of the cabal functions.

'Now observe too what else Mac secures during his tenure as UK premier. He frustrates Butler by steering Douglas-Home, an appeasement hero of twenty years before, into the premiership in order to keep the seat warm for Heath some ten years later. It is Heath who will take the UK into the Common Market, again on whatever terms are available, in order to fulfil the geometric symmetry of the UK's new strategy, which consists in placing itself at the centre of four, not three, overlapping circles – the US, Russia, Europe and the Commonwealth. Membership of the Common Market is essential if only to destroy it, the role Thatcher attempts to play twenty years later. As I said to you, Joe, you have to run everything the UK does at this stage at different speeds in order to establish exactly what the strategy consisted of. Not content with moving the empire's world goalposts, Mac also destabilises the Treasury by imposing his man at FO, Sir Roger Makins, as joint boss of the Treasury. Then finally, in a little known but very significant move, he restates the UK's classic mantra by elevating in a formal manner the Bank of England into a pre-eminent position vis-à-vis the chancellor and the Treasury. It's back to the nineteenth century in a way that is quite crucial for what is about to happen in the sixties and seventies. But this is not romantic nostalgia; this is tough-minded business for the cabal. For the cabal's US strategy to succeed, it is quite imperative that the Bank of England should remain independent within the confines of its 1946 nationalisation.'

'You'll forgive me, Joachim, but I don't quite follow all of that. Am I being quite stupid, or something? Surely those two statements are quite contradictory?'

'Not at all, Joe. I'll outline it for you. In the late fifties Thorneycroft is chancellor and worried about inflation, which he views as a monetarist phenomenon. He wants to instruct the banks to reduce their advances by five per cent. Thorneycroft turns to the governor and finds that the Bank of England is unwilling to issue such a directive. Thorneycroft is then advised that he has neither the power to force the bank to issue such a directive nor the power to dismiss the governor, both of which courses he was contemplating. In other words, the chancellor has only very limited jurisdiction within the City where the bank's writ runs with as much force as ever it did in the past. The hidden part of the unwritten constitution is as powerful as it ever was in the eighteenth century. Nonplussed, Thorneycroft appeals to his prime minister who to his consternation backs the bank instead of his chancellor. Not long afterwards Thorneycroft resigns, which is hardly surprising under the circumstances. But that is not all. There are even better times ahead for the cabal and for the bank, courtesy of Harold. In a surprise move, Harold appoints Lord Cromer, a Baring, to succeed as governor the retiring Cameron Cobbold. Same stable, of course, as most of the other governors so far this century – Eton and Cambridge.

'Now, the points to grasp about Cromer are these: first, he is an outspoken patrician who dislikes with some intensity, and will not hesitate to say so, the man who appears to be the incoming Labour prime minister in a year or so, Harold Wilson. Those two hate each other, not least because Wilson has poured such public scorn on the City during the bank rate tribunal in 1957. In these circumstances Cromer can be relied on. No one but no one is going to spoil his game, still less a footloose, rootless politician. Second, as well as being a member of White's naturally, Cromer is married to a Rothermere and therefore is guaranteed a favourable press platform whenever he happens to opine. Result? A foregone conclusion. The bank two: Wilson nil before the game has even started. This move by Macmillan is, I venture to suggest, one of the finest examples you will ever see in British politics of nobbling the odds-on favourite before it is even out of the horse box. The Wilson administration goes round in ever decreasing circles during the sixties. As a political force for change, it is quite negligible. Wilson himself is gradually driven mad by the sheer dottiness of it all and thus the cabal triumphs in the most unlikely circumstances. And most important the Bank of England has retained its traditional role. It is still quite free to formulate its own view of credit irrespective of what the Treasury might say. And this is very important.'

'As you say, Joachim, all these things have been overlooked. Macmillan was quite a dashing blade in his own way.'

'One of the finest fencers of all time, I humbly opine. But we must press on, Joe. We are nearing the end of our story. It is time to see how the great plot is sprung and how the cabal manages to push its way into the very highest circles in the US and then how it all goes wrong. Ready for the last lap, Joe?'

'I'm all ears.'

'Fine. Now to compress a great deal of data; it takes place in four or five precisely articulated stages. First, a group of corporate commandos is bred up in the London market, the likes of Slater, Goldsmith, Gordon White, with whom you will be familiar.

'I know these men, Joachim.'

'Of course you do. They cut their teeth on asset-stripping and drive a swathe through British industry in the process doing it more or less irreparable harm. But that as we know is not a powerful factor. The asset-strippers build up in the process formidable expertise and viable balance sheets, helped, I think, by credit lines from the Bank of England, or other forms of help that are even more intangible. That is why Mac is so concerned to protect the bank in its traditional form. This all happens in the sixties and seventies. But it is all home-based activity because the UK still has exchange controls in place. The asset-stripping of British industry takes place in a sense within the City of London itself through the stock market.'

'I follow.'

'Next comes the oil gambit. Now no one can say how or why for certain but in the early seventies, post the Vietnam War which the US finances in a highly inflationary way by borrowing, the price of oil rockets and OPEC gets its act together for the first time ever. Very, very hard to ascribe causality anywhere convincingly in this instance. But the fact remains that overnight more or less the oil price goes from $3 to $30 a barrel. *Mirabile dictu*, that oil which I hinted the quiet doge has known for some time lurks in the North Sea suddenly becomes commercially viable.

Assuming it can be extracted, which it can be, then for a time at least Britain's balance of payments problems will be a thing of the past. The oil is scheduled to start flowing around 1980. Before that the awkward matter of the sterling balances is tidied away during the great sterling crisis of 1976 when the IMF is forced to take charge for a time of the UK economy and the old Labour Party with its clumsy socialism is taken out of the game for at least a generation. But no matter; all is primed and ready for the great lift-off of 1979. It all goes according to plan and the cabal pulls it off. Callaghan does his bit and throws the election and in come the Conservatives led by Mrs Thatcher, to be followed a year later by Reagan as US president and with whom Mrs Thatcher starts what is practically a political love affair. That is important in the light of the other move the Conservatives make as soon as they are elected – they scrap exchange controls. So what happens then, Joe?'

'You tell me, Joachim. I'm not going to ruin your story at this point by stupid speculation.'

'The money smashes into the US in an explosion of exported capital, spearheaded by those commando groups that I mentioned a second ago. Think of Venice and Byzantium and think of the sack of Byzantium by the Crusaders in the thirteenth century and you have an almost exact historical parallel – except that New York is not put to the sword. According to the published figures, which almost certainly understate the true position, Britain invests many hundred of billions of dollars over a decade in the US, spearheaded by the likes of Goldsmith and James White. It asset-strips the American continent. The commandos buy company after company, rip them apart, and then move on. That is the only way to describe the process. The UK sees the fastest build-up of overseas assets in world history and in the process reconstructs its US asset base to what it had been before World War I. So what does that amount to, Joe? Think hard, Joe. Think of the income that will accrue from those US investments over time.'

'Very cautiously, Joachim, I would suggest that this onslaught on the US amounted to a reconstruction of the UK's invisibles base, which as you have pointed out is the offset to the perpetually poor UK industrial performance.'

'Quite correct, Joe. So you have been listening all along in that quiet way you have. Correct. I am very pleased. Those streams of income increase exponentially throughout the decade, but, as we will see…' Joachim fell silent briefly. Joe said nothing, waiting for him to continue.

Joachim spoke musingly. 'You know, Joe, it is almost incredible to look at what has happened to the UK during the twentieth century. The currency goes from top status to master currency, then to negotiated status, and then almost to a shadow currency position relative to the dollar, falling from around $5 to the pound before World War I to a level now of some $1.50. And it has been lower. It hit parity against the dollar at one point in the eighties, and all this without the slightest ripple effect in terms of social consequences. And without any improvement in the country's industrial performance. It is nothing short of incredible, like a dream sequence. Other countries which see their currencies decline in this way incur revolutions and worse as inflation grips, but not the UK. Everything just soldiers on as before. It is unbelievable. There must be extremely powerful control factors at work that even I cannot fathom wholly precisely. But to our muttons, Joe. Our story is nearly finished now and the denouement is not long delayed.'

'Denouement, Joachim?'

'Joe, it will not surprise you to hear what happens to British industry, once the Thatcherites get into their stride.'

'Decimated?'

'Perhaps a fifth of capacity is lost in about eighteen months as the pound rockets ahead briefly, in order to make those capital exports cheaper. But that is only a part of the story. Industry is unnecessary now. The Thatcherites also rip out all the wiring in structure which has had the long-term effect during the century of tying the cabal to the rest of UK society in terms of social commitment. The cabal is free again, and freer than at any point in the whole century in terms of domestic responsibilities. Free to roam about the world as it did in its heyday in the eighteenth century. There is a massive return to the status quo ante of pre-World War I Britain. But then just when the timing of everything is working to perfection, it all starts to go wrong. Very, very wrong. Down comes the Berlin Wall, right on cue, as the Soviet empire falls apart according to one definition. But by then the Thatcherites have gone completely crazy. They have got their snouts into the trough so deeply they cannot be dragged away from the rich feed.'

'Explain, Joachim.'

'Defence, Joe. The Thatcherites are new boys on the block, parvenus in the corridors of power, and they have never seen such money as can be generated by the defence game. They have big expectations and short purses. So they need money. They start selling arms here there and everywhere, in short wherever they can, and this in turn starts to destabilise the planet as the world and his wife get their hands on very, very advanced weaponry. Iraq is a case in point, which I will not go into. Meanwhile the third leg of the Macmillan strategy – Europe – also proves to be just a bridge too far. Thatcher falls out with her chancellor, Nigel Lawson, just when he is scheming to take Britain into the European Monetary System at a cheap rate. Entry at that level would help rebuild the industrial base, but from within Europe as Britain beds down in a new structure of concentric circles. A very stable structure too with lots of scope for change and development. But it cannot be done at any price. The quiet doge's great scheme falls apart because the new boys are just too greedy. Thatcher has too many self-interested advisers and she listens to them too much. Besides, she hates the Europeans. And she loves the Americans, especially the far right of America, with its love of very high defence expenditures. So Lawson is forced out as chancellor.

'Worse is to come. The current account goes haywire and the deficits explode, so the overseas assets base is not quite the nest egg it promised to be. Meanwhile the bribes and scandals and kickbacks on the defence front create an almighty stench. Eventually the Americans grow so alarmed by the whole process that Thatcher is unhorsed in turn, but by then the damage is done. The opportunity has been lost, especially over Europe, and this gives the traditional post-war elements in the equation their chance to regroup. The old military–industrial complex, which we know and love, moves back into town. And regroup it does – with a vengeance. And it is very dangerous now. Very dangerous indeed. Very dangerous for everybody. Things are just out of control.'

Joachim fell silent. Joe waited for him to resume speaking. But he remained obstinately quiet.

# PART THREE

# STRIP SQUEEZE

# Chapter Twelve

Tuesday evening had come but not yet gone. Joe stood in a large, airy well-lit room, with mirrors running round every side, feeling conspicuous in tight shorts. Knots of slim, scantily clad women lounged around him. Some were seated on the floor reading in apparent oblivion of their surroundings, legs the length of eternity splayed everywhere. Silence in the room. Joe gazed with interest at the pale face and under-exercised torso he could see in the mirror. He realised with a start that this frail and frightened looking male he glimpsed was in fact himself. It was a shock to find he even existed at all.

Ichabod, he said to himself and thought about Berlin. He was waiting for Marcello. Such an expensive errand of mercy he was pursuing. But he was grateful for the interlude. He was deep in the mission now and as ever he was confused, just as the effort was starting to take its toll. A dangerous combination. It had been like that in Berlin. Always. Missions took their toll. It was the uncertainty of it all. You gazed at the situation and it looked threatening, with towers and rocks and furnaces breathing smoke and thunder. Then you looked away and looked back and it had all dissolved into innocent little paper boats floating on a tranquil pool.

Intelligence work is always like that, Joe told himself. The reality is ever changing, ever elusive. You can never quite pin the reality down and nor indeed should you ever hope to. Don't speculate and don't get smart. Just play down the line, that's all you need to do, he told himself again. Reality is too demanding for understanding by mere mortals, and intelligence work is very nearly the same; it is like a myriad of crystals at the bottom of the glass, capable of a trillion rearrangements. It all hinges on time and perspective and it is impossible to predict just how the combinations will fuse together. And as Berlin, likewise now in London.

On the surface he was doing brilliantly. He'd got close to Lady C, no one had busted his cover, contact had been re-established with control without fuss, he'd made some money through Tom and the structure was set up. In principle it was just a matter of pushing on to the end of the road. Maybe he'd even get his money back as well some day.

But it was just not that simple. Perdita, he knew, had been the motivation behind his getting involved again with control, despite their blandishments, and the evolution of the Pugh situation threatened disaster to the whole enterprise. Rivers the psycho was quite capable of having him killed – so much was abundantly clear. Rivers was a grinding threat to the whole thing, because the more he disapproved of Joe, the more Lady Pugh would dig her heels in and then of course the keener Perdita would get, because he and Perdita had some form of intuitive understanding, and so Rivers… It was like watching a time bomb tick slowly towards the point of explosion.

Worse, Joe had a feeling about it all. He was starting to feel hemmed in and he knew that feeling. It was depressing. Such reactions generally portended a worsening in outlook and a deterioration for the mission. It was like stiffness in the knee ahead of a storm.

So that was your reality for you – one thing and then another thing, all at the same time and never a pause in between. Had that reality in the back last week and couldn't get a word of sense out of him…

Joe was grateful to the girls for just standing around in the gym like so many pieces of statuesque modern architecture. Clumps of beauty on the strand. Silent poses of dryads. Joe found himself rewriting the daft blurb of an art catalogue to describe the girls in the gym and it made him feel better. Proximity to a more straightforward and uncomplicated version of reality always had that effect. Not something to reach out and touch, though. Briefly he thought for a moment about Lucy-Miranda and then dismissed the reflection. There is just no room at all for that kind of sentiment in this game, he mused.

Movement among the statues. Joe came to with a sudden awakening. The gym was abruptly crowded. Women had come from near and far for the class. Perhaps about sixty girls now thronged the floor. A massive air of expectancy. The girls straightened up, the readers raised themselves from the floor and the books were put away. Lines of girls, with one solitary male in their midst, formed across the gym floor.

In strode the kings of the dance, Marcello, relaxed, carrying a bag and a box of tapes, accompanied by Jean-Paul, who slunk into the gym in a black and enticing one-piece outfit that ended somewhere just below the knee, looking exactly like a modern Pan. Gleaming smile and coffee-coloured skin. Born beneath the stars as the caravans trekked along, straight from the sands of the desert. He carried the whiff of the desert storm and sun with him as he and Marcello came to a halt in front of the assembled throng. Jean-Paul's genitalia bunched in confident protrusion like an affirmation of masculinity as he stretched expansively in front of the girls. The girls looked on with appraising detachment.

Greetings all round the class from the habituées, and then a huge smile from Marcello as he spied Joe, hidden and alone in the grove of budding girls. Marcello nudged Jean-Paul and pointed Joe out to him, which was hardly tricky, and Jean-Paul smiled and waved, and then shouted through the mike that he was busy strapping around himself, 'And a big hello for our brave new-comer, our brave male newcomer, who has come to provide us with reinforcements.'

A laugh ran around the class and Joe raised his arm in gladiatorial salute. Then they were off.

Clap hands and a move to the left… clap hands and a move to the right, and then back with the legs and forward with the legs and Jean-Paul screaming all the time at the girls, as if they were cattle. Joe could feel the breath running smooth and free within him as he kept his eyes fixed on Jean-Paul's small smoothly rounded butt which moved here and then there. Joe found Marcello at his elbow, and Marcello spoke to him as they both moved in time to the room.

'Good to see you. Glad you made the class.'

'No problem,' Joe gasped.

'Don't worry if you can't do it all. This is an advanced aerobics class. Just do what you can. Let's meet up afterwards for a coffee.

I'll see you in reception after the class.'

Joe nodded and Marcello seemingly swam off through the whirl of legs and arms and regained his spot at the front. Joe was too flustered for the time being to enjoy the full easy significance of his rendezvous with Marcello. Somewhere at the back of his mind he grasped it though. Meeting, yes... Betty would be pleased, yes... Meanwhile, where had his legs gone?

Joe could see what a huge turn-on the Marcello and Jean-Paul double act must be for the girls in the class. The boys were like dervishes. They wiggled and screamed and exhorted and danced in front of the milling girls, waving their bodies and wiggling their butts at the maddened class moving in strict unison to the heavy pounding bass of the tape, with the girls responding through grunts and shouts and a more concentrated, savage stomping tread at the provocation. In line, moving in unison, moving in line, losing self-awareness in the strictly disciplined throng.

Joe lasted just seven minutes before he quit. It all became too much. He had no breath left to give. The legs had gone totally. He almost crawled to the back and both the instructors and most of the girls waved farewell as they danced on. He was in agony. The class sailed on into time as the music pounded away and the girls danced.

I may be gone some little time, thought Joe as he staggered to a halt outside and gulped some water down. That was very tough indeed. So much for mercy dashes.

An hour later he was feeling warm and tranquil and well showered. Neat and together. A cool and relaxed Marcello sat next to him in the Chelsea Potter and they sipped their lagers. Hullabaloo by the drinkers all around them. But the pain had mysteriously vanished from his limbs. Marcello looked as if he'd been out for a slow stroll. Quite unfazed by the aerobics. Remarkable.

Joe remembered Betty's last message to him that afternoon. In high excitement, she had called him for about the fourth time that week and relayed the final message from her daughters – they particularly wanted to know if he had a girlfriend. So far as Betty and her girls were concerned, Marcello was back home safe and sound. And who was she? Anyone they knew? Was she nice?

Would they like her?

'Be sure and find that out, Joe, they're dying to know,' said Betty. 'We'll all be waiting for the call and we'll all be saying a little prayer for you and him. Good luck, Joe. And thank you.'

Joe took another swig of his lager and asked whether Jean-Paul would be joining them. A shadow passed across Marcello's face. He paused in slight embarrassment.

'No, not this evening. He wanted to but he couldn't…'

Sensing an opening, Joe persevered. 'I'm sorry about that. I was hoping to talk to both parts of the duo.'

'Yes, it's a pity.'

Further pause. Here it comes, thought Joe. Easy does it. The urge to confide is sempiternal.

'You see, Jean-Paul has a rich lover, who collects him now after the class and whisks him away.' Not a long statement but a highly significant one.

'That must be a bore for you, Marcello, if you can't sup a few jars with your oppo, after provoking sixty women to terminal orgasm.' Gently does it, thought Joe. It'll come out by degrees.

'Well, yes, it is a bore. More and more, but there you are. It's…'

'I'm sorry to hear all this.'

'I'm starting to get used to it. You see, Jean-Paul and I have made common cause along with Ateh against the world for quite some time now, and it's quite a blow to find that it's starting to break up. A big blow in fact. Ateh is quite devastated but then she's fairly paranoid about relationships anyway. She always thinks they'll break up, but that's because her background is so odd.'

'Ateh?'

'There are three of us in this fight. Jean-Paul, me and Ateh. Ateh is really the force behind the whole thing but that's because she's had such a hard time. She drives us all just as she drives herself. Over time, we've all done pretty well, all things considered. We've dragged ourselves out of the lower depths, as Ateh says. And it's true, it's been a great partnership. Ateh's got her shop now, Jean-Paul's got his lover and I…'

'You've got an aerobics class?'

'No, trickier than that; I've got a decision to make.'

Joe admired the way that Marcello handled his sentences. They were light but well balanced with a high information content, always a good sign in a person. Good verbs, he noted. Marcello impressed him. Joe waited for him to continue.

'Another lager, Marcello?'

'Yes, why not. Here, let me get them, it's my turn.'

He shot to his feet and strode off to the bar. He'll be back in a flash, thought Joe. A well-built guy like that gets served immediately. And he'll have thought about what he wants to say while he's getting the drinks in and he'll say it, no more and no less. Nicely judged and nicely delivered. Marcello's problem is that he's outgrown all this aerobics and he's ready to come home. But he doesn't quite know how to arrange his withdrawal in the nicest possible way. I can see that it might be difficult. He and Jean-Paul must have had quite a hard time together. You need to be a real man to have a friend like that and carry it off. Interesting though that he should have landed on his feet in London quite so spectacularly. Marcello strikes me as a survivor.

Marcello returned with the drinks. He sat down and started talking. He knew what he wanted to say. 'Forgive me if I burden you with my problems. The next lager's on me by way of recompense, if that's any help. But we're talking as complete strangers and that's a great help. I can suddenly see a way to resolve all this. So, happy days…'

'Happy days.'

'My problem is whether I return home or not. You see, I ran away from home a few years ago because, well, the reason doesn't matter, because people do run away, don't they, all the time… Anyway, I ran away and now that I've actually done something for myself and in London, which has been tough all round, I think I ought to be thinking about going back to my parents and family. It's just a thought but it's one that keeps coming back. I can't put it off for ever.'

'Tricky, isn't it? How do you think they'd react? Have you had any contact with them at all while you've been away?'

'Yes, I call my mother once a week on her mobile. She, I know, wants me to return immediately. The problem was with my father…'

'It frequently is. But surely all that is water under the bridge now. Old men forget, don't they?'

'Most likely. But let us just suppose that I do decide to go back – how do you think I should go about it? We're talking as complete strangers, you understand, so no comebacks on you if I decide to do the complete opposite of what you suggest, but what d'you think? Talking to you just for this small amount of time makes me realise just what an enclosed life I've been leading with Jean-Paul and Ateh. It's refreshing, chatting away like this.'

'That's just the lager talking.'

Marcello laughed at the gag and Joe warmed to him some more. He envisaged a very reassuring message back to Betty at the homestead later that evening.

'What you really mean, Marcello, is that you'd like a spot of exhibitionism about the return of the prodigal. Bands playing and guns going off all round to celebrate the return. That kind of thing, yes?'

'Well yes, you're quite right, if only to make the point that I'm being welcomed back by everybody – and that includes him as well. But I don't want it all to be so overstated that it just becomes a farce.'

They both laughed. It was a good moment of discussion. Lots of good drinking enthusiasm all around them in the Potter.

'How many other people in the family?'

'I've got three sisters.'

'And you left when?'

'About three years ago.'

'Seen nobody since then?'

'Not a soul. I've been making my way in London. They don't know where I live at all. It's been cold turkey all the way through.'

'Marcello, you're a young man of remarkable character. All this is very impressive. A lot of people would have weakened by now. I think my counsel would be – oh, forgive me for asking, but got a girlfriend at the moment?'

Joe slid the rogue question in when least expected. But those were Betty's instructions after all.

'Not really. There's Ateh, but she's not a girlfriend, more a soulmate if you like. With Jean-Paul in the offing, running a girlfriend would be quite difficult. He's very possessive.'

'I rather got that impression too. So there's not really a great deal of baggage to take back home?'

'Precious little.'

'Marcello, you may disagree, but I think what I'd do is quite simple. I think I'd let the women in your family look after it all. That's not a cop out even if it sounds like one. There are four of them after all. They'll see to it. They'll arrange the welcome for you. So leave it all to them. After all, it's they who are taking you back in. You can't really dictate terms at all. So let it ride. Leave it to them. What could be more healthy and spontaneous? Just say you've decided to return in some way that I can't quite see just now. Say it in some neutral way. Employing some symbol. Yes, I've got it. I think you need to make a gesture, just that and no more, and they'll do all the rest.'

Marcello nodded thoughtful agreement. Joe could see that the decision to return had been taken in principle a long time ago. But Marcello wanted to take soundings. He struck Joe as a business-man in embryo. He didn't like taking decisions without further discussion. He was cautious, most likely a consensus man. He wanted to carry the team with him on his thoughts. More than likely the son of his father, in business at least. How ironic that he'd been forced out of home by his father. Maybe they were too much alike. Perhaps they both sought consensus and failed to find it in each other, for the time being.

Joe pressed home his point but quite gently. 'Tell you what, Marcello, as we speak, I've had an idea. No problem if you tell me to take a running jump when you've heard it but listen to me. Why not do this – why not just send an enormous bunch of flowers back home to everyone, without saying who they're from, and use that as your calling card? That'll defuse everything. A few days later, quite casually, when they've got over the flowers, but they're still chattering about the identity of the sender, you can ring up and say you're on your way. As a matter of course. Quote a time and a day and the women will do the rest. I guarantee that.'

'You know your women.'

'And you must know yours…'

'Touché. I asked for that didn't I? Very well.' Marcello looked thoughtful for a second. 'Look, what are you doing for the next half hour or so?'

'Drinking with you, in principle.'

'I've got an idea as well. One idea begets another. This is the night for them. Why don't I call Ateh on my mobile, see if she's still in the shop, and if she is we can shoot over to see her. She's only in Notting Hill Gate.'

Joe nodded, experiencing that same sense of trepidation he always felt when penetrating another person's domestic life. Marcello fiddled with the mobile. Then he got through.

'Ateh? Hi, it's Marcello here. Yes, yes, fantastic; but of course Jean-Paul's disappeared. Oh yes, he did a very good class... What d'you expect? He's a professional, after all. But that's not why I rang. No... Look, Ateh, you remember I told you about that guy who turned up at the gym last week. The one who looked as if he'd dropped in from Mars... Yes, well, he did come to the class this evening.' Here Marcello winked at Joe.

'Yes, and we've been talking about the great topic, you know, the return home and he's come up with a really great suggestion, so I thought... Yes, yes, you're still there? Yes, in about fifteen minutes. That's terrific, we'll be there. See you in a quarter of an hour.'

'Ateh catches on fast, Marcello.'

'Well, yes she does, mind like a razor, heart of a – I don't know what. She's a very driven woman and she never stops working out the numbers. But it's more to do with the fact that we always discuss everything endlessly, all three of us, before any of us take a decision. We all have the same hang-up – families. So she knows what I'm thinking about.'

They were out in the street now and Marcello hailed a passing cab. Typical London, thought Joe – as he briefly rediscovered its endless series of possibilities – one moment you're alone in a crowd and the next you're bosom buddies with someone you barely knew at the start of the week. Sharing thoughts you hardly knew you had. About plays you're supposed to have seen and books you claim to have read. Bullshit capital of the world, *sans pareil*...

Joe decided to keep very careful counsel over all his dealings with Marcello, who grew more talkative and relaxed as he warmed to the stranger's presence. Joe didn't want to appear to be acting the part of copper's nark for Betty at any stage. That might destroy any trust between them. Best, he thought, if he said as little as possible and just let events take their course, so that the rapprochement between Marcello and his family took place with the minimum of fuss and disclosure. And then he, Joe, could get on with the more difficult business of staying alive to complete his mission. Already Joe's mind was straying back to Rivers and Lady C and the implications of his next and impending Thursday morning appearance at the bridge with the girls, now that he had apparently become a permanent fixture as Lady C's partner.

Marcello talked some more about Jean-Paul. 'We met in a railway station. We were both running away and we were both in tears. I'd left home and didn't know what I should be doing in London, while Jean-Paul had had a row with Ateh and decided to leave her. For ever, as he said. That was before she got the shop. She was working all hours just to get the money together to buy the lease and she was looking after him and I guess things were strained between them. Anyway, I persuaded him to go back to her and make it up and I tagged along and that's how we all found ourselves living together in this happy families set-up. It's worked very well for me, but it can be quite fraught.'

'Because she works so hard?'

'Partly that, and partly because Jean-Paul is so incredibly manipulative and promiscuous. He really is just like a female in some ways, always tempting you along a certain path, gauging your reactions and then claiming that you led him on. He is very good at disclaiming all responsibility for his actions. I'm not telling tales out of school, because Jean-Paul knows that's exactly what I think about him, but when I accuse him of any of this, he just shrugs and says, "What can you expect, I am from the desert. My heart is not your heart," or something equally fatuous. And then goes and picks up yet another lover. He is completely irresponsible in that respect. Ateh is very good at keeping him in order, but on this occasion I doubt if she'll have much influence over him. I think Jean-Paul has made his final bolt for freedom. He is besotted by this new lover he's picked up. That's what's driving him. And if he does make the break, then that means, I fear, that our wonderful little *ménage à trois* is finally over as well. Which explains, in turn, my dilemma about the return home. That's what London is about, isn't it? It flings people together and then it forces them apart. There's a kind of demonic energy running through this city which is simultaneously very stimulating and highly destructive.'

'Very perceptive of you, Marcello. Not many people get that far in understanding London. And the lover?'

'Oh, he's some big shot from the City. Or so he claims. A broker, I think. Big shot, red braces, and big cock, according to Jean-Paul. Terribly suave and terribly dapper and terribly in control and well connected. He's even got a wife somewhere, according to Jean-Paul, but the big shot only sees her occasionally. Or so he says. The wife plays around too; it's an open marriage. The big shot says that his life has changed totally since he met Jean-Paul. He's found all he ever wanted, that kind of thing. There's a lot of money there too, as well as the lust, but Jean-Paul says that he's only going to take and spend what he thinks is his by right. Power sharing, according to him.

'But you can tell from that kind of comment how it's all developing, can't you? Jean-Paul can't believe his luck. He spends most of his time now in the big shot's flat in Knightsbridge or going to incredible parties all over town and the Home Counties. Complete orgies from what I can gather, with some very surprising people there. Jean-Paul really thinks he's launched on the international circuit, but I'm not so sure. To these people, he'll always be a shoeless little Arab boy, to be taken up and then thrown aside, but he can't see it that way. But then Jean-Paul doesn't know much about my background either, since I've always been a bit discreet about it, so he doesn't really know how I can make that judgement. But I think he'll be discarded. That's the whole point about being rich – you can do exactly what you like and to who you like. It's partly because of all that that I left home in the first place. I can't really judge further in Jean-Paul's case because we see so little of him nowadays. He just about turns up for the aerobics classes. We get calls from castles somewhere in the Midlands with lots of shrieking in the background, with him sounding as high as the sky. He has changed a lot in the past few months and I'm very sorry to have to say that.' Marcello paused in his harangue.

'I'm sorry all of this came out in a rush, but it's sad to find the little haven breaking up with such speed after I'd just started to get used to it... especially after I'd survived the rigours of home as well. But enough of that.'

The cab crunched heavily round the corner.

'Here we are. This is Ateh's shop. Prepare, oh aerobics person, to meet thy doom in the shape of Ateh.'

The cab was paid off and Joe and Marcello stood in front of the shop, located just behind the Notting Hill Gate tube station. It was called simply Ateh. It was a fashion shop. Very little in the window.

'Ateh was a Nigerian queen a couple of hundred years ago who conquered most of the local tribes, according to our Ateh. That wouldn't surprise me,' said Marcello as he pushed open the door of the shop.

A tall slim woman with very pale dark skin, high, high cheekbones and a reserved, rather withdrawn smile came to meet and greet them. She wore jeans and was sparse in appearance, but still opulent in her impact.

'Ateh, this is Joe, who I mentioned to you over the phone. I brought him over to discuss his suggestion with you. Joe, this is Ateh.'

Did Joe have a flash of partial recognition? Something in her smile or her walk possibly. Joe couldn't be sure. He dismissed the idea as foolish.

'Good evening, Joe. How kind of you to spare the time for Marcello and for me.'

Ateh had a charge to her presence in a subdued but insistent way, as if a lamp of one million kilowatts burned perpetually but discreetly within her. It was like a knot within her. That presumably was the pack of power that had forced her to get and stay ahead. That was what drove her to such ferocious feats of endurance. Joe discerned, rather than saw, the power. None of it showed; it could only be gleaned by inference. Ateh had the perfect grace in her manner of the true aristocrat. She slowed it all down. She created space around her and she left time for the others in the circle. She behaved like an ambassador for a different culture where nothing ever happens at all in the deep sunshine of the day, but where gesture and suggestion are all important. Joe felt mildly airborne in her presence. He was dealing in a different kind of currency here, and for the first time. The trade was exotic.

'So, Joe, just what is the big suggestion for Marcello's dilemma?' Ateh murmured. Unspoken questions hung between them. Who are you? Friend or foe? Describe yourself further. Her eyes kept glancing round the shop as if to protect it from the intrusion of the new as she interrogated him. Joe nodded. Then she moved back just a fraction, to let some air into their circle. It was instinctive.

'Marcello talked about his family and the problems he thought he'd run into if he got back in touch with them. I suggested he send a bunch of flowers and leave it to them. He's got three sisters and a mother. That's surely enough women to take care of the problem.'

'You think the women should take care of the problem?'

'I gather there's only one male in the establishment and since he created the problem in the first place, he's hardly likely to set about resolving it, is he?'

'Well replied, Joe. Marcello, I like your friend. He is very quick. Joe, I'll ask you about the women in your family in a moment. But first, how do you like my shop?'

'Very beautiful, but then I'm no judge. When did you open?' He pushed the question back to her but with difficulty. He saw that Ateh had a genius for slowing things down and leaving time for everything to be talked over, just so. She was hypnotic in her power to do this. She lived in different, sweeter time. But she still drove a chariot to work. Joe could see that as well.

'Two months ago. I count the days we've been trading. It's like being in heaven. It took me nearly ten years of really hard heavy work to get to this point. Not a penny was made but it was directed towards the shop. I bent all my efforts in this direction as the boys will tell you. I drove them as well as myself. And now that it's open I can hardly believe it.'

Joe made a slight slip. He asked a technical question. 'How's the cash flow?'

It was an automatic response, but he should not have said it. He was a hick bridge player to all the world and at all times. He'd broken that convention and he felt annoyed with himself. He'd dropped his guard with Ateh, in a way that he had never faltered with Perdita.

Ateh picked up on this comment immediately. 'Marcello, just what have you brought home here? This man knows about cash flows. What are you, Joe, an accountant?'

'No, a gambler more like. But I know about cash flows. Or lack of them.'

'Joe, to tell you the absolute truth, the cash flows are wonderful. Beyond expectation. Marcello and I did a lot of work making the projections before the shop opened and we thought we'd break even after about six to nine months. But we're there already. New kids on the block maybe, but the locals seem to have taken to us. They just troop in and out all day long, and they're buying as well. Real shopping, not just in the window. And booking appointments, which they're keeping. Ordering clothes and putting down their deposits like dutiful little citizens. So we've been quite a hit in our own little way.'

Another little idea tugged at Joe's mind. 'Ateh, Marcello, forgive me for interrupting again, but I have a tiny idea. Marcello, couldn't you enclose with the bunch of flowers you send home the shop's card, so that when you ring your mum up, you could invite her down to London to see the shop. In a natural kind of a way. I'm sure your sisters would enjoy the trip to London and the clothes and all that jazz. It could all go with quite a swing. That would mean you could all meet on neutral ground in this further round of tense diplomatic negotiations and perhaps—'

Marcello broke in. 'Spend some money in Ateh's shop. That would be nice. I owe Ateh a lot. It would be nice to repay some of it.'

They all laughed together. It had been a happy thought of Joe's. Marcello popped in a question for Joe. 'Joe, your family? How would they react if you sent a bunch of flowers saying you wanted to come home?'

'Impossible to say since I have no family.'

'What none at all? Not even a wife?'

'Not even a wife.'

'How come?'

It was difficult at such points in the discussion to admit that as a full-time operative for British intelligence, ready as such at any moment to risk the tender neck in the chase, wives and sweethearts constituted excess baggage. 'It never happened, I guess.' Joe said this very carefully. He was conscious of Ateh's close scrutiny.

'And you never knew your family?'

'Hardly.'

'I know the feeling, Joe.'

Marcello interrupted. 'Joe, don't get her started. She'll go on all night. She was abandoned, or rather fostered and then abandoned and that's the long and short of it. She knows nothing about her real family. It mucks her up if she starts on it at all. Keep her off the topic. That's what we talk about the entire time once she gets on her hobby horse, accompanied by more than just a few swigs of gin. Then she becomes suicidal. The whole thing just rips her up. She knows where she's going but she doesn't know where she's come from. And now the shop is doing so well she feels worse because she has no pedigree to present to her new circle of friends. So, Joe talk to her seriously, be stern with her and don't let her get on the hobby horse.'

Ateh deferred to Marcello for the first time in the discussion. Her eyes looked incredibly sad. 'He's right, and I must not discuss it. It makes me so vulnerable. All my punch goes out of the window and I just feel like sitting down and weeping. It leaves me feeling so bereft. Marcello, I authorise you to take away the gin bottle. I can feel a session coming on. Which I mustn't allow, because I have things to do.' She was brightening up now as vitality returned. 'Like closing the shop up.'

The power pack was suddenly functioning at full throttle. 'It's been a good day in the shop and I must look no further than that. Hence, loathed melancholy, and be gone. I must go. To read some poetry or something soothing and uplifting. I will rise above it all. Joe, I'll say thank you now for all this conversation and ideas and then I'll say goodnight. I'm sure we'll meet again shortly. In fact, we must. We have things to discuss, don't we? Now,

Marcello, have you eaten tonight? Do you want me to cook you something?'

Marcello was feeling and looking good. And hungry. 'No, but don't cook for me, Ateh, let's go out and have a meal somewhere.'

She nodded. It was time for Joe to disappear. The tribal council was about to get into plenary session. He'd already overstayed his welcome by a large margin. Taking telephone numbers aplenty, he stole away.

He telephoned Betty from a call box a safe distance from Ateh's shop. It was late now and Betty sounded sleepy as she took the call.

'Joe, how did it go? You're very late. The girls have all given up and gone to bed. They were so disappointed not to get some news. We were all so anxious.'

'Betty, I've got nearly the whole story. It's all good.' He heard a sharp exhalation of breath. 'He's an aerobics instructor in London.'

Betty laughed. 'That's very funny. He never even played games when he was at school. Do you think he's any good?'

Joe thought about his aching calves and replied that Marcello was very good.

'He's in a very secure set-up and he's thinking very seriously about coming home to you all. Don't be surprised if you get a mysterious delivery in the next week or so and an odd invitation.'

'What on earth d'you mean, Joe?'

'That's diplomacy for you. Ask no questions and...'

Betty laughed, a rather croaking, post-hostessy late night laugh. 'You'll tell me no lies. God, nothing changes, does it? Joe, you're as evasive as you ever were. Which reminds me, I meant to ask you – just how is your job going right now? We never ever talk about you. How is the job?'

Joe hadn't bothered to bring Betty up to speed on such tedious matters as his total poverty.

'Betty, it's late. That's enough chat. I'll talk you some more tomorrow. Just rest content that the news is good.'

'Hmm. I'm not so sure that's enough for me. But goodnight then, Joe.'

Joe decided to spare Betty the revelation that Marcello had acquired a surrogate mother in the shape of Atch. That would have been too much for her to cope with at that late hour. Joe also decided not to talk about the new idea that had crept unsummoned into his head. He would keep the idea in reserve. But it would mature held in bond. An ounce of knowledge was worth a ton of speculation, as the Fat Man had never tired of telling Joe back in Berlin. Joe had about six pounds of pure gold, so he surmised, from his encounter with Marcello.

Yet again Joe was playing a treacherous game.

## Chapter Thirteen

Thursday morning. A beautiful morning. Clouds were flung across the sky in lazy sleepy ease, soothed by the wind.

Annie was awake from an early hour. She was thinking about Bootface. This was the day for their second meeting. It was cards on the table time. Twist or stick? Would she do the deal with him? Would she shop Joe for the money and hand over her half of the computer code? Was this the start of something quite new for her? Cards on the table time it might be, she thought, but sometimes you can't see a blind man. Can you? Did that mean anything? Adrian would know. But Adrian was far away. Meanwhile, did she have any winning cards at all?

She wriggled under the bedclothes seeking just a further inch of sleep. And searching for succour against time that was marching to meet her. Annie knew that she had no ideas as to how Bootface should be handled that evening. Her mind was a blank on tactics. But she knew also that, come what might, she was not handing over the code. That was fact. Set in stone. 'No, Bootface, I'm sorry, but no code.' That was what she would say. That was an axiom and infrangible. So it was stand-off time. It was down to Bootface to blow the whole mission, something which she was quite certain he would do, in his greed to get at Joe's money.

And where did it go from there? A whole dreary series of fail-safe and messy manoeuvres on her part, she guessed, to safeguard Joe and abort the mission. Or perhaps that too was impossible. Events were speeding up. Time was not on her side at all.

The previous day, using the agreed procedures, she had been alerted to a message impending for her which would come that day. The message would be about the mission. Very discreetly she had to make a progress report. To the Top via Another Anonymous. In the process, did she shop Bootface? Impossible – it would make no difference to his freedom to manoeuvre in the time available. Did she say nothing? Most likely, although that would be compromising as well. She thought she should say nothing to her bosses and bluff it out with Bootface. But it was a perilous avenue to pursue. She knew that.

She knew what the message would contain. It would be to the effect that time was running out now. That was the nature of the mission. It was about dates and time, nothing more. Simple big things, things that anyone could grasp. So, how far advanced was Joe? Had he got to Sir David? How far into the household had he penetrated?

The answer to all that was simple. They were running on schedule. All communication lines were blasting away and structure was in place. Joe was nearly there. He had his foot in the Lady Charley door. The mission so far was a success. And Annie knew what the reply to that gobbet of data would be. An uncompromising order to speed it up. Take it up a gear. Get a move on. There's been a change in tempo. We're running late to the switch. We are running out of time. We're on go now and it's getting tight. The Russians are about to make their move. We have to know the date.

The date? The date? The date? That was all the mission was about. Treason was a matter of dates. So too was the mission. Sir David was the only one who knew the date. That was why they had to get to him. Joe was the only agent who could do that. That was why he was in the frame.

Irresolute about the correct approach, Annie got out of bed and made one final and irrevocable decision about the day – she would wear her best clothes to the meeting with Bootface. She disliked the idea because it sounded too submissive to circumstances and too wholly female, but that was what she was going to do. In propitiation? In a charm bid? Because she didn't care any more? Annie couldn't tell.

The decision was a mystery to her conscious mind as well. But she knew she was going to that drink with Bootface as dolled up as she could make herself. Like a million dollars, only more so. And then once there she would say as little as possible, letting him come to her. No girly chatter at that point, no sir, far from it. She would practise the silence of an enclosed order, the inscrutable reticence of a medieval mystic. Nothing forthcoming.

She rebuked herself for her empty head but that was all she could think of doing. At least it was something. And perhaps it was more than that. Perhaps the mannequin gambit was really an act of war, and she was really dressing for the fight, like Joan of Arc in an oblique kind of way, employing the weapons she knew she could use best. Perhaps it was a deadly stratagem. She doubted the rationalisation, but she knew that she was not handing over that computer code to anybody. Shotgun or no shotgun.

And now it was time to get out of bed properly and go to work. She felt composed and resolved and determined as she showered. Impenetrable, like old jade. And underneath it all she felt a growing anger at Bootface.

She laid out all her clothes carefully across the bed ready for her return in the early evening. All the chain mail of the female warrior was there on display.

Thursday morning was becoming quite the little social whirl for Joe.

First, there was the excitement of Tom Stone's column. This gave him an immediate fix on the morning ahead because of the billet-doux it might, or might not, contain for Ursula. After the first fiasco of the Latin tags Tom had concentrated a little harder on his linguistic techniques – or possibly he had acquired a book of classical quotations. No matter. The quotes had been accurate, drawn mainly from Ovid, and they fitted both the context of the article and the hidden subtext of his relationship with Ursula. It was all done quite skilfully, although the information content of Tom's column was not what it was; it had suffered since Tom had started canoodling with Ursula again. He just had no time, that was clear. But no matter again. Joe had made enough out of Chaebol Trust to keep him in funds for a month or so.

But that morning, as Joe scanned the *Chron* for market trading ideas, he glanced at Tom's column and eventually tumbled to the fact that it was different. No Latin. Not a tag to be seen. Strange, thought Joe as he ripped through the paper. Perhaps Stone fell out with his editor over his bid to go upmarket. As if...

Next, the chat with Sid about the markets. The Chaebol coup

had made Sid slightly more relaxed about Joe's market acumen, especially since there were funds in the account. Sid had done well out of Joe's ideas. He was hungry for more tips from the same stable that gave him Chaebol. Joe called Sid but there was no reply from his phone. Later, thought Joe, I'll make the call later when I have something substantive to talk about. That'll get him gagging for chat with me...

And then finally there was Emma, who had developed quite an interest in the stock market after her own dealing coup. She was helpful to Joe in a quite unexpected way. Brasenose, spotting Emma as a potentially active client, had started feeding her more market-sensitive ideas which she dutifully passed on to Joe, who thus and in turn had a more accurate picture of what the shifts and turns of expectations were in the market. Apart from Tom's column, the *Financial Chronicle* didn't succeed in covering market expectations. Emma had started doing a little trading on her own account, not the desperate kerb stuff, of course, where Joe trafficked, but in situations with a fair degree of risk nonetheless. Emma was discovering that she liked risk. Early reports about profits were favourable. Joe was impressed by her progress. She had a feel for the market.

After all this early morning palaver, then it was time for Joe to amble down the road and play some bridge with Lady Charley, not quite as her new best friend but nevertheless as someone with a relatively secure niche in her social hierarchy, perhaps as the reliable domestic card player who lived by the chimney, almost a noble Mellors proxy, who could be relied upon to bring home a good score for the partnership. Playing with Lady C was still a total nightmare but at least it helped Joe fulfil his local rationale – to get as close to her as possible.

They had played again together one quiet afternoon in Trish's house in Flood Street and she had smiled at him occasionally during the play. Sadly though for Joe's interest, Lady C had been more guarded and they had played without the accompanying revelations, like the gurgling laugh and the sluttish demeanour, concerning the secondary Lady C lurking ever present beneath the surface. Lady C was very pleased with her new and budding partnership and had broadcast her satisfaction in a fairly discreet way among friends.

In consequence, Joe had even been invited to play at a couple of glamorous houses in Pimlico, much to his dismay. Joe was not over-enamoured of the Pimlico crowd. It meant a waste of time for a start, because the bridge was poor, but it also amounted to a loss of revenue. Joe was losing money by all this social frolicking. To play with Lady C and the like meant that he did not play with Joxer, who for his part had started losing money playing with less reliable partners and was mightily miffed about Joe's defection. Joe had the impression that Joxer was down heavily on his recent bridge. That was crucial for him. A reduction in Joxer's revenue reduced his ability to keep up with his expensive girlfriend and that in turn entailed certain adjustments. And so on and so forth. And so the long domino of social cause and effect rolled from piece to piece down to the sea.

Emma, Joe noted, made a point of ringing at around ten in the morning just before he set out for the Playfair establishment. Nothing was ever stated explicitly but Joe had the impression that the timing was not accidental. Emma was jealous about his play at Liz Playfair's, he imagined, and she wanted to join in. So instead of staying well clear of such dangerous and potent sensations, she chose to feed her anxieties by making her call at just that awkward time for Joe – and holding him on the phone. It was artfully done.

No more so than on the morning of Annie's impending meeting that day with Bootface. Annie had done an hour's work already when Emma rang Joe. Joe saw that it was just before ten. She chattered on about the markets and Joe reckoned he could spare five minutes. But he sympathised that morning with her call. Her anxiety was forgivable and understandable. Later that day was the meeting with Gregory scheduled for a pub in Earl's Court, O'Neill's, just up a little from the Troubadour, on the corner of Earl's Court Road.

Emma thought she would be reconciled with Gregory but Joe knew otherwise. Joe knew that it was a mistake for her to meet Gregory. Knew for a fact because he had more intelligence than she did about the Gregory situation. Only tears would flow from the meeting. But she was adamant and determined. Gregory and she must meet. It was her way of confronting her past. Joe was riding shotgun for her; he would see her to the pub, wait for her and either take her home alone and in tears or make a discreet exit as she reconnected with Gregory. Joe knew that he would be escorting her home alone.

To conceal her apprehensions about the evening encounter, Emma talked about the markets, testing Joe's reactions to her ideas. He watched the clock as she talked down the phone. Emma wanted to trade Mexico, and as she went through the idea Joe's mind started moving in another direction. He was in a hurry as well. He had half a mind on Emma's talk and half a mind on the trip down the King's Road to the bridge, so that in consequence he had no mind to spare for the little toe-curler of an investment proposition that leaped into his mind and started chirping with all its strength. Joe failed to consider everything from every angle. That was what he told himself later after the catastrophe.

The idea was simple. Emma liked Mexico as an emerging market play and Joe thought about the play underpinning Mexico, which was oil. The oil price was bombed out, like the gold price, because the dollar and the Treasuries were strong. But the US Fed, under Greenspan, was running a soft money policy in order to revitalise the credit standing of the emergings. Countries like South Korea and Mexico were starting to respond to the US promptings and their economies were beginning to recover. What would feel the impact of their recovery first? Why, oil of course. It stood out a mile. Demand for oil would rise if the emerging market economies started to bounce.

That haze over Malaysia had a macroeconomic justification and stood for something, Joe thought, as Emma banged on about Mexico, parroting no doubt the Brasenose recommendation of the day. But the oil price had troughed to something like thirteen dollars a barrel, which was a crazy price level, if demand started to pick up. Oil was cheap up to eighteen dollars a barrel at least.

This was the trade of the century, at least until Joe's next one. Hence and ergo and *primo*, he should be in oil. Now. He should be buying oil futures hand over fist. He looked at the clock, wondering if he'd have time to trade after Emma had stopped talking. No way. It was after ten already, and she was in full flight, but if he got to Liz's early or just a little after ten thirty, he could ring Sid from Liz's office and buy some stock from there. The dames would be sitting down and fingering the cards in their usual restless urge to start playing; they wouldn't overhear him. He was going to do it that way. He knew the idea was good. Oil was cheap and there was value in those prices at that level. He was in the market for that one. If he took four dollars a barrel out of the market on about ten thousand oil futures contracts, then he could forget about all his money worries for the rest of the year, he calculated. It was all so simple. The arithmetic wasn't even challenging.

Joe had overlooked gold. It was that simple.

Finally Emma stopped talking about the markets and allowed Joe a word in edgeways. She hadn't finished yet, she said. She wanted to talk to him about Mrs Poole.

'Emma, I have to run. Can we meet earlier than we planned this evening to talk about Ma Poole?'

'If you must. But why do you have to run? Is it bridge?' She wanted him to admit his priorities.

'Not exactly, Emma. I have an investment idea that I want to put into play…'

She was interested immediately. 'What is it? Tell me.' She was all ears.

'Tell you later, Emma. Now I must go. Talk to my broker, if he's there. I'm going to miss the offers. Six thirty at the Troubadour?'

'See you then, plunger. Don't be late. I'll have bought half of Mexico by then but I'll leave some room in the portfolio for you, never fear.'

That Emma is a caution and no mistake, thought Joe as he caught his usual bus in a hurry down the King's Road. But plunger? That's a really insider market term. I wonder who else she's been talking to. She must have been talking to someone to learn about plungers. Maybe Emma has a whole secret agenda that she hasn't even mentioned to me. Ma Poole rings a bell somewhere. Perhaps she holds the key.

The bus hurtled down the King's Road, driven presumably by the same driver as usual. Same old structure – must be Thursday. Only the cards will have changed. Everything else will be in its place. This is the beauty of the toff kingdom, thought Joe; nothing ever changes once you've got over the high walls and found your way to the chateau. One of these days I might even think of staying…

Dismissing the concept as juvenile, Joe fell to thinking about oil and the chart patterns and how Sid would react. Meanwhile the bus charged over the new set of lights at Old Church Street and then made a dash for it by the Fire Station. It made good time, shooting past Marks on its right and then swung round the bend and into the straight with Peter Jones lying directly ahead. Nearly ten thirty but not quite. Just on time as usual, he thought as he galloped up the stairs, after sprinting down Lower Sloane Street.

But Joe was wrong about this particular Thursday. Things had changed. The atmosphere was different for a start. It was strained but it was also concerned. The women were arranged in new poses. They stood not in single statues, teacup to chin, but ranged in a form of crude and protective circle round Ursula who on this occasion had reverted to her traditional uniform of jeans and a blouse. Much murmuring and quiet susurrations of soothing sound. It was like a meadow blown across by the wind, thought Joe.

No Ursula best clothes this morning and hence no cosy lunch with Mr Stone, Joe surmised as he wandered into the room. No precautionary phone call either, he guessed. What a bore for her. Nothing to look forward to at all for the anguished mother of five – or was it six? So that was what the absence of Latin tags signified. How sad for Ursula! She'd looked so happy and contented the past few weeks. And now! Busted! Joe knew the feeling, but he too was concerned for her. It was hard not to belong, albeit by proxy, to a circle like the Thursday bridge set and not get involved in some way with the others. The sympathy went back and forth; it was a mutual support system, about as powerful as Battersea Power Station at full blast. Even Joe was aware of it.

Ursula must have invested hugely in that particular situation, thought Joe, his mind swinging back to the oil trade as he wondered just how long it would take for the office to get clear of bridge players so that he could make his call to Sid.

Liz was also distressed. She was not her usual lithe, blonde, hip-swinging and discreet self, fresh from the really heavy hand weights in the gym and the aggressive workout. She was seated in a corner by herself, staring at the floor in what looked to Joe like utter disbelief. It was as if a bomb had exploded in the room.

But it was not for Joe to make enquiries. This was not his territory. He held a temporary visa in this land and he was already way beyond the frontier. He could be taken by guerrillas at any time. Or see his visa annulled. All might be revealed by the women in due course or on the other hand they might decide to say nothing. Even money either way. In the meantime he wanted to get to the phone and place his order, if they would only just move it up a bit and start fingering the cards as normal.

Joe hovered around, disregarded by the women, waiting for the office to clear. It was there that he received his own special bombshell, one so powerful and devastating in its impact that he almost staggered under the impact.

One of the women asked Lady C about her husband, doubt-less in a bid to switch the subject away from the stricken Ursula. 'And how is David? How is he coping?'

'Very well indeed. He's off next week for a week in the USA after a couple of days in the Midlands, but then he's back for our bridge soiree. That's in – let's see – yes, a fortnight's time… Oh yes, David's feeling very confident about the business. The contracts are rolling in, especially on the US side, and he's just found a marvellous man to deputise for him while he's away. Yes, it's marvellous. David smiled last night for the first time in a month. That will ease the burden considerably. Deputising very informally, of course, so no noses are going to be put out of joint but he's definitely managing director material according to David. David's bringing him along very rapidly which is not difficult because he's very easy to promote. It'll take about three or four years to push him through which is no time at all for a young man… Yes, a real boon in a way, because the new man is from the same stable as David. Yes, a Sloane School man, too… Yes, they all are, aren't they… Fits in very easily because he knows exactly how David goes about things. This new one will make four of them on the board, and three of them are from the same house, which makes it even better. Yes, one of the Pughs, Rivers Pugh.

Yes, that's the one, his father was under-secretary, I think, or something very close to it. A pillar of the FO anyway, one of the really stalwart families there. Rivers has just left the FO, so he'll be invaluable for the contact on the diplomatic side. David's delighted... No, I think he just got bored with the FO and decided to look around for something new. And he found us, or rather we found him.'

Joe felt exactly as he had done in Berlin, walking down a dark street late at night and cringing away from the headlights as the cars flashed by. He felt like a street Arab, a scavenger, an object of putrefaction from the gutter.

So Rivers Pugh worked for Lady C's husband! He should have guessed, but then again he wasn't trained to guess. He could not have divined that fact from any piece of information he had unearthed. He couldn't be faulted there on that count.

But this was very bad news indeed for Joe. It made the chances of him being unmasked that much higher because two people could now compare notes about one individual and thus pool their knowledge. If Lady C pushed her 'taking Joe on board' gambit any further he might even meet Rivers at Sir David's house. Now that would be fun and games, wouldn't it? Joe blanched at the thought. If Rivers had been provided with a heavy to look after him after only a few months with the company, just think of the squads of minders Sir David could call upon just by pressing a bell.

Separate worlds were drawing together, like ice flows, and he was going to find himself crushed between the two huge masses of ice and water. Crushed completely. And his chances of survival were correspondingly diminished still further by the Pughs, because, like Lady C, Lady Pugh wanted to bring him into her circle, much against her son's judgement. That move would almost certainly bring him up against people he had known in another life. So Lady Pugh would do the social business at the same time as Lady C. Someone in Lady Pugh's circle would recognise him and that information would be transmitted to Sir David via Rivers who was the connecting link between the two circles. Worlds joined and fused and created fire.

Joe could hear the question already. 'So tell us, Joe, in your own words, how is it that the brightest man in the City is masquerading as a hick bridge player? Do tell us. We'd like to know now. Yes, here, this instant.'

Sir David plus Rivers plus Lady Pugh: that was the infernal triangle within which he now found himself pirouetting in some macabre dance of death. It would take just one slip now, just one comment out of place by any number of people and the jig would be up for him. Rainbow bridge time. He would find himself quickly and efficiently battered to pieces within a matter of hours by Sir David's thugs. It took about three seconds to reduce Norman to a quivering hulk of senseless jelly. It would take about the same amount of time to reduce him to the level of a moron, he calculated. The Black Pimpernel was not a man who asked questions for long.

At that exact moment, Joe reckoned he was doomed. He could see no way out. It was simple. The algebra was irrefutable. The very success of the mission in so far as he got further into Lady C's circle meant that it was doomed because the risk of exposure was enhanced. And with exposure went almost certain death. At that moment he was as dead as the Fat Man.

Not lost, oh Fat Man, but merely gone before. Keep that cloud warm for me, old son. I'll be up there soon.

Joe could see Rivers giving the instruction to Marty, in his mind's eye. For Marty it would be a pleasure. 'Consider it done, Mr Pugh.' In Joe's mind's eye he could also see what a God-awful mess Marty would make of him in about two and a half seconds flat. It didn't bear thinking about.

Lady C interrupted his anguished reverie by calling on her partner to sit down at the table.

'Now come along, Joe, it's time to play some bridge. Why, what's the matter? You look as white as a sheet. Are you going to faint on us and add to all our troubles?'

Joe shook his head and pointed to his throat and motioned for a glass of water. This Lady C brought to him. She muttered to him as she handed it across the glass, 'I know you're feeling faint but it's the high pollen count. Don't worry, you'll recover. But remember this morning, you have to be very nice to Ursula and Liz. They've both had awful shocks and they're both very fragile.'

She lowered her voice still further and hissed into Joe's ear. 'This must be very confidential. Liz's husband has threatened to leave her if she doesn't give up her bridge, which is dreadful with her just on the edge of the England team. It's appalling. And he means it, the swine. He's threatened to do this before, but this time he's serious. I'll ring you later and tell you more.'

Joe nodded, again in silence. His mind was a long, long way away from Liz and her problems. He could see Perdita's smile from between the trees, and beneath the sunlight. Then he could see Marty's boots smashing into his face at one and the same time. It was not a happy vision. He felt sick. The moment he rescued Rivers Pugh from the thugs in the Fulham Road was turning out to be a very ill-judged piece of philanthropy.

But now it was time to play some bridge. The protective circle round Ursula started to break up its formation. Like a defeated army, they all heaved themselves slowly and reluctantly into line in order to play the cards. Liz sat at her accustomed place in the centre, as invigilator, with eyes downcast. Miles away. No joy for her in the endless combinations of the cards. Ursula stared straight ahead without a word. Joe felt his hands flutter every time he touched the cards. Lady C glanced at him sharply.

The atmosphere was sharply supportive and quite gracious in its ambience. No one snapped away as the bidding went haywire, or when cold contracts went off because attention had wandered to that evening's dinner party. The women heaved away at morale that morning like a roped-up rescue team pulling shipwrecked travellers from the sea.

At one point, just around eleven thirty, the phone rang in Liz's office. Every head in the room rose to attention. Little hopes danced from face to anxious face. Could Tom have relented? Was this the tom-tom call of peace-making? Ursula's eyes were protruding from her head in anxiety as Lady C skipped to field the call.

Dead silence in the room. No card was played. With compassion, Lady C turned to Ursula as she answered the phone. She shook her head, dealt with the call and then returned to her seat. Nostrils ceased to dilate. The play continued. A little acerbity began to creep into the morning.

'Damn these bridge novices. They always ring to book an appointment at the wrong time,' Lady C said in a matter-of-fact voice as, in full confidence and to the surprise of Liz, she played the ten of spades to dummy. It was the right card as it happened, and she made her contract.

Liz raised her eyebrows in surprise at the skill in Lady C's play, about the only sign of life from Lady Playfair that morning. In a most socially incorrect gesture, Lady C then blew on her fingernails and rubbed them in triumph against the small lapel of her cardigan, closing her eyes at the same time. Ursula smiled at her antics.

Bridge the truth machine struck again. It was not quite the gurgling laugh but it was just as revelatory. Joe was not so devastated as to miss her telling gesture, another small indication of another life led elsewhere by Lady C. So she did go down to the village and socialise with the butcher's boy, he told himself. She wouldn't have learned to blow on her fingers otherwise. This constant process of slow revelation about Lady C is both fascinating and also completely galling, Joe thought, since I am just about to be shoved through a mincing machine and probably won't be alive to see the end of it all and tell the tale. You can't learn to whistle through your teeth by watching television. That is fact.

But apart from Lady C's lapse and his reflections thereon, he struggled to get through the morning. Joe had a bad session's bridge. Lady C clucked away at him. But she enjoyed herself hugely. Misfortune was her mistress that day without a doubt.

Joe noted that she was particularly solicitous throughout the morning to Ursula, cajoling her in many delicate ways that were calculated to force her morale upwards. Joe wondered about all that too. Lady C and Ursula were obviously as thick as thieves and had been so for years. And what portfolio of secrets did both of them maintain? There had to be something there. Perhaps his conversation that afternoon with Lady C might amount to more than just tittle-tattle, who knew?

Annie's briefing was terse, just as she had expected. The Top was in a hurry and he was nervous. Nervous about getting the factors on his side correctly adjusted so that he could play to the situations as they developed. Getting the timing right was quite crucial. As usual he was balancing the world on the top of a pencil, pushing one situation ahead, after allowing a myriad of others to slow down, so that the evolution of the different situations did not conflict in their timing. They were in convoy. Even espionage had its own timetable, normally four-four waltz time and desperately slow. But it could go faster on occasion, breaking into a foxtrot or even a tango when pressed. It could be a very stately affair, except at the death.

'Sir David is the only one who will know the exact timing of the move. This is why. He was spotted at a cocktail party in Moscow a year or so ago and he was talking in a very special way to the Russian deputy prime minister, formerly, of course, one of our friends from the KGB. They were wedged in a corner, and Sir David was nodding, not through politeness but because he was getting a briefing. And he would be briefed because he's the head of one of the biggest arms suppliers in the world. He'd have to know about the whole thing. He's one of their main suppliers.

'Our man got very close to the pair, close enough to hear Sir David say, "So when do I hear?" and for the Russian to answer, "Shortly. But the sign will be obvious to all." But then he was forced to pass on by in the swirl of the crowd. That was all he got. By the time he'd edged his way back again, they were out of their corner and chatting away to all and sundry. It was sheer luck that he got that close at all. The implications of the whole thing are enormous and, as I've said to you before, they reach right up to the president of the USA himself. Yes, Clinton's involved right up to his neck in this. If we can find the date when it all goes up, then we can position accordingly and minimise the damage. We can also save the US presidency into the bargain.

'It sounds far-fetched and fantastic, but it isn't in the slightest bit. That's the hit of the modern for you. Everything inter-connects in a way that it never did before. With huge unforeseen consequences. Now, philosophising apart, from the same stable that gave us the steer on Sir David comes the information that whatever is going to happen to the Russians will happen very shortly now. I will know more, and I will tell you more, very shortly, but the bottom line so far as you are concerned, Annie, is this: you have to get Joe right into Sir David's household and if possible into his confidence within the next fortnight. I know that's a tall order but it has to be done. That's what the situation requires. He has to get that date. I will tell you more, as I say, very shortly. Now what are the chances of Joe getting that close?'

Annie admired the Top. He didn't beat about the bush. And she felt pleased also because she'd positioned well for the change in the mission's tempo. So far the briefing was going well.

'I would say that Joe has a fairly good chance of getting there. He's well entrenched in Lady C's bridge circle and he's quite sure that he's manoeuvred in such a way as to create a springboard for what you're after. He plays all the time with Lady C now. She's bound to have some social functions that he'll get invited to, and that will give him his chance.'

'How can it go wrong?'

'He's very likely to get himself killed in the process. The weak link in our chain is the fact that Joe has managed to get himself mixed up with the Pugh family, and Rivers, as you know, is now working for Sir David. I think that Rivers wants to get rid of Joe because Joe intervened recently – and quite by chance – to save his life; Rivers feels beholden to Joe, not something he enjoys or indeed feels he has to endure as he pushes through the rivers of blood in Sir David's organisation and becomes more hardened. Any opportunity to dispose of Joe will be seized upon and utilised by Rivers, I think. That's my opinion but I've done some work on his background and there's a history of sporadic and temperamental violence there which means you can't rule out what I'm suggesting. Apparently there was a series of incidents when he was at Sloane School when he lost control completely. All hushed up of course but the record is there nevertheless. He's a petulant man who's been spoiled and shielded by his family in such a way that he cannot tolerate any infringement of his self-image, because the ego is just too sensitive. If he gets so much as a sniff of what Joe is really about, then Rivers will go completely out of control over it. I'm afraid we're risking losing another agent.'

'I thought that's how your analysis would end. Any way of shielding him?'

'None,' replied Annie, thinking of the pleasures and dangers of

Bootface to come that evening. Someone else needs shielding as well, she thought in despair. But she refused to whimper her fears. She was not in the mood for that. The heat from the kitchen was not yet scalding her.

The Top continued. 'So we have to go with it and hope for good fortune, knowing that we risk losing Joe?'

'I think so. I see no other solution. We're going to have to move fast anyway. There can't be more than a fortnight in all of this from my angle, before Rivers and Sir David tumble to Joe, and that is more or less what you're saying about the whole thing from your perspective.'

'Correct.'

'So we're well placed to go for it, although the outcome is far from clear.'

'It never is, Annie. And when it does look clear, then beware.'

'I gathered that from your tone. Cries of old Century House. Tell me, just what will happen if the whole mission blows? What's the downside? Not that I'm contemplating slacking off, but I would like to know what the edge on this amounts to.'

'Again it sounds far-fetched, but conceptually the whole of the West, most likely.'

'That's quite a downside. You and me against the universe. Quite a mission.'

Down the line came the voice again. It was calm, measured and explanatory. 'The West doesn't go down immediately, of course not, but the risk of it exploding is dramatically enhanced. If we fail on this one, there is a big risk that we regress to the old cold war stand-off situation and in the process a new arms race is started, just after the old one finished. But we start the new arms race without any of the safeguards that were built into the old US–Soviet structure. Those traditional safeguards worked; there was no nuclear war. But Russia is a different place now and so too is the USA. Both are reassessing their post-Berlin status and both are pushing into the new without much thought for the consequences. Both are in a hurry. Both in a sense have unfinished business to complete with each other and with the rest of the world. Most important, there are elements in both Russia and the USA which feel that their cause is best enhanced by joining together, by fusing. So this is not a mission against Russia, nor one against the USA, it is a mission against those elements in both countries which refuse to believe that the world has changed from its post-1945 structure and which are intent on pushing back the clock. The return to the status quo, if it happens post the fall of the Berlin Wall, means arms, arms for everyone, arms in the Middle East, in India and Pakistan, in Europe, or wherever you name it – that's where the proliferation will take place, with eventually everybody armed to the teeth with nuclear weapons.

'So that in essence means the world becomes a fireworks factory and we know what happens to those. Our mission, if we're successful, more or less brings an enforced halt to the arms proliferation, partly because of the reasons which I have told you already, and partly on account of factors which I will explain in due course. Our mission, if successful, enforces an adjustment in attitudes. But assuming we fail, the arms race escalates exponentially without safeguards. To give you the flavour of all this, let's take a typical arms dealer, a big man in his field. Take someone like Sir David. He's survived everything and grown in the process. And grown his business. He even managed to emerge from the Scott Report unscathed. Do you think he's a man who is going to consider the future of the planet when he looks at an arms deal?'

'In all honesty, no. He's a bottom-line man who worries about his profits and—'

'It goes further, Annie. He has developed a racket that strikes right at the heart of the UK in a very effective way. Sir David is lethal. He has discovered a very nice little line in blackmail, which cannot actually fail, because it's built into the fundamental structure of the country. It starts with Sloane School and the FO. Sir David knows both organisations well. He was at Sloane School, for Christ's sake, and he has retained very close links with his alma mater. So what does he do? Easy – he spies out the likely candidates for his business in the FO, all of them more or less from Sloane School anyway, arranges for them to be smeared by some report at the FO, and then recruits them direct into his business and promotes them. He's working with the UK system, and more dangerously working with the hidden part of the system, the part that never gets spotlit and which just carries on doing what it has always done for centuries. The dignified Bagehot ceremonial bit that is always deferred to, the untouchable part of the UK that lies above the snowline. His victims can't say no to the offer because, like Rivers, they have nowhere else to go, and the job looks too tempting to turn down. And so they accept. Suddenly family prestige is restored. The prodigal can hold up his head again, and he's making money into the bargain. An enormous amount of money. It happened to Rivers, who was framed at the FO, but no matter now, because he's taken the David shilling and so it's on with the motley, now that he's on Sir David's payroll and doing the business. Rivers can't actually get out of any of this now, no matter how hard he tries.

'That's the beauty of Sir David's scheme. Everyone makes what they most expect. Sloane School looks brilliant because it has this perpetual flow of money-making geniuses to boast about while the FO meanwhile just turns into a front for the arms business. Neat, simple and brilliant. Sir David does just exactly what he wants. Always has done. Always will do. You're not seriously going to tell me that a man like that will be deterred from his trade by tender considerations about what happens to plant life post the explosion of a few nukes in the Kashmir?'

'Exactly.'

'Especially since he is about to clinch the final leg of his business strategy. You know that he's tipped for a cabinet post in the next reshuffle?'

'I do. The House of Lords beckons.'

'Guess where he's going?'

'I can imagine. Don't tell me. It's all got an awful symmetry to it. It must the Ministry of Defence. Procurement Minister or suchlike.'

'Right in one, Annie. On the nail. Think of the leverage for him and his business if that goes through, especially since he is actively trying to merge the whole corporation with a US defence company.'

'Game, set and match for Sir David. Not much left of the Middle East, after all that, if anything goes wrong with the timing switches.'

'Precisely. So that's the big picture to the mission. You see how crucial and extraordinary it was that our man eavesdropped on Sir David's discussion in Moscow. Without those few throwaway sentences, we'd have known nothing of all of this. It is a very carefully hatched plot and one which is about to blow the whole world upside down, including Clinton, in a kind of dress rehearsal for the real thing a few years hence, with the nukes.

'Now, Annie, to the details. I want you to sound Joe out very carefully about the next leg in the mission. Not quite concerning morale, more about the feasibility of getting right to the heart of Sir David's existence – into his house. Can he actually parachute in there in some way? Speak to him and get him to talk, now that you've got a good line to him. Time is running short as I said. Joe's the front man and he may have some good thoughts about it all. I think we have to think in terms of moving very fast. We're talking about a change of tempo and that's exactly how it all looks now. At worst this will all turn into some kind of SAS-style operation right at the death. I can't quite see how that squares with the rather statuesque world that surrounds Sir David. So talk to Joe, and we'll discuss it in more detail again very shortly, certainly no later than early next week.'

Annie thought again about Bootface and the evening ahead with a sort of sick dread. She felt stupid. The best clothes ploy against Bootface suddenly seemed stupendously childish before these harsher global realities of greed and power which the Top had outlined. And she was meeting him that evening! No time for thinking up any more Girl Guides' little stunts. What a stupid bore Bootface had turned himself into. She was just going to have to sit it out in the bar and play for some kind of time, as he tried to maul her in one way or another. Oh, what a fucking bore!

Typically, the Top left his best comment until last. 'Annie, don't get upset by this, but you may find that there are additions to the team. We'll talk again shortly.'

No more. He clicked off and was gone.

At the end of the Thursday bridge, everything purportedly took place according to tradition, just as it had always been before.

First, Lady C slid her envelope across the table to him, discreetly but meaningfully, and the women went off for lunch, dragging Ursula with them. There was practically a fragrance of well-cured female solidarity in the air as they milled around her protectively. Joe felt that as the sole representative of the male sex, which in the shape of Tom Stone had done the dastardly towards Ursula, he might find himself pretty surplus to requirements if he tried to crash the lunch party. He didn't even try to get himself invited along for a drink, but left them to cascade, in a merry and determined throng, out of Liz Playfair's.

He spoke briefly to Liz, who was close to tears. 'I'm very sorry, Liz. I'm very sorry you're upset. A woman's place is in the wrong, I know, but...'

'Don't worry, Joe, it's not your fault. Just things, you understand, just things. It all needs thinking about, that's all. I just have to go back to square one and think it all out again. But it is so upsetting. Just when I thought I'd got it all settled, the home, the family, and the man bit, so that I could squeeze some more bridge in and get into that England team, along he comes with his great spanner and chucks it into the works. And for what? Just to gratify his stupid ego. Nothing more. He's done it just to show me who's boss. I am truly...'

'Gobsmacked, Liz.'

'I wasn't going to say that, Joe, since it's a forbidden word so far as the ladies of Sloane Square are concerned; they think it's a common word. But yes, in a word, I'm gobsmacked. Now does that satisfy you?'

Joe could always make Liz laugh, if only for a second. That was why they got on so well. He grinned at her and rolled his eyes in mock derision at her use of language, and then dodged as she went to throw him out of her bridge studio. Liz was strong because she worked out constantly. Joe had no desire to get involved in trials of strength with Liz. She could break his neck with a finger if she really tried.

'Get out, you scallywag, and don't come back with those dreadful finesses you made this morning,' she shouted at him as he escaped her lunge and danced down the stairs. She was right about the finesses. He'd played like an oaf. But he had managed to make her crack her face, if only for a few seconds.

The noise and bustle from the street hit him squarely as he emerged. Recalling his unfinished business, he dived into the quiet phone booths inside Peter Jones. Berkshire ladies, shopping carefully on their monthly trip to town, were examining garden furniture across the store as he called his broker.

'Sid, it's Joe, I want some oil futures. Now.'

'Price? Size? Really, Joe, you get worse. I think you're going native. You sound exactly like a private client these days.'

'I'm in a hurry. Ladies who lunch must eat.'

'Always makes for a bad trade, haste. They can wait for just a moment. How many do you want?'

'About half of what's in the account. I leave it up to you. I don't know the technicalities. I just want the stock.'

'That's better, Joe. More humble. Trust your broker. I like your oil idea and I think you're just ahead of the market. Some of the boys were talking up oil at our morning meeting today. Next week it could start to fly. Yes, I definitely think you have picked a good one.'

'Sid, you're a saint. You give me such encouragement.'

'We, as you know, do not canonise. That's a vile Christian practice. But we do have our own special way of recognising talent and worth.'

'That I can imagine, and it starts with an l.'

'Followed by an s and then a d. You catch on fast, Joe.'

'It's talking to you, Sid, that keeps me young and on my toes.'

'One of these days, Joe, I'm going to invite you home to north London so that—'

'You can introduce me to a nice Jewish girl?'

'So I can give you the time of day right across your backside. For your information, there are no nice Jewish girls any more, not for the likes of you anyway.'

Joe laughed. He admired the rigour of the Jews. 'On form, Sid. Slay the goy. And spoken like a true broker. I'll call you later, yes?'

'With pleasure. Bye, Joe. And congratulations on a good idea.'

It being early in the afternoon, Joe took a trip on the tube across London, eventually venturing south of the river, partly to escape the pressures of the mission and his mortal fears of Rivers Pugh, and partly in an attempt to try to search for new ways of understanding the mission. Joe could sense the pressures building. He wanted to be ready to cope with whatever was flung at him. He wanted to feel ready. He also wanted to check a few things out.

Above all, he wanted to live long enough to get out of the country with whatever assets he could take with him. Nagging away at him also was the suspicion that his oil trade was just a fraction too obvious for it to be really profitable. If it was that good, the market would have been into it a long while since and oil prices would be substantially higher. He sensed that he'd goofed on the oil idea no matter what words of comfort Sid flung his way. Sid was only a broker after all.

Now that he'd dealt in stock, and he was presuming that Sid had completed the bargain, it all had a kind of flat feeling to it, as if the bounce in the idea had gone out of the price's future the moment he'd gone long. He knew that feeling; it was like being becalmed in an empty ocean. Nothing happened until the price started to sag on yet another idea that was too clever by half. And so, what if he'd got it wrong and he lost money on this one? The prospect was too terrible to contemplate, although he saw the satirical side to it all too, as he roared along on the Victoria line beyond Pimlico to Stockwell.

Perhaps he might be bankrupt and hence unable to participate in the mission, in which case he might avoid getting himself killed through sheer indigence. The prospect was too macabre to contemplate. Joe did some more thinking and some more mooching about and checking in south London during the afternoon and then returned back to familiar haunts in the King's Road. It was getting close to the time to take the telephone calls and prepare for the trip to Earl's Court with Emma.

The office was an empty desert after Annie's discussion with the Top. She wanted to catch up with Joe and initiate a new level of dialogue with him, but it was too early to find him at the flat. She would try later in the afternoon. She contemplated a trip to the Tate but doubted whether even art could hold her attention long enough to distract her from the business in hand. She discarded that idea. She discovered she had no other initiatives to take that seemed remotely tempting. The concept of an afternoon off all rather petered out. A call to Betty perchance to whom she had rarely spoken these past months? Too risky because of the unpredictable human contact. Betty's bubbling chat might provoke the juices of humanity to start flowing through her again at a time when she preferred to become the most flawless and most adamantine marble. She failed to ring Betty.

Eventually she wound up back at her own flat in mid-afternoon, conscious that she was living through dead time, and aware that time had no meaning ahead of the encounter with Bootface. Until she actually started the interview with Bootface, her existence in a purist sense was pre-temporal. There was nothing else. Nothing else had any mass of reality. She sat for a long time in the quiet and cool of her sitting room, watching the sun fall through the curtains, doing nothing, drinking in the rich stillness around her, emptying her mind as her imagination dissolved into the room and its objects.

Should she have mentioned all of the Bootface imbroglio to the Top? Perhaps, but she doubted it. It was too late now anyway. His intervention would be a catalyst not a placebo. Far better to have kept her own counsel and try to resolve the issue herself. That was what she had decided and that was how she was going to play it. She was sticking by her original judgement. That was final.

From time to time she wandered into the bedroom and surveyed her garments neatly and prettily laid out for the fray that evening. All she needed was war paint, she thought, to complete a picture of total aggression. Then she retreated back into the sitting room for more solitary contemplation.

The hours passed slowly and inevitably.

Lady C rang Joe at about four in the afternoon and she caught him immediately on his return from his trip. Joe felt more courageous. His spirits were rising after some contact with the unfamiliar.

'Joe, you were very good this morning at the bridge and I

congratulate you. You didn't say a word and you were very discreet. Well done. It was all a bit fraught, but I thought we did rather well. So, first things first, are we well organised for next Tuesday at Savage's?'

'I'll have to check, Lady C, but I rather think I may be tied up that afternoon. Did we actually make a firm date to play?'

'Not exactly, but I thought it was understood…'

What was understood was that Lady C wanted a good score at the duplicate so that she could show off to the circle. But Joe boxed more clever and harder to get.

'I think I may be busy…'

When Joe said ambiguously that he was busy, what he actually meant was that he was supposed to be gambling at the Jack of Hearts with Joxer; that he hoped to come away with about five hundred pounds in notes; and that his winnings at some point would finance a delicious tête-à-tête with Perdita, life and Rivers and Marty permitting. Joe had decided that Rivers could go hang. He was going to make a play for Perdita as soon as the coast looked clear. To hell with the risk!

'Well, that's a bore, Joe. How inconsiderate of you to have booked that afternoon. So our next opportunity for meeting will be next Thursday morning?'

'That's how it looks, Lady C.'

Quiet pause from Lady C. Joe wondered what that slight break in the proceedings might have meant. Hard to tell. Lady C knew how to use a phone and give nothing away. A professional, in Joe's opinion, when it came to concealment. He thought of the way she had dealt with Sybil – Sybil never so much as glimpsed the assassin's knife in the air.

'Well, I'll just have to try Ursula, if she's fit and well, that is. You may have noticed that she looked a trifle abstracted this morning.'

'Run over by a number 22 bus, more like.'

'Yes, well, that's as may be. I don't know much about buses, but she was certainly not her normal self. Very confidentially, and this is not for repetition, Joe, under any circumstances whatsoever, something has gone rather awry in her private life and she's finding it difficult to come to terms with it all.'

'Not her children, I hope. There's nothing wrong with them is there?'

That was the correct reply. Joe could sense Lady C's fears about grooming abate slightly. So Joe was sensitive to these things and knew how to make the helpful comment! Very interesting...

'No, Joe, not at all, the children are all very well, at least they were at lunchtime today. No, Joe, it's something to do with an old beau who's suddenly erupted back into her life and who's being something of a nuisance one way and another. He is being quite tiresome. I know him of old so I can say that with insight. And authority.'

'I'm sorry to hear all this. And I'm sorry about Ursula. That's the problem with old beaux – they don't seem to realise that time has passed and life has changed. They won't beaux out.'

Lady C did not react to the atrocious pun. Nor did she bat an eyelid at such a blatant misrepresentation of the facts. She countered by taking Joe's untruths as a cue to launch into the real business of her call.

'Now, who is this Emma that is talked about so much these days?'

'She plays at Savage's, Lady C.'

'A friend of yours, Joe?' The question came down the line like an arrow from a bow.

'A very distant acquaintance, Lady C. So long ago that I can barely remember how it was that we were acquainted. I think there was a mutual friend involved somewhere along the line. But it was all a long time ago.'

Lady C sounded pleased by all of this. She didn't press the point. But she staged another pause. Joe grew puzzled. Did she really have something else to say to him at this precise stage? Was her agenda even more corkscrewed than he had imagined?

'Thank you, Joe, for being so frank. I was hoping to get my mind round the Emma situation. I would hate for us to get our wires crossed at this stage now that we're playing together so well.'

An average of fifty-three per cent in Savage's duplicate did not constitute good play so far as Joe was concerned. But he let it pass.

'And Liz, Lady C?'

Lady C's tone of voice changed. It grew more impatient.

Suddenly she was finding she had things she had to do urgently. 'Well, yes, that is Liz's affair in the end. I don't think I really want to get so heavily involved. If her husband tries to ban her from playing bridge, well, I think she just must learn to stand up to him and fight for what she thinks is right. She has to convince him that bridge is important to her and that... Of course, it would be very inconvenient for all of us if he did decide to carry out his threat, because we'd have to find another club to play in. But I'm sure we could manage that if we really had to. I'm sure that Savage's would accommodate us if we went and asked.

'In fact, Joe, I wondered if you wouldn't be an absolute sweetie and do us all a favour by asking the Savage man very discreetly if he has a couple of tables spare one morning when we could play. I know all this sounds very callous and heartless, but it is a good, happy group and we've played together for a long time, although our bridge hasn't got much better. Anyway I'm sure you understand. The Thursday morning group has become such a haven for some rather nice people, of that there can be no doubt. So would you do that for us, just in case there is an explosion at the Sloane Square end of town? Would you be an absolute angel and ask him for us?'

Joe readily assented and Lady C, mission accomplished, rang off almost immediately. Joe was amused by Lady C's bartering methods. He reckoned she was working on a straight two to one ratio or even higher in terms of feudal favours granted and acknowledged. She was warming to those terms of trade. After all, it's not every day that you pick up a domestic on the cheap who can do some vital gofering and also play good bridge. But there was more to it than that. Joe mused away at what else might have been on Lady C's mind when she telephoned him. She had other things to plot too, hence the hesitation. He didn't think he'd heard quite the full story yet about her plans.

His phone rang again. It was Annie. She came straight to the point. She sounded busy. And tense. No introductions. They knew each other's voices, although Joe did not know the name of his caller. He never did and anyway who cared what the name might be? Survival was more important.

'Joe, we have to hurry up. The tempo is changing. We have

about a fortnight in order to get everything we need. You have to get to Sir David – and fast. Keep going through Lady C, sure, but you have to reach Sir David now. That's the switch. What ideas do you have about that? You're in the front line. Give me some estimate of how feasible you think that might be.'

'When you say get to him, what exactly do you mean?'

'Dining terms, talking terms, that degree of intimacy.'

'The Lady C entrance route is paying off handsomely. I had her on the phone just a second ago... We're getting very close and on terms that she enjoys. She's certainly keen to have me on call as some bridge-playing home help... But that's no help to you, is it?'

'Joe, you have to get beyond her now. Can you do that?'

'Bypass her?'

'If necessary.'

'Impossible. It doesn't work like that. One merest suggestion that she's expendable and I'm out on my ear. This is worse than Venice and the Council of Ten. In fact, she's even more likely to throw me into the Adriatic now that I've been clasped to the bosom than she was beforehand, when I was just a silent face at the table. Outraged *amour-propre*, that sort of thing. No, the bypass ploy won't work. She'd see it coming a mile off. She's the Richelieu of social precedence. Forget that angle.'

'What else then?'

'Just give me the parameters again. Let me think about it.'

'You have to get to Sir David. Talkie-talkie stuff. And within a fortnight.'

Annie did not tell Joe that once he had reached Sir David another leg of the strategy kicked in. One that made life exceedingly difficult for Joe. Annie made a point of concealing that from him. It was not for him to know. It might discourage him. There was always that risk.

'You know, we might just be able to do it. It depends on a lot of factors, but we might just get lucky. Lady C has a bridge soirée in about two weeks' time – that's about your time scale, isn't it? And she's planning to invite half the top people of west London and all points south-west. I haven't been invited but there again I might still be placed on the list since I'm now viewed as her permanent bridge partner and she likes getting good scores at the bridge table. And it's going to be an evening of duplicate because they're all madly competitive now that they've got the bug. So I might well get invited. There is a window there for what we're after. In fact, now that I start thinking it all through some more, because we've just been idling about until now, I think that's just about our only window because they depart for the Seychelles a few days after that. I know that because the bridge is cancelled for about a month. That's what half the chat was about this morning.'

'Okay, so far so good. Now, can you guarantee getting an invite to this soirée?'

'I thought you were going to ask me that. Just how tough do you want me to play it? Do you want me to go truly nuclear and burn all my boats in this part of London in order to get that invitation?'

'Explain.'

'I can see a way of securing that invitation – okay, let me rephrase that – of possibly securing that invitation because there's no absolute guarantee I'll get it. But the approach involves a play on the psychology of Lady C which in turn involves a piece of straight manipulation of two people, using a piece of information that I think I'm going to get tonight, and another piece of data that I think I'll get by the weekend at the latest. But it's very tough, this approach. People, some people, will get burned and quite badly. So, let me ask the question again: how tough do we have to be?'

'Joe, we have to go nuclear. The mission is very big. I have about half of it. It's not about individuals, it's about something far bigger than that.'

'One death is a tragedy but one million deaths is a statistic?'

'Exactly.'

'Let's temporise. Let's take it by degrees. I'll call you tomorrow and tell you how tonight goes. That way, we can check part one of the operational strategy. If that holds, then we push on to the second part. If that holds as well, then we'll be close to the centre of the whole thing and the decisions will start taking themselves. But I want to push into that decision-taking part slowly so that I can gauge whether there's any damage limitation potential at all. Some of these people are really very nice indeed. They will be shocked and they have not been brought up to field that kind of exposure. If they get hit by the kind of hurricane I have in mind then half the husbands in the City will be going without their breakfasts because their wives will be so upset by what will have happened.'

'That sounds about the strength of it.'

'Let's talk tomorrow. I'll tell you more about my plan, if tonight holds up. Which it should. I'm about nearly one hundred per cent certain that I will report no change to the basic assumptions tomorrow. So I'll call you early, say ten thirty and report in.'

'Thanks Joe. Much appreciated.'

Emma rang Joe very abruptly.

'Joe, you must help me. I don't know what to wear. Do I turn up in jeans, and give him a picture of the past Emma, because I wore jeans all the time with him, or do I turn up in a good suit, as the new Emma recently ennobled? What do you think? I can't decide. Decide for me, or at least give me a hint. Please, Joe.'

'Emma, you know what I'm going to say before I even start.'

'Which is?'

'I think you're going backwards because you're afraid of the future. The clothes question proves it. It is an impossibility. You cannot turn up in jeans. That Emma, who wore jeans and slopped around at weekends and hoped about buying a house at some point in the future, is now dead. And has been dead for about five years. You have to provide an authentic representation. You have to turn up as you are now, as an affluent young woman with all her future before her in London or in the rest of the world. Anything less than that is just cowardice. And misrepresentation.'

'Thank you, Joe. I thought you'd say that. I don't agree with you, but I'll follow your advice.'

'It maybe sounds harsh but I think it's true. You could switch back into jeans and your old self once the initial point of contact has been made and the old rapport re-established, but not, I think, until then. I don't think it would be diplomatic somehow.'

'Joe, what on earth do you know about diplomacy?'

'Next to nothing, as you can gather, because if I did I wouldn't be telling you such home truths so boldly.'

'Hmm. You're like an avenging angel, Joe, when it comes to tough dialogue. You should be in the movies with all those good lines. I can't compete at all as you can gather. Now changing the subject, do you remember me mentioning Ma Poole to you?'

'Vaguely. Refresh my memory. It does ring a distant bell.'

'Wine glass, Teddy, mother rings to apologise, coffee in Peter Jones…'

'I remember now. Long and detailed explanations of her daughter's temporary insanity. You had to go to lunch with her if I remember right.'

'Yes, so you do remember. Fine. Now do you want me to tell you what happened?'

'Didn't you want to talk to me about this at the Troubadour?'

'I don't have time for the Troubadour. That's why I'm calling now. I have to wait for Ma Poole's phone call. One of the reasons why the daughter was so upset was that she and Teddy had got themselves mixed up in one of those investment opportunity schemes, you know, the ones with open-ended guarantees.'

'I do indeed. Vicious little things, they are.'

'At one stage it looked as if Ma Poole was going to find herself and all the Poole assets dragged through the courts. This all came out over lunch. What Ma Poole didn't realise, of course, was that I had experienced another life.'

'You were a partner in your firm, weren't you?'

'I was indeed a partner, much to Ma Poole's astonishment. She gawped at me when I told her. "But my dear," she said to me, "I thought you were just—"'

'A man-chasing bimbo from Norwich.'

'She didn't put it exactly like that, but something similar was running through her mind. So she spilled the beans after my revelations and I was able to put her on to someone who knows just how to frighten the life out of the opposition. The final meeting was this afternoon, so Ma Poole informs me suddenly. I have to wait until she phones to give me the outcome. So no Troubadour.'

'I'll meet you outside Earl's Court tube station. What time will suit?'

'Joe, have you no interest in seeing where I live and perhaps picking me up from my home?'

'None whatsoever. Too painful for me. We'll meet where the rest of the world meets, by the telephones at the tube station. This may be an evening of surprises, so let's start off with our feet on the ground.'

'You sound like something out of the Old Testament sometimes, you know, Joe.'

'Words fail me in your case. Try the Apocalypse.'

'You've done it again. Until later, oh witty man.'

Annie dressed very slowly after a long soak. Her bath had set the tone. She had used lavender salts from Penhaligon's and had lain there in silent immobility for about half an hour, staring at her toes. After that, and very slowly, thinking the whole time about what was to come that evening, and trying to contain her mounting chagrin at the insolence of Bootface and his wholly disgusting disloyalty, she slid into her underwear, La Perla, a present from Beta at the end of the last great mission on which she'd served. She started to feel better immediately at the soothing caress of the materials against her skin. She liked the way that her boobs fitted in the cups and were held there snugly. She felt more comfortable immediately and yet still in control. The tights were from Harvey Nichols and clung to her legs very prettily and the suit was grey, from Joseph, with an oyster silk chemise, purchased under Betty's surveillance.

She watched the transformation from nude body into elegant young women take place stage by stage and still her rage grew as her outward appearance became more and more stylised. She felt like a priestess complying with an ancient ritual of destruction as she brushed her red hair, now cut very short, with great vigour and then eased her feet into the shoes from Ferragamo. The shoes seemed to move around her feet like gloves, such was the softness of the leather. Earrings from Adrian, a kind present from a kind man who was far away, and she thought of him fleetingly as she packed her handbag, also from Ferragamo. Sweet kind Adrian, who had no part in this alternative existence she led. Who would have been horrified had he known just the half of it. He thought she was rather clumsy and always needed looking after. Which she did up to a point. Sweet Adrian.

She would have liked a pistol in her handbag but that was not the mode of the service. With mirrors, that was how they worked, and by exploiting dissent, the natural dynamic that ran between the cracks. Nothing more. Most of the time it worked, but in the quick and the now... As for the missing sheet of explanation she had left between the two clocks, she dismissed the thought of any help from that quarter. She was on her own and most likely the sheet had blown up the chimney or some such similar and ridiculous explanation.

It was time to go. On her own.

She locked the door behind her, leaving the flat in darkness, and went out through the main entrance of the block, a young women like many others in London, out for a fine evening on the town.

Joe met Emma at Earl's Court tube station and they walked down slowly to O'Neill's, the pub on the corner. Going to meet Gregory the man. Walking backwards through time. Emma wore a well-cut charcoal grey suit and by trying to look inconspicuous managed to appear ultra-smart. Joe, in his jeans, approved. Emma was pleased by his approval, and even a little flirtatious.

They sauntered slowly down to the pub, and Emma talked about her trade that morning buying Mexico. Had Joe considered buying Mexico?

'No, I bought something else but I think I may have boobed. It doesn't feel right.'

'Poor Joe, and if it goes wrong?'

Slowly, with great aplomb, Joe drew his finger across his throat.

'I can't stand the idea of that. I'll split my Mexico profits with you. My broker's are convinced it's the cheapest buy since the fourth crusade. Lots of profits.'

She was nervous and she swung her handbag. They had reached the entrance to the pub.

'Good luck, Emma. I'm sure it'll be fine.'

She kissed him on the lips. Nice lips, thought Joe.

'Oh, Joe. I hope so. I'm having second thoughts about all of this. I feel suddenly that I may be in the wrong place.' She stamped around a little, looking a trifle bulky but trim at the same time.

Melodramatically, Joe drew his finger across his throat again. 'That one is for you.' He smiled at her again. 'Don't forget, it'll only hurt for a while, if it hurts at all. Think of Teddy and all those marvellous people just waiting outside for you. Don't forget also that he's not expecting to see you at all. He's expecting to see a benefactor. So he'll be all keyed up.'

She nodded. 'You will still be here, won't you, Joe? You will wait for me won't you?'

She was panicking. He gripped her by the elbow in encouragement and she recovered. Then, vintage Emma, she stuck her tongue out at him and vanished inside the pub. Gone in search of Gregory and her lost past.

The plan, as it stood, was for Joe to wait outside for her and to make himself scarce if she emerged with Gregory. On no account was he to go into the pub and witness what was happening. Joe had given his word of honour that he would stay outside.

Joe gave her about five seconds start and then slipped into the pub behind some other drinkers. He stood at the back of the pub and watched the scene evolve.

She tripped around the pub in search of her man. Then Joe saw that she had fixed upon someone seated at a settee with his back to Joe, and invisible to him behind the high back of the furniture. It had to be Gregory. Joe could still see Emma's face. A look of utter bliss spread across her face. She lost about ten years in that moment. She'd seen him. It was Gregory.

She stopped, took stock and then with a smile as forgiving and clement as the Blessed Virgin advanced on the invisible personage. She was almost on tiptoe, she moved with such delicacy.

Joe watched her bend forward towards the seated being and saw her lips move. Endearing and beseeching, lips that framed the most awful and momentous question. Do you still remember me? Do you still love me? Is there anything still between us? Are we still together after all these years? The only questions that really counted.

Some slight confusion across Emma's brow, and a slight recoil, but she sat down nevertheless and sank from sight. The watching was over. Through the semi-darkness, Joe saw another form from across the other side of the pub move swiftly towards the settee.

Joe left the pub and settled down to wait outside. He amused himself by taking the square roots of the passing number plates of the cars. He had no idea how long he would have to wait.

Annie sat at the same spot at the same table at the same point of the day in the same pub as she had the last time she met Bootface for an evening drink. She sat perfectly still and alone at the table. A large gin and tonic partly consumed was on the table. Normally she drank white wine. But tonight was special. It called for something stronger than the grape.

She had nothing to say to Bootface and nothing to offer him. No presents, no bribes, no appeasement. There would be no meeting of minds tonight, that was for sure. It was all a complete void.

Attracted by the sight of this pretty woman, dressed so expensively and with such good taste, sitting alone, the waiter hovered, hoping for the compliment of a glance and a smile. Annie stared straight ahead at the entrance and watched the clock tick.

And here he came. Dead on time! Bootface stepped through the door, was framed for a second in the light, and then advanced towards her across the more or less empty space of the main bar. He was smiling at her. He looked very confident. He had spent a good week planning his getaway. Now for the final clinching details and Rio here we come!

Suddenly the whole revolting nature of what he had suggested overwhelmed Annie and she felt her face twist for a second into a snarl as the rage mounted inside her from the toes upwards. It was unbearable. She controlled the rictus with difficulty. He was still walking towards but now with a broad smile on his face. The smile enraged her.

Bootface reckoned he had it made. So she had come to meet him for a drink. So she was sitting there all submissive like little Miss Pretty! That was good enough for him. The plan was working. Her presence signified assent in Bootface's book or at least a willingness to parley. Bootface could see two million pounds and freedom for the rest of his life sailing toward him as he advanced across the bar to Annie's little table.

Still grinning, he bounded up the short flight of steps with his hand outstretched. A puzzled look overwhelmed the smile. The hand dropped. Fear sprang into his eyes. Terrible, terrible fear. He went to turn away swiftly but he was too late. Annie caught the flash of a shadow on the wall and a gun pointing from somewhere. From behind her, she thought. Then the flash was gone. No noise.

A hole appeared in Bootface's forehead, just above the nose, and then the back of his head just blew away from the skull. Still spinning, he fell to the ground and lay in a crumpled, lifeless heap at Annie's feet. She looked around startled. Was she next? Behind her there was nothing. Only a long deep velvet curtain. The drapes hung undisturbed. A very professional job.

She looked again at the body of Bootface and took a deep swig of her gin and tonic as waiters and drinkers alike ran to the table in a panic. Annie did not panic. She stared straight in front of her. Hope and life and possibilities and integrity had been restored! Bootface still lay there with his hopes, like his brains, dead on the carpet. No more flying down to Rio for that particular Caesar, not any more.

So the clocks could read and talk and organise, thought Annie. That was nice to know.

Emma clung to Joe outside the pub. She was in tears and she was very upset. She was almost helpless. Great screaming sobs in the street. All her make-up, so carefully applied an hour before, was running down her face. She was howling on Joe's chest. The sadness was running through her like an epidemic.

'Joe, it was horrible, horrible. He was there and he wasn't there. Joe, I can't bear it. He's gay. Yes, gay. I can't believe it but it's true. Oh God, just think of it, he's gay. With a man. In love with a man. He's gone from me. I can't reach him. It's too terrible for words. Just take me away instantly. Anywhere. Just let me get out of here and somewhere else. I cannot stand it for one moment longer. Just cannot stand it. D'you hear…'

She was starting to screech hysterically. Joe pushed her into a cab and she lay on the back seat, weeping. Eyes stared round at the scene passing swiftly outside, without registering.

'He looked just as he ever did, tight and stringy like a rapier, with that quiet little look he always had. He hadn't changed, he'd just become more like himself. He was drinking a Coke. So I saw him sitting there alone on his bench, and I said very softly so as not to frighten him, "Gregory it's me, Emma, I've come to commission another poem from you, what do you think?" He looked very startled at seeing me, but it wasn't as if he was afraid of me, it was more that he had something to hide. His eyes flew off at a tangent. So I said, "Gregory, what's the matter? You don't need to be afraid of me, it's only me, Emma, come to see you." But he was nervous and he wouldn't speak. And then – oh Joe, it was awful, I can't stand it, there's nothing I can do about it. I can't fight this. It's not like another woman – it's something utterly different. Joe, d'you understand that?'

Joe nodded. Nothing she had said surprised him. The dedication on Gregory's poem which Joe had spied in the Troubadour had said it all. No room for doubt after that fulsome and public tribute to male love.

'Then as I tried to get him to speak, this man came up and sat down beside him and then he kissed Gregory. Yes, he did. He kissed him. Right in front of me. Proprietorially. As if to say: He's mine. Keep off. And Gregory kissed him back. Yes, full on the lips. They were embracing there in front of me. And they knew each other. They'd been to bed together. They'd fucked each other, it was obvious. They were of the same flesh. And Gregory was somehow submissive to him, as if he was dominated. Yes, I mean that, dominated by this man, and guarded by him from me, so that there was no way that I could get in and get him away. No way that I could find him…' Her voice tailed off into fresh sobs and her head was in her hands. Her shoulders shook with grief and loathing.

London passed by outside the cab, a series of snapshots of people frozen in mid-action, of roads, houses and buildings, all standing quite serenely in their own space and time, oblivious to the heart-rending sobs of Emma, another victim of its caprices, in the back of the cab.

'Oh, Joe, what do I do now? What do I do? Is there anything I can do at all? Come on, you must help. Is there any hope for me at all with Gregory?'

Joe shook his head. In his view Gregory was lost to Emma for ever now. The embrace of male love would be irreversible for Gregory, he reckoned, not least because it had brought him some success as a poet. Not every poet got to be quoted in *The Sunday Times*. More sobs from Emma who was almost hysterical.

Joe managed to get her close to home and then paid off the cab and took her into a bar. He filled her so full of alcohol she was practically cross-eyed. She sat there drinking and the fine clothes gradually turned into rags that barely clothed her. But he said as little as possible. He merely bent an attentive ear to her ranting and her rambling.

Joe was playing a treacherous game. He kept reminding himself about one death a tragedy, one million just a figure on a page. He didn't like what he was doing one little bit. Emma in her usual frame of mind was one thing to him. But Emma in her distraught state was something quite different. She was useful to him now. She had blundered into something that was too complex for her to understand at first glance, because it was devious and underhand, and she had fatally misunderstood the real underlying agenda of what Joe was all about. All of this notwithstanding her brilliant legal skills. Like most people, she had a blind spot – Gregory – who had become her Achilles heel. She had faltered. Now she was vulnerable. She represented possibilities for Joe and he was determined to exploit those possibilities to the limit.

He regretted what he was thinking but he was determined to pursue the logic of his position and his discoveries to the bitter end. Only the mission counted. Only for the mission was he lacking some two million pounds, plus, plus, plus of his fortune. Cause sufficient in itself for him to be rigorous. Only after the end of the mission, which was near enough at hand, could compassion supervene. Only then could he pause to pick up the pieces of Emma – if there were any left.

Emma carried on drinking, regretting the past, regretting Gregory, regretting her huge fortune, regretting every step of the way, paved with excited expectations, which had borne her through the years to this exact moment of her destiny.

Joe said nothing. He kept his own counsel. But he was proud of the fact that even in her gross misery he did not try to mulct her of any of her fortune. He stuck to the rules of the game. Some vestigial integrity remained. Spying was a treacherous game. Some people thought espionage was a cab ride. Not true. For those who knew, it was a journey to the end of the road. No stops, no putting down and no turning back. Anything less rigorous and the entire enterprise would founder. Along with everything on board. Emma was not his friend now. She was his quarry.

Eventually Annie arrived home. She went straight to bed, leaving her clothes on the floor. She was too tired to tidy them away. No need for the vestments, now that the priestess had triumphed. They could slumber along with the rest of the flat. She fell asleep at once. Just before her eyes closed she reminded herself that she had urgent business with Joe for the next day.

Then she was out cold.

## Chapter Fourteen

Joe had barely opened his eyes the following day when his phone rang. It was just after eight thirty. He picked up the phone slowly. His head was sore from the boozy company he had kept the previous night with Emma.

It was Betty calling him, a very excited Betty.

'Joe, I don't know how you do these things, in fact it beats me completely, but the most amazing thing has happened this morning.'

'What's that, Betty?'

'The most enormous bunch of flowers I have ever seen has arrived at the house. But no sender's message at all. Just a huge bunch of flowers. Now, Joe, you have to tell me the truth – is this your doing?'

'Well, I did say...'

'Yes, I know you said something, but you say lots of things. Now answer the question, is this your doing? I want to know about these flowers. Are they for me? I doubt it. For the family?'

'One moment, Betty, you catch me asleep. Let me raise myself into a semi-recumbent posture.'

Joe heaved himself on to his elbow, thinking what a good little egg Marcello was turning out to be. Sooner or later he would be a credit to his father. That Joe knew for sure.

Betty jabbered at him reproachfully down the line. 'You should have been awake hours ago, Joe.'

'There are lots of things I should have been doing hours ago, Betty. Now tell me, are your girls up yet?'

Betty scoffed at him. 'What, at eight thirty? Are you crazy? Two of them have only just gone to bed, I think. I heard them rolling back from some party or other at about six this morning.'

'So they haven't seen the flowers?'

'What is this, Joe, a game show? No, of course they haven't seen the flowers.'

'Good. Now are you sure that there is no message of any sort with the flowers?'

'I'll look again.'

Sounds of scrabbling, of cellophane crackling. Betty returned to the phone. 'No, there's nothing. Only a card with one word on it. It looks like a business card.'

Marcello, you really are a good boy, Joe thought. You carry out your instructions to the letter. I can see possibilities for you on the dark side of life's valley. My side of the valley.

'What's the word on it, Betty?'

'I don't know how to pronounce it. It's spelled A-t-e-h. Maybe it's an acronym of some sort.'

'It means happiness in Nigerian, Betty.'

'Fascinating, Joe. So what's that to do with the price of fish? And what's it to do with my Marcello?'

'You know, Betty, on your home ground you're nothing better than a bully. A playground bully.'

'All mothers are like that on their home ground. It's allowed. Indeed encouraged. Come on, Joe, talk to me. Stop playing the giddy goat with me.'

'Tell you what, Betty, ring directory enquiries, ask them for Ateh's number, and call me back in three. It's a business. Bye now.'

And he put the phone down. Tottered out of bed. Put the kettle on. Sat in his armchair, waiting for the phone to ring. It rang. One minute and twenty seconds had elapsed.

It was Betty, surprise surprise. She sounded suspicious. And truculent. She breathed rage and frustration down the line. 'It's a shop in Notting Hill Gate. It's not open yet. It opens at ten. I've already rung the number.'

'Well done.'

Pause.

'Well, Joe? What now?'

'Betty, I want to put a proposition to you. Let us assume that you had a son – which you do – who had gone missing, which he has. He's called Marcello, incidentally.'

Snort from Betty.

'Now let us further assume that the son turns up again, which as you know he has—'

Betty interrupted him. 'Does he live there, Joe?'

'Not at all, Betty.'

This was a lie, Joe's first untruth of the day. But it served its purpose. Betty backed off.

'Let me continue, as before. Let us assume the son turns up again posing the further problem which I have hinted at to you on the phone – how to handle the reconciliation? Tricky situation, don't you agree? The family will make a huge leap to fold him back into their collective embrace and to such a galvanic extent that this may in turn, although perfectly understandable, serve to trigger off all sorts of defensive mechanisms on the part of the son. He may flee again, and this time for good. Which, I'm sure you will agree, would be fatal for all concerned. Bad outcome that, further flight. Don't you agree?'

Betty mumbled some form of grudging assent to the basics of what Joe was saying.

'So why not arrange to meet on neutral ground in London? Ateh, who is a friend of mine, has just opened her shop – it's a clothes shop, a very fashionable clothes shop – and so you, in all artlessness so far as your daughters are concerned, can propose this trip to London for you all in order to visit the clothes shop. A big expedition to a shop you've just heard about. What girls in the world could resist that as an offer? And if you do that, I, for my part will guarantee to produce Marcello. In the shop at the same time that you are there. Now how's that for a deal? Just picture the scene for a second and then tell me if you agree with what I'm suggesting.'

'Joe, I would strangle you at this moment if you were standing next to me. But I have to admit that your reasoning is good. I see a very joyful scene before my eyes.'

'Good. Now you understand why I was so concerned to find out whether your girls were up and about. If they so much as get a whiff of what is planned they'll be down to London like lightning – and miss Marcello.'

'Joe, what do I say about the flowers? Where did they come from?'

'From Marcello, of course. They're a peace offering from him to you, for causing his poor old mum so much grief and pain.'

Short, very pregnant pause. Some heavy breathing. 'Good God! I'm flabbergasted.'

'See what I mean about the age of miracles? Now, Betty to business. Tell me what is a good day for you all to come down to London, and I'll fix it from the other end and we'll all have a very wonderful time.'

'I'll get my diary.' Pause. Then the rustling of pages. 'Wednesday next is best. After that it gets very tricky, because not all of the girls will be around. But I can transport them all next Wednesday from here to London. No problem. What time shall we be there?'

'Early. On the dot of ten, I would say, just as the shop opens. There's going to be a lot of talking to get through, so the sooner and the earlier the better.'

'You really are a little miracle worker, Joe. How can I thank you?'

'Don't even think about it. It was all a matter of seizing the day. Pure good fortune from end to end.'

'One final thing, Joe. What do I tell the girls? I have to give them some degree of warning.'

'Easy, I've worked all that one out. You tell them about the flowers and you say they're from Marcello. That will set their heels tapping. You tell them that you've heard from me. You say that you're going to meet Marcello in London next Wednesday, but that you're going to treat them all to new outfits in this special shop you've heard such good reports about, Ateh, and so you're making a visit to the shop before meeting Marcello and me for lunch. How about that?'

'Brilliant. It covers everything. And it's nearly true.'

'As true as it gets in this nasty old world.'

'Joe, you're a genius. We'll talk before Wednesday?'

'If necessary. I have to tee everything up from the other side but that shouldn't be a problem. We can talk at our leisure over the weekend to confirm everything.'

One very happy and reassured mother clicked out, to spend the rest of the morning wandering about in a kind of daze of ecstasy, thinking about the return from his travels to his well-beloved home of her dear, dear son Marcello.

And Joe for his part reflected on the recent look of gaping astonishment on her dear, dear son's countenance, as the truth of Joe's role in the search for Marcello had been explained. After Marcello had absorbed the small point that his family loved him enough to send someone in search of him, he had broken down and sobbed like a child. Head in hands, eyes streaming and heavy tearing sighs coming from deep in the pit of his stomach. Not wholly unaffected, Joe had wrapped his arms around the young man's taut muscular shoulders to soothe him, and thought of another role for Ateh, this time as comforter.

Joe rang Sid to check his oil futures price. No change and no improvement. Mexico by contrast was roaring ahead. Joe felt mortified. Sid was reassuring but Joe was not consoled.

'I'm going to dump them, Sid, if they don't improve. I'll call you this afternoon.'

'Look forward to that.'

Then Joe took a call from Emma, who wanted to see him urgently for some coffee at Peter Jones, their natural meeting place as she said with rather undue emphasis. Joe readily assented. She was giving him a perfect opportunity to put his twisted little scheme into operation.

Finally Joe rang Ateh and gave her the news about Betty and the trip to London. Joe gave particular instructions that Marcello should be congratulated on following Joe's instructions to the letter. So far it had all worked well. Ateh sounded delighted and mournful all at the same time. She invited him to come round and see them all that evening at the shop. It might be a wake but it wouldn't be dull, she promised.

'Jean-Paul is going away for a long weekend with his lover. I wish him well but it does somehow portend big changes for us all. We somehow don't think we'll see much of him again for some time. It sounds like a very long weekend plus some consolidation of the relationship somewhere in the South of France. What with Marcello going back to his family, I feel rather bereft. Our whole little circle is breaking up after being so solid for so long.'

'Not for long, Ateh, not for long. I have other things in mind which you will enjoy, although they may take time. Incidentally, what is the name of this dreadful City chap who is taking Jean-Paul away from you?'

'Barthomolew, would you believe?'

'That's a mouthful.'

'Quite. Jean-Paul can't even pronounce it correctly. He calls him Barf. So right now, it's Barf this and Barf that, because Jean-Paul is so excited about it all, and it's driving Marcello insane. You know, we've never even seen him. This home-breaker just sits in the car outside and beeps his horn when he arrives and Jean-Paul goes rushing out like a two-year-old to climb into the car. Then they're gone. I feel so diminished by it all. Marcello has had to be very stern with me these past few days.'

'How's the shop?'

'Booming. We seem to have become an absolute hit in the neighbourhood. We'll show you the books tonight. You'll be amazed. We're really making lots of money. People pop in and out all day long and we've already collected what you might call some regulars – about ten of them so far. They've taken to assembling around eleven and asking for coffee, which I give them. Or rather which I make and Marcello serves to them. They love all that and they can't get enough of it. Then they sit around and chat for a quarter of an hour before I shoo them out. But they buy, buy, buy. And so do their friends. And so do the friends of their friends. And so do the daughters of the friends – and maybe their daughters as well. The telephone never stops ringing. It's as if I have become overnight a part of all these different people's lives. It is quite breathtaking. I, Joe, quite frankly, am nervous about all this success so quickly. I would have preferred it to have come a little more slowly. But how can I argue with success?

'And then there's the money. There is oodles of the stuff. It seems to be flowing in from all directions and somehow reproducing itself. Wherever I look there is profit. It's like a golden stream flowing towards me. It seems somehow quite wrong for us to be making so much money for doing so little. After so many years of struggling, you understand, followed by the switch from poverty and dreams to affluence. But it's also a very agreeable sense of guilt. I feel as if I'm floating on some kind of cloud and I'm getting nervous about it all because I'm not feeling nervous. I'm so worried that I may be letting my defences down too soon.'

Her voice tailed off, and Joe let the pause grow down the line before adding some more words of reassurance. He promised to be at the shop by eight for some drinks.

Ateh added as an afterthought, 'Why don't we meet you in the pub at eight instead? We have a little favourite haunt just round the corner from the shop, where we go and chat; it's called The Leopard and we drink in the bar at the back. We'll shut the shop up early and prepare for Jean-Paul's departure in the traditional way, by having a few drinks in our little snuggery. Meet us there if that's okay with you, Joe.'

That suited Joe very well. He was planning a long slow return to reality that afternoon. He was playing bridge with Joxer at the Jack of Hearts. Both of them needed money urgently. Both were hoping to run into a couple of mug punters from the country with lots of loot to lose. It was rumoured there had been a sighting of such a rich target earlier in the week. It promised to be quite a session, waiting for the rustics and then fleecing them.

Just before he set off to see Emma at Peter Jones, Joe called his special number. A very easy number to call because it was arranged in such a way that his fingers could tap it in anywhere, even blindfold, in the dark, in the heart of Moldavia. His fingers danced to the automatic tune on the dancing pad. He was through immediately. It was like old times. He rather wished it was somehow different from old times, but no matter. He would always get through on that number.

'Hello, Joe.' The usual cool voice, the same one in fact that he had chatted with the previous day.

He tore his mind away from thoughts about the fortune he was losing by not working in the City and ignored as well his bleak reflections about the fortune that had been abstracted from him. He was in again with them and that was all that counted. No sense in bottling now; that way lay death. This was after all the trapdoor mission. He wanted desperately to get through it all and escape on the other side.

He made his report. Or rather put forward his suggestions. Control was not negotiable. His ideas got the usual noncommittal response, which was exactly what he had anticipated. Until he had secured his position with both Emma and Ateh, it was far too early to go firm on his plans. But the plans sounded good as he pushed them down the wire.

He left the flat at a run and caught a bus down the King's Road with ease. Same road, same driving style, same people, or more or less, getting on and off. But not the same thoughts. Normally on this journey he would have been thinking about bridge with Lady Charley. But not today. He was plotting something unexpected for the stricken Emma.

Emma was waiting for him at Peter Jones. She had purchased some coffee for him ahead of his arrival. Two cups steamed together on the red-topped table. She was seated by the window overlooking the square, wearing shades and looking anonymous. Her shoulders were hunched. She looked sad and crumpled. But the outfit had a kind of rich diamanté look to it that was reassuringly affluent, suggesting that her grief might be purely temporary. Distraction could be made available, should madam so desire it.

'Thank you for the coffee, Emma.'

'Don't mention it, squire.'

'Don't call me squire.'

'Of course not, my lord. The coffee was a pleasure. Thank you for last night, Joe. I was distraught. Very, very unhappy indeed. I think if you hadn't been there to look after me I might have done something that I would have regretted. You were a good friend to me last night and I appreciate that very much indeed. But it was my own fault and no one can say that I wasn't warned. I should not have taken that initiative about Gregory, or made that démarche, as we sometimes say in more formal legal circles. It was stupid. You told me more or less what would happen and you were right. I deserved to be punished – and I was. That's all there is to say about it.'

They drank some coffee together in silence. She sounded dull. Hopes of reconciliation quite crushed out of existence.

'Emma, I think you're being too hard on yourself. You would always have wondered what happened to Gregory, especially if he continues to publish poems. Just imagine how you would have reacted when you saw his slim volume of verse.'

A flicker of pain went across Emma's face. 'Poetry. Gregory never wrote verse. He despised it. Like Betjeman.'

'All right, his slim volume of poetry. Same impact though as it glared at you from the shop window. Every shop window, in effect. You would never have been able to resist buying a copy, reading it, and speculating. "What does that poem really mean, and how come he's phrased it like that. He never used to use that verb at that position in the sentence" – you know his composing style better than he does himself. Isn't that true?'

Emma nodded unhappily. 'Down to the last semicolon. He used to recite his poems to me when I was in the bath after I got home from work. I would float in the bath and he would sit on the loo seat and blaze away. We reckoned that it was a good poem if I didn't fall asleep in the middle of it from the fatigue of the office. As for Friday night... He used to compose a special stanza for me on a Friday night. We used to call it the Friday night special. And if I fell asleep to that? He would get very, very angry and accuse me of ignoring his great endeavours. Yes, you could say that I knew his style pretty well. He hated using the first person singular and yet – I have to mention this – in the poem that he had published, he used it all over the place. The poem is riddled with I–me–my. That's a big change. He would not have written like that in the past. Very un-Gregory, that stress on the I.'

'That rather ties in with what you perceived the new relationship to be, I think, doesn't it? Doesn't that prove my point? You would always have been tempted to find out where he was and what he was doing. The past would have pursued you up hill and down dale. All that happened yesterday was that you found out all that you needed to know quite brutally and in one fell swoop. But at least you've made one major advance...' Joe let the end of the sentence hang in the air temptingly.

She snapped away at the words. 'What's that, Joe?'

'You've discovered that the past can be self-liquidating. There's no going back now on that. Gregory now is not for you what Gregory used to be. That is self-evident. He is not there for you any more. The past is closed for you and only the future beckons.'

She looked at him imploringly, asking him mutely whether

there was any remission from the pain of that realisation.

'But, Joe, I could always commission a poem from him and stay in touch with him that way. Couldn't I do that? Couldn't I? That wouldn't do any harm, would it?'

'Well, yes, you could, I suppose. But you run the risk of getting thumped by the angry boyfriend.'

Another shocking spasm of pain across Emma's face. 'You sound very hesitant, Joe. So you don't think that's a good idea?'

'No, but perhaps only because I had another idea.'

Again Joe let the thought hang in the air. Just as temptingly as before. He had no doubt that Emma would snap at the bait on his line. She was up for it. But he wanted her to gulp it down so fast and so greedily that she could never in the future accuse him of leading her on. He wanted her to forget that it was he who had arranged her extended and bruising encounter with social reality.

'What's that, Joe?'

'I wondered if it might be a good idea for you to chat to one or two of the women in my bridge circle…'

She brightened at the Liz Playfair suggestion. Joe felt better. So she was just ever so slightly a snob? But who could blame poor Emma for a touch of snobbery. To persevere? And why not!

He carried on talking. 'You know, talk to them, get a feel for how they might react to what you're going through… These are rich and powerful women in their own right and they're used to running things, and they run them well. They've been through this kind of thing a thousand times, or their daughters, or both at the same time, and they should be able to advise you far better than I can. Don't underestimate the problems of wealth and its burdens as well as its privileges. This is something that I am not qualified to examine with you on your account, Emma, first because I am not rich now, and second because the money that I made I made fast and in the City so that it was never put to the social test, if you understand what that means.'

Emma nodded her understanding of his comments. Joe rejoiced as he spun some more verbal nets for her to stumble into.

'It's not as if you're some waif and stray, suffering from a broken heart because your swain has gone off with someone else. Far from it. You have sway in the community. You have pull.

You're a wealthy young woman who also happens to be one of the best lawyers of her generation but who for very special reasons is caught precisely between two modes of existence. This seems to me quite normal. Not surprisingly, this paragon of super woman-hood feels confused as her two lives struggle to coexist. That problem, I fancy, is exactly what the dames that I play bridge with know a lot about. So how about it?'

'Joe, you really do come up with them, don't you. You cut to the chase very easily. You should be an agony aunt, not a bridge player. That's exactly what Ma Poole said to me the other day and now here's you saying just what she said. Not in so many words but the gist is the same.'

Joe cut in quickly. Now that the idea which he had planted was flowering fast in fertile ground, he wanted to push it all along. Without at the same time being too precise with details.

'I'll fix it with Liz Playfair for you. I'm so pleased you like the idea. Just turn up next Thursday at her club and they'll fit you in somehow.'

'I'd be very nervous going there on my own. It's got a fearful reputation, the Thursday morning group at Liz Playfair's.'

'Bring a friend then. One of you might have to kibitz for part of the morning but that's not the object of the exercise, is it? Who could you bring along with you?'

Joe wondered what he might have to say if Emma proposed bringing Sybil along with her. Doubtless some sophistry would spring to his lips.

But Emma produced the correct solution. 'I'll bring Morka. She's a good player. A very good player, in fact and far better than I am. I'll get in under the net of her good play. Yes, Morka would come. She doesn't speak English hardly at all, so she won't understand much if they give her a tough time. She speaks mainly in French at Savage's – it's hilarious watching those women practising their schoolgirl French on her.' Emma paused. Her intuitive caution and good manners started to hold her back.

'But now, Joe, you're sure about this, are you? I don't want to put up any backs unnecessarily with these women. They're famous for treating outsiders very roughly. They're known as the Furies at Savage's. I'm not going to get turned away, am I, like the little match girl?'

'Quite the contrary. I happen to know that they're very short because of holidays, and it'll be first come, first served. Leave it to me and I'll make the booking. Liz wants to bring in some new faces. She's been saying that for months. Yours will be the first.'

Emma was very struck by Joe's endeavours for her. She reached out a hand and took Joe's, bringing it up to her lips. She kissed his hand in the bright sunlight streaming into the coffee room from outside. She looked better as the thought of working the social ticket – and getting on a bit in London society – appealed to her industrious nature. She also looked very alone at that moment, as if there should have been some male in attendance.

Ignoring his Judas words, Joe thought about Anne Boleyn emerging from the Tower on the morning of her execution, surrounded by her ladies, giggling and laughing hysterically as she traipsed on to the sward. There where the expert French swordsman, brought over by special request, awaited her... Two minutes later he had removed her head with one mighty and accurate slash of the sword, after she stood patiently on the scaffold, blindfold, awaiting the blow. And a great spume of blood jetted from the headless, lifeless trunk in the sunshine... Thus Emma, if she went to Liz Playfair's without a formal invitation. Joe had no intention of securing her an invite. Emma was being set up. It was part of the plan which Joe had concocted. But Emma would be very badly hurt in the process. Joe reminded himself about one death and a million deaths. Too bad she was from out of town and didn't know the ropes too well.

Emma kissed him tenderly on the cheek and asked him if he would like some more coffee.

'Please, Emma.'

'For my guardian angel, anything. Just anything at all.' She removed her shades and showed him her eyes, swollen and puffy from crying throughout the night. 'See, they're getting better, now that you're looking after me. All I need now is a trip to the chemist for some eye lotion.'

She trotted off to get more coffee for the two of them. Joe watched her go, and thought about Berlin.

On his way to the Jack of Hearts, Joe called Annie.

'Yes, Joe, how did it go?'

'Well, I think she's bought the idea. That's half the story. I'll be able to firm up the other half this evening. We'll be in touch first thing Monday. That will give us plenty of time to position for Thursday. I won't call you before then after this call.'

'Well done, Joe.'

Annie was enjoying watching the strings of the plot draw tight around the victims. All the lines were working, and pulling together just as the need for speed and acceleration mounted. She was also enjoying some freedom from the fears which had haunted her over the last long and tedious week.

Bridge with Joxer at the Jack of Hearts was a long drawn-out affair. They failed to find the mythical mug punters from Gloucester. Instead they ran into a couple of Indians from the hill country somewhere in the Punjab. Very tough customers, and one with the most impressive facial scars. Joxer took a professional interest in the tissue. They spent most of the time cursing each other in a guttural dialect, but this was just a blind. They played the cards together very skilfully. Joxer was rattled. He misbid his slam, got himself doubled, he redoubled, and then went one off, when the slam was cold. Expensive. Joe started worrying about his losses.

Joe didn't like the look of any of this. He was worried too about that position he was running in oil. He didn't like the look of that either. The price should have started to bounce by now, if the idea had any vitality in it. He thought of calling Sid and rejected the idea.

Then Joxer got even further into trouble in a two spades vulnerable part score and lost control of the hand. More losses. Joe decided to take a view on the whole thing. He was occasionally superstitious, and this was one of those occasions. He excused himself from the play for one second, went to the phone in the hall, called Sid and told him to sell at best. Sid demurred but Joe was insistent. He said he didn't like the feel of it, neglecting to mention that Joxer was now down two hundred and fifty pounds after thirty minutes' play in the notorious Jack of Hearts gambling den. Sid said he'd sell; Joe said he'd ring back to check the price. More or less breakeven, he estimated.

The cards improved immediately after Joe returned. The two of them got back to something approaching square but that happy state of affairs did not last. It was now the Indians' turn to hold good cards. The swing of the good cards was in full flow. They held, bid and made three slams on the trot, which made for a very good afternoon for the bad guys. Joe and Joxer were now down about seven hundred pounds with no mug punters to be seen. The only dudes around that afternoon were tough dudes, the kind from whose wallets of a session it was hard to chisel more than about a couple of monkeys – and even they came running with pain in their eyes.

Around five o'clock Joe remembered Sid and his deal and nipped back into the hall to check the selling price.

'You are a very lucky boy, Joe. A very lucky boy. I still can't believe it.'

'Why? Sid, what happened?'

'I went to sell for you as instructed. I did it immediately. So Joe, let's say, two minutes elapsed from your call to my deal. Okay?'

'Okay. So what then?'

'About one minute after I'd dealt, the Bank of England announced it was going to halve its gold holding in the UK's reserves.'

'And that?'

'Torpedoed the oil price because oil fell in sympathy with gold. Had I waited another minute, I think you might have been wiped out on that little trade, Joe.'

'Born lucky, Sid, with nerves of steel and balls of brass. What is oil now?'

'About five dollars down on the session so far.'

'How about a little bear trade?'

'Yeah, okay, that might work, but do you really want to run this position? I don't think you should, not with your fragile cash position. Where are you right now, Joe, so that I can get back to you?'

'Er...'

Sid pounced on him in his avuncular Jewish way. Joe had no time to lie. 'Joe, where are you?'

'Nowhere special, Sid, just playing a little bridge.'

'And you're down what on the day so far, Joe?'

'Nothing, Sid, it's been a very successful session, but I think you have a point about that bear trade. Let's forget about it. I'll talk to you tomorrow. No, it's been a very good session so far but I think I'll forget about any bear trades.'

Joe put the receiver down swiftly and returned to the play.

Afterwards as he toiled up to Notting Hill Gate from the squalid depths of Earl's Court, Joe started to shake just a little with the uncertainty of it all. The gambling with Joxer had not been a great success, but not exactly ruinous either. Anyway, Joxer would shoulder more or less the bulk of the losses. Just a bad boys' afternoon when all was said and done.

But the oil trade! Wheeeeee! It was as if the great axe of probability had swung down in its curving arc and missed him by a hair's breadth as he jumped clear. He took a few long deep breaths as he thought about the escape from total disaster. True, he had no ongoing stock market position which might help pay the mortgage, but at least he'd managed to hang on to what he had. That was something. He still had a tiny bit of money. Like a diligent ant, he could still try to build on that. If he'd been wiped out by the oil trade, he doubted if he still had the guts to try to come back again and make enough money to survive. Mission or no mission, it had been that close. He couldn't stand that sick feeling in the guts a second time round, when the bills came in and there was no money about, and no money coming in, and just no chance of money coming in either; no, he couldn't go through all that dull throbbing pain of poverty all over again, after the first gross shock of discovering that all his assets were mysteriously blocked and inaccessible and that he, the great Joe, had literally no money at all.

But to our muttons, he kept telling himself, to our muttons; the oil trade wasn't a wipe-out. Still in business. Still trading although not as yet thriving. Where there's hope, there's life, even if it does include such paranoids as Rivers Pugh and Marty. Well, there should be life, even with such crazies in the offing.

He felt a little more cheerful. After all, the mission couldn't last for ever. It should even now be starting its downward descent towards the runway. There were limits to the amount of time he could be suspended in mid-air, at forty thousand feet up, and in mid-animation as well.

Surely there were limits?

He found his way to Notting Hill Gate and made his way to where he thought The Leopard pub was located. Up a turning to the left, or so he thought. It was late now and well after eight. Well, Ateh had said to him that it was an ultra-casual date. He wondered if he'd catch a glimpse of Barf, in silk foulard, doubtless, and other slightly outré accoutrements.

He hastened his step and strode past a Jaguar about the length of a row of terraced houses, parked hard against the pavement with a man, expensively dressed, just emerging from the driver's seat. Joe glanced into the car at the leather seats. Maybe he really should turn to car thieving. Then, after a frantic piece of clock, clock, clock in his head, Joe carried on walking in an anonymous slouching way that in no way resembled his normal gait.

The sense of recognition was so strong it almost knocked him over. The blood pounded in his head. It had happened so swiftly.

Joe spotted The Leopard pub but then walked on past it and crossed the road in order to double back and take up a vantage point. He was confident that he knew the man emerging from the car. Knew him very well. Hated him in fact. Joe stood in the shop doorway on the other side of the street where the car and the man and the pub were clearly visible.

He was back in Berlin, watching as ever. Gumshoe time. He could almost feel the Fat Man beside him, the sensation of recall was so strong. Only this time…

Joe carried on watching from his hiding place as the man very cautiously went to the pub, edged round the back and peered in through the window. Satisfied, he then returned to the car, opened the door and tooted on the horn. Three clear blasts. Then triumphantly, with folded arms, he stood beside the bonnet and waited. The closer to resemble a down-and-out, Joe sat down on the pavement and stretched out. He did not want to be seen. It was absolutely imperative that he was not seen and recognised.

After a little while Jean-Paul came running out of the pub, alone. He wore a pair of white jeans and a yellow shirt open to the waist. Brown body and dark points of the nipples high on the chest. Joe could see the delighted smile on his face. His man had called for him and it was all going to go without a hitch. Jean-Paul was delighted. So was his older lover. It being London, the man and the young man embraced with a fulsome grappling. Hands and arms and lips, everything just folded together. They were long-term, passionate lovers and happy to be together again. The kiss between them suggested an immediate melting and blending of their bodies in some short space of time ahead, just as soon as they could find their way to some space and shelter.

Then they were inside the car. The engine purred into life, the Jaguar reversed a few feet, turned, zoomed into the main road and then shot off towards Holland Park and out of sight.

Joe clambered to his feet. No, it was not true to say that he felt as Emma had done when she witnessed a similar scene between Gregory and his lover. No, that was not a true statement. Joe had seen such sights in Berlin and elsewhere. They meant nothing to him. He was unmoved by them. Male love was male love so far as he was concerned. He had no prejudice either way. What people did to each other was their business.

But what was an issue for him was the identity of Jean-Paul's lover. It was none other than Sir David, Lady C's husband and a future cabinet minister, and the man to whom he was programmed to move closer. His quarry, on one level of interpretation. The end to his mission. And his quarry was gay. Very, very gay. His quarry had a full-blown relationship on the go. His quarry was maintaining a passionate relationship with a young aerobics instructor. So how about that, then? And how did that help the mission, if at all?

Joe took some long turns round the block before he dared enter the pub and resume his usual posture of balanced nonchalance. There was just so much to think about and analyse after his quite unexpected discovery. It was like the blink of an alternative reality via the divorce case of the next-door neighbour, a familiar and jolly drinking companion, always full of japes; it transpired through newspaper reports that he had forced the wife into unmentionable activities with the family dog every week for ten years. And this man had always been so eager to buy his round and trade jokes with the barman!

Worlds had collided for Joe in a wholly bizarre manner. No one could have foreseen any of that, if only because the strength and brutality of Sir David's personality gave no clues away at all about the possibilities of an alternative Sir David, of a Barf's Sir David in fact. Love of any kind was not linked in Joe's mind with Sir David. Death, yes; love, no.

Finally Joe composed his thoughts, deciding to reflect on the whole business later, and went into the pub. He found Ateh and Marcello huddled together in the back bar and he tried at once to introduce a note of gaiety.

'Guess what,' he said, 'the bridge was very profitable. I made some loot. Milky bars on me. Come on, what are we drinking?'

Ateh tried to rouse herself to respond to Joe's presence. 'I'm sorry, Joe, but we're a bit knocked out. Jean-Paul really did give us the impression that he'd gone for good. He couldn't wait for his toot on the horn. Then he was out of the place like a shot. He hardly said goodbye. It all leaves you feeling a bit...'

'Used?'

'No, I wouldn't say that, Marcello. Inadequate, more like. You know, what's Barf got that we haven't? After all, we're the ones who've looked after him.'

Marcello was quite fierce with Ateh. 'The only reason why you're saying all of this is through your own misplaced sense of motherhood. Yes, you know I'm right. You've been mothering him all along because you're so neurotic about your own background. You were doing it before he went just now. "Have you got everything, Jean-Paul? Will you ring us, Jean-Paul?" I thought you were going to wrap him in swaddling clothes. At any rate you fussed over him something rotten. So you leave yourself wide open to get kicked in the teeth when he goes. Look, Ateh, you're going to have to toughen up. You're going to have to tell yourself that something has changed. Gradually you're going to have to get used to the idea that you're a success and that if you can manufacture a future for yourself, the past will take care of itself.'

Ateh still looked quite distraught. She looked alone and uncomfortable in her isolation. Marcello turned to Joe and told him the shop had had a record day in terms of sales and indeed in terms of everything. 'We have to get a different kind of focus into all this.'

Joe heard the self-confidence of an affluent well-brought-up young man ring through his tones. But it somehow didn't work for Ateh. She didn't have the Anglo-Saxon kick-ass mentality. She was more delicate on the outside and more profoundly wounded deeper down inside her. Unconsolable. Certainly not someone to respond at once to Marcello's breezy injunctions.

Something in Ateh's system just failed to function. This she was little by little starting to understand. She had tried extending hospitality, to Marcello and to Jean-Paul, and somehow that had failed. They had behaved like young men, not the creatures of unfailing affection that she had hoped for. Meanwhile, and amazingly, the shop was a great success. She had received money in return for that, but not consolation, again to her surprise. Again, somehow, the system failed to function. The outputs resembled the inputs in nothing like the expected batches. Eventually the money was scant reward for her. She needed more. Joe could see that Ateh wanted, indeed needed, to think it all through again, this time coming up with a wholly different answer, like flight into a convent, or stylitism. Marcello and the shop had given her what she wanted for a time, but that time was starting to draw to a close quite rapidly.

But Joe wanted her to stay around for just a little while longer. He had some business to transact which involved her. Joe just wanted to make doubly sure about it all.

Still jabbering on about his bridge, and getting some fresh drinks in, he succeeded in switching the subject to Betty and the impending visit of Marcello's family next Wednesday. Joe congratulated Marcello on following his instructions so faithfully and Marcello meekly accepted his warm commendations. They discussed the details of the visit and some giggles began to creep into the conversation as they wondered just how Marcello's sisters might react to the changes in his body. Marcello confessed that before coming to London he had never so much as run a step in anger. He flexed a sinewy forearm and they all laughed.

'I'm nearly a stone heavier now. They'll think I've turned into a brute.'

More laughter, and then Joe, very carefully, went through his strategy. He requested a pack of cards from the bar and dealt out the cards as for a bridge hand, indeed, one very like the hand he had just played at the Jack of Hearts. He asked Ateh how she would have played the hand.

She looked at him shyly, her dark liquid eyes wide with embarrassment at her inadequacy, a dappled fawn among the rocks, and confessed she knew nothing about bridge. But she was interested to find out how he could help her.

'I'm told it's a marvellous social game.'

'Yes, my mother plays it all the time,' Marcello broke in with enthusiasm.

Joe put his fingers to lips at Marcello and pointed again to Ateh. 'Look, there are hundreds of bridge clubs in the area. If we can get her to just one of them, and she could start to learn, that might help in some way.'

Ateh fingered the cards delicately, her long black fingers toying with the edge of the pasteboard. 'So what happens now?'

Joe told her just a little bit about it, and saw that she registered some enthusiasm for the whole mobile machinery of the bridge table. She was staring at the cards. They intrigued her, like well-cooked food on a plate. She was concentrating hard. Then came the moment Joe had been waiting for.

'So to play a card from dummy, you just do this...' He reached out and pulled a card from dummy and tossed it into the centre of the table. 'Now you do that, Ateh.'

Marcello had looked away, his mind busy with thoughts of his mother's visit. But Joe was wholly attentive. Card play was like fingerprinting: it defined a person exactly and precisely. No two people played the cards alike. But Ateh played the cards as he had expected, and hoped, she might.

She stared at the dummy for some time. Then abruptly a long arm ending in a claw advanced like a hasty crab across the table, grabbed the card in haste and deposited it on the pile of other cards in the centre.

'Very good,' said Joe encouragingly.

What she had done was wholly instinctive and distinctive as a mannerism, just as in the same way Joe always picked up his cards, looked at them and then replaced them face down on the table. Such a style of card play as Ateh possessed could not be practised. It was inherent, the legacy of generations of breeding and reproduction, even if as Ateh said she hadn't the faintest clue where she came from. She played the cards her way, just as a bird might fly.

Joe now knew pretty well for certain what the origin had been of that inherited mannerism. He knew where it came from. Nature couldn't lie. All it could do was repeat itself in an infinite series of progressions. Nature was a stickler for accuracy and heavily distrustful of change and alteration. And so it had proved now. Ateh was the daughter of someone. That was self-evident. But not someone who formed part of the nameless billions inhabiting the planet. She was the daughter of someone a lot closer to home.

Joe knew someone else who played the cards from across the table in exactly that way. How uncanny it all was. Same stabbing claw of a hand, same widow's mite style of reaching across the table, same mechanical grab of a hand. Same rapt concentration.

After Ateh had discovered and admitted that she might have found bridge a touch late to become world champion, but had added that she would very much welcome taking a stab at the concept, and after Joe had promised to see what he could do in that direction but without undertaking any specific commitment, and after Marcello had said lazily that he must go to bed soon because he had two classes to teach the following day, given the absence of Jean-Paul, and after they all enjoyed a couple more drinks, the evening started to peter out following its delightful and mellow interim period.

Joe put his thoughts on hold for a while. The snuggery had worked its magic and likewise the alcohol. They had recaptured that elemental sense of a small group huddled together against the mighty unknown outside the door.

It was time for Joe to get on his travels. They said their good-nights and their promises for Wednesday and their best wishes for the weekend and Joe wended his way down towards the river. He was full of thoughts. He decided to walk part of the way home. He took a bus from Notting Hill Gate to Lancaster Gate, the better to saunter beneath the stars of a clear London sky, through Hyde Park and the Serpentine, and to mull his discoveries of the evening.

In the event, the fact of Sir David's relationship with Jean-Paul mattered far less than the dynamic which it represented. Joe had got that far already into his analysis of the discovery, as he stared at the Serpentine running slowly beneath the bridge. The sky stretched high above and the roar of London was a distant muted rumble in the dark of the night. A few cars shot past him as he stared at the stars and reflected, a small figure in the middle of London close to midnight.

That was what he had concluded – it was the dynamic that counted. By an astounding coincidence he had stumbled upon the fact of the relationship. But what mattered was not the sexuality of it all but Marcello's report of what Sir David intended to do. Jean-Paul had said that his Barf was going to take him to the South of France and start a new life. Now Barf was Sir David, incontestably. Barthomolew was most likely his first name, the one he had suppressed at school for fear of ridicule. He had been a closet Barf from day one. So now Sir David was planning a flit. It all fitted, especially the rapid promotion of Rivers. There would be a number one already groomed to take over from Sir David at Global, also a Sloane School ex-alumnus, and Rivers would slot in comfortably and easily as his number two, the heir apparent. Hence the succession would be secured, as regards the business, the Sloane School connection and all the other elements of the web which bound Global's arms business to the key parts of the British Establishment. Meanwhile Sir David, who had pledged his humanity many years since in the service of his career, was poised to withdraw that humanity from bond. Any moment now he would turn up waving the pawn ticket and demanding restitution. The South of France, oblivion with the boyfriend and a new life beckoned.

Joe had no doubt that Sir David would make it to his Shangri-La. He was too clever a businessman to leave anything so important as his new life to the hazard of circumstances. Everything would have been plotted and planned, in secret, down to the last few seconds before lift off. He would get there where others had failed.

That left Lady C, the other part of this shaky and fragile constellation. Joe had more or less worked out the whole of her background now as a result of the evening. He could always check with Tom Stone at some point in the future for confirmation of some of the finer details but the story in essence was clear.

Ateh played the cards in exactly the same way that Lady C did. Not approximately but exactly. Thus had nature repeated itself. It was irrefutable. Ateh was Lady C's daughter from a long way back.

It was easy enough to picture the scene. Just as Ursula had had some kind of heavy knee-trembler going with Tom Stone, so too had Charlotte, as she would have been known in those days, with a man from the warmer parts of the colonies. These flighty headstrong young girls in Camden Town, living alone in their beautiful flats, what do you expect, for heaven's sake?

Along came Sir David, tough, aspiring and respectable product of Sloane School, a real marriage prospect, and with his arrival came the news that Charlotte was pregnant by Everton, or Clyde, or whatever his name had been. Charlotte had the baby under conditions of total secrecy most likely after telling Sir David that she was off to Brazil for a holiday with the girls, or some such similar lie, and had placed it in care. Hence the weekly letter which Joe was obliged to send under his own auspices. That was cash for the foster mother. Most likely a very tiny amount of cash, knowing just how tight-fisted Lady C could be, but cash nevertheless. Babies didn't just obligingly disappear at the end of a news bulletin. The care had been continuous and, to do Lady C credit, pretty hazardous over all these years.

More thoughts by Joe looking out across the Serpentine at the folly of the Hilton Hotel. Lady C was in humanity deficit too, although in a different way to her husband. Ursula knew all about the baby. Of course she knew. That was why Lady C had been so solicitous when Ursula had fallen out with Tom Stone. She was afraid of Ursula just as Ursula was afraid of her. The two of them hung together as they had done for years. Hence that odd frieze effect that he had glimpsed one day when Ursula looked ready to murder Lady C. The two of them were like Goneril and Regan. But then, was that strictly fair? Joe passed on the causality, the taxicab nature of their escapades. They were what they were. That was all that could be said with certainty at such a juncture.

As regards the foster mother, well, what could be simpler? Joe knew all he needed to know. He had both the name and the address, courtesy of Lady C, once he'd worked out the connection. So, as well as posting Lady C's precious letter last week, Joe had taken a trip down to south London to the address itself and staked out the premises. Nothing startling about the house, except for the fact that Joe was now poised to take the whole business up a tempo.

He was about to pay the minder a visit. That was the deal, as he saw it. The mission came first; he had extra firepower now and the shooting started very shortly. There was no other choice available to him. He just had far too much artillery.

He thought his plan was foolproof. Hence into this delicate cosmos of Lady C and Sir David, wheeling and turning about itself under the most perilously exact calibration of gravitational pull, had come Joe, the pressed man, the agent, and the killer, a kind of downmarket Bruce Willis. It was his role to blow it all apart. Which he would do. He had no choice. Now that he'd unravelled the skein of happenstance, it was clear that soon the Sir David and Lady C show, which had enthralled London society for years, would be no more. Joe would see to that. That was his role.

And after he'd finished doing his Bruce Willis bit, what would be the consequences? Incalculable, he reckoned. The social chain reaction, once set in motion, would roll on for ever. But one thing was certain. Both Lady C and Sir David would regain their humanity, and rather more rapidly than perhaps either had assumed. Humanity was going to be forced upon them, especially on Lady C. By the looks of things she was simultaneously going to lose a husband who was one step away from a cabinet post and acquire a long-lost bastard child, now fully grown into a svelte Creole beauty and desperately in need of social reassurance, that is, long-term TLC from her mother.

How's that for a fairly mind-blowing rate of exchange, Lady C, he thought, under the stars, leaning on the bridge.

Joe ruminated about the repercussions of the whole chain reaction that he was poised to unleash. He preferred to duck precise formulation of the myriad outcomes that he could envisage. He had other thoughts pressing on him, because he too had a date with some form of destiny. He had urgent thoughts that required satisfaction. He too must reconcile himself to an event, lasting no more than a minute or even less than that but still nevertheless an event, something which had happened years ago in an obscure street, something irreversible which Lady Pugh in her deep wisdom had spotted instantly the moment he had stepped over the threshold of Pugh Park. Something from which he now required enfranchisement.

It is time, it is time, he thought. It cannot be delayed much longer. It is all over now. It is time. To forget is not to forgive, but to forgive is always to allow oblivion a chance to begin seeping in under the door...

Lady Pugh was not wrong to bracket Joe with death. Nor would Joe now ever deny such a connection, even to Lady Pugh. The time was fast approaching when he must reveal what he was and what he had been, if only to one or two people. He wanted to be rid of it all. It was time to wash it all clean, if possible. The integrity of his humanity required it.

Sir David and Lady C were not alone in their need to redeem their humanity. Joe had a pawn ticket too. Even as he stood staring in the midnight dark at the Serpentine, feeling the awful sad forlornness of the unshriven, under the midnight stars, he was fishing through the memory bank, looking for his own ticket which he had briefly mislaid, wondering at the same time if it all could have been different, if the deep regrets over the years, now rising rapidly to the surface, could have been allayed in any way.

Perhaps not and perhaps so; he had no way of telling. An event was always an event. They happened, even to the best and most astute of politicians. And to think he had been haunted all these years by an event that grew out of a few petulant words spoken in the heat of grinding tension. Just too, too stupid...

He still thought that Perdita held the key. A future beckoned with her. With Perdita he might survive, ridiculous as it seemed.

He could grow away from the wound with her. They could move together in sunlight and grateful shade, although, tormented by the natural instincts of the spy, he somehow doubted it. Perhaps the impending elevation of Rivers, after Sir David departed from Global, might make access to the well-beloved Perdita easier. Or perhaps not... That was more feasible. But perhaps Lady Pugh had a role to play. No matter, but Joe felt pledged to Perdita, come what might, as the guilt of years rolled round his shoulders. He also felt deeply vulnerable as he made that pledge. Spying was a treacherous game and it left its own mark of Cain, plain for all to see.

Eventually it was time to depart and leave the park to the night and other thoughts. Joe trudged home. Phantoms, unbidden and unwelcome, assailed him as he followed the road away from the park, down past South Kensington and into the King's Road. Back to the rickety block of flats and the crack in the wall. He saw the door again in his mind's eye, the door behind which death lurked, the door which he must perforce open, to be greeted by the blast of a pistol full in the face. The door which he had opened and behind which had lain a precise nothingness, while behind him... Ah, such a different kind of tragedy. Human, personal and sad...

He reached his flat. He fell asleep fully clothed on his settee with its ripped covers and contours exactly moulded to his body.

# Chapter Fifteen

Come Wednesday, Betty rang Joe at just after seven o'clock in the morning.

'We're all ready to go, Joe, and we're all bursting with excitement, and I don't think it's entirely to do with the clothes. We're setting off soon.'

'Good, I'll be there. See you in three hours.'

'Stand by for a front-line report on the perversity of human nature. Now that they've got over the initial shock, the girls are going to give him such a roasting. I heard them talking about it last night. They are going to give Marcello hell for leaving them alone for so long. They've decided that he's thoughtless, selfish and self-centred. Unworthy of their love.'

'Didn't his father thrash him?'

'That as well.'

'Well, he won't expect his sisters to react in that way. He thinks he's going to be welcomed with open arms. He's like a puma in his anticipation. He's looking forward to the cheers.'

'It may be a touch rougher than that. They don't quite see it all the way that you and I do, now that he's been found.'

'Warn them to go a bit easy on him. We don't want him in flight again, but this time from his sisters.'

'I will do my best, Joe. But my girls once roused are implacable. They believe in women.'

'Don't we all.'

'Yes, but not always with the same motives. Until three hours' time, then.'

'Drive carefully, Betty. I'll think about your devil's brood.'

'I will do the same. Thinking about the girls and how they might go for him has quite taken my mind off the real thrill that lies ahead, which is just getting my boy back safe and sound again. I can't believe that in three hours' time I'll be seeing him again. Do you believe it, Joe?'

'I don't believe in many things, but I do believe in this meeting, if that's what you want to hear.'

'Joe, you're impossible. One of these days I'll find a way of thanking you for what you've done without provoking a rejoinder like a cannonball.'

'Early training, Betty. That's what does it. That and a good dentist. Bye-bye, and drive well.'

'I will keep my eyes on the road and my thoughts to myself.'

'With three daughters in the back! I don't believe it.'

Three hours passed quite smoothly. With five minutes to spare, Joe stood outside Atch's shop, waiting for it to open. He had walked at a slow pace from the King's Road, taking in the air and savouring the piquancy of the situation. Now, as he paced about in the street in front of the shop, a fine specimen of a Chelsea tractor glided up behind him and then stopped. A head poked out.

'Hello, Joe, it's Betty. My, you've lost weight since I saw you last.'

She halted the car and turned off the engine. Doors opened and girls tumbled out from all directions, flowers from Betty's garden.

Betty had three tall, poised and very well-groomed daughters, with identical broad brows and slim pretty noses, all on open display like gunslingers in the street, and all armed to the teeth with injunctions for Marcello. They looked slightly grim as if on the journey down the conversation had turned against Marcello, tending to the view that he needed to be put right on his incredibly quixotic follies, so that he wasn't tempted to do it ever again. Just told quite calmly what was right and correct for him. Of course we love you, Marcello, but there are limits… Don't go away again without telling us where you are because it's just too hurtful for us all and just too hard to bear. In other words, just put in his place. The family was foregathering round him to administer a first-class duffing-up.

They glared rather at Joe as if in some obscure way he should be held to blame too for Marcello's escapades. They were impatient to get on with things. First the shopping and then lunch with Marcello. If that was the itinerary, well then, let's go for it.

Now for the shopping…

The door swung open and Ateh stood in the doorway. She had been primed for her part. She said nothing. To the girls she was just a shopkeeper and they bustled in, thanking her as they plunged into the grotto within containing one thousand delights at least. Ateh winked at Joe and Joe with his head and eyes indicated Betty, who in turn smiled at Ateh. The circle was nearly complete. The conspiracy was working.

The girls fanned out across the shop, two of them in search of tops while one stood transfixed by an ethnic Indian skirt. She held it up to the light, scrutinising the fabric, and then checked the quality of the garment by testing another skirt against the first. Lost amid the reds and golds, she was wholly absorbed.

Time for go…

Sliding into the shop came Marcello, lithe and limber, wearing a white T-shirt and jeans and looking like a beach boy. Stealthily and unseen, he approached his sister, still frowning over the skirt, as Betty and Joe and Ateh hovered in the background saying nothing. Marcello did not exactly resemble a hungry prodigal. This was the moment of all time for everybody.

'Can I help you, madam?' said Marcello in his best assistant's voice.

'No, that's quite all right, I can manage…' Her voice tailed off. She paused. Then she spun round. Her eyes widened. 'Marcello, is it you? Is that you, Marcello? It is isn't it? It's Marcello!'

Marcello nodded, too overcome to speak.

'Oh, darling Marcello, how absolutely marvellous you look. You're like a film star. Oh, you great big… boy…'

She flung her arms round his neck and hugged him and shouted out his name. The tears ran free down her cheeks. The other girls came running and they too sprang at him as Marcello embraced them one by one in turn. Bitter thoughts of reproach had been laid to one side as they all burst into tears, Marcello included, and they wept freely.

'Oh Marcello, you bad, wicked person, but it's so good to see you. And you're back with us now. We've missed you so much all day and every day.'

And now they were dancing through the shop, arms round

each other's shoulders and singing at the sheer joy and excitement of it all. Ateh and Betty watched with huge smiles. The flowers from Betty's garden were in full bloom.

The door opened and a genuine customer entered, then made as if to leave because of the hullabaloo. Ateh restrained her. 'No, don't go. This won't continue for very long.'

The customer stared in bemusement at the rowdy figures dancing through the racks of clothes.

'You see, what was lost has been found.'

Mystified, the customer shook her head but took it all in good faith. She began searching for something she wanted for her daughter. Joe congratulated Ateh for her fortitude in speaking those words. Not easy for someone as fastidious as Ateh to be so crazily adrift on the London seas without so much as a rudder. But, Ateh, it's not over yet, he thought. The fat lady hasn't even started her aria yet.

At the far end of the shop Marcello and his sisters had sat down among the clothes and he was telling them about his adventures. They sat like children in a circle. Every now and then one of them in sheer enthusiasm would fling herself at Marcello, kiss him and then subside into breathless shouts of laughter while the others looked on, awaiting their turn.

Joe explained to Betty that Ateh had looked after Marcello for most of the time that he'd been away. He told her about the shop and its genesis. He told Betty how well the shop had done since its very recent opening as Ateh, in some shyness, hung back from more open disclosure about herself. The two women were slightly distant from each other, separated by a common bond with Marcello. But Betty worked hard to close the gap. With incredible tact, she listened to the saga and thanked Ateh and made much of her, emphasising that she was not taking her son away from the ambience which had sustained him. Such self-possession in the midst of such desire to repossess, although Betty's kiss, hug and long silent almost greedy look into Marcello's eyes just for a moment as the girl's circle opened up gave powerful sight of her true feelings. Then using all the sagacity of experienced and protracted maternalism, Betty produced her master stroke. Addressing Ateh, who winced a little at the direct attention, she invited her to come back home to Hertfordshire with them all, the shop permitting, adding that provided Ateh had no objection, she would like to ask her girls whether any of them would work in the shop, along with Marcello.

A two-way trade, thought Joe. How elegant. Not a bad little deal for Ateh.

No need for Betty to take it further. Her words had been overheard. A chorus of agreement came from the floor some-where to her left: the shop was a big hit with the girls. Ateh beamed. She was going to belong to one family at least, Joe thought, and stole away. For him, the party was briefly over. Time now to get into contact with the Gents. Time to check in. There wasn't a great deal of time left before the great denouement, part one, scheduled for precisely 10.20 a.m., give or take a few seconds, just before the Thursday morning bridge started.

Also Joe felt he had outlived his usefulness in this particular situation. Besides, he had work to do. He had a trip to make in the direction of south London. Now that one situation had been resolved, it was time to move on to the real Gordian knot of his preoccupations. Time to take the tube again down to that address which Lady C had so foolishly given him.

Nevertheless it still remained true – what was lost had been found. Marcello was safe and well and reunited with his family at more or less the right time for him.

On Thursday morning Joe awoke with a start. Just before eight but he was awake at once. He knew what he was about. Twenty minutes past ten that morning loomed large in his mind. It was all set up to go. Before that, though, he had some time. Time to glance at the *Chronicle*, to take in Tom Stone's piece, enjoy a laugh over his fumbled attempts to understand the markets, perhaps call Sid and shoot the breeze about stocks…

His phone rang. It was Perdita. Perdita the impatient. Perdita who wanted information urgently.

'Joe, just what is your address? We just don't know it. Mummy has gone crazy trying to track you down so that she can invite you to her lunch party, but she doesn't know where to send the invite. Do you live in a hole in the ground or something?

Come on, Joe, no stalling now, so out with it. The details please, and pronto.'

Joe laughed, a pleasant enough sound even so early in the morning, but he felt grim hands fold round his throat. Invites meant something different to him now. Perdita's next comment did nothing to allay his fears.

'She's even gone so far as to ask Rivers where you live. He didn't know either, although he's ordered one of his henchmen to find out. He's mightily pissed off at not being able to run you to earth.'

And the name is Marty, thought Joe. I'm sure he's pissed off. It means the kicking I so richly deserve has had to be delayed for a few more weeks. The mere thought of Marty tramping up and down the King's Road looking for me is enough to drive me into the Thames with fear. To die bruised and battered to death or to die physically unscathed in the soft fires of drowning? Which do you prefer? Which one do you want? You have a choice and we know it's a tough call but you have to choose. Which do you want?

'To tell you the truth, Perdita, there's been a bit of a domestic catastrophe recently and my whole block has been condemned pending renovation.'

She was suddenly sympathetic. 'Oh, poor you. That must be so upsetting.'

'So we've all had to move out... Yeah, a crack in the wall suddenly became a chasm and the council got to hear about it.'

'So where are you living now?'

'In a hostel owned by the council. They put a jack into the room so that the phone still works, which is just as well, otherwise I'd be completely uncontactable... So you could ask Lady Pugh to send the invite care of Zorba's in the Fulham Road; it's bound to reach me because that's where I spend most evenings after bridge.'

'Zorba's, you say, in the Fulham Road?'

'That's right.'

'I might just pop up to town and deliver it myself so that we can have some dinner together. How would that suit you, Joe?'

Joe could see death striding over the horizon.

'Marvellous, Perdita, provided you don't wear that white

trouser suit again. I really wouldn't be responsible for my reactions if you wear that. A dishcloth round your loins would be less provocative.'

Joe thought he had to play the next few seconds very carefully. He carried on talking. 'Look, Perdita, tell me when the lunch date is.'

Perdita quoted the date. It was the day after Lady C's famous bridge evening, when the great denouement, part two took place. Not long to go now for all of that.

'How would you fancy having dinner with me the night before that, at say ten thirty, at Zorba's? I'm playing bridge that evening, but it will finish at around ten. So I'll meet you at Zorba's, you can give me the invitation then for the following day, and we can have some fun. Zorba's can be very jolly. How does that sound?' A restaurant thronged with drug dealers was not exactly an easy room to work but Joe had overlooked the menace built into Zorba's in his urgency not to reveal his address.

'Can't we meet before that? I'm missing you and I want to see you.'

Joe could feel Marty's boots smashing into his skull as he pictured the aftermath of a meeting with Perdita. But it was Thursday morning and he felt like living dangerously.

'That might be possible, but let me do some juggling and ring you back this afternoon. Is it okay if I ring you at home, or is that tricky?'

'Ring me on my mobile at three o'clock exactly. I'll be there.' Perdita was getting the hang of the mobile.

'Tramping the fields?'

'Something like that. I hope it's not raining, that's all.'

Joe promised to call Perdita at three and replaced the receiver. It rang again instantly. It was Emma.

'Now, Joe, are you sure this is going to be fine? I'm ready and Morka's ready and we're both looking forward to it.'

'Of course, I'm sure. It's all arranged. They can't wait to meet you. Just make sure that you're there a little bit before ten thirty so that the places can be allocated. See you then.'

'Joe, you have been good to me about all of this. I feel like a complete lemon now thrashing about in London. I'm completely out of my depth at this end of the pool. As I now realise. I miss all the nuances and all the coded messages. Miss them completely. Without your help…'

'See you there, Emma.'

Joe settled down to read Tom Stone in the *Chron*. I should give him a call, he thought, and pick his brains for a change and see if he has any ideas about the market. He deliberately thrust out of his mind all thoughts of the messy fate awaiting Emma at Liz Playfair's. Like most things, it wouldn't hurt for long. Well, not for very long.

He flicked through the paper looking for the column in its normal spot. And there it was… and there it wasn't. What a surprise! He could see at first glance what Tom's column comprised. It wasn't so much an investment column as an extended billet-doux to the distant beloved, in this case Ursula. Ostensibly about the US bond market's aggressive search for five and a half per cent yields, it was in reality a yearning paean to their rediscovered love for each other, judging by the number of pet phrases which littered the column. Phrases like 'us people', which Joe had actually heard Ursula use on one occasion, or 'searching without success' – another favourite – or 'the very rightest thing to do' lay like signposts to their mutual ardour. They had kissed and made up quite obviously. Probably more than that, judging by the breathless tone to the column. It had plainly been written on the hoof, perhaps even dictated down the line as Tom sat sweating with apprehension in the cab on the way to Ursula in their love nest. It all read in a kind of hugger-mugger way. Joe's imagination ran riot.

As for Latin tags, the column positively sparkled with them, with Tom's choice of apophthegms running from the tasteful Virgil to the racy Ovid all in the space of a single column. Joe wondered what book of quotations Tom used in order to appear so wordily-wise and yet so literate in such a handy portable way.

Unfortunately there was precious little about investments in that column, which was what Tom was paid to do and the reason why Joe bought the paper on a Thursday. To whet his appetite for the mighty storms of the morning which lay ahead and also to tweak the tail of the besotted Stone, Joe decided to put in a call to his office, chaff him a little about the Latin and then pick his brains for a few minutes about the US bond market. They were still on speaking terms. Joe could make that call without taking too much of an initiative. The bonds might still be cheap. Sid would trade them like a shot. This might be a good, simple and obvious idea which would bail him out of a little hole for a month. He needed a good sound dealing idea some time in the next fortnight, Joe reckoned.

He put in a call to the *Chronicle*, asking for Tom Stone. The switchboard was sympathetic. 'No, sir, you won't be able to talk to him at all today and not for a week or so either.'

'How come? What's happened?'

'We've just had confirmation from the hospital, sir. There's no paralysis.'

'What? What's this about paralysis?'

'He had a stroke last night, sir. Fortunately he was with someone who knew what to do. He was rushed to hospital and in the way of these things he should be fine in a week or so. That's what the hospital just told us. They rang not five minutes ago.'

'Oh. I'm very shocked. I didn't expect to hear this. I rang him up about his column.'

'So is all the paper, sir. We're all very shocked. He's very popular on the paper, is Mr Stone. But what was the query about his column?'

'I wanted to complain about it.'

'I'm surprised to hear that you're ringing to do that about his column. We've had a deluge of calls today and everybody has been saying what a bright read it was. They all love the Latin, you see, sir, it really strikes a chord with the readers...'

Eventually the babbling seemed to be drawing to an end. Joe thanked the *Chronicle* switchboard for its help. Switch had one last nugget of information. 'Yes, he got to hospital in time because he went on a fire engine. Obviously the person he was with knew all about these things and got the fire brigade out...'

Joe laid the phone to rest. No disputing the British taste for rubbish; that was always and obviously self-evident. Tom's column that morning was a disgrace. But poor old Tom! Hospitalised! Borne there on a fire engine with all bells clanging.

Such a fate could only befall a hack. And at the end of it all to find himself alive in a comfortable hospital bed. What a calling is the newspaper business!

Joe called the *Chronicle* back, winkled out the hospital where Tom was laid up, and resolved to send him some flowers at least to speed his recovery. He wondered if a certain other party would be doing the same.

Time to depart at last. Joe sped from the flat, ignored the crack in the wall, which seemed to have shrunk during the night, and caught the usual bus at the usual spot to arrive at the usual place where he was accustomed to spend his Thursday morning. Everything was moderato cantabile as usual.

He arrived at ten fifteen. Nursing their cups of tea, the women stood in clumps against the walls, chatting away about events before dispersing to prepare for the play. A general air of contentment. Liz looked desolate and kept slightly apart from the group but Nancy was in high spirits. The cookery book was ready. Everyone had contributed. All the recipes fit to print were due for publication very shortly and heaven help Nancy if there were any misprints. But Nancy was confident, stressing to all who were listening that she had checked the proofs at least twice. She hadn't been able to find a single mistake.

'Not one. The printers have done very well for us. It goes on sale at the gift fair next week, but I have a funny feeling that we may do rather better than just raise the money for the scanner. Yes, it's true now, and I can say it with confidence, I've had an approach from one of Clive's business friends who likes the sound of our cookery book and who wants to relabel it and repackage it and market it really aggressively. He thinks it will sell really well. So, Sophie, if there's anything wrong with your leek and stilton tart, the whole world's going to know about it shortly.'

Sophie sniffed and rolled her eyes in disbelief that there could be anything remotely imperfect about her leek and stilton tart, not in this universe anyway. Eighteen minutes past. Not long now, Joe thought, before all of this just changes shape quite drastically. He noticed that Lady C was paying particular attention to the news about the cookery book. Her contribution had been mushroom and chicken filled pancakes.

Nancy had more information to impart. 'The hospital may get more than just a scanner. It might get a whole new cancer ward, if we're lucky and the book really takes off.'

Twenty past. The phone rang. Bingo! Right on time.

'Charlotte, it's for you.'

Joe held his breath as Lady C took the phone nonchalantly, holding a mug of tea in her left hand. She held the phone to her ear while still participating in the chat about the cookery book. Then she listened hard. She went pure white and then puce after about five seconds.

'I really don't know...'

As she spluttered, her mug of tea crashed down on to Liz's desk and she gulped in a huge lungful of air. Joe could understand that. She would need the oxygen by this stage. Her eyes had started to bulge.

'But where? How?'

Ursula slipped into the room unheeded as Lady C struggled with new ideas equally unheeded by the throng of women off duty, poised for their charge at the bridge.

'Yes, I know that, but...' Lady C was getting very angry now. 'That alters nothing.' The voice was becoming more clipped.

Joe noted that Ursula if anything looked even more distraught than Lady C. Hardly surprising that, he mused, when your long-lost lover has experienced a heart attack in flagrante. But the fire engine showed quick thinking.

'I thought I'd made it clear that under no circumstances was there ever to be a call.'

Twenty-five past. Now for it, Joe thought as Lady C slammed the phone down and retrieved her mug and started mopping up the pool of tea on Liz's desk. Lady C was in the vilest of moods.

In through the door and right on cue bustled Emma and Morka with eager faces looking forward to their first session of Thursday bridge. Joe saw fit to make himself scarce through the throng of the women. This was not going to be pleasant for anybody. He stood beside the door quite concealed from Emma's immediate gaze.

Lady C was in no mood for explanations. Again hardly surprising after she'd just heard unexpectedly about her bastard daughter not ten seconds previously. That had rocked her. Lady C would also have recognised Emma and Morka as emissaries of the hated Sybil, not something calculated to improve her sweet and sunny temperament. Joe had organised the whole thing around the conjunction of the two events – the phone call and the illicit arrival, uninvited, of Emma and Morka.

'What are you two doing here?' She sounded like a barracks room sergeant.

'We've come for the bridge.'

'Oh no, you haven't. Nobody comes here without an invitation and you haven't got one. If you think you're coming in here uninvited, well, you've got another thing coming.'

Emma sagged.

'You're not wanted here so out you go. Go on, out you go this instant.'

Lady C knew how to dish it out on request. Her words were like a whiplash across the room. Joe felt the women around him stiffen in dismay. This was not how things were supposed to happen on a Thursday morning. Surely some mistake somewhere?

'Go on, out you go, I said.'

A murmur of dissent began. The murmur was directed against Lady C. She hadn't paused for a second to explore the situation, had she? Nobody merited this kind of treatment.

Joe could see Emma's face through the reflection in the mirror. She looked aghast. Morka by contrast was quite calm. Where she came from, this was par for the course. But Emma was quite shocked into speechlessness by Lady C's outburst. Her mouth hung open and she looked ready to burst into tears. After the fiasco of Gregory, this was just far too much for her to bear. She was in social disgrace.

Another slight murmur of sympathy before Lady C, eyes rolling a touch in front of this show of defiance by the peasants assembled around her who so far had not been cowed into submission, prepared to give voice once and for all and dispatch these excrescences. She gathered in a huge breath of air and seemed ready to fly at Emma and Morka. Emma gazed at her, like a rabbit hypnotised by a snake.

Then the unexpected happened. Nancy intervened. Very forcibly. She spoke from the corner of the room. 'Charlotte! Charlotte! Will you please be quiet for one second!'

Nancy spoke in upper case. The first stress landed on the 'Char' like a bomb explosion and then the voice rose sharply towards the final syllable. Nancy sounded like a foghorn. The words shot out of her. It was not an instruction to be denied. Lady C spun round to glower at her. Joe saw her eyes. There was some element of terror in them at the prospect of insurrection. Her face was quite pale. Now she was being assailed from all sides. She looked surrounded by her enemies. A new regime threatened.

'What!' Worlds in distant galaxies collided and exploded into millions of particles.

'For goodness sake, Charlotte, will you be quiet for once?'

Lady C looked terrified at the insubordination. But Nancy was not to be deterred. 'There has obviously been a mistake and poor Emma here has come on a fool's errand.'

Lady C was breathing hard. She was unhappy about the reference to poor Emma.

'But no matter. It does not excuse your behaviour. That is no way to speak to anyone, still less someone who is here because of a misunderstanding. She and I can go and do some shopping together and we can arrange for her to play another time with us. That is the least we can do. Meantime, Morka can take my place at the table. That way we can still make up our numbers.'

Lady C was staring at the ceiling and nodding in blank bemusement as if to suggest, to anyone who might be fool enough to believe her, that such had been her idea all along. It was quite a coup by Nancy. The fight had quite gone out of Lady C.

'Don't forget, Charlotte, this is not a concentration camp. Other people might want to join us occasionally.'

Nancy's torpedo had smashed right into her magazine. But it was not yet finished. Nancy had another card to play. An even bigger card, it transpired.

'And while we're about it, hurry up and invite Joe to your soirée instead of keeping him hanging on like that. It's just too ill mannered for words.'

Lady C, no fool by any stretch of the imagination when it

came to social gunslinging, had by now recovered her sangfroid sufficiently to regain her footing. The revolution had been short-lived. She returned to the charge with vim.

'Nancy, it's my soirée and I will choose my own time for making the invitations. I think that choice is still left to me, isn't it Nancy? I was planning to make the invitation a happy surprise for Joe this morning as we played, but since you've insisted on pre-empting me like this I'll make the invitation now, so that all the world can hear. Joe? Where on earth have you got to, Joe? You were here a minute ago. Yes, there you are, I can see you now.'

Joe waved a pathetic hand from the clump of women sheltering him.

'Joe, will you please come to my party next week and make two women at least very happy?'

'I'd be delighted to, Lady C.'

'Well, that's settled then. Now what are we waiting for? Isn't it about time we played some bridge?'

The peasants trooped to the bridge tables and Lady C was back in control. But the object of the exercise had been achieved – Joe had his invite to the party the better to get closer to Sir David, now presumably swanning about with his lover Jean-Paul in some obscure part of the Côte d'Azure, his whereabouts unknown to the shaken Lady C.

Nancy led a shocked Emma from the room and Morka prepared to take her place at one of the tables. Joe noted that her expression had not altered from start to finish of the exchanges between Nancy and Lady C. It was strange that she had been quite unmoved by it all. Joe recalled the glimpse he had snatched of Morka laying down the law weeks ago to her bunch of toughs. Could there be yet another twist to this odd, many-headed saga? Had Sybil really boobed, in her hatred of Lady C, to find herself mixed up now with some truly unsavoury creatures in her desire to get even?

It was possible. Joe refused to rule it out, the more so since there was another odd feature to the morning's horseplay and rough words. Joe had primed the situation by organising, in quick succession, the call from Ateh's south London foster mother and the arrival of the uninvited Emma. But none of this would have worked without the dramatic intervention of Nancy. Nancy had clinched the deal for him. But who was Nancy? She had come into the fray too precisely for it to have been accidental. So whose side was she on? Back-up for Joe? A freelance? As if he'd be told...

Joe went to the tables with Lady C, still brooding about the extra dimension that he could sense to the morning's events. If Nancy was working on Joe's side, as well as collating recipes, then she had observed him the entire time that he'd been smuggled into this hallowed sanctum of the dames playing bridge. Now that was a thought.

How sad, mused Joe as he pulled out the cards for the first board, that she will have found so little to report on me. My behaviour here has been exemplary.

Ursula shuffled over for a quick word with Lady C, as Joe continued his thoughts.

'Which is more than I can say for some people.'

Joe overheard Ursula's muttered comment to Lady C.

'No, he wasn't at all well. But at least he was still breathing. No, the fire people came almost at once. It was very frightening. He just collapsed like that...'

Ursula's table shouted for her to hurry up and come back to play but she insisted on a few more seconds, to add extra words of comfort to the stricken Lady C.

Ursula hissed at her friend, 'Just think, though, what the situation might have been if he'd actually died. Worse than embarrassing... How could I have explained that?'

Lady C hissed back, 'I know just what you mean, Ursula. Something rather similar just happened to me this morning.'

'You don't mean...'

'Yes, I do. I got a call. Here, at Liz Playfair's, can you believe?'

'My God!' Ursula's eyes widened in horror and she was about to speak some more when she was physically yanked back by the skirt to her table. She vanished like Eurydice.

'Come on, please, Ursula, we're all waiting for you. You have to start the play. You're declarer, as if you didn't know.'

Then Lady C started to play her Thursday morning bridge. Joe observed her closely and found her behaviour surprising. She was different and she was cool. The frenzy of ten minutes ago had abated. Instead of agitation, which he had expected after the phone call from Ateh's minder in south London, Lady C seemed strangely calm. Even relaxed. Even enjoying herself. She shrugged off the spat with Nancy without a second thought and unbent sufficiently to behave with cordiality towards the opposition. She even smiled at Joe. This was surprising. Normally when they played together on a Thursday morning, her eyebrows spent most of the morning tight closed as she expressed disapproval at Joe's imaginative play. Or efforts in the direction of the same.

Traditionally, Thursday morning was an opportunity for Lady C to reinforce the iron laws of correct behaviour, common to her caste, through the bridge. Social custom and obligation took precedence over subtleties of play and delicacy of interpretation. Winning was nice when it happened. But it had to happen correctly without any show of desire to win, such as excessive concentration on where the queen of spades might be lurking, a quest which in turn entailed pausing for a fraction to work out some basic probabilities. Lady C didn't like pauses in the play. She didn't want any of this thinking stuff. Winning the contract was less important than behaving well. Most of all this was sheer gobbledegook to Joe, and totally incomprehensible to him. Hence he spent most Thursdays wincing at Lady C's withholding pattern as she in turn tried to wrong-foot him over the bridge and preserve her social edge.

But not on Nancy's Thursday morning. Not this time. Lady C's gurgle of laughter, first heard at Savage's, came back, to such an extent that Joe could see players at the other tables looking across in surprise at her merriment. Her outburst at Emma could be excused on almost any grounds but the girls were frankly puzzled by the subsequent switch to excessive good humour. That was not exactly in the programme. They knew their Lady C and she was not the forgiving sort; moods continued from whence they started until they changed. The glances went back and forth from table to table, but the atmosphere in the room undeniably improved. Shoulders started to fall, cards were held lower and the usual bickering returned – Joe had never realised that the phrase 'cashing out' had quite so many syllables.

Lady C's timing improved dramatically. She paused in her play, reflected – in her terms – for an age and actually held up instead of covering. She also returned Joe's suit back to him, something normally she refused to do almost on principle. That 'can do' aspect to her play, that 'well, come on then, let's get to the next board' feature, was quite absent that morning. Lady C was enjoying herself.

Had something happened which she had long dreaded but which secretly, withheld even from herself, she had desperately wanted to take place? Was she now prepared to flout society and its laws, laws which she had strenuously and forcibly enforced all her life, in order to secure a little happiness on the human level? Was she, Joe wondered, willing to take a chance on all this? Was she going to insist on something in the face of certain social disapproval? Or was she going to retreat into her shell, deny the whole incident on further reflection, and clam up completely?

The jury was out on this one, he realised, as she played a winning club very sweetly and, leaning forward, gathered in the last trick in the contract with a beautiful and cheeky grin, a grin which harked back years. Almost an urchin's look. It showed in all its splendour the alternative Charlotte such as had not been allowed a peek and a run from its hidey-hole for nearly a quarter of a century.

What a waste, thought Joe. She's actually quite a good sport. In real life and in real time she buys her round. But what can you expect from her, married to Sir David for all that time? Before my eyes I can see the ravages wrought by good behaviour and conformity to the norm. And also, amazingly, the survival of the human spirit underneath it all. Desperate survival, but survival nevertheless.

He played a confident middle spot spade, which held, and then cashed out, before switching to a diamond as an exit to get off lead.

For some reason, in the course of the morning, the Lady C bosom became less pert and more inviting. It became a living thing, not an inert thing moulded out of marble, existing merely to be gaped at. The bosom seemed to expand as the play contin-ued. Her whole shape appeared to alter at the same time and become more alluring and more feminine. Less mechanical and more shapely. Lady C was transforming herself before his eyes. She even moved differently in her chair, not heaving herself around like an ill-tempered frump, but shifting elegantly from haunch to haunch. Eager for the dance. That all mystified Joe. He couldn't fathom the process of thought transmission which proceeded from brain to breast and it left him floundering as a mere male, unelected to these Eleusinian mysteries.

But how, he wondered as he bid an easy three no trumps, have her tits suddenly taken on human form? I thought they were made out of alabaster the moment she was born. Any more play under these conditions and these bristols will be heaving by this afternoon, he told himself, as he ducked a spade for the second time and waited for the inevitable and wrong switch to a diamond.

The liberated and partially reborn Lady C smiled at him again as he played the hand and quite unnerved him. Joe was very careful about smiling in return. He looked solemn by design. Partly out of fear and partly too because there were other developments taking place which he wanted to observe. These too contained the seeds of a new radicalism.

Something very unexpected was taking place to his left. Morka, he could see, was playing like a professional, sitting there quietly and waiting for the cards to be played, conserving her energy for the struggle over the contract, doing nothing that might cost. She was playing in exactly the same style as she had used at Savage's, when she partnered Sybil.

Liz was transformed. She hovered over Morka like a mother hen, scrutinising her play, nodding at the turn of the cards, and wafting encouragement to her in a most obvious and uncharacteristic way. Liz normally sat in the centre of the morning's play like a sphinx, studiously preserving her neutrality. Not so today. Sister spirit called to sister spirit.

Again Joe found his imagination faltering before the chameleon possibilities of these women. It was extraordinary. Liz had transformed herself into suppliant. The mighty, proud and almost Amazonian Liz was practically on her knees to Morka. Joe could see that. Her eyes never left Morka's face. She was hungry, almost ravenous, for approval. She was quite desperate to win

Morka's respect, to the extent of abasing herself there in public in front of her and all the other women. A process of communication was establishing itself between the two women like a scent, which defied any attempt at analysis by Joe. But the affinity was quite palpable. By inference, and Joe had to look quite hard to discern this, Morka was queenly in her acceptance of Liz's abject deference. It was sovereign to subject stuff.

Morka played the cards very well, always with a calm almost deferential air. Her bidding was impeccable. She was in a quite different league to everyone else in the room, Joe included. She placed the cards on the table with a definition of presence that was incontestable. No claws stretching out for her dummy, no sir.

Could all that account for Liz's apparent infatuation? Hardly, to Joe's mind. This was like a clarion call, something far more powerful and sustainable. This looked like love at first sight, trite though the phrase might seem. Or if that failed as an explanation, how about Morka as the simple answer to a maiden's prayer from out of all of Liz's difficulties? With Morka, Liz could perhaps see a way out from the conflict between her bridge and her children and her husband. An escape route. Certainly society would not be allowed to stand in her way as it might be in the case of Lady C. Every boat that Liz possessed would be burned over Morka. There would be no holding back over this.

No doubt about it; they seemed like a unit already, after just an hour of play. Liz was bursting to speak to Morka, privately, about every card that was played and every bid that took place. There was communication at every level. No one else in the room mattered. They were superfluous and the sooner they departed the better.

Something quite irreversible was happening in that room that morning. These women, married to men who owned the country, were not used to being shouldered to one side so that their bridge coach could chat up some refugee nobody. Society was not flouted in that way without dire retribution taking place.

Even more astonishing to Joe's eyes was the fact that Liz also seemed physically altered, along similar lines to Lady C. Her hangdog look had gone. So too had the bent and bowed shoulder and the sluggish manner and the impression of utter hopelessness she conveyed before the harsh dictates of her husband. For days the hair had been lank. Now suddenly her eyes were sparkling and she was actually moving round the room, although never very far from Morka, with a spring in her step. She was almost like a schoolgirl in her excitement.

And Morka certainly reciprocated her feelings so far as Joe could judge. She nodded at Liz and she inclined her head every now and then in acknowledgement of her presence, both secret and public, and she did not appear to reject her. It could be argued that quite calmly Morka accepted her destiny as part of a unit with Liz. The two seemed to be together against the room and the street and the town and the world, so far as Joe could judge, as yet again Lady C smiled at him. A complicated dance of love was weaving its complex steps in that quiet little room in Lower Sloane Street on a Thursday morning like any other Thursday morning, while the women played their bridge as they had done for years.

At the end of the session, by tacit consent, the women left the room almost immediately without Liz and without Morka. There was no invitation to stay. The tension in the room was strong as Liz appeared to will the whole gang of them to depart. She tidied the cards away as soon as the last hand was played as quickly as possible and her rooms were no longer a place to chat and gossip; they held the welcome of a Macedonian transit camp to be left as quickly as possible.

Liz looked acutely unhappy at the prospect of talking to anyone before she had communed with and confided in Morka. She was more or less silent after the play. Such was the shattering power and force of instant love. Liz was no longer in control of anything until she had received sanction from Morka. None of the usual lunch together for all the girls after the rigours of the play. No high jinks today with the bread rolls and the weight reduction programme. They were bereft. As the girls tumbled down the stairs, Liz and Morka stayed behind together.

Everybody was too surprised at the instant change in Liz to comment immediately. A common idiom had not yet formed. It had only taken a matter of hours, and not a word exchanged between them! This surpassed anything by way of unsavoury that daughters had brought home for the weekend without luggage and unannounced. It was unbelievable! An era drew to a close in a flash. How soon was structure that defied time with apparent ease destroyed and rent asunder!

For the first time ever on a Thursday morning Joe found himself talking to Lady C in the street. She babbled a little at him in her confusion. So did the others. Joe made a small and successful bid for control of the situation. He spoke firmly. They listened to him.

'Look, you obviously will want to discuss all this amongst yourselves. I don't think there's much I can contribute. It's unfathomable. There's no precedent for it in my experience. Why don't I take you all to Oriel round the corner, buy you all a drink, let you all sit down, and then disappear? How's that for a deal?'

Lady C said that they might want him to stay with them all at Oriel. She was almost coquettish, although in a wooden way, as though she'd only half remembered the body language. Breaking the old Eve out of the cupboard would take time.

Joe demurred. 'Not this afternoon, Josephine.'

She stared at him disbelievingly. Joe continued. 'This is neither the time nor the place for a male to interfere. This is a female event and I'm quite out of place. I would only make stupid comments that might be misunderstood. Something happened this morning and we might as well accept it and position accordingly. I think. I don't know for sure but I think that's right. And don't forget that Liz is quite free to do whatever she wants with whoever she chooses. It's still a free country so far as that's concerned. We shouldn't be too hard on her. It's not as if she's sinned. She has merely sprung a modification to familiar reality upon us, which has shocked all and sundry.'

'You can be quite eloquent when you choose, Joe,' said Mags, a touch appreciatively. 'So far I agree with all of that.'

Joe did not respond to the interruption but bowed acknowledgement in her direction. 'So shall we go and have a drink? My shout of course. I'll disappear after that and leave you all to it.'

They followed him around Sloane Square to Oriel, chattering excitedly. He led the way inside, hosting the throng, and then stood at the bar and ordered three bottles of Sauvignon. Glasses were produced and tables clattered and the ladies were seated. 'This is more like it,' they were saying amongst themselves, 'a bit of service from the local male who should have been doing this the whole time, a glass of wine and the weight off my feet. Yes, maybe some bits of old reality remain. Now, Sophie,' – after a gulp of Sauvignon went down very sweetly – 'what exactly do you think took place this morning? Wasn't it just extraordinary?'

Only afterwards did Joe realise that some form of acceptance had been conferred upon him. That was equally disturbing for someone resolved to quit as soon as the mission was over. Lady C had insisted on talking to him all the way to Oriel. She averred how much she was looking forward to playing with him at the bridge soirée. Something was breaking out of Lady C, something dark and dangerous. That was even more frightening.

Annie rang her aunt at home later in the afternoon.

'So what happened, Nancy?'

'It went like clockwork. Joe had set it all up very accurately, so my intervention, when it came, was one hundred per cent effective. So he's in now. He's got the invitation.'

Nancy knew about these things. She had spent her late teens in post-war Berlin, tending fugitives from the brutalities of the Russian espionage drive. She had traded in the desperation of sanctuary many times, although now of course she was seen as just a silly old woman, busying herself about stupid recipes.

'Your Joe is a cool customer. He knew that something was missing from his plan and he just had to hope that something would happen to clinch it. He never batted an eyelid when I spoke out, though. I could see him in the mirror as I spoke. Not a flicker, not even in the depths of his eyes. He was very impressive.'

'And Emma?'

'Very shocked, but not blaming Joe at all. We had a coffee and a little cry and then she started to recover. She's very resilient. I told her that there had been an invitation but that Lady C had had one of her little turns. I said they happened occasionally. Emma has no way of checking the truth of any of that so it will stand. Meanwhile she cheered up considerably when I told her that her name would go on the list. She can come and play some other time. Suffer but join – that kind of thing. That really did reassure her. I gather that she's come into a huge fortune recently, so it's hardly surprising that she feels somewhat at sea with all of this.'

'But she's also a very successful lawyer?'

'Not only that, but she's also been instrumental behind the scenes in saving someone quite a small fortune, she told me. One of the Pooles, I believe. The word will get around. She'll be fine. It won't take long before she's accepted. I think there's a boyfriend story too somewhere along the line and that doesn't help at times like these. She's a very brave girl, I think. She might even...'

'Especially because of the boyfriend angle, Aunt Nancy.'

No more words were needed.

Annie read her aunt very well. Her aunt had been responsible from a distance for Annie's induction into the service in the first place. They spoke the same language. Might not Emma prove to be a possible recruit? Perhaps but the vetting process was inevitably thorough and took time. Agents were like rare and beautiful paintings – unique, indispensable and also irreplaceable.

'And Adrian, Annie?'

'Very well when I last heard from him. Blooming. It won't be long now.'

That was all that Annie would permit herself to say about the imminent conclusion to the mission, even to her aunt. But it was enough. The end was looming, now that Joe had secured his invitation to the ball. Meanwhile Annie had work to do on that whole scenario. She had laid very careful plans indeed. They had to mature with the same successful precision as the gambits of Aunt Nancy's Thursday morning bridge. And, provided she left nothing to chance, they would mature as she wanted. Espionage's best weapon was still – and always would be – total surprise.

Joe rang Perdita at exactly three o'clock. She answered the phone. He asked her if she was Sean by any chance, an old joke by now between them.

'Mummy says yes, we can meet but she wants to come too, if that's acceptable?'

'By all means, Perdita, she's very welcome.'

'Aren't you just a teeny bit disappointed that we're not going to be alone, Joe?'

'Part of me, the sensible part, is very relieved, Perdita. I won't talk about the other part, not over an open phone. Quite, quite disgusting. But every time I speak to you I fall just a little bit more in love with you. It's like falling out of the sky. Very soon it will be fatal for me to be apart from you. I will both cry and die at the prospect. So your mother's presence, when we meet, will be just the prophylactic I need.'

'The proffer what? What's that, when it's at home?' She didn't sound too upset at Joe's protestation of love.

'Oh, you know what I mean, garlic, that kind of thing, to ward off evil spirits.'

She paused a fraction. 'Joe, are you sure that you're just a bridge player?'

His heart went cold. Pimpernel time again.

'I'll tell you why I ask. We went, mummy and I, to the local bridge club last week just to check it out and we didn't find anyone there like you. They were like corpses. We thought they'd all been dead for about one hundred years.'

'Hampshire bridge is famous for its conventions – of all kinds, Perdita. London bridge is very different.'

'And so is London Bridge, ha, ha, ha.'

She went off into peals of laughter. Joe felt a fool. But relieved. Attention had been diverted. The joke would divert her swiftly from any further searching questions about his true identity. With the directness of youth, Perdita was getting through Joe's defences like something out of the Long-Range Desert Group. And he for his part felt increasingly reluctant to lie to her. He was wearying of the shams and subterfuges of espionage, the closer she came to him. The glow of her body warmth against him, even down the line of a mobile phone, made him resent the awkward inadequate creature that he presented to her. He wanted to tell her about his great fortune, yes, the one that he had made and lost, that one, but still he wanted to describe it to her, just so that she could gauge what a great man he used to be.

Like an idiot, he wanted to tell her that he could speak French as well as German; that he had read good books and that he wasn't a social moron, as her vile brother imagined; that he had spent his formative years dodging the bullets in Berlin, over and under the Wall; that he had been chief executive of Martins Bank in the City; that his whole outlook had been conditioned by his desperate and dangerous life working for British intelligence; and that even now, as he spoke to her, he was involved in the greatest of all missions... As a spy. Against her brother, no less, because that was what it amounted to now. That was how it all stacked up, now that Rivers worked for Sir David. And that he had done something else...

Truly for him this was turning into the trapdoor mission. His own emotions were making him completely vulnerable. One part of him still cleaved to the isolation of the mission but the rest of him – oh no! – that part that remained wanted none of it. The rest of him craved the fireside and the gentle touch of Perdita. The sooner the mission was over the better, before Joe came to grief. He felt his senses slipping. He was losing control. Perhaps he only had a few weeks left as a real spy before he became utterly useless at the job and rejoined the human race. There came a little flash of the resentful Fat Man into his mind at that precise moment.

'Oh, Joe, I feel so much better now. I got one over on you. That's the first time ever.'

More giggling and screeching. What had started out as a serious conversation became very silly indeed very quickly. Joe felt a lot better for the London Bridge gag. He had very nearly fallen down himself at that point.

At the end of the discussion, just before Perdita rang off, she said thoughtfully, 'I don't think mummy is going to tell Rivers about our dinner with you, and I'm certainly not going to breathe a word about it to him. He's very busy anyway that night so all he needs to know is that we came up to town early. He made such a song and dance about mummy inviting you for lunch with some of our friends that she became quite vexed with him. He really doesn't want you to come to that lunch at all. Which is very strange, seeing as you saved his life. Very odd. Very unlike Rivers too, but we've been into that. So, any road, as I heard someone say on television and nearly did myself a mischief as mummy would say after I heard it, any road, lad, eh up, if tha don't talk to lad bart it, there's nowt wrong done.'

'Perdita, you sound so exquisite when you try to be vulgar.'

'Eh up, lad, tha's tryin' tah git ararn me. No, that's wrong, I've gone into cockney. I'm going to try again. Too many soaps, you see, Joe. Wait for it, while I twist my throat round...' Silence. Then laughter. 'Joe, I think I've lost my glottal stop. I can't do it. What do I do now?'

'Wear a smaller bra.'

She laughed a lot at that. 'Now who's being vulgar? What an idea! And what a thing to say to a young girl, especially over the telephone. All my gals have been very carefully trained... That's my Jean Brodie voice. Ah, there we are, I've got it back again. Yes, it's definitely come back. I can talk dirty in broad Yorkshire now – for about fifteen seconds before I lose it again.'

And so the conversation continued until they both ran out of steam and had to cease the conversation because they were both helpless with laughter. But each time they talked together they inched just that fraction closer. Now that they were talking dirty to each other about underwear, Perdita's underwear, even in the most incredibly genteel way, it could only be a matter of time.

# Chapter Sixteen

In the run-up to Lady C's bridge soirée, Joe acquired an inkling of just how incredibly chatty the SW3 grapevine could become when there was a local issue to be debated. Discussion about Liz and Morka never ceased and his phone never stopped ringing. He was on the phone for most of every morning. The calls whizzed back and forth like meteorites. What did it all mean? Was anything going to change? What happened now?

Joe learned the hard way that women understood a situation by gnawing into it through relentless discussion, night and day and then more besides, without, however, reaching any clear conclusion. Their appetite for forensic analysis of the Liz–Morka axis appeared to be insatiable. All of this was new for Joe.

The lovelorn pair were spotted walking down the King's Road hand in hand; they were seen together at Harrods and they were observed lunching and dining together in full public gaze so frequently that it was no longer considered worthy of comment.

That was only part of it. That was the tittle-tattle bit. There was another more sinister aspect to it all. Fresh sources of information about the women at the Thursday morning bridge circle appeared to have become available to all and sundry, courtesy of Morka playing at Savage's, which she still did in what seemed to Joe to be a rather brazen triumphalist way. It was all a touch like going on the Internet. The whole world, for example, knew about the recipe book that Nancy had prepared, knew when it would be on sale, knew what it was expected to raise. Sophie's desperate and very, very discreet battle to save her poor alcoholic sister became the talk of the town as did a couple of business problems encountered by husbands of wives who played at Liz Playfair's. And much else besides.

Now that she was in the middle of what looked like a gigantic affair, Liz had been enormously and uncharacteristically indiscreet in the context of her spider role at the centre of a vast web of information that fed in and out of the bridge club. Liz had been the repository of all this information for years. She knew every home phone number, every au pair's number, every cousin's address, the direct line to every husband whose wife played there, most of their bank accounts and club membership details, and all the addresses. She had the lot, either in her head or in her diaries, of which she kept a very copious number, because Liz was very meticulous.

It had always struck Joe that, in her own way, had she ever contemplated defection, Liz would have been welcomed with open arms by the Central Intelligence Bureau of every power hostile to the UK in the globe. She was passive intelligence power incarnate, like a little hidden GCHQ all on her own – and all completely overlooked. Not only did she have the vital, hard information, like birthdays and holiday homes, but she had the background to it all as well by sheer dint of familiarity. So she could sift the raw intelligence material as well. The databank just lay there inertly in the shape of Liz's contacts book. It had built up simply and organically over the years as trust in her had grown throughout London SW3.

Now in her infatuation she had simply opened up the treasure trove of information to Morka, a treasure trove entrusted to her on the basis of absolute trust and confidentiality. It was like watching a bank open its vaults and simply distribute its reserves to anyone who happened to be passing at the time. Liz laid a carpet of gold on the pavement, gold that was not hers to distribute, and invited all and sundry to take their pick.

Joe was greatly saddened by it all. He remembered a discussion years ago with an old Jesuit, a veteran of the confessional, who said quite quietly but with great force that most people had a blind spot – most of the time it was sex – and when it happened that the blind spot was touched it was tragic to observe. The consequences could be very grave. Joe felt he was watching a simple human tragedy, in all its grand and sublime aspects, as a youngish woman, through loneliness and frustration, went completely off the rails. Morka sailed through it all like a proud queen with Liz stumbling after her, shackled by a halter to her chariot.

The old jokey ambience had broken down completely;

everyone was very pissed off; and to all pleas from the women for mercy or compassion Queen Morka had turned an inscrutable but unrelenting implacable eye. She was enthroned in Liz's affections and durst no one forget it. That she was out to destroy something or somebody was clear to the entire world with the exception of poor doomed Liz Playfair.

Joe could see more trouble looming. Liz's husband was reportedly cutting up very rough indeed as the doors which had been opened to him by virtue of Liz's bridge cachet suddenly slammed shut. The domino effect was in full tilt. Worse, Joe thought it was only a matter of time before Morka insisted on becoming a permanent feature of the Thursday morning session, which in turn meant that somebody somewhere might have to drop out. It was as crude as that. What Morka wanted Morka got. Someone somewhere was going to get pressured. One way or another.

Ursula certainly saw the potential for mischief. She rang Joe and asked him whether he'd heard anything about Tom Stone. Joe was mystified by the call at first.

Ursula sounded crisp but brittle. 'He's a friend of yours, I know, Joe, and I happened to hear at a dinner party last night that he'd had a mild stroke. I wondered if you'd heard any news.'

Joe wondered about that lie. Why be so obvious? But she ploughed on regardless. She was a desperate woman.

'So have you heard anything?'

'I'm sorry to hear that, Ursula. I had no idea. I must contact him.'

'Yes, do ring me back with any details if you get any.'

'I will do that.'

Then Ursula came to the real point of her call. She was obviously very worried. 'I've heard some absurd story going the rounds that I used to know Tom rather well. I wonder if you've heard that at all, Joe?'

Double or triple bluff from Ursula. What she was saying was complete bollocks, obviously. The whole world, or that part of it that counted, knew full well that Ursula had done a spot of joystick canoodling recently with Tom. Although it had become life-threatening and landed him in hospital, that setback counted for nothing, forming part of the normal rules of engagement. Some knew that and some didn't. Most were indifferent, thinking it none of their business. But did Morka know? That was the crux of it. Had Liz split on her? That was the object of Ursula's call. Had Liz, who knew full well what had been taking place extramurally at her bridge salon, told Morka, en passant, about this dalliance, to such an extent that she, Ursula, would now receive the blackmail call from Morka, telling her to fuck off and die in no uncertain terms from Thursday bridge so that she, Morka, could take her place?

Joe played it straight. 'I've heard nothing on that account, Ursula.'

Ursula sounded very relieved. 'Thank you, Joe. You will tell me if you hear any of this malicious gossip, won't you?'

Joe promised faithfully that he would keep her posted. Joe knew what would happen if the news broke. Ursula had her plans well laid by now. If Liz did split on Ursula, she, Ursula, would immediately suggest to her husband that they fly overnight to Tahiti or somewhere similar out of harm's way, to renew their marriage vows to his delighted surprise in a romantic tryst which would avoid at the same time Mr Ursula taking delivery, by the next post and by registered letter, the tapes, the pics, the notes, and presumably the used condoms as well, of her recent meetings with Mr Tom Stone. Hardball, Morka style. No question but that she'd play it that way. Joe had met her type before – angels with a fist of steel.

And so Ursula, mightily relieved for the time being, rang off. Joe heard no more from her for a few days until the next big topic of discussion came to dominate minds in London SW3. Should Lady C withdraw her invitation to Liz for the bridge soirée, now that Liz had gone native? Would Liz try to extend her own invitation to include Morka? Was that even feasible, given that the Lady C bridge soirée was one of the smartest invitations of that part of the year? Could Liz have sunk so low so fast as to even contemplate such social delinquency? It was a very knotty point indeed. It had lots of moving parts to it. It permitted no easy answer.

No question of theology, not even the Filioque dispute which divided Christendom in the early Middle Ages, separating the Eastern and Western churches for ever, was so hotly debated. Tempers were at boiling point. Liz and Morka's names were on the lips of all and sundry. They were reviled and they were the compassionate objects of sympathy all at the same time. Joe, fully in the swim so far as the discussion was concerned, found his opinion canvassed by all and sundry. To some he said, 'No, Liz shouldn't go; the invitation should be withdrawn,' – and he was howled down. To others, he said, 'Yes, she should come; Lady C should contemplate no such thing as a blackball,' – and he was howled down. Opinion was united on one point alone – that it was divided.

One bridge player, Trish, said darkly, 'She's been bought,' and left it at that. By whom? With what? And who had been purchased? She did not say. Like jesting Pilate she did not stay for an answer. But she was right to be so brutally emphatic and yet so ambivalent. She spoke for them all in SW3 when she made her pronouncement.

Lady C preserved a careful silence and refused to be drawn on her decision. She was the sphinx incarnate. But it was accounted a triumph for her subtle backstairs version of the old diplomacy when suddenly Liz withdrew from the evening, alleging a prior engagement. She sent in her place one of her young trainees, Mary Caldecott-Smith, accounted by those who had played against her as one of the best and most level-headed young players around, and known to all and sundry in the bridge world as Mimps. Joe knew her well; she'd tried a diamond switch against him at Young Chelsea one evening that very nearly succeeded. Mimps with her bright good humour and penchant for flowing, apparently unsupported, gowns was deemed a good choice as Liz's replacement. Deuce so far between the forces of light and the other chaps.

Then another far more terrible rumour spread amongst the ranks of the SW3 ladies, notably that Liz was declaring *force majeure*. This piece of intelligence exploded on the very day of the soirée itself. The story was remarkably consistent in all respects. It had the ring of truth. Liz was leaving her husband and going abroad to play serious bridge with Morka. She was closing the academy shortly, so there would be no more supervised bridge practice and, worst of all, Thursday bridge would be scrapped.

The bridge dames were aghast. On every floor of Peter Jones, on all levels of Oriel, up and down Cheyne Walk, from Chelsea Green to Waitrose and then after Habitat on to the Farmers Market, through all the libraries, in and out of Old Church Street and round and about the Blue Bird Café, from gym to gym and even during the aqua aerobics and the body conditioning classes, the talk was of nothing else: Liz was going.

That the story should detonate on the very day itself of the Lady C bridge soirée was seen as no more than appropriate, symbolic according to some of the real split that had taken place in the area between what local bridge demanded by way of commitment and the superior overriding demands of caste. The two by now were seen as irreconcilable. No terms of trade possible between them, and the rate of exchange was simply unquotable.

Joe spent a few hours of total repose during the afternoon ahead of Lady C's bridge evening. He tried to drain himself of all superfluous feelings, sensations and thoughts. He needed total focus to survive the evening. This for him had to be his last great engagement. Afterwards a slow decline into normality and a gradual withdrawal from theatres of warfare such as he had always known. He wanted to come out alive.

He lay on his settee, which moulded itself with loving comfort to his body, and, emptying his mind as far as possible, thought about what would be happening on the following day, after the meeting with Sir David was over. The post-mission world, how would that look? Bridge, normality and the usual quest for money to stay alive? Certainly. Perdita? A flash of sunlight on a face with a grin threaded its way through his imagination. He grimaced at the pain of it. Perdita the Perhaps; later that evening he would receive the full flavour of his relationship with that young lady. He knew that he was quite capable of behaving completely out of context and character now with Perdita, losing his concentration in the process, and he feared for the time being her influence on him. She might ruin his timing and his focus and he refused to think about her at all except as a pleasant somehow future sensation, as a whisper of heaven. He deferred gauging the dimensions of all that until he was actually striding through the doors of Zorba's to meet her. And Rivers? Rivers would certainly be a factor in all of the Pugh element that related to him. The Pughs came in a tight high explosive package. No two factors were the same. Collectively, they were nuclear. He ducked thinking about Rivers. It made him feel uneasy. Lying on the sofa and staring vacantly at the sky through the dirty window, letting the hours and minutes pass in their ebbing silence, he started to focus on what he was actually committed to achieving during that evening – the mission! At last, denouement time.

And the mission itself? What was it about? Joe knew nothing. He was a cog, nothing more and nothing smarter. Who knew? Someone, somewhere. Who cared now, now that it had gone on for so long? Somebody cared, but not Joe. His commitment was clear. He wanted out, alive. That remained his staple unchanging position. He knew that he had to get close to Sir David and he knew that sooner or later that afternoon, probably later, he would receive his briefing. Briefings always came late. So much could happen in the run-up to a denouement that by the time battle was joined they might have become outdated. Joe liked a late briefing.

His phone rang and he shifted position to take the call, ranging his mind back into mode.

It was Emma, a rather breathless but reassured Emma. Joe winced at the sound of her voice. Now for the bollocking, he thought, after he had misled her so wantonly over the Playfair bridge. Mega-bollocking on the way, and one he richly deserved. No doubt about that. But Joe was wrong. Emma had called not to rebuke him but to thank him. Astounded, Joe remained silent.

'Joe, I rang to thank you.'

'It was nothing, Emma. A trifle, a ducat from my purse.' Why was she thanking him?

Emma continued. 'I know you had nothing to do with that terrible dressing down I got on Thursday. Nancy explained it all to me.'

Nancy, thought Joe, well, fuck-a-doodle-do, here's pics and tricks because that Nancy has more to her than meets the eye. Had it not been for Nancy…

'Joe, she's been terribly nice to me. She explained that Lady C

452

had had one of her little turns and that I just happened to get into the firing line. But I wasn't ringing to thank you for that. Just for looking after me during the past few weeks.'

'This sounds a trifle valedictory, Emma. You're not leaving us, are you?'

'I'm off for a long weekend with Nancy to her place in the Cotswolds. She couldn't make it to Lady C's soirée and she's invited me to keep her company. She's going to give me a crash briefing on life and times in SW3, so that I can find my place, as she puts it, more easily among the women. The Pooles are coming too so it should be quite a party. They want me to look over a few documents for them. It should be great fun.'

'It sounds it, Emma.'

'Did you know, Joe, that Nancy has had such an interesting life? She was in Berlin just after the end of the war and she's promised to tell me all about it.'

Lights crashed on in Joe's head and just as quickly were extinguished. No wonder Nancy wouldn't be there... He refused to rationalise for himself what he had just been told. Not even for a second. He talked to Emma as he played down that line in the conversation.

'I'm told Berlin was a very exciting place just after the war. I've never been myself but I'd love to go.' A big lie was always a good lie in such circumstances.

'She was involved in the Berlin airlift when the Russians tried to take over the whole city.'

And involved in a good deal more else, thought Joe as the conversation maintained its bright chatty timbre and Joe's mind slunk into a corner. One part of the intelligence world just touched at the furthermost tip of its arc another segment of the same world. Touched but did not intercept. That was always against the rules.

'She sounds like a very good person to know, Emma. I'd cultivate her if I were you.'

'I plan to do just that. Thank you for the guidance. Joe, I'm off now. I promised Nancy I'd catch the early train. I'll call you when I get back, of course, but can I ring you from Nancy's, if I find myself getting into hot water? Just so that I can ramble down the line at someone? It will take my mind off Gregory and what he might be up to.'

'Feel free to do so, Emma. I'd be delighted to hear how you're getting on. And I'll come and collect you if you want at any time, provided you give me just a little bit of notice.'

She paid Joe some very handsome compliments for his solicitude as she rang off and Joe wandered about the flat, thinking with awe of the skill with which British intelligence selected and then inducted its recruits. A kaleidoscope of realities... And then disposed of those recruits. Its proudest boast was that it always got the body back...

Numb now with anticipation, he awaited his briefing call as the sky gradually filled with long traces of gold, flung haphazardly against the brilliant blue and making for a magnificent evening for Lady C's soirée. In the Little Boltons, where Sir David and Lady C resided, the evening would be heavy with musk, dark shadows, and the brilliance of the lights against the gathering blackness. And the chatter of the play would fill the house...

After Emma's call, Joe barely moved for an hour, filling his mind with thoughts of his next investment move. Nothing sprang to mind of its own accord. Russian bonds were a possibility but then again they were risky. And they'd done so well recently. How about following Emma into Mexico? A bit late, he thought. He'd be filling in someone else's bear position more than anything else.

Joe was called at five thirty exactly. No words were wasted. This was business now. They were on line. It was go time.

'Joe, you're going to have to play it more or less by ear because it's a pretty volatile situation. Object of the exercise? First, get close to Sir David, who will find himself put under some very considerable pressure during the evening. We'll take care to put you up close to him so don't worry about doing any of that. We've got that well in hand. Second, listen for a date. Just a date. That's what you're after, a date. Sir David is the only one who knows this date outside the obvious enclaves. The pressure will be put on him so that he reveals this date. In all kinds of ways that you too will find surprising. Whether he will reveal all or not remains to be seen. That's what the mission is all about. You're there as front man, so just be yourself. It's important that your reactions appear to be spontaneous, although you may want to switch around a bit as the evening progresses. Questions so far?'

'None.'

'Good. Now, downside bits and pieces. Well, not too bad for you. You should get through, we think. Your friend Rivers will be there and you must be very, very careful in your dealings with him. He is very dangerous so far as you're concerned, especially since he is becoming a very big shot indeed in Sir David's entourage, nearly next in line now, we gather. And, of course, there will be friends of Rivers there too, hence, *ipso facto*, no friends of yours. So all that downside is pretty obvious. Don't get yourself killed without purpose is what I'm saying, by stupid provocative behaviour. Questions?'

'None.'

'Topside for you is pretty good. We've got good watchers on this one, so that we can cover you pretty well all the way, especially during the break for dinner. That's when we plan to go for it. Be prepared for some disturbance as the bridge breaks for dinner. Again, don't risk anything yourself; we can take care of the initiatives. It's important that you're ready for anything at that point because it may get rough. So as we see it, some ding-dong as you get there, with a reprise in the break. That's optimal for us and we think we can do it. Questions?'

'None.'

'Some background for you. Sir David's little plan to flee the business and the country has come unstuck so he is, to put it mildly, volatile. That's good for us but maybe bad for you. Rules of the game, nothing more. He lost his little boyfriend during his dirty weekend.'

'Jean-Paul left him?'

'Not exactly. They finished up at a fairly wild party together in the South of France and it got out of hand. Wrong kind of people for Sir David. The boyfriend died because he was fucked and strangled to death in a massive gang rape. Not only was Sir David forced to watch all of this, but it was also filmed. He may be on the film. He was the only one not wearing a mask as the snuff movie was made. The body was dumped at sea. His entire project lies in ruins. Sir David is now back in the UK, minus his boyfriend, and you can work all the rest of it out for yourself. There may be even more to it than that but we can't be sure. But tonight, be very careful, Joe. He's waiting for the blackmail call, obviously, and we plan to trade on that. But he's afraid, feels threatened, and he is very nervous – in fact he's a total unknown quantity. He's never found himself in this situation ever before. Everything has changed for him. He has no bearings. So it may get rough. Understood?'

'Understood.'

'Reactions?'

'Neutral.'

'Good. Here's the number to call just as soon as he spills the beans, if he does. The minute you get the date, just make as if to go. Stand up and plead a migraine. You'll be overheard. We can get you out easily enough as soon as you've got the info. Don't forget, there are plenty of watchers there tonight, so you should be fine.'

'Good.'

'One final question. Have you got all the kit?'

Joe had his dinner jacket to hand, borrowed from the charity shop.

'Yes, I have.'

'Good. Now, don't go out again until it's time to go to the bridge. Don't stir. Just get some sleep or something. Here's the route we want you to take from your flat to the Little Boltons.'

The route was relayed to him down the line. It was almost the route Joe might have taken; almost but not quite.

'Joe, leave at exactly seven fifteen. No sooner and no later. Then start walking.'

'Why can't I take a cab?'

'Don't be stupid, Joe. We want to see where they are just as much as you do. This is the only way we can find out.'

'Thanks very much. At least, I'm a free-range sitting duck.'

'Not a bit of it, Joe, you're battery reared like all of us. You just think you're free-range.'

Pause.

'And good luck, Joe. We think you'll be fine.'

'Talk to you later. Bye.'

There was nothing left to say. So far, so procedural. After the briefing call, Joe fell asleep. There was nothing else to be done. End of the mission, so full steam ahead.

At six forty-five he awoke with his head clear. That was a comfort. He showered at some length, shaved, and then donned the rented soup and fish. He wondered about his own dinner jacket, now held in store for years, so much so as to be quite unfashionable now, but the speculation wearied him. He dismissed the thought from his mind and pottered about the flat for some minutes. Then, at seven fifteen exactly, he left the flat, ignoring the phone which rang just as he was locking the front door. Most likely Ateh calling to say that she'd had no news yet from Jean-Paul.

The crack in the wall outside was reassuringly small. Best to leave the phone to ring. Otherwise that crack might start to grow again.

He followed the route as outlined to him and was gratified to see a familiar escort swing into place very discreetly for most of the time – the boxed formation of two in front and two behind. All at a distance but still there. Someone was taking no chances on this one. He was pleased to see the escort. It gave him some hope. Walking at a steady pace, they tramped along. No words together and no communication. It could have been the escort to a firing squad. As they neared Little Boltons, the escort peeled off, but Joe guessed that most of the parked cars would provide cover. Many of them contained drivers smoking idly with, most important, open windows.

That was the killing detail, the open windows. The second it took to break the glass was the second it took for the bullet to go through a brain. A second too long…

With one minute to spare he entered Little Boltons. The suit felt fine – its original owner must have been a bulky kind of cove – and he was walking freely. He was in that dreamy state when any attempt on his life seemed inconceivable. Floating free. He approached Lady C's residence without breaking stride. Just about a minute to go before the bridge began.

Shock number one was the appearance of Mimps at the door.

She appeared to be wearing nothing more than her pyjamas, which covered very little of her firm young flesh and left very little to the imagination. Joe goggled for a few seconds. Then he congratulated her on the cut of her jim-jams and she kissed him on the cheek for his compliment.

'It's a hot night.'

'Indeed it is, Mimps. But you'll find it hard to hide your cards in that outfit, you know.'

'You'd be surprised, Joe,' she replied and disappeared down the hall in a flurry of chiffon. 'There are hiding places everywhere. They're like tax havens.'

Why does every young woman I meet have a cute line in dialogue, thought Joe as he prepared to ascend the stairs to the first floor, where the tables were laid out for the play. It must be the TV they watch.

He looked to his left in the palace of Lady C. Food on the ground floor, acres of the stuff, with tables laid as far as the eye could see, and an army of flunkies and tweenies ready to ladle it all down the throats of the starving masses in an hour's time. Joe looked about him with some interest as he climbed the stairs; this didn't seem very menacing.

He laid a hand on the baluster. A familiar voice broke in on his reverie, a voice that he last heard many moons ago as he left Martins Bank when to be precise he had winkled a monstrous compensation package out of the Gilston family. It was George Gilston, now in charge of the entire financial empire. The last time Joe had heard that voice he was clutching a cheque for two million pounds in his hot little hand. Joe had liked George. He was perhaps the very last person that Joe would have wanted to meet at the bridge soirée. Joe felt his poverty now very keenly.

The figure of Mimps flew up the stairs ahead of them like a fairy on wings. George gazed at the drifting vision philosophically. 'I'd like to show her my grand slam force some time. One of these days…'

'Didn't know you were a bridge player, George. But I warn you, she'd finesse it, George, she's an expert.'

'Not with my stiff ace, she wouldn't.'

They both laughed. George sounded like a friendly native. Joe fell naturally into discussion with him. It was a long time since he'd talked business with anyone. It all came back very fast.

'How are the markets treating you, George?'

'Not as well as they should, Joe. We miss you.'

'What happened? You get the euro wrong? It was obvious that it was going to collapse. Forward euro against the yen told you that, surely. It was obviously going to tank.'

George hung his head. Joe dug him in the ribs, quite forgetting that he was a proscribed being in this neck of the woods and had been for many months. The old habits of market goz came back very swiftly.

They were reaching the top of the stairs where their hosts were assembled. Mimps had just floated through the assemblage. Joe made out Lady C vaguely. He also saw Sir David, looking much the same but tugging slightly at his collar as if it had become too tight. At the same time, Joe also realised that in dinner jacket it was impossible for George to realise that he was clearly bankrupt. That emboldened him.

'Come on, George, tell me. Where are you long? $1.12? $1.13? Higher?'

'It's not a currency, it's a nightmare.'

George, palm outstretched, made an upward motion with his hand.

'Christ, you must be idiots to be long that high.'

They had reached the welcoming party. Joe was still talking to George. They waited to greet the pair.

'You know, George, you're nothing but a blockhead. A complete fucking blockhead. You shouldn't be in charge of a pram, let alone a bank. You should have known better. It was all obvious. So what's the position you're running? Come on, total damage? Tell me. And the truth, mind…' Joe was back in the old routine.

A voice broke in on their dialogue. 'So who are you calling a blockhead, Joe? How dare you? Are you all right, George, or shall I have him thrown out for his rudeness? I'm very sorry about this man's conversation. Please forgive us.'

Rivers Pugh made his own introduction. He was part of the welcoming party, along with Lady C and Sir David. Rivers gave

Joe a fine and spirited fusillade of toff rude. Identities, past and present, came into headlong collision with a crash. Joe began to understand just how cleverly the denouement had been set up. Meanwhile Lady C's jaw was hanging open at her surprise and her eyes were startled. So just who was this person opposite whom she played bridge for many many months? Talking this way to one of their most honoured guests!

George Gilston made a typical no nonsense reply which helped to muddy the waters still more. 'Rude? What is this? What on earth are you talking about? This is Joe, our former chief executive at Martins Bank, who's obviously been hiding himself away incognito, having himself a very good time and leaving us all in the lurch. I must say that you look very well rested, Joe. Very well rested indeed. I hope you've been having a good time, Joe, because we haven't…'

Collapse, at least temporarily, of toff rude. Rivers's eyes were indescribably vicious. Pure hatred at the deception visited upon him. No quarter there, thought Joe. Not for a split second.

Further reaction was not possible. The bridge was starting any minute. As George made his comments, the momentum of their arrival and the jostle of other late arrivals forced them to push through the knot of greeters and into the bridge room itself.

Joe saw that Sir David's eyes contained a curious blankness, almost the look from another world. Another tug at the collar and another impatient movement of the neck which strained to find release. I suppose, thought Joe, if you've just witnessed the gang rape and slow strangulation of your boyfriend and you think you're captured on film doing all that, you'd feel that the present proceedings lack a certain brio. Or something.

Joe also glimpsed Marty seated in one corner near the entrance. Marty, the incarnation of diversified corporate services. Marty saw him and nodded at him in a speculative kind of way as he and George were swept into the room. George carried on talking to Joe.

'Look, Joe, it's perfectly true, we've missed you. One of the reasons I came here tonight was to catch up with you. I want to hear from you Monday without fail.'

Rehabilitation verily and without a doubt. The spring in Joe's step grew more pronounced.

'George, just what is this? Just explain it all to me will you? I don't understand.' More from Rivers, who had followed them into the room. Rivers was not happy with these revelations. He buttonholed George and ignored Joe, who was standing right next to George. Toff to toff, toe to toe.

George looked at him for a second, and seemed to hesitate. Then he took the whole thing up a tempo. 'You mean Joe didn't tell you what he was about? How stupid of you not to ask. Joe is one of the smartest people in the City today. He was probably doing some undercover work on your company. I've always thought the quickest way into a company's secrets was through the wives. Joe has gone one better. He's been playing bridge with them. I reckon he knows more about your company than anyone else on the board. Isn't that so, Joe?'

Joe nodded. It seemed the only correct thing to do. Without a word, Rivers turned on his heel and stomped off back to talk to Sir David. Sir David nodded as Rivers spoke to him, the two of them glancing in Joe's direction as they conferred, with Rivers then making the obvious hand gestures of a B-movie hero: shall I have him thrown out now by Marty? Or shall we wait until the pause for dinner and then I can arrange for him to be beaten up well and truly? What are your wishes, my liege lord?

George asked a gentle question. 'Morale, Joe?'

'First class, George.'

George nodded in silence.

Further analysis of the situation had to be deferred because Lady C, begowned, bejewelled and stunningly well coiffured, swept up to Joe and suggested that the two of them take their places for the bridge. He led her to her table. He saw Sir David and Rivers still conferring together at the back of the room. The interval would not be easy. Rivers would become very tiresome.

It was time to play. The room stretched the length of the house, occupying much of the first floor, overlooking the garden at the back and the quiet of Little Boltons at the front. It was a mass of crimsons, blacks, browns and greens, with the flash of the men's white dress shirts at regular intervals breaking up the frieze of heavy, highly substantial colour.

A beautiful balmy evening – what better setting than for Lady C's bridge soirée. She had indeed been blessed by the weather.

Annie dispatched her message of love and death to Joe, the only thing control could send. It all hangs in the balance now, she thought as she replaced the phone. We are engaged in the battle now with all our resources committed. No room whatsoever for retreat. It's win or lose.

She stared out of the window at the Thames running by. Like all great commanders, she did nothing. She waited for the news.

The play began and at first, as the guests settled, the evening was a study in contrasts. Those who were used to this level of fine existence were expressionless and they lolled in their chairs, seeing it as nothing beyond their norm, while those to whom this level of grandeur seemed sumptuous gazed round with startled grateful eyes and sat bolt upright. Bidding styles reflected these two attitudes. Joe fully exploited the sense of deference which inhibited the bidding of those springing from lower down the hog's back. He and Lady C started the evening well, securing some good scores.

Lady C was playing at her best, more as the alternative Lady C with the rich gurgle of a laugh than as the mindless robotic he had squabbled with over many hours of play. She did some clever things with the hearts on the second board and Joe was impressed. She was pleased that he was impressed and gave him a mock bow and curtsy with her shoulders from the other side of the table. Joe smiled in return, and his mind drifted for a few seconds away from the bridge towards the soft-toned glamour of the evening. He found himself watching Mimps away at a distant table as, sadly, she hitched up an errant strap yet again.

He came to and found that Lady C was talking to him as the move was called. 'So what is all this about your being a City big shot? You never told me about any of this?'

'It all happened a long time ago, Lady C.'

'Joe, I think it should be Charlotte at the very least, just for this evening. You can't keep calling me Lady C, not when we're playing bridge like this. It's absurd.'

'You mean that if I play really well I get to call you Charley?'

'Only once or twice, or my husband will start getting jealous. But yes, let's be slightly less formal with each other, shall we, this evening?'

Joe laughed at all of this and it startled the next pair coming to sit at their table. Laughter from Lady C's partner? Such a thing had never been heard of since before the Napoleonic era. They must be having a good time – unheard of! Watch out!

A messenger was bumbling along from table to table carrying an envelope looking for someone. He stumbled from table to table. Finally, he accosted Joe. 'I'm looking for a Mr Joe. Have you seen him anywhere?'

'That's me. What have you got there?'

'Letter for you, Mr Joe. Just arrived by courier for you downstairs. Special instructions to give it to you immediately.'

'Amazing. I'm sorry about this, Lady C.'

'Charlotte.'

'Yes, Charley. I'm sorry about this, as I say.'

Lady C's eyebrows rose at the familiarity. The messenger was insistent. 'Sign here, sir.'

'Will do.'

Joe signed and the messenger clumped off. Joe stuffed the envelope into his jacket and picked up the cards. He was thinking about his bridge. Lady C stopped him picking up the cards. She glared at him.

'Joe, you can't go through all of that and just put the envelope away. You have to open it. Otherwise we'll spend all the boards wondering what on earth it is that you've just taken delivery of. Now go on, open it.'

The opposition smiled at each other. This was more like it. They thought the laughter couldn't last. Lady C was born bossy.

Joe opened the letter. It was in French. *Mille regrets… problemes d'administration… Mille excuses*. The upshot of the letter was that he was now worth as from that instant four million. The account was unblocked. His fortune had been returned to him! He was rich again.

Joe felt Lady C's eyes upon him and he passed the letter across to her. She fumbled in her bag.

'I can't read without my glasses, you know that, Joe.' Out came the spectacles. 'Now what have we here? Oh, blast it, it's in French. Translate for me, Joe, what does it say? Really, this grows more astonishing by the hour. First a messenger for Joe and then a letter all in French. Amazing scenes. Quite unprecedented for our little bridge evening. Now come on, Joe, what does it say?'

'It's about some money that I was having difficulty in obtaining. It's come free now.'

'Is that good news, Joe?'

'Quite good news, Lady C.'

Something in Joe's tone made Lady C start. As they picked up the cards, she said to him very softly, 'How much, Joe?'

He scribbled the figure down on a piece of paper and passed it across the table to her. She opened the scrap and her eyes widened as she read the number.

'Not a bad figure, Joe. You are going to become very popular all of a sudden. Now the tables are truly turned, Joe. I must refer to you in future as Lord Joe. The girls will be truly happy for you when I tell them about your good fortune. I think you're going to need some protection with that kind of money.'

She meant that most sincerely, Joe was sure of that. She smiled and made a thumbs up sign and gave her gurgling laugh and Joe laughed a bit as well. The play began and continued as expected, with Joe feeling his chest swelling with pride as he settled back in his seat and digested the information that he was no longer the indigent, the unloved and the outcast; the cash was back in his account and he was a rich man again, fully entitled to take his place at any bridge table in the land.

So fuck you, Rivers Pugh, and all those who sail in you. Exactly the reaction that Annie had planned to create by sending the messenger at that moment, after the first encounter with Rivers had taken place. Joe was not the first front man to find his control manipulating his responses. Nor would he be the last.

As the play continued, Joe glanced across occasionally to see how Rivers and Sir David were enjoying the evening. Definite signs of agitation from Rivers and truly quite alarming signs of discomfort from Sir David. More pacing and more tugging at the collar and the jacket as if he wanted to jump out of his clothes entirely. He looked unwell.

The dinner interval came and the guests rose for their food. By tacit agreement Joe, George, Rivers and Sir David assembled in the middle of the room. Unfinished business to be transacted, most definitely.

Rivers was in a tearing rage and went for Joe at once, accusing him of spying on the company. Pure company man stuff. He was hysterical. Or pure Sloane School stuff, since in this case the whole thing was interchangeable. An outsider was tampering with their game, and woe betide him for doing that thing. Sir David looked on uneasily. He saw deeper into the situation. He sensed something more profound happening. He looked old. Rivers was out of control but Sir David was powerless to check him. Nor did he want to and nor did he care. Sir David was abdicating. Before Joe's eyes. The panache had gone. He wants out of it, thought Joe. All of a sudden the face seemed to be falling in upon itself, so that the outlines of the skull were prominently visible. The wrinkles on the skin were piled up like ridges in a field. Grim Reaper time and fast arrival of same? Certainly he seemed to lack the punch of firm control that Joe had always seen him exhibit in the past, that dancing sense of sheer God-given authority and nastiness sanctioned for the sake of it – to impress the others – that he exuded at all times. No more Black Pimpernel for him. It was over, all of that business for Sir David. He looked more like a paper bag now than a human being.

Joe could sense some violence coming up on the horizon. He had a feel for this kind of thing. The whole business now smelled fisticuffs in some way or another. But fortified by his good news, Joe rode the venomous attack from Rivers, delivered in such high pitched tones as to attract attention from the diners waiting patiently in line with their plates for food from the buffet which had risen from the depths downstairs. Joe sneered contempt at Rivers's accusations and this enraged Rivers even more. George hovered protectively. He kept glancing towards the door.

Then Joe counter punched. It was done purely intuitively, and it was based as ever on the concept of the big lie. That, and a bid to impose divide and rule.

'Look, Rivers Pugh, none of this discussion would be taking

place if you hadn't been so lippy and gabby when we first met. You were the one who first talked about a US merger and so naturally I got interested after that. I'm a market man after all, and that's a big company Sir David's running. But he won't thank you for spilling the beans. You should learn to keep your mouth shut tight in future.'

The reactions in the little group showed that Joe had hit the ammunition dump with his lie. Right on target, so direct.

Sir David aged about twenty years at the mere mention of a US merger and Rivers danced from foot to foot in quite uncontrollable anger. Joe thought he was going to spit at him or even strike him. But he was stuffed. Joe's speculation about the merger was clearly true and so by inference was the smear that Rivers had blabbed about it. A lie, once it registered, was very hard to shake off. It had to be countered straight away in such tense discussions. But it was not denied. Rivers failed to nail Joe's untruth. The lie was now established as truth. Rivers had spilled the beans about a merger. George drew closer. He was very interested. 'Joe, this really is turning into a very fruitful evening. You have done very well. Sir David has been talking to us as well about a deal but he never mentioned that he was in separate talks.' The cat was out of the bag well and truly. Sir David's schemes were unravelling fast.

George was still focused on the door and now Joe could see why. Marty started to bear down on them from his original spot just outside the room. Rivers looked happier. Marty's orders were obvious. Joe wondered about the protection the bridge guests might afford him. But George just nodded, still watching Marty. He'd been watching someone else.

A small figure appeared in front of Marty. It looked like a young girl. Marty motioned her out of the way but she refused to move. He moved forward to push her aside and found himself seated on the floor, after describing what appeared to have been a double somersault. The girl had not moved. Guests who saw all this pantomime laughed, thinking it was part of the entertainment. Amazed but still in disbelief, Marty rose to his feet, moved forward… and the girl twisted a fraction from the hips and Marty fell to the floor a second time.

George said very evenly to Rivers that if he didn't call off his heavy, Marty would have his neck broken next time. No threat but a simple promise. Rivers looked across at Sir David who nodded at Rivers to tell Marty to back off. Joe seemed to be winning. George came from older City stock and he had better, more skilful heavies.

George moved in now on Sir David. He sounded menacing. 'You'd better explain your side of the story, Sir David.'

Sir David looked shifty and uncomfortable and unwell. The eyes darted about restlessly like those of a man in a fever.

Lady C appeared at his side. She chirruped her news to him. 'Guess what, David, Joe has just had very good news. He's had some trouble with his bank but it's all sorted out now and guess how much they owed him. Four million pounds, that's how much they were holding out on him. Isn't that shocking!'

No reaction at all about Joe's good news. Rivers looked appalled. But more shifty eyes from Sir David. First they played on Joe, then on George and then on Rivers. Finally on Lady C. He said nothing. He paused. He was assessing everything.

They all waited for him to speak. Again he remained silent. Guests stared as he ruminated. Then he seemed to make up his mind. A more familiar light flashed into his eyes. He moved a fraction apart from them. He took a knife and tapped it against a glass on a small table nearby. Silence fell. It was a little early for Sir David's traditional speech, but then again he was a busy man.

Sir David started off confidently enough. He was standing quite close to the window looking out over the quiet street. The soft evening wind through the window blew the curtains around behind him.

'I'm sorry to have to say this but something has cropped up and I'm going to have to curtail your bridge.'

A general wail of disappointment. Lady C looked furious. What was this, a joke? It was ridiculous and a joke in very poor taste, if it was.

Sir David paused again. A manic look came into his eye. He looked quite deranged, just as if the light had changed. His voice rose to a scream. He looked like a creature from hell, silhouetted against the open window.

'And the reason why the bridge is curtailed is this. Look...' He tore off his shirt, throwing it to one side, and exposed his chest. It looked normal enough to Joe. But not to Sir David. Sir David saw it differently. In his mind's eye, his chest and indeed his whole body were covered with angry vicious red weals; and open suppurating sores, so that his skin glowed with pain. But inner pain. Sir David had lost the balance of his mind from shock. Joe saw that. 'Oh, it's all over me... Look...'

He stepped out of his trousers. Sir David, now nearly naked, was breathing hard and he advanced a step into the room. The guests retreated from the Evil One.

'Yes, I'm HIV positive and I think I've got full-blown Aids. I'm going to die from it.'

A terrified whisper ran round the room.

'Yes, but that's not all. You'll all be dead more or less very shortly, and 17 August is when you'll all go. Ruined anyway. Mark my words, that's when you'll all suffer. But I'll be there before you.'

Sir David turned and ran at the open window. He seemed to fly through the air and then disappear. Seconds later there came a terrifying shriek, then silence. The guests rushed to the window.

It was all over.

Joe did not follow them. He knew full well what had happened. Sir David had fallen from the window on to the railings and his ravaged body, apparently so full of life and power just a few seconds or so ago, now lay draped along the steel points punctured throughout and still radiating its savage heat from the disease. A piece of rotting meat, no more no less.

Joe found a quiet corner and made his call. 'August 17 is the date. I'm still here but that's the date.' Joe explained what had happened.

'Inevitable, really. We thought he had the virus before the weekend but Jean-Paul's death won't have helped. But thank you, Joe. The date's 17 August, you said.'

'Correct.'

'How do you feel, Joe?'

'Richer and poorer.'

'Where are you going now?'

'The safest place, maybe, in London. Zorba's, for dinner with the Pughs.'

'No Rivers?'

'If he does turn up, I think his family will protect me.'

'Well thought out, Joe. But be careful. You don't want to lose that money a second time, do you?'

'As if. Goodnight.'

George saw Joe off the premises and rode shotgun for him down to the Fulham Road.

'Until Monday, Joe?'

'Until Monday, George.'


Annie called the Top in Washington.

'It's 17 August. Joe just rang me. Joe's alive but Sir David's dead. He killed himself because he had Aids but he gave us the date before he died. Apparently it was quite spectacular.'

'Congratulations, Annie. We can get to work now. Time to take some leave.'

'Thank you. That's exactly what I plan to do.'

The office was very empty, now that the thrill of the chase had evaporated. Just a chair and a table and a telephone. Nothing else. The objects in the office had been drained of their dramatic content. They were nothing more now than what they had always been.

She left the office hurriedly. It was all over for her. Time to book that flight. Time to get back into life. Now about that Adrian...

She reached her flat and just before she turned the key in the lock she paused. She had the strongest sensation possible that someone else had just left the flat, not more than a few minutes before. There was just a strong sense of another presence around. She pushed open the door of the flat and almost immediately saw two clocks on the mantelpiece, pushed tightly together and both an hour fast...

Time I wasn't here, she said to herself. Now what's that Adrian's number?

# Chapter Seventeen

Same table at Zorba's and about the same time in the evening as they always met.

After the passage of a few days, Joe sat waiting for Joachim. Final briefing, or debriefing, on the mission. He wasn't sure. He was there at Joachim's request. He was tired. The mission seemed to push away from him now like a wall as the pressure eased. He still had some energy left but not a great deal.

As he waited for Joachim, his mind rolled back to his great evening with Perdita and Lady Pugh, which had started at that very table after he arrived from the terrifying experience of Lady C's bridge soirée.

Joe glanced round the restaurant as he recalled the evening. Same drug dealers as always. Same air of watchful tension. But he was a world away from all that. He wondered what had happened to the mad-eyed blonde.

Charley had been tricky throughout the evening. Hardly surprisingly. His parents' village had been machine-gunned by rebel forces the previous week and he still had no news about his family. Charley just sat in the corner of Zorba's, speechless and stunned.

Rather apologetically, after he had arrived feeling flushed, Joe explained that there was rather more to him than met the eye, and they listened carefully. He explained about the French and the German and, as he did so, mother and daughter exchanged those knowing looks which indicated a considerable intelligence between them about a certain third party. Then he got on to his erstwhile position in the City and he'd rather spun that one out, dotting the i's and crossing the t's more for the benefit of Rivers, he explained, than anything else, because Rivers at the party that evening had been somewhat sceptical of Joe's claims. None of these revelations appeared to surprise them.

Lady Pugh was brightening at this stage. She could see that her lunch party the next day was going to go with a mighty swing, now that Joe actually turned out to be somebody worth knowing. A hobo bridge player could be passed off as somehow worthwhile and possessing intrinsic merit but he would require extended introduction, whereas far less would be needed by way of preamble if he did actually have his own calling card. As Joe undoubtedly did… Oh, iron laws of the social game. Lady Pugh looked radiant.

Perdita broke in boldly at this stage, eyes glinting in the candlelight, to say that whatever explanations Joe came up with about his past now, she was fully determined to stick to her man.

This flummoxed Joe, who looked to Lady Pugh for help and clarification. She looked away. 'I think she means what she says, Joe,' she said vaguely.

Whereupon Joe pushed his little piece of paper across the table. That clinched it. Nobody needed a lot of help with the translation.

Lady Pugh's lunch party the following day was a great success. It was just as well Joe had been so forthcoming about his City existence. A couple of ex-colleagues from Martins Bank were present at the lunch and most of the chat was about doings in the Square Mile. Not to have gone through with his explanations beforehand would have been fatal. Perdita sat beside Joe the whole time over lunch, beaming and holding his arm. Rivers was too busy intriguing and manoeuvring to attend.

But now waiting for the man in Zorba's it was back to the familiar hard tack of Joe's world of espionage and life on the line and living dangerously. Perhaps not for long, but Joe felt the sinews stiffening in the old familiar way.

Joachim entered the restaurant followed closely to Joe's surprise by another man, of medium height, smartly dressed in a lightweight pale grey suit. The newcomer had a light step and an easy manner. He was American. Joachim introduced him as Gatsby.

'Why don't you have a white suit, then?' Joe asked the question provocatively.

The stranger was quick to reply. 'Robert Redford had a better wardrobe than I've got.'

Joachim explained that as part of the sign-off briefing process, it was quite important that the American should be present. Quite why this should be so was left unclear. Joe prepared to take Joachim's points on board. But he was very tired. He listened with half an ear.

Joachim wasted no time. 'So you see, Joe, after the war, the UK found itself in a very strange position. It was caught in the web of US politics. It wasn't strong enough to go forward on its own account and neither could it back off from its engagement. By degrees, the UK found it was enjoying the sensation of being a small part of a larger operation because it found that it could actually function quite well in this subservient position provided it toed the line. That meant keeping everything unchanged in the UK and this suited the forces of inertia in this country very well; you know, monarchy, privilege, et cetera. A winning global formula in the nineteenth century but not apparently in the twentieth. It also meant spending heavily on arms but this again was hardly a problem since the UK taxpayer paid up unhesitatingly on the arms account. Fast forward forty years and very nearly nothing had changed in the immediate post-war scenario in the UK. Cold war still going on, the West still spending hugely on arms, the balance of terror still neatly sewn up between Russia and the USA.'

The American was looking idly out of the window and Joe was wondering whether the mad-eyed blonde still turned up for her fixes. Joachim continued. 'But subtly things were starting to change in all directions. China was beginning to emerge as a world power with the capacity to deliver in terms of nuclear weapons and this added a further twist to the Kissinger Doctrine which said that the US had to get closer to both China and Russia in order to prevent them getting close to each other. The US had to take account of this new factor in the game and this in turn meant adopting a fresh attitude towards Russia. The US and the UK were spending massively on their defence programmes and so too were the Russians. But the UK in a bid either to burst into US preserves or merely to reward greedy freelances in the Tory Party was selling arms to literally anybody in the world. The arms business was out of control. But meanwhile, additional key fact,

Russia started to alter its borrowing programmes with regard to the West. This was one of the crucial factors…'

Joe began to wake up. He started to concentrate. He could glimpse a pattern starting to emerge. Not quite the pattern he had expected, but he could see something afar off. This was pay-off time.

'Until the mid-eighties, Russia had always paid the West in cash. At some point around the mid-eighties, it started to borrow from the Western banking system in a bid to try and build up credit lines outside the Soviet Union after exhausting the savings of the ordinary Russian people. The West would not lend while the Russian empire was still organised on its traditional system of terror and repression. Very well, said the Russians according to some, and obligingly trashed their entire empire in exchange for fresh borrowing. Hence the fall of the Berlin Wall. But the Russian credit line started to grow. Russia started to owe the West money. For some this was a cynical move because the old Russian nomenklatura was still in place and still calling the shots. During glasnost the Russian espionage drive into the West intensified by a huge exponential factor. The top jobs still went to graduates of the security services. Equally, while the Russians withdrew from areas of empire, the US perforce was forced to try and colonise those recently vacated areas, leaving itself potentially exposed to global overstretch.'

Joe was concentrating hard now. It was too soon to reach for a phone. But it would not be long before he put through a call to Sid. He thought he knew what all of this was building up to.

'We can sum up what I have said so far in a simple phrase – the cold war was over but long live the cold war if perestroika was just a sham.'

Gatsby nodded. He was seemingly paying more attention to the drug dealers whose phones were now starting to buzz with evening orders.

'Now let us factor the UK into this global equation, the UK which had fought two world wars in the century and experienced economic defeat in both of them, and most important of all had been forced to dispose of all its portfolio of US assets. That weakened its hold on the US which the UK had maintained throughout the whole of the nineteenth century because of its massive investments in the US.'

Gatsby nodded again.

'The UK discovers North Sea oil, digs it out of the North Sea, and engages in the most rapid build-up of overseas investments during the 1980s that has ever been seen. The bulk of North Sea oil revenues are invested in the US and indirectly the UK repurchases its position of influence in the States.'

Gatsby interrupted Joachim. 'I'm going to run. I'm happy so far with the story but don't deviate from that line. I know the rest as told previously. I'm going to run because I really don't like to be seen in this café with those people just so close.' He stood up and shook hands with Joe. 'Well done, Joe. Great mission. We'll meet again. Bye for now. It's good to put a face to a voice.' Then he was off walking swiftly out of the café.

'Joachim, what on earth was all that about?'

'Ask no questions, Joe, and you will be told no lies. I'm relieved he's gone. I was just getting to the really tricky part which I can now alter around a little bit. Now where was I? Yes, the UK investment build-up in the US. Well, of course, as it takes place during the 1980s, it does not take place in isolation. The UK is not only purchasing US assets, but it is consolidating its influence on a political level.'

Joe could see a face peeping round the corner of the door, a face that was prematurely aged, ashen grey, with hair sticking up on all sides like a scarecrow. Then the face was gone again. It was just recognisable – just – as the face of the mad-eyed blonde. But the deterioration process was total. Hers was now the face of an old women. She had got through her entire life cycle of experience in just a few months. She was now an old penniless hag. Joe knew too that the face would be back very shortly. It couldn't stay away from the dope.

Joachim suddenly seemed to become very shy and coy about his disclosures. Perhaps he feared the return of the American. 'Some people argue that the UK went out to buy the US presidency, saying that Reagan and Bush and Clinton all worked for the British and that these men were steered into position by the British after their earlier success in getting rid of Richard

Nixon. Certainly yet again there was a certain congruence to events like Thatcher bracketed with Bush as well as Reagan, and then characters on both sides of the Atlantic dumped. Bush should have won that election against Clinton and it is still a mystery why he failed. Who knows? Many odd things go on in politics. Others say all this is fantasy. Again, who knows?

'Anyway, suffice it to say that in the late nineties Clinton arrives at the White House and he is just the man – indeed the only man – to alter the terms and conditions of the post-World War II arms race. A Vietnam refusenik, a dope smoker, and a political genius of the absolute primary category. He wants to reverse the traditional US equation and put butter before guns and he is capable of doing just that, if we assume therefore that at the world's most senior tier of decision-taking there is a school in favour of peace, as opposed to war, and that Bill Clinton is their candidate.'

'Hence Monica Lewinsky?'

'That's what some people say. They say the president has been set up by the arms industry across the world and that includes the Russians, which absolutely refuses to alter its traditional mode of dealing with the rest of the world.'

There was something here for Joe to grasp. It would not be spelled out for him. But it was there. Joe thought that Joachim would take questions now but that he would not advance any further. The briefing was drawing to a close.

Again that head came round the corner, and now emboldened the body followed, a wizened shrunken corpse of a thing. Playfully, like a child, the charred remains of a once beautiful human being tiptoed into Zorba's and advanced up to the drug dealers. Joe followed this charade with fascinated eyes. He was aware of a slight commotion to his left but he ignored it.

The shrunken person approached the dealers who roared with laughter at her antics. She went to kneel in front of them to beg and implore them for drugs but one of them soon wearied of it all. He stood up, picked her up like a child, advanced towards the door, opened it with his foot, and threw her across the road and into the street right in the path of an approaching bus. The bundle of rags went flying through the air and the bus braked, but it was too late. The girl had finished up beneath the wheels.

Joe looked round. The restaurant was empty. The dealers had fled, although they would return the next day. But Joachim had also gone…

Annie had said aggressively that she didn't object to the American being present at Joe's briefing but that was as far as it went. The Top reminded her of a certain evening and a certain smooth disposal of Bootface. 'Gatsby is a very good shot,' he said, and Annie fell silent.

Joe reckoned it had to be right. He was still at Zorba's. He rang Sid at home and caught him in mellow mood. Sid chaffed him.

'Now that you've become so rich again, Joe, I'm surprised that you bother with an old hoofer like me as a stockbroker.'

'Stuff it, Sid, I'm in a hurry. You've got a New York office, haven't you?'

'We've got offices everywhere, Joe.'

'And you know how much money I'm worth, don't you?'

'Yes, because you told me.'

'Right, I'm going to pledge all of that capital in one deal. I want you to go short for me to that whole amount on Russian bonds. Buy and then sell them if necessary, but I prefer to go an uncovered bear with the cash as collateral.'

'My God, Joe, that's a big punt. In fact that's an enormous trade.'

'If you're wise, you'll follow me. I know to the date when Russia is going to default on its foreign debt. You can take the entire firm out of Russian bonds if you're smart. Now that'll look good on the sheet, won't it?'

'Indeed it will.'

'If we get this one right, Sid, I'll take you to as many football games as you like, wherever you like, irrespective of what Clinton does.'

'And, Joe, why not…!'

And to do him credit Sid did the business for Joe even at that late hour. Somehow Joe felt that he and Sid were almost quits now.

## Chapter Eighteen

It was the last night for the Liz Playfair Bridge Academy. Morka and Liz were catching a plane the following morning for Lisbon and a new life together. No more Thursday bridge, indeed no more bridge at all *chez* Playfair. This was the final session. End of an era. Joe had attended out of sorrow, sadness, duty and a sense that things might have turned out more equably for Liz. None of the usual crowd were there. He had liked Liz very much indeed. She had a smiling presence and a fine upstanding and optimistic look to her. He thought she was a fine bridge player with great cards judgement although, if the paradox could be tolerated, almost wholly lacking in common sense about the ordinary matters of life.

But time spent at the final Liz Playfair session was time spent in vain. His gesture went unrecorded. Liz was not there, busy presumably packing. Morka, the blonde Asian queen, was in full control and she welcomed Joe with a flick of her head, assigning him to the lowest table of all. Not much joy here, he thought. And the clientele seemed different. The denizens of SW3 had long since fled, to be replaced by hungrier and rougher bridge players – women with longer jawbones and less refined expressions, women who smoked at the table and who disputed the bids unceasingly. It was a rough old house now, quite unlike the calm and well-established finishing school for the dames of SW3 that it had been. Somehow the chairs seemed to be set at a more louche and crazier angle. They swung about freely. Undeniably the subtler edge of gentility was now missing.

Joe had wished Liz the very best of luck on her travels by phone. He doubted whether such switches, born out of desperate passion, worked so well later in life but she was welcome to try. He hoped she'd enjoy the flight. Meanwhile he played the bridge as best he could and looked forward to his meeting with Perdita later that evening at Pugh Park. Joe's life had had more than its fair share of valedictory moments. He could cope with farewell.

It was 7.55 p.m. With a thirst coming upon him, Joe slipped into the back kitchen to brew himself some tea. Morka was away from the room as he did this, otherwise he would have asked her permission. Morka treated him fine but he liked to go by the rules with her. As camp commandant to the manner born, she was that kind of autocrat.

As he started the kettle and prepared to drop the tea bag into his cup, he dropped it on the floor and bent down to pick it up, flicking the kettle off as he did so. He heard Morka walk swiftly into the kitchen, pick up the phone and begin dialling a number; it was a long number. It was not a local call. She did not hesitate. She was ringing at a pre-arranged time. Joe heard her fingers drum on the desk. She was anxious and she was busy. Full of curiosity, Joe stayed put, quite invisible from where Morka was making her call. She connected immediately. She spoke very quietly so as not to be overheard by anyone. It was a private call. Deeply private.

She spoke unhesitatingly in French. '*C'est toi, chérie. Tiens, c'est ta voix. Oh, quelle merveille de te parler même si ce n'est que pour un instant, c'est v'raiment un bonheur, tu me manques tellement. Tu n'as pas la moindre idée de combien tu me manques… On n'a pas longtemps maintenant à attendre. Non, je dois prendre l'avion jusqu'a Lisbon mais après je vais la laisser tomber et c'est fini… Mais non, c'est ridicule… Je te le jures, j'ai horreur du poulet anglais qui me dégoute tellement… C'est abominable… Mais, je t'aime passionement, et tu le sais aussi bien que moi… Quoi, l'amour?*'

Poor Liz, thought Joe. This is horrible.

Morka continued. '*Sa façon de faire l'amour me fait chier, c'est complètement le bordel tu sais et de plus ce n'est pas toi qui est là avec moi au pieu… Mais je te le jure… Mais non je compte les minutes… oui, mais à huit heures trente ce soir c'est fini, oui on va les faire fusiller tous, ces cons de marchands d'armes… C'est fixé, c'est reglé ca aura lieu et après, pouf, ils sont tous morts… mais bien sûr c'est pour ça que je couche avec le poulet… Mais après ce soir, tout est fini et foutu et je reviens a toi… Oui, j'ai toutes les adresses, ça a été tellement simple et c'est Pugh Park qui va se faire exploser le premier… Oui, dans une demi-heure…*'

Morka finished the call, replaced the receiver and returned to the bridge room. Joe knew everything now. Poor Liz... And poor Perdita.

Joe waited a second or so and then edged himself through the door of the academy and rushed down the stairs in silence. Out into the street. He found a call box. He rang a number. It too was a long number. It took time to compose.

The call was answered. Joe felt calm and cool and determined and detached yet still focused on the business in hand. He spoke very clearly. No time to lose. 'Request clearance.'

'Colour?'

'Blue.'

'Code?'

'Fat Man.'

'Wait one.'

A pause.

'Destination?'

'Pugh Park. Hampshire.'

'Time of arrival?'

'Eight thirty.'

'Wait one.'

A pause.

'Clearance granted. Proceed slowly up the King's Road away from Sloane Square.' Click and out.

Joe had gone nuclear. Those codes and that request for clearance were to be used only in matters of the gravest emergency. Perdita Pugh was strictly personal. But no matter. Perhaps it was a national emergency. Joe left the phone box and began walking along the King's Road. After perhaps a minute a car glided to a halt beside him. The door opened. Joe climbed in.

'Where to, Joe?'

The engine was moving into steep revs but they were only just above stationary. Moving very slowly. Two cycle cops swung into position on either side in front of the car. Then they were away, travelling shortly at over one hundred miles an hour, following the cycle cops who had their horns on at full strength. They screamed down the King's Road, swung a heavy right through the backstreets and found themselves on the Cromwell Road, still travelling at high speed. No time to pause now.

Joe's driver was balanced at the wheel like a dancer, moving in time with the car. Now they were smashing down the Cromwell Road and out of London, still hitting it hard with the cops ahead still driving with speed and panache.

'Just keep on down the motorway, Sandy. It's Pugh Park we're after. I'll navigate. It's not hard to find.'

'And when we get there?'

'Death roll, I think.'

'How long, Joe, since you did death roll?'

'Two weeks since.' Joe said that with assurance but he lied, and his driver knew he lied. Death roll was tricky. It could be a very brief encounter.

On and on they sped into the night. On the outskirts of London the police escort left them. They continued into the dark. Swish-swish went the tyres on the motorway as they smashed along at maximum speed. The lights scythed a way through the darkness. Joe thought about the destruction to Perdita that was coming not later than ten or twenty minutes hence as the crew of Morka's mercenaries hit Pugh Park. That was what Sybil had organised so carefully in her malice; she had allowed Morka and her crew to penetrate the weakest link in the whole social chain. And Morka had taken full advantage.

He thought too about the way that he had now burned all his credentials with intelligence. But so what? End of the road time. End of Fat Man time as well.

They drove on. Eight fifteen now and still miles to travel. Clearance such as he had requested was only granted for matters of state emergency. He had never done this kind of thing before, he said to himself over and over, knowing that to be a lie as well and knowing also that a reckoning was approaching with the past. Time to square the books and time to get out of the way of the Gents. And fuck you, Rivers Pugh, again and again for being an arms dealer.

'What's the story, Joe?'

'No story, if we're early. No story, if we're late, they'll have burned the place down. If we coincide, then it's death roll.'

'Looks like we'll coincide.'

'To the second. It's death roll, I think. There's a front entrance and a side entrance to the park. We'll go in by the side and they'll come in by the front. You drive right across the front green if they're there and we ram them. There's no time to fuck around because the girl always runs down the drive to meet anything coming in by the main drive. We need about thirty seconds on our side, no more and no less.'

Joe fumbled in the glove compartment for some weapons and found a heavy machine pistol. Loaded. In good working order. It sat in his hand, familiar to the touch. Berlin was never very far away, at any time.

'As we go in, I'm going to start firing as we drive at them. That may halt them a touch. But we should be fine. They're just mercenaries. They may have got lost anyway. Hampshire's a confusing county at the best of times.'

They drove on through the night and Joe thought about death and Lady Pugh and then death roll. Some Fat Man recall but not much.

Twenty minutes past. Joe thought about what was to come. Death roll needed split-second timing, he knew that. The driver rammed the oncoming car and flung himself backwards, just before impact. He was covered physically by his colleague who shielded him from the shock of impact and who then tumbled out of the car by the driver's seat to start firing at whatever was left alive in the other car. That was the theory. The practice was harder. One second's wrong timing and nothing was left alive in either car. Joe felt his pulse quicken. He was up high on the trapeze and waiting to perform his very own triple somersault, without a net – of course.

Eight twenty-five and they were getting there. Joe thought they were running some two minutes behind schedule but Sandy who recognised the route now, thought they were on target for eight thirty. Two bends taken very fast, some straight road, another long curve, and then they were running down the long road beside the estate.

'The side entrance is coming up now, in a very short while, so slow now… Now swing left very sharply and we're in.'

They curved through the side entrance and took in the scene. Nothing moving at first, and they were there on time before the assassins. Joe looked again and screamed at the driver to hit the speed very fast. The car almost took off with the acceleration.

Another car was just crawling through down the drive towards the house. Some few hundred yards separated them. As Joe's car screeched across the green, the front door of Pugh Park opened and a familiar figure appeared and started running down the drive, towards the enemy car. Like a butterfly on the wing, Perdita was skipping in high spirits towards what she thought was Joe's car arriving early.

Joe smashed the side window of the car and leaned out with his pistol aiming to Perdita's left as she ran to the right. As he aimed to fire, the car jolted on the turf. He fired and she fell. A butterfly falling to earth...

They were closing on the other car now very fast. It loomed huge. Faces at the wheel and beside the wheel... startled expressions. Joe pulled the driver's seat back and just before impact shouted, 'Now!' and flung himself on top of Sandy, falling back as the car hammered with a great crash into the other automobile.

The din was tremendous. A ripping and tearing sound of metal. So too was the thump of the shock of the two cars striking. Now Joe was out of the car, on the grass, struggling to find his feet and then up, pistol in hand and raking the other car with fire.

'Sandy, Sandy,' he shouted. 'You, okay?' He fired round after round into the other car where nothing was moving.

A voice behind him to the left shouted, 'Joe, I'm fine. Time to go.'

Joe ran back and clear of the two cars and then commenced firing into the tanks of their car, which promptly exploded.

Pugh Park was lit up by a huge orange glow and Joe sank to his knees, sick, dead with nervous fatigue and emptied of every emotion. Sandy helped him to his feet and tried to calm his shaking body. Lady Pugh stared at him as he entered the house. She wanted to know where her daughter was. Joe sat shaking violently in the entrance. Outside the two cars burned on the lawn in front of the house. Lady Pugh stood over Joe. Sandy sat beside him, holding by the shoulders. Nothing else moved.

'Easy boy, easy.' Sandy knew about these situations.

Some minutes passed. But Lady Pugh was not to be placated.

'Come along, Joe, we're going to find my daughter.'

Joe stared at her with sightless eyes where thoughts failed to register. She tugged him to his feet and Sandy left them to it. Together the two of them, the aged aristocrat and the agent who used to be a sensible human being stumbled out of the house and trudged down the drive, Lady Pugh supporting Joe who shook with trauma as he walked.

They found her lying down a small culvert, quite motionless. She lay in perfect child pose at total peace. Not moving at all. But not wounded either. At first they thought she was dead, but then they looked again and saw a tiny regular movement. They realised she was breathing and alive but heavily concussed. But alive.

Joe reached for Lady Pugh's hand and folded it within his own. Her hand was cold to the touch.

'So you saved our lives, Joe. You didn't bring death as I said. You brought life.'

'Not quite, Lady Pugh. What you said was quite right when we first met. But it all happened in the past. That was where the error lay. Come on, let's get Perdita back into the house and get her to hospital. I'll tell you as we go.'

Lady Pugh took the legs and Joe carried her by the shoulders and together they struggled to transport Joe's beloved, and Lady Pugh's darling daughter, back to the house. She lolled between them like a doll. Joe panted a little but Lady Pugh walked ahead stolidly, clutching her daughter at both of the knees. Like a nurse in the trenches in World War I. The fires now abating from the burning cars caught them in tragic silhouette, like gravediggers on the march. But the image was wrong. Perdita lived.

In the ambulance, Joe leaned forward and told his story to Lady Pugh who heard him out without a word.

'I'm an agent, Lady Pugh, and I work for British intelligence. Always have done, between doing other jobs. But that's what my training is about. I worked with a man called the Fat Man mainly in Berlin when it was the centre of the cold war and he and I did many jobs together. We were a fine team and we survived. We shouldn't have done but we did; we craved life when everyone else was going crazy with fear. So we came through.'

The ambulance jolted along. Perdita was silent on her

stretcher between them. Lady Pugh said nothing but listened.

'The Fat Man was my father figure in all our espionage and he taught me all I knew at the time. My mind even now always rings with his phrases in any given situation. I will never escape his influence; it's a fact of life. His injunctions were pithy to say the least, but they worked. He was my guru. We always got through. As a team we worked well, as I said. Eventually we were so successful we were posted back to London for a particularly tricky job involving a break-in at one of the national newspapers. I won't tell you which one, but it was difficult because we thought the Russians were on the other side. And heavy with hardware. Very dangerous.

'So come one Saturday morning I'm standing on one side of Fleet Street with the Fat Man, and I have to cross the street and open a door. Nothing more and nothing less, but twenty yards is an eternity when you think there's a Kalashnikov on the other side about to blow your face apart.

'I had to cross the street, and I hesitated. The Fat Man may have panicked or he may have simply blown up after too many missions, but he suddenly altered and started screaming at me. "If you don't cross that street and open that door, I'll kill you here like a dog!" was what he said and he pulled out his pistol to reinforce the point. He was hysterical. Maybe I'd done too many missions as well, because Berlin was very tough, but I snapped when he pulled out the pistol and gave me that abuse. Love or something like that was being abused. "Fuck you," I said and I took his pistol. Then I shouted at him, "Well, we'll go together then!" and blew his brains out. Then I marched across the street. He was dead and I expected to be shot. But there was no sniper behind the door. So I did the job, and I lived and so for many years and… and… I wish I hadn't done that to the Fat Man… and…' His voice tailed away. He'd said it all. There were no further words to use. His head went down.

Lady Pugh leaned across to him. 'And came to save us, Joe. To save you and Perdita. That is all you have to think about now. Nothing else counts. Now be a good little boy and go to sleep, will you, and I'll watch over the two of you.'

Joe looked at her. Then, obediently, he put his head down and the blackness rushed in from all sides.

Lady Pugh looked over them both like an old war veteran.


Russia's financial crisis began around mid-August, when the rouble came under extreme selling pressure. Russia, in the throes of seeking a $23 billion aid package from the IMF, was forced to disburse some $1 billion weekly from its foreign exchange reserves in order to support the currency. Panic set in among Moscow investors, despite the dispatch by the White House of top Treasury officials to Russia. Russian bonds fell very sharply and yields touched a crisis level of some one hundred and fifty per cent. The Moscow stock market dropped so swiftly that trading was suspended for forty-five minutes during the afternoon session. Talk of Russian default on its bonds began almost immediately, because of the evident shortage of Russian options for raising fresh finance ahead of the year-end maturing of some $19 billion of bonds due for redemption. The deputy prime minister stoutly denied that default was an issue.

Problem was that Russia's problems were not confined to Moscow. The contagion of investor panic began to spread. New York was very shaky, dropping some ten per cent from July highs. Asian stock markets started to reel. The dollar soared against regional currencies appreciating in particular very sharply against the yen. The D-mark also came under selling pressure because of the German banks heavy exposure to the Russian economy. The flight to quality by investors over the next few sessions impacted heavily on emerging markets across the world, as funds were switched out of the peso; the baht; or the forint and into the dollar. Central European markets were special casualties of the Russian financial crisis. Venezuela was rumoured to be on the point of going belly up. Meanwhile the rouble continued to come under heavy selling pressure.

The crisis accelerated over the following week until on 17 August, just a few days after Russian President Yeltsin had proclaimed that a change in parities was not an option, he announced a devaluation of the rouble and a moratorium on Russian government debt – in other words a default. Many Russian banks by this stage were on the brink of closing their doors. Russia was in the throes of financial meltdown as indeed were many other countries, Japan included.

At around the same time, almost to the hour in fact, US President Clinton announced that he had had an inappropriate relationship with a White House intern, Monica Lewinsky. His tenure of the presidency was seen to be in immediate danger.

The Russian financial crisis continued to rumble through the markets over the next fortnight as the USA found itself engulfed in a fresh political crisis concerning President Clinton which seemed almost as grave as the sell-off in markets. The dismissal of his entire government by President Yeltsin was viewed as an ugly yet potentially prescient augur for future developments concerning the White House. By this stage, the Dow Jones had dropped some two thousand points from its July peak and US banks were beginning to count the cost of their Russian exposure. Losses were heavy. Confidence was very low.

Then, some two weeks after the crisis detonated, it was lifted into an entirely fresh dimension of peril and danger by the problems of a US hedge fund called Long-Term Capital Management. Run by the charismatic John Meriwether, late of Salomon Brother and its ultra-aggressive trading mentality, LTCM had produced dazzling returns of some forty per cent in its second year of operations. LTCM believed in using complex mathematics to exploit market anomalies. It was also a devotee of leverage – its ratio of borrowed funds to equity was around thirty to one. But the difficulty for Meriwether and his team was that a collapse on the scale of Russia had simply not been foreseen. When liquidity in markets evaporated after Russia's debt default, LTCM was left with large positions it simply could not manoeuvre. Western markets now positioned to crash dive because LTCM had become a forced seller of a massive portfolio of dud holdings.

There was a real fear in markets at this point that the entire Western system of credit was poised to default. Nor did the problems of President Clinton make for a settled atmosphere. America was tottering.

But forewarned is forearmed. The crucial knowledge which Western intelligence agencies had gained concerning the exact date of the Russian debt default, courtesy of a grand bridge soirée in London's Chelsea, gave the world monetary authorities a slight breathing space when it came to coping with first, the problems of the world banking system in the aftermath of Russia's move, and then later the LTCM debt mountain. They needed all the time they could get.

When the storm broke, they were well positioned and could move on to the attack against the markets without initially surrendering too much of the initiative by making the wrong signals. It was a delicate business.

First, they injected massive funds into the mature markets in order to prevent liquidity drying up, a development which in turn would have provoked a complete seizure in trading. Then in September, mindful of LTCM's difficulties and moving very quickly, the New York Federal Reserve brought together a consortium of fourteen Wall Street banks over a weekend. The banks bought ninety per cent of LTCM's portfolio and put some $3.6 billion into the hedge fund. In effect they transferred the market's potential losses from a smaller trader on to their own far larger books. The banks were standing behind the markets.

That move lanced the boil of investor panic. Markets began to recover. And President Clinton did not resign. That is the key point. It is worth repeating it – the president did not step down amid political as well as financial chaos. American politics failed to go through the ringer yet again after the traumas of the two Kennedy assassinations, Nixon's Watergate and the miseries of the Carter presidency.

Clinton stayed put and the coup failed. That in itself may well have been Clinton's greatest political conjuring trick. Caught in flagrante as he had been but well briefed as he subsequently was by Western intelligence, again courtesy of that bridge soirée, he seized the optimal moment to admit to a relationship that was damning for him politically and potentially fatal to his presidency – that is, the moment that Russia defaulted. But as world financial markets rode into a complete typhoon, he was invulnerable. It was arguably the one and only moment, in the context of his imbroglio with Monica Lewinsky, when Clinton was wholly unassailable.

But it was all a damned close run thing. Just a small matter of knowing the correct date for a certain event and then positioning accordingly, as a very senior New York central banker was heard to remark as the colour returned to his knuckles and the storm slowly began to blow itself out. For a few days it looked as if the West was back to nylons, cigarettes and sea shells for money. It came that close.

# Chapter Nineteen

Joe slid into his chair opposite Lady C and prepared to play some Wednesday bridge. Not Thursday morning bridge. That was still off the menu, courtesy of Liz Playfair's defection, the defection that never was. Liz had failed to make her Lisbon connection, Morka had disappeared overnight and somehow the bridge academy had failed to get off the ground a second time. Liz left the area quite shortly afterwards. The Thursday group as a bridge-playing ensemble was no more for the time being. But it would return again, no one had any doubt about that. There was talk of a summer trip to Sicily where Nancy had a villa, with, significantly, a spot going spare for Emma now that Liz Playfair was no longer one of the group. But in the meantime the girls played mainly at Savage's although for the most part as a smaller group slightly apart from the other players. Sybil was not invited to play with them.

The cookery book had been a great success. It had sold many thousands of copies. Somehow the idea of women who played bridge actually rolling their sleeves up and getting on with it in the kitchen had appealed to the vast mass of the British public somewhere there outside in the exterior cosmos.

They teased Joe a lot now because of his respectability and his wealth. He nearly had a job, a lucrative troubleshooting consultancy with George Gilston; he had a girlfriend and rather more than just that, in the shape of Perdita; and, as Lady C hinted darkly, he had literally millions in the bank. He was very nearly one of them. They teased him that he might have made the grade although he was still very much an apprentice gentleman. Not tamed at all...

Joe took good care not to make any reference whatsoever to his stunning dealing coup over the Russian debt default. He had more than doubled his fortune as a result. He took care to appear more or less as the old Joe, sharp-eyed but withdrawn at the table.

They accepted him as such. He fitted in and they all rubbed along together quite well in a casual way. But even now, so soon after the whole cycle of tragic events, Joe was restless. His addiction to risk was chronic. He craved more excitement than just conformity to the SW3 social round of bridge and dinner parties could provide. In low moments he even missed Berlin.

Lady C was different. She seemed wholly at ease with her new status as a much respected widow after the tragic death of her husband. Nevertheless she was still not wholly clear on the precise sequence of events surrounding the winding up of the Liz Playfair Bridge Academy; she required some extra information. Lady C had filled out a little in the aftermath of Sir David's funeral. Her hair had not quite turned gold from grief but it was certainly cut and styled very becomingly.

'So what happened in the end at Liz's on that final evening, Joe? I'm still not clear.'

It suited Joe very well to talk about Liz because he had one final trick up his sleeve for Lady C. It was scheduled for that afternoon.

'Morka was part of a group of freedom fighters who had come to London to try and get even with the arms dealers who were supplying their government with weapons.'

'But why us?' Causality was not Lady C's strong suit. It had not occurred to her that Sir David, as head of one of the world's largest weapons companies, might be in some way involved in that kind of business.

'She wanted to penetrate the whole group in order to get all the names and addresses. That way they could pick off whoever they wanted.'

Joe spoke soothingly. No point in trying to draw obvious conclusions. This was an afternoon's bridge, not a seminar on moral relativities. Besides, he was as entangled in the confusion of the moral undergrowth as anyone. Why otherwise should he have gone haring off down to Hampshire to save Perdita when her brother was even then angling for a seat on the board after Sir David's death? And to continue the business in much the same way as Sir David had always run it. It was very much the affair of Sloane School and would remain as such indefinitely. It was a fief of the school. Joe had no claim to speak at all. He was just as embroiled as the rest of them.

The cards were shuffled and dealt and Joe looked at the clock. Two forty-five. Yes, it should be happening about now. About now... It sounded as if Betty had done her work well from the progress reports he had been receiving.

On cue, a figure in shades and a wide straw hat entered the room and stole over to Joe's table. Delicate steps from small feet. The figure sat beside Joe very quietly. Joe introduced her as a friend to Lady C who glanced at her and then forgot about her.

'She needs to do some kibitzing to get her bridge up to speed. She's at the crucial early learning stage.'

The cards went back and forth and the play swung from one end of the table to the other. After a while, Joe asked Lady C if she minded the kibitzer playing a hand or two. Lady C assented and Joe changed places with the silent watcher. Still shades and the hat. The cards were dealt and Joe slipped away from the table. Standing behind Lady C, he motioned to the rest of the room to gather round. Very quietly the play ceased at the other tables. Sybil was left alone at one of the tables. Joe got a quick shot of the Sybil bulging eyeballs show before he looked away. She was not happy at the movement away from her table, if only for a few seconds.

Lady C was declarer in the first hand. Dummy went down. Shades and a wide hat opposite to her across the table above the dummy. Lady C played the cards in her usual fashion, the hand coming out like a pecking bird to the cards opposite, very fast. Gathering in the harvest. End of the hand. The cards were dealt out again. This time shades was declarer. Down went Lady C's dummy. Shades prepared to play the hand.

Joe looked at the crowd assembled in silence round Lady C. All were intent on the first card to be played. And then, there it came again from the other side of the table. As shades played, out came the pecking claw of a bird towards the cards opposite, playing them very fast. Gathering in the harvest, like Lady C.

A sharp intake of breath from all gathered around. Lady C was rigid. And speechless. She could not fail to take the point on board concerning the resemblance.

Someone said very softly to Lady C, 'Why don't you ask her to take off her spectacles, Lady C?'

With a graceful flourish, Ateh removed her hat and shades and stared at Lady C. Who stared back across the heap of cards piled on the table. And stared and stared. Taken together, they were mother and daughter. No shadow of a doubt.

Then it was too much for both of them as recognition slowly dawned, and the realisation that they had met each other at last. Great rivers of tears ran down Lady C's cheeks as Ateh began to sob. Their friends closed in on the pair from all sides.

Lady C made a last effort before she surrendered to her emotions. 'Come over here, Sybil, and introduce yourself to my daughter. Who was lost and has been found... And who is much loved.' Then her voice choked on the emotion.

Joe stole away softly to keep his appointments. He was playing bridge that afternoon with Joxer, unbeknown to Perdita who thought he was working. Joe had somehow failed to inform Joxer about his fortune. But he was working on the idea of persuading Joxer to play at the higher stake tables. Meanwhile, Joe had talked Emma into setting up a stock market dealing operation for just the two of them. Before he started playing with Joxer, he would put in a call to Emma just to check on the progress of prices.

One of these days – and he knew it in his bones – he and Emma would play together at the Jack of Hearts. And do a great deal else besides... Meanwhile he had a bet to fulfil with Sid. The two of them were going to see Spurs play Manchester United that Saturday – and splitting the cost of the tickets. It turned out that Sid really didn't have the time to fly down to Rio...